JULIA GRICE

DAUGHTERS OF THE FLAME

PUBLISHED BY POCKET BOOKS NEW YORK

For Sean

Permission to reprint from the following is gratefully acknowledged:

Circus Days, by Jill Freedman, copyright © 1975. By permission of Crown Publishers, New York, N.Y.
The Christianis, by Richard G. Hubler, copyright © 1966. By permission of Little, Brown & Company, Boston, Mass.

Another *Original* publication of POCKET BOOKS

POCKET BOOKS, a Simon & Schuster division of
GULF & WESTERN CORPORATION
1230 Avenue of the Americas, New York, N.Y. 10020

ISBN: 0-671-82320-5

First Pocket Books printing April, 1979

10 9 8 7 6 5 4 3 2 1

Trademarks registered in the United States and other countries.

Printed in the U.S.A.

"YOU'LL HAVE TO DEPEND ON YOUR BODY TO KEEP YOU."

Dr. Arthur's taunt echoed unpleasantly in her head.

"I . . . I don't love you," she heard herself say.

"It doesn't matter. Love will surely come. . . ."

"All right," she heard herself reply. "I'll marry you, then, if that's what you want."

Adam's eyes widened. He gave a start, and then she saw triumph spread quickly over his features. He started to reach for her. "Under one condition," she said. "Under only one condition will I marry you."

"I will marry you if you will buy me the William deBord Circus and let me run it and do with it whatever I please."

"What?" Adam threw his head back and emitted a great peal of laughter. "You, running a circus? A girl of seventeen with both legs in splints?"

"Yes." Carisa squared her jaw and stared at him defiantly. "Your Dr. Arthur told me there would be ways for me to make money," she said in a low voice. "I . . . I suppose I could find them. I'll do what I have to. And one way or another, I'll buy that show."

"You're a little witch," he said. He gave a harsh laugh. "A money-minded, hungry little witch. But I want you anyway. God help me, I want you anyway. . . ."

PUBLISHED BY POCKET BOOKS NEW YORK

All characters and events are completely fictional, with the exception of Richard Sands, who was a real circus man, well-known in his time. The city of New London, Connecticut is real, of course. But Hearts-ease is not, nor, to the best of my knowledge, did a circus ever make its winter quarters there. But if it had . . .

I am grateful to Robert Owen Decker for having written his detailed history of New London, *The Whaling City*, to which I referred often. I am also grateful to have been allowed to use brief passages from Jill Freedman's circus-photo book, *Circus Days*, (Crown Publishers, 1975) and material from *The Christianis*, by Richard G. Hubler (Little, Brown, 1966).

Don't you wish that we could both go back to 1870 and see a real circus parade, a solid mile of it, with calliope and clowns and beautiful equestrienne riders? I do. . . .

"The circus is an exuberant place, like childhood; a celebration of the joy of just being alive. It's a magic place, full of the mystery, terror and ecstasy of childhood . . . a place you feel more than you remember, where things imagined are as real as things happened. Preposterous things that streak too fast across the corner of your eye. . . ."

—Jill Freedman, *Circus Days*

"In equestrian work . . . nothing is stable or truly synchronized. The solid ground is exchanged for a 2-foot-square platform. It is rounded, heaving, slippery, five feet off the ground, moving in a tight circle at about eight miles an hour. . . ."

—Richard G. Hubler, *The Christianis*

"From the first, Papa Ernesto had a vision of his own circus. The spangles and tights were to clothe his own flesh-and-blood. Everything except the audience—from animals to canvas—was to be Christiani. Even the audience was to be owned by him as long as the performance lasted."

—Richard G. Hubler, *The Christianis*

Prologue

By the time the little circus caravan came to the stones, Benicia was tired from walking beside the wagon, and her belly ached. It was a long walk for someone heavy with child, and now the wind was coming up, blowing dust in their eyes.

"Stones!" Anna prattled. "Look at stones, Mama!"

Benicia looked. She felt the hairs raise on her arms and neck in a rippling shiver. She had heard of these stones, called the King's Men, and now here they were, arranged in a jagged circle, some of them leaned to one side, catching and splitting the sunlight like ancient teeth.

How had they come here? she wondered. Or the ones further below the church, the ones called the Whispering Knights?

This site had once been used as a meeting-place for witches, John, her husband, had told her. And she could sense it. There was evil here. Evil as strong and touchable as the sheep-cropped grass which grew spiky beside the stones.

Just then Anna, who had been clutching Benicia's hand, released it and went toddling up to touch one of the monoliths.

"No! Baby, no, don't touch!"

"Mama?"

Benicia felt touched by some nameless dread. "I said no, Anna. Don't touch!"

Anna started to cry. Then it came, the picture in Benicia's mind. Fragmentary, as all of her visions were, it was the image of a woman. Small, with high, exotic cheekbones in a delicate face, she had strawberry-gold hair and was in the full bloom of her maturity. And she

1

was running. Stumbling terror-impelled across a field burned and charred by fire.

Benicia caught her breath. How familiar this woman looked! As if—yes, almost as if she might be——. Unconsciously Benicia's hand touched her belly, mounded now with pregnancy.

And alone, her thoughts went on. How alone the woman seemed, how desperate. Calling out for someone, in a voice made frantic by loss. Crying out a man's name. . . .

It had been a long birthing, too long. The odor of blood, sharp, hot, vividly salty, filled the air of the circus wagon where Benicia now lay, her eyes fastened dully on the sides of the wagon. At times the wood, marred by a hundred scrapes, seemed to recede from her in a mist of red.

She was bleeding to death. There was already, she knew, blood puddled on the floor of the wagon, seeking the lowest level of its uneven boards.

"Push down, woman. Push, can't ye?"

"I . . . I am pushing. . . ."

The village midwife crouched by the side of the high, narrow bed, her face shiny with perspiration. One baby had already been born. A healthy girl, it lay in a basket swaddled in flannel, emitting mewing, kitten-like cries. It was the second twin which presented its foot and would not be born, no matter how hard the midwife pushed or how desperately Benicia struggled.

"Pushing? Eee, don't look it to me." The woman's voice, thick with village dialect, seemed to come from an enormous distance. "Eee, and I'd of thought you circus women would have an easy time of it. Birth a babe like a litter of puppies. Like a *gypsy*," she added contemptuously.

"No . . . we're not . . . not gypsies. . . ."

Benicia fastened her eyes on a shaft of May sunlight as transparent as ale, which streamed through the center door of the wagon. She clenched her jaws together, willing herself not to scream.

Arriving an hour ago, the village woman had stared

2

curiously about the wagon, showing by her sniffs that she disapproved. The wagon, sixteen feet long and ten feet wide, had wood sides braced with brass and iron which slanted outward as they reached the roof. The roof itself was made of canvas, and showed the stains of years of storms and leaks.

There were two doors, each with fold-up steps. There was a large black wood-burning stove, its vent pipe extending through the roof. There were wooden chairs and tables, built-in cupboards, and two high beds, each four feet from the floor, with storage underneath. Dried food and sausages hung from the room supports, to be used when needed.

But all of it was clean. And Benicia had dried bunches of wildflowers and hung them from the roof, too, to add a bit of color.

Now she could hear voices coming from outside the wagon, and she knew that the others were waiting there anxiously. Marta Taggart, the half-crazed woman who could gracefully walk a wire, and who, because she could mix curative potions, many called a witch. Young Rolf, Marta's ten-year-old son, about whose father Marta would never talk. Duddie, the misshappen youth who was their Harlequin. And, his voice rising angrily above all of theirs, John Phillips, her husband.

The Phillips' were traveling mountebanks. They had been so for two hundred years, moving from village to village with their trained horses, their equestrian act, their small roundabout and peep show, their pantomimes and juggler and Harlequin.

Benicia herself read the Tarot Cards and specialized in thought reading and second sight, when she was not riding. Everyone in the caravan could do something, could ride or do flip-flaps or work on the bar. John Phillips had been trained at Astley's Royal Amphitheater in London. He was a deft, muscular rider. He could leap over three horses at once, could do quick costume changes while riding, and a rare double somersault.

John had brought the fourteen-year-old Duddie with him from London. The boy, small, dwarfish, was nonetheless a superb rider, and had told them he was the fourth son of an Earl.

Someday, John was fond of saying, the Phillips Show would not be small and shabby. Someday the circus would be a proper one, with elephants and tigers and a long parade. It would perform before kings and queens and receive the adulation of the world.

Dreams, Benicia thought, sinking further into the red haze that surrounded her. *Nothing but dreams.*

The reality was this caravan wagon, in which they ate, slept, cooked and carried their equipment. Reality was the food hastily cooked, the roads impassable with mire and mud, the hoodlums who attacked the small group of wagons, delighting to overturn one into a ditch or to attack some lone circus man.

Reality was the stolid villager who, one day during the performance, had announced loudly, "Them be witch-taught, them be!"

Witch-taught. Benicia felt the moisture standing heavily on her forehead, and knew that her hands and feet were growing cold. In a way, she thought, the man had been right. The villagers sensed it; they always knew.

For uncounted generations it had been in her own family, passed down from woman to woman. Sometimes skipping a generation, it was always there. *The knowing.* Erratic, undependable, fleeting, sometimes fading as the woman grew older. But there. The awareness, the catching, somehow, of what was still to happen. . . .

Pain, red pain, caught her and lifted her. It swept her in its elemental force. Distantly she was aware that the midwife's mouth was open and working like a fish which has been removed from a bucket, that her husband John had forced his way into the wagon and shoved the woman aside.

"Get out of here, you fat old cow, and let me do it. You're killing her."

"I'm not killing her, *ye* already done it," the woman hissed in her thick, country dialect. "That be the truth! You men an' yer filthy desires . . . *you're* the one done it to her. . . ."

4

"Get out!"

"*Ye* are the. . . ."

"I said get out, you old harridan!"

He shoved at her, and the woman was gone, cursing and muttering about "devil's spawn" and "gypsies."

"I'm going to die," Benicia whispered.

"No! I tell you, you're not. I won't have it. You'll bear many children yet. And now I've got rid of that old witch, I'm going to do this myself. I should have done it from the start. I'm going to reach in and turn the child."

"John!" she gasped. "John, how can you. . . ."

"Don't worry. I'll do it." He stood for a moment flexing his fingers, his big, hard hands which could discipline a horse or repair a roundabout or erect a tent.

"All right . . ." she whispered. "My feet . . . John, they're growing very cold."

"Never mind about that." He moved down the bed and crouched at the juncture of her thighs and began his work. Benicia did not scream because she was too weak.

"Anna?" she muttered, fighting the pain.

"She's fine. Duddie has her. He and Rolf are amusing her with the dogs. Don't worry about Anna."

"Yes. Good. . . ." She felt her eyelids flutter, and she pushed back the old hurt, the thought of ten-year-old Rolf, the thin, sharp boy with John Phillips' eyes. "*This* baby . . ." She touched her belly and grunted against the stabbing, grinding, incredible pain. "She's . . . a girl too. . . ."

"No!"

"Yes. You'll name her . . . after my mother . . . Carisa. . . ."

It was as if Benicia could see it, could see it all happening. How odd, she had time to think. That moment at the stones, the evil plucking at her.

"Daughter . . ." she muttered, unable to get her thought into words.

"Hush. Don't talk. You're wasting your strength."

Benicia closed her eyes against the tide of red which seemed to flow in front of her vision.

"I see . . . oh, John, I see. . . ."

She shivered convulsively. The coldness was creeping

5

up her limbs. Soon it would reach her heart. She tried to say it, to speak urgently.

"I see . . . accident. . . ." She had to stop, to gasp with pain. "Oh, dear God. John . . . you must tell her . . . must tell her. . . ."

But John Phillips, intent on his task, was not listening to his wife's barely audible words. And by the time he had finished and the small, dark, matted head of the baby emerged, Benicia had already lapsed into unconsciousness and would not waken again.

-‡ 1854 ‡-

1

NEW LONDON, CONNECTICUT, 1854

It began with a bad-luck feeling, a prickling of the skin along Carisa's neck and shoulders.

"Now, don't forget," her sister Stephana ordered. "Don't forget what I told you, Carisa. Do it just the way we rehearsed, just exactly, and there shouldn't be any trouble!"

Carisa nodded dubiously. She wriggled her shoulders, which felt sticky in the hot American June sun, so different from the paler English one. But this wasn't England. It was New London, Connecticut, one of the country's proudest whaling ports, its sun hot and vital, its air full of the tang of the sea.

The three sisters stood apart from their father and Rolf, by the "back door" of the large circus tent, waiting for their cue to go on. Patient beside them were the great gray Percherons, the rosin-back horses with their broad backs, soft eyes, and great, arched necks.

Now, Carisa glanced upward toward the sky nervously. Although it was still early in June, the air was full of humidity. It seemed to push down on them until Carisa wanted to gasp for air. Even the clouds seemed flat and ominous, as if a thunderstorm might be brewing.

But she knew the danger today did not lie in the sky but in the horses' backs. Because of the moisture

7

in the air, these would be more slippery. Papa had always scorned the customary pads, and thus the animals' bare backs provided for their riders a platform full of heaving and joggling. Even a liberal coating of rosin would not provide much security.

Why couldn't her sister see that?

Carisa stepped closer to her twin so that their father, who was talking with Rolf, would not hear. "Stephana, you're being a fool. At least you could wait until Papa has seen. . . ."

"Papa! That old fogey! If I wait for him to approve what I do, I'll be an old lady and too feeble to ride." Stephana said this defiantly, but in a half-whisper.

"But, sister, the double somersault is risky! Duddie said so. It takes great skill, and Papa hasn't approved it for you yet."

Circus smells rose up about them: trampled summer grass, horse dung, sawdust, wagon oil, perspiration, the jungly smell of Herod and Barabbas, the show's two Bengal tigers. Both girls furtively eyed their father. Deep in his conversation with Rolf, John Phillips looked stern and rather like Beelzebub in his red costume and cape, sewn by Carisa and Anna during the long winter evenings. Stephana refused to sew.

"Oh, rot!" Stephana burst out. "Papa never approves of anything for me. He won't even let a man look at me, much less talk to me. Well, I'm going to show him I'm a woman. I'm seventeen, I'm not a baby, and I've been training all of my life for this. Once he sees what I can do, he'll *know* I'm a star."

Carisa pressed her lips together. "He already knows that, Stephie, we all do. Please, I just don't want to try it today, that's all. It doesn't feel right. I had a very strange dream last night. . . ."

A dream. Carisa could still picture it vividly, the ugly images which had swirled about in her mind. Flashes of red. Phoebe's hooves flailing. Someone screaming. And mingled through it all had been a picture of the large, sprawling house on the hill which they had seen when the caravan had first rolled into New London. Proud among its grove of hemlocks, occupying

8

its rocky land with easy arrogance, it was, she knew, the home of the man who had rented them this circus lot. Adam Hartshorn was a man who loved the circus, Papa had said. And in her dream, Carisa had seen him, too. His eyes were as yellow-gold as Barabbas', his hair as tawny. . . .

"Oh, a dream!" Stephana scoffed. "Another one? Fiddle-faddle!" She tossed her head and gave an irritable tug at the sleeve of her red, ballet-length costume, which did nothing to hide the lines of her tall, superb body.

"You're always having those feelings, Carisa," she went on. "Dreams! Mooning and imagining, that's what I call it, and that's what Papa says, too. Pull your head out of the clouds! We've practiced this new act dozens of times. Hundreds! With the mechanic belt and without, We're perfect, I tell you. Papa will say so, too, when he sees us."

"We shouldn't have kept it secret," Anna, the older sister, put in. "Duddie says. . . ."

Duddie, the small, misshapen clown, had been with the Phillips' since before the twins were born. He had taught them all they knew about riding, and he had taught them to read and write as well. None of them could imagine life without him.

"Duddie is a silly old fool then," Stephana replied sharply. "And so are you, Anna."

"But, Stephie. . . ."

"How dare Duddie say I'm not ready? I *am* ready. I don't want to wait any longer. I want to do this now, today. And I'm going to!"

Carisa stared at her twin sister. Although the two girls shared the same birthday, they were not identical. Stephana, older by one hour, was also taller. Her figure was curving and regal, and there was no movement of her body which was not graceful. Her hair was a yellow so pale that it might have been plucked from a harvest field of grain.

Carisa was much smaller. Her body was slender, her hips slim, her strength more wiry. Her hair was reddish-blonde, "strawberry gold," as Duddie called it.

9

It was so fine and silky that when she performed it always flew out of its ribbons and formed a nimbus around her face.

Where Stephana's face was oval and fashionable, Carisa's was arresting, irregular. She had a square chin and a wide mouth and slanting blue eyes. Her cheekbones were high, so boldly sculpted that an artist they had met in Atlanta one summer had begged to paint her.

Anna, the older sister, had brown hair, and eyes of a deep, soft blue. She was plumper, smooth and appealing and soft. All of the sisters agreed that of the three, Carisa was the most striking, Anna the prettiest, and Stephana the most beautiful.

"It's Stephie who's the best of the *Flying Flambeaux*," their father proclaimed critically. "You, Carisa, you're too light and small. It takes a larger woman to really ride well. As for Anna, she hasn't the fire. She's content to be ordinary, and therefore she'll always be just that."

The ordinary was something for which John Phillips held contempt.

Now the tiger cage was coming out, drums still rolling in the tent where Duddie did his "clown walk" stunts. It was almost time.

"Stephana . . ." Carisa began again, knowing that she had only a few moments left to persuade.

"Oh, hush up!" Stephana gave a spring, landing deftly on the back of her horse, King. The tiger cage rattled by, emitting the strong stench of cat.

Otto, the animal trainer, nodded at Stephana, whose statuesque figure he admired.

"Not a bad day today," he remarked. "Good crowd. But old Barabas here, I think he's got worms. Wish this was a decent show and I could get me some decent cats, instead of these mangy old beasts that are ready for the tanners'."

With that Otto stumped on toward the equipment wagon and Carisa and Stephana looked at each other.

"See?" Stephana whispered. She patted her horse, King, on his smooth, rippling shoulders. "This whole

10

show is like that. Old, shabby, tired. We need a good act, something to get people's attention. Papa is too cautious. Practice, he says. Practice! Well, I'm tired of that."

"But we always have to practice." The heavy feeling in Carisa's belly had not gone away. In fact, it felt heavier than ever, like a sodden lump of canvas. She could hear the second roll of drums, their cue to get ready, and she swung onto Phoebe's back.

"No, Stephie," she said. "Not today, please. Let's wait a week or two. Give it some more time. . . ."

"No! I won't wait. And you do what I told you, Carisa Phillips, or I . . . I'll scratch your eyes out after. I swear I will!"

"You will not! You . . ."

"Girls, girls, what is this? We're on in twenty seconds."

John Phillips moved up to assume his place as first in the procession, glancing at Carisa as he rode past her. He was a thick-chested, stern-looking man of fifty-two, wearing a flamboyant red costume which only accented these characteristics.

Behind him rode Rolf, a knife-blade of a man, boldly handsome in his scarlet cape. Women always stared at Rolf. Sometimes they threw flowers at him, or handkerchiefs.

"Yes, Papa," the girls chorused. But from lowered eyelids Stephana shot a commanding look toward Carisa.

Oh, well, Carisa thought. Her sister was determined (willful, Duddie said), and it was too hot to argue. And perhaps her feeling of foreboding would go away once they began riding and she had to concentrate only on movement and timing and balance.

Besides, there wasn't time. The drums were urging them, and inside the tent she could see Duddie's feet flying as he completed the last in a series of rapid flip-flaps.

Bud deBord, the aging circus owner and equestrian director, blew his whistle. But still Carisa hesitated. Perhaps—

11

"Carisa!" John Phillips' face had darkened. "Stop daydreaming and get in line. And mind your concentration. I've had just about enough of your airs and graces. You're not a great lady, you're a circus performer, and don't you forget it."

The words stung, and Carisa felt an instant's squeezing hurt. Why was it that nothing she did ever seemed to please Papa?

"Yes, Papa," she said quickly. "Very well."

Her lips parted into a curved, stiff smile. Then they were moving forward into the tent, and she reclined gracefully on Phoebe's back as if she were a nymph and the animal's flesh the silkiest of water. She heard the crowd noise and glimpsed the faces, hundreds of them, disembodied rows of eyes and opened mouths among which the candy vendors moved, hawking their wares.

It had begun.

"Practice," Duddie always insisted. "*That*, my girl, is what will keep you from getting hurt. Practice, practice, until you can do your act in your sleep, until you don't even have to think about it. Until your body takes over and does all of the work as easily as it breathes for you."

Now, as she rode into the ring behind Stephana, it was as if Carisa could almost hear Duddie saying that. And he was right, she thought. Now that she was actually moving, she didn't have time to think, or to plan, or even to be nervous. She could just *be*.

She couldn't even remember when she had not been a performer. She, like the other girls, had been started as a baby. Duddie had been given the job of seeing to her training. Limber muscles, fearless balance, willingness to please—these qualities had been seized upon and used, exactly as if she had been some very intelligent animal.

Like most circus children, almost before she could walk she learned to do back-bends, bringing her head up easily between her knees. She could pick up handkerchiefs with her teeth. And she could lie upon the ground and coil her slim little body around her head like a snake.

Later, when she was six, she was taught to walk the "globe." This was a large, brightly painted ball made of pieces of sectionally glued wood. The girls would balance on top of it, and, by taking tiny steps, guide the ball in circles or up a ramp to a pedestal. The red-white-gold-blue globe taught exquisite balance and control—skills the girls would need all of their performing lives.

Stephana and Carisa learned to make themselves into a human wheel, catching each other's feet and rolling along the ground. They all learned split jumps, flips, cartwheels.

During their training, Papa would come often to inspect their progress.

"No!" he would shout at Stephana, or Carisa. "No, no, no! Your balance was off and your legs are sagging. I want to see good form! I want to see beauty! Or you might as well go off and get married to a greengrocer or a dray driver," he would add in contempt. "You'll be good for nothing else."

Somehow, it seemed that Carisa made mistakes more often when Papa was present. Perhaps it was because she was so nervous, or because his voice was so deep, his look so piercing. And then the scorn would be directed at her alone.

"Don't worry," Duddie would console her later. "He is a perfectionist, that's all. And perhaps he has never gotten over your mother's death. He loved her very much, you know."

"I know," Carisa replied somberly. "Once I heard him say that Stephie looks like her. I don't. Oh, Duddie . . . sometimes I think that he blames me."

"Blames you? For what?"

"Why . . . because she died giving birth to me."

Duddie's round, homely face, heavily coated with white clown makeup, creased in the sudden smile which could transform it. In a lightning-fast motion he produced a paper-wrapped packet of hard candies from his sleeve.

"Why, look," he exclaimed. "Where did these come from?" He gave her the packet. "Don't talk nonsense,

13

Carisa, child," he added. "How could you, a babe, have been at fault? Your Papa delivered you himself and I'm sure all he wishes is that you make the very best equestrienne you can. You see, sweetheart, your Papa has dreams. Dreams of a glory you're too young even to imagine."

"Dreams?"

"Someday your Papa wants to have his own show. Not just any show, mind you, but something large and stupendous. Who knows? Someday the *Flying Flambeaux* may very well play before the Queen. How would you like that? They say the Queen adores the circus."

Carisa, entranced by this picture, was distracted, and skipped away happily. Herself, Carisa Phillips, performing before Queen Victoria? Could it ever really happen?

As the years passed, the girls' skills grew. Papa hired a ballet teacher for them. To the horror of this ardent Frenchwoman, he gave orders that they were to learn to dance on a small, wooden pedestal two feet square—and to dance flat-footed. Ballet was the foundation of all bareback riding, he insisted. It would teach them balance, recovery, and graceful movements.

The dark, thin little teacher threw up her hands, argued—and charged them a bargain rate, because there were three. They learned.

One morning Papa ordered Rolf to set up a wire for them to walk, five feet high and thirty feet long. With the security of the leather mechanic harness, operated by Duddie, they began to walk it, to do jumps and twirls in their homemade canvas slippers.

Until one day when Stephana slipped and fell on the wire, and came staggering into the wagon, bleeding copiously from between the legs. Duddie took one horrified look and shouted for Marta Taggart. Then he went hurrying off to find Papa. The next morning the wire was gone and they were never asked to walk it again.

Every bareback rider has to learn to train her own horse, and the three Phillips girls were given theirs at the age of twelve. Carisa spent two months teaching

14

Phoebe to pace at an even gallop around the ring, until her gait was as dependable as a metronome.

She spent another month learning to "side-sit." This was the art of balancing on the back of the horse—without using hands or feet—so that the rider seemed to float effortlessly.

"It looks hard, but it really isn't," Duddie told her. "All you have to do is learn to use the horse instead of fighting him. Use the centrifugal force, the rosin, the friction of the horse-hair, even Phoebe's own instinct. She loves you, she wants to please you, and she'll do her best for you, if you'll let her."

Years. Of daily practices, of caring meticulously for Phoebe, sandwiching it all between performances and travel from village to village.

There was so much to learn. Rolf taught her to sell tickets, to bark out a spiel to attract an audience, to dicker with shopkeepers and farmers for food. Marta Taggart taught her to rove the fields and hedgerows, plucking wild plants to crush and mix into potions, or boil for infusions. And there was Duddie, too, to give her books, to fill her head with circus stories, with talk and dreams.

One spring in 1850, after a disastrous season in which six of their baggage horses died of disease, and bad rains and mud had eliminated their profits, Papa made a sudden decision. They would emigrate to the United States. Americans loved the circus, and the country was an enormous one, sprawling thousands of miles from the Eastern seacoast to Indian Territory. Surely, Papa said, they could find work. . . .

Now, as the *Flying Flambeaux* rode into the ring, Carisa pushed away her worry and felt the familiar lift of joy that always hit her when she saw the audience for the first time. Faces, she thought. Happy faces. Children, adults, even very old people, all kindled with the excitement and release of the circus.

That man there, for instance, she thought dreamily. The man in the reserved seats with the small boy. *He* loved the show, she was sure. Or was it just herself he was staring at, with those deep-set eyes? He was, she realized abruptly, the man who had been in her dream.

Rolf and Papa sat erect, riding with swaying, muscular grace. Then came Stephana, wild and willful and beautiful. Behind her, Carisa and then Anna, capable but ordinary. They circled the ring, as they had done thousands of times before.

But this time it would be different.

"Papa! Papa, I want some more candy. Papa, buy me some!"

Julian's voice was high, whiny and demanding. He bounced up and down on the wooden bleacher seat, plucking at Adam's sleeve.

"Julian, you've had candy. And you've had lemonade, too. You've been so busy eating that you've barely watched the circus at all."

Adam's voice was annoyed, colder than he had meant it to be. To make up for it, he reached over and put his arm around the boy.

"Look, Julian! Pay attention. Watch the clown!"

Below, in the ring, a short, squat, oddly misshapen clown was pantomiming with a chestnut horse. He pretended to slide off the animal's rump, catching himself just in time. Then he performed a series of rapid flip-flaps, landing first on the animal's back and then in the sawdust of the ring.

The little man (was he a dwarf?) was remarkably agile. His body moved with a fluid elasticity. His spine was as pliable as rope, and under the white clown make-up, his eyes gleamed like black marbles.

"Oh, I hate the clown," Julian said in his high, slightly harsh voice. "I want the tigers back! I want to see the tigers growl and roar and eat the fat man up!" He struggled to free himself from his father's grasp.

"No, you don't." Adam held tighter to the squirming nine-year-old and tried to push back his surge of irritation. "Blood-thirsty little beast, aren't you?"

"Blood-thirsty, yup," Julian agreed. He drummed with his heels on the flesh of Adam's calf. "I want the

16

tigers back, Papa! I want them to bite the man! And I want some more candy!"

"No. You're not having a bit more candy. You've had all you're going to get."

Adam sighed. He supposed the circus had not been a very good idea. But Katherine, the boy's grandmother, had had one of her headaches today. She could not bear the noise of the child's shouting. Besides, since Adam owned the pasture on which the performance was being held, he wanted to be sure the land was left clean and undamaged. Adam himself had been captivated by the circus since he was a small boy and, one day when a caravan was in town, had been paid a penny to water the elephants. . . .

He moved slightly away from his son and hoped that Julian was not going to treat them to one of his tantrums. Since the boy's mother had died six years ago, he had been left mostly to the offices of his nurse-governess, Poll Henry.

Adam's eyes darkened as he thought of the slim, wild beauty of the girl, a daughter of one of Adam's whaling captains who had perished with his ship. Poll could be sullen, yet exciting, too, in a strange, avid way. And—but, with an effort, Adam closed off the thought. Poll, it was certain, had been able to do nothing about the boy's temper.

Even Katherine, the boy's grandmother, had been able to do little. When she attempted to discipline him, he would throw himself full-length on the floor. *"Grandmama,"* he would howl. *"I hate ugly Grandmama!"*

It might have been easier, Adam thought now, if the child had been homely. Then he might have been easier to dislike. But he was not. He was a beautiful boy. When he smiled, dimples flashed in both cheeks. His hair was a honey-colored, curly cap.

That was one reason why he got his own way so often, Adam thought sourly. People could not believe that such an adorable little boy could be so single-mindedly determined to have the world run exactly as he wished it.

If only the influenza had not come, he thought. It had

17

taken away Mary Elizabeth, the boy's mother, in just one short week.

"Papa, Papa, Papa, look! Look what's coming now! Look, Papa! Look at the red people!" Julian's fists were hammering at Adam for attention.

"Yes, Julian, I see them. They are the *Flying Flambeaux,* I believe they were billed."

"They're red! Red people! Are they going to fly? Really fly?"

"Perhaps. Let's watch and see what they do."

A line of riders was entering the tent, dressed in costumes the color of flame. First came the two men, dark, their faces much alike, capes flying behind them. Then came the three girls, wearing ballet-style dresses with short sleeves and knee-length skirts. Their bodies seemed to sway in perfect accord with the motion of the horses.

Like naiads, Adam thought. Or perhaps Cleopatra, in her barge on the Nile. Three Cleopatras, each lovely.

His eyes fastened on the second girl. Slimmer than the other two, she held her body well. The lines of her face were bold, yet delicate, her cheekbones high. Her smile was fixed, as were those of the other *Flambeaux,* but Adam, watching her, had the impression that her eyes were anxious.

Why? he wondered idly. Why would a circus girl have reason to look anxious? A girl as beautiful as this one, and as skilled?

The two men performed first, riding standing, balanced across three horses. Then the girls began to perform a ballet on horseback, their movements fluid, their bodies tilted slightly inward.

The taller, wheat-haired girl began quickly to dominate her sisters. It appeared that she would slip off her mount—would have to! Yet she did not. With each *arabesque* and *jeté* her power seemed to grow. She seemed like a brilliant red flower, blooming there upon her horse's back, a swaying flame-blossom which could defy the laws of gravity.

Although he liked the smaller girl better, Adam could not help watching. *This one is brilliant,* he

18

thought. As gifted a performer as any to appear in Paris or London. Why on earth would she be here with this deBord show, a shabby affair with only a few wagons and a parade so pathetically small that it was over almost before it had begun?

"Candy," he heard Julian demand beside him. "I *said* I want candy."

But Adam did not hear him, so caught up was he in the magic of this performance. In the ring, the tall girl had moved deftly from pirouette to *arabesque penchée*. Now the two men had rejoined the girls, their capes flying, and were leaping from horse to horse.

And then (Adam was aware that the smaller girl had suddenly tensed) the tall girl suddenly arched her body and turned a cartwheel from her mount to the back of the one behind it. Almost instantly she spun into a series of somersaults.

In the hot, close tent there was a hushed silence, broken only by the roll of drums.

Beside him, even Julian had stopped his whining for candy. In the front row a candy vendor had paused in the act of selling a cone of sticky pink to stare at the girl, too.

Then it happened, so quickly that Adam barely saw the scrap of paper which the front row child threw toward the horses.

He was only aware that horses' bodies were lunging and falling, that people were screaming. The spinning girl was a blur of red.

Then people and horses lay sprawled in an ugly mound, and already the clown was running in their direction. The big man in the red costume came running too. He stared downward in horror.

Pain and confusion and people screaming and shouting.

But mostly pain.

Carisa lay with both legs pinned under Phoebe's back, and knew that she had broken her bones. She had felt them snap in the nightmare moment when Phoebe had landed on her, nineteen hundred pounds of struggling animal flesh. Now Phoebe still struggled,

19

emitting high cries of pain. Each time the mare moved, she sent more pain rocketing through Carisa.

Faces blurred above her. Men had jumped from the audience to try to help. Duddie was there, and Papa. Rolf. Mr. deBord. They were trying to drag Phoebe off her, to ease the savage agony that ripped up her legs.

A flash of wild grief ripped through her for her horse.

Stephana, she thought wildly. Was that her sister nearby, that crumpled, oddly bent heap of red? And Anna. Dear God, Anna. What had happened? She could barely remember it now: a flash of white across the corner of her eye and Phoebe's startled jerk. Then everything tipping, tilting out of control.

She heard her own voice screaming.

Abruptly the pressure across her legs was gone—they had lifted Phoebe away.

"Was this your fault?" a voice said over her. She looked up to see Papa's face bent over hers, his complexion drained leaden gray. Two red spots colored his cheeks like paint. "Was this *your* fault, Carisa?"

Then, mercifully, Papa's accusing face receded into the background of excited, hurrying people. The pain faded, too, and then she was unconscious.

She awoke to find that she was in a room, lying on a soft bed. She could smell beeswax, and the crisp odor of linen stored in lavender.

"Phoebe," she moaned. "Phoebe . . . my horse. . . ."

"You'd better take this," a woman's low, husky voice said. A spoon nudged at her lips. "It's opium. Dr. Arthur is seeing to . . . to your sister, and then he'll be back and tend to you."

"It . . . hurts. . . ."

"Of course it does. Both your legs are broken. It's a wonder you're alive at all."

"Anna . . . Stephana. . . ."

"Hush. It does no good to think about them now. You've your own injuries to worry about."

Carisa thought of the gentle mare whom she had loved and trained herself. She tried to lift her head so she could see where she was. But as she did so she felt an agonizing wrench of pain in both legs, and she sank back helplessly.

"You mustn't move," the woman said. "You'll only make it worse. You've a wound in your right leg with the bone sticking through. It's very serious, I'm afraid. You won't be riding horseback again." She sighed. "Open your mouth and take this medicine as I told you. I've put it in honey."

Carisa obediently swallowed and tasted the cloying sweetness of honey, mingled with some bitter flavor. She gazed upward at the woman who had given it to her. She was about fifty-five, clad in black *moiré* and wearing a lace-trimmed collar. Her voice had been of the deep, husky timber that strikes certain women of middling years, and her face seemed to match it. It was long, sallow-skinned, rather masculine, yet with a faded handsomeness.

"I'm Katherine Hartshorn," the woman said. "You're in my son's house. Adam owns the lot on which you held your circus." Her eyes regarded Carisa disapprovingly.

"But . . . I don't understand. . . ."

"When the accident happened, he ordered that you and your sister be brought here. The doctor is attending to her now. Then it will be your turn."

"My sister? Do you mean Stephana?"

The woman, Katherine Hartshorn, looked away, her eyes evasive. "No, I believe that the other girl is called Anna. That is what she told Dr. Arthur. She has a sprained arm, I think."

"But . . . But Stephana. My other sister. What happened to her?" Carisa's voice rose.

"Now, you mustn't excite yourself. You are very seriously hurt, my dear, and I would suggest. . . ."

"My sister! She's dead, isn't she?"

"Well. . . ."

"She's dead!"

"Why . . . yes, she is. It was very unfortunate. But you mustn't upset yourself any further. You've enough ahead of you as it is. Try to swallow another spoonful of opium. That should. . . ."

Carisa pushed away the spoon. Shock was flying through her, slapping at her in wave after wave. "She died of a broken neck, didn't she?" she heard her voice say mechanically. "And they had to shoot my horse, as well, my Phoebe, didn't they?"

"Yes."

"I dreamed it," Carisa said dully. "I knew it would happen because I dreamed all of it, last night. But Stephana wouldn't listen, she was determined. I . . . Oh, I should have told Papa. I had the chance to tell him and I let it go by. . . ."

The opium must be taking effect, for she could hear her voice slur, and she began to feel detached, removed from her surroundings. The bedroom—dark furnishings, oak paneling, framed engravings on the wall—began to assume a blurred aspect, like watercolors which have run.

Stephana, her thoughts tumbled on. *Stephie, why did you do it?* It all seemed impossible, not real at all.

And why did she feel so dulled and numb? Even her legs didn't hurt very much any more. She couldn't react, she couldn't weep, she could barely even think.

There was a rap on the bedroom door.

"Yes?" Katherine Hartshorn called out sharply. "Come in."

By turning her head, Carisa was able to see the two men who had entered the room. One, short and balding, was evidently the doctor, for he carried a worn leather bag. The second was a handsome man of thirty-five, with tawny eyes that seemed to blaze yellow at her. His face was rugged, the nose bold, the chin clefted, strong and determined. His wide-shouldered, rangy body was clad in a dark broadcloth suit now stained with dust and straw and blood. His walk was arrogant, as if he were used to giving commands and having people do his bidding.

"I'm Adam Hartshorn." He came to the foot of the bed. The amber-gold eyes regarded her. "This is my house, Hearts-ease, we call it. I had you brought here.

A circus wagon is no place for a girl in your condition, I'm afraid."

Surely it was only because the room was blurred, surely she did not see pity in his eyes.

"The medicine is taking effect, I see," the doctor said. "Which is just as well. When I examined her in the tent I found she has a compound fracture of the right leg, plus an ordinary simple fracture of the left. I stemmed the bleeding, of course, but the wound is a dirty one and I am sure it is going to suppurate." A pause. "I feel we should amputate at once."

"What! Amputate!"

The big, lion-eyed man had whirled about to face the doctor. Even in her stupor Carisa could sense his horror.

"I'm afraid so, Hartshorn. It's a customary procedure in cases like this where the wound is so ugly, and contaminated by dirt and horsehair, as this one is. These kind of wounds usually turn gangrenous."

A customary procedure in cases like this.

The words seemed to echo around the room. Even Katherine Hartshorn drew in a sharp breath.

Carisa wanted to open her mouth to say something, to protest, but her jaw muscles would not move. A cold gray fog seemed to be rolling from the corners of the room. She felt her eyelids flutter shut. With infinite effort, she forced them open.

"No," she whispered. "No. Please."

Then her eyes closed again and the fog took her.

2

Adam Hartshorn felt his fists bunching at his sides. He resisted the urge to grab Dr. Arthur by his high, starched collar and drag him bodily from the room.

He had not realized just how captivating he found the girl until he had seen her lying there in the bed.

23

Helpless and in pain, she seemed diminished, fragile, completely at his mercy. She had been a naiad, perched on the back of that magnificent horse with the arching neck. He could not imagine her stumping about on only one leg. The very thought tore at his insides.

"Dr. Arthur," he said. "If we must argue, we will do so outside this room where she can't hear us. And we will do nothing, nothing whatsoever, until we have her permission and that of her family."

He said this very clearly so that if she were still conscious she would be able to understand.

"But surely. . . ."

"Outside, if you please, Dr. Arthur."

Grumpily, the doctor followed Adam out into the corridor, wiping perspiration from the bare dome of his head. "Of course, of course. But I was only thinking . . . I mean, she's only a. . . ."

"Only a circus girl? Of course she is, and a superb one, too. Dr. Arthur, had you forgotten that this girl's livelihood depends on her legs? And you want to amputate!"

They were in the wide, upper hallway, its paneling painted in pale cream and hung with family portraits. This was the post-1724 addition to the house; the original section had been built by the first Adam Hartshorn in 1715. It was one of the few in New London which had escaped burning by the British in 1781.

The faces of his ancestors, done in crayon and oil, looked down at him. Many of the Hartshorns, including the first Adam, had died at sea. They had been whalers, sea captains and ship builders for generations.

One portrait, in particular, stood out from the others. This was the painting of the first Adam Hartshorn, a man with a stubborn, arrogant face, a chin of iron determination, and eyes which blazed out amber fire. This first Adam had hung seven men accused of piracy on Long Island Sound and had been, it was said, as bold as any pirate himself.

Now it was Adam who fought to build the family fortune—sometimes quietly, sometimes ruthlessly, sometimes against the opposition of his brother, Samuel.

24

Now, he realized that Dr. Arthur was speaking to him.

"She objected? Oh, pshaw, anyone under those circumstances would say no. She was under the influence of the opium I gave her and she barely knew what she was saying. Besides, she's a mere girl. She can't be more than seventeen. A child, really, and a female as well. What can she know of her own needs?"

"As much as any other person, I'd say. What will happen if you don't amputate? If you just set the bones and let her remain as she is?"

"Why . . . Why, the wound will probably develop pus and grow gangrenous." The little doctor was staring at Adam in surprise.

"Probably, you said. But not certainly?"

"Well . . . I don't know. Many things are possible in medicine, and nothing is certain. I have seen men recover from truly grievous wounds . . . and I have seen them die from simple things, like a scratch, or a cut to the hands."

"Then it's conceivable that we could care for her leg so she would not need amputation?"

"Oh. Well. . . ."

"Can you tell me how to do it?"

"I suppose I could. But, Hartshorn, I just wouldn't recommend it. Odds are we'll fail and the girl will die. It's common . . . *common,* I tell you, to do amputations in cases like this."

Adam scowled. "I don't care what's commonly done. I'm going to save that leg."

"But good heavens, man, you're taking a frightful risk. These circus people . . . why, they're no better than gypsies. Gypsies and vagabonds. Chances are they'll just go off and leave you with the care of her."

"Perhaps. Nonetheless, I'm going to go out and find her family and talk to them."

"But, Hartshorn, even if we do save the leg, she's ruined for the circus. The bones . . . the severity of the break. . . ."

But Adam was not listening. He was already halfway down the corridor toward the stairs, and as he passed the small oil portrait of the first Adam Hartshorn, he

25

fancied that the arrogant yellow eyes of the sea captain, so like his own, turned to stare at him as he went by.

But that, of course, was only his imagination.

Adam's study was a big, comfortable room smelling pleasantly of old leather book bindings and Havana cigars. It was paneled in white-painted pine and contained an English walnut desk-bookcase, comfortably upholstered chairs, and a Turkish rug woven in deep reds and blues. A fanlight arched over the door which led to the garden. Here Adam conferred with Mr. West, his whaling agent, transacted business, and held tense late-night meetings with other New London businessmen, both friends and enemies.

He had always pursued the Hartshorn fortunes with singleminded determination. In doing so, he had made more than his share of enemies. This room, he reflected ruefully, had seen more than a few shouting matches, and several times there had been drawn pistols. . . .

Now, pacing up and down, he could not stop thinking of the interview he had just had with the girl's father, ten minutes ago in this very room.

A big-chested, arrogant man with the lithe body of the circus performer, John Phillips had still been wearing his red woolen costume, crumpled now and stained with the blood of the daughter who had died. The man's full, springy gray-black hair flowed back like a crest from his face. The blue eyes held a look that was near to madness.

"Take her then, damn her hide." The voice, with its English intonation, was resonant and impressive, as flamboyant as the man himself. "And do whatever you wish with her. It doesn't matter to me."

Adam could not believe he had heard him properly.

"But she's your daughter."

"She's also a traitor to my name. Do you know something?" John Phillips leaned closer, and Adam could smell whiskey on his breath. "Do you know what she did? She *knew* what was going to happen! Oh, yes, she knew, she must have, and she *didn't tell me*. She

26

was aware that Stephana intended to disobey me and she kept silent!"

"Oh, surely that's not the case. And surely the other girl, the other sister, also knew. . . ."

John Phillips made a savage gesture. "Anna knew nothing of it. She has already sworn it to me on the grave of her mother. No, it was Carisa who betrayed me. She who destroyed the *Flambeaux* by her silence. She and no other."

He turned, and with stiff dignity began to walk out of the study.

Trying to control his anger and dismay, Adam strode after him. "Betrayal or not, she's still your daughter. What do you wish to be done with her? And what about her care? Surely you do plan to see to that at least?"

"I'll leave you some money. She won't be a public charge. But beyond that, I don't care. The show is leaving in the morning. Anna is well enough to travel and we've already posted our bills for the next town."

"But. . . ."

John Phillips' eyes were glittering with moisture, his mouth twisted. "Leave me alone, young man. I don't wish to hear anything more about Carisa Phillips. To me, she is dead. Dead like her sister, whom she killed."

Now that implacable voice seemed to echo against the walls of the study. Adam paced back and forth, trying to quell his fury. Like a patriarch from the Bible the old man was, he thought disjointedly. Stubborn, iron-willed. How had such a man fathered a girl like Carisa?

And now, exactly as Dr. Arthur had predicted, he was left with the girl on his hands.

The door of the study swung open and Adam's mother swept in, her petticoats rustling.

"Adam Hartshorn," she said in her harsh, raw voice. "Don't tell me that you have really volunteered to take that circus hussy in."

"Yes, I have. Her father consented to leave her here."

Katherine Hartshorn's mouth opened in dismay. "Have you completely flown your senses? To keep a

young girl here in your house for months on end . . .
because it *will* be for months, don't you realize that?
Bones don't mend in a week or two. And with two legs
broken she will be quite helpless. A total invalid!
Which means more work for the servants . . . we'll have
to assign her a personal maid, and. . . ."

Adam stared coldly at his mother.

"I will provide all the extra servants she needs."

"Servants! Oh, yes, very well, you'll provide them.
But that's only a bare beginning. Adam, what are people going to think? A girl with that . . . that bold appearance, and you not even married to her. . . ."

Adam shrugged. "As you know, I have never cared
over-much for the idle chatter of the townspeople. Let
them think anything they wish."

"What?" Katherine stared at him. Then she threw
her head back and laughed, the muscles of her throat
working. In her youth she had been a handsome woman;
now occasional flashes of her looks remained. This was
one of those moments.

"Oh, Adam, you are joking, I do trust! A girl like
that! Oh, I'll grant you she's pretty . . . she's very striking indeed, with those high cheekbones and that mass
of red-blonde hair. And she has courage, too, I'll admit.
Hardly a whimper out of her, and her legs must have
hurt her terribly. But those things are neither here nor
there. Surely you can see that."

"See what, mother?"

"Why . . . Why, it will look as if. . . ." Katherine drew
herself up. She picked up an equinoctial dial from the
desk, which had been owned by Adam's grandfather,
and stood turning it in her hands.

"You *know* what it will look like, Adam, do I have
to spell it out in detail? And what sort of debased,
barbaric people must she spring from, that they would
go off and desert her like this?"

Adam thought of the granite face of John Phillips.
"I don't think they are debased, mother. Stubborn,
perhaps."

"Stubborn! They are animals, Adam, and you know
it. To leave her in the care of strangers . . . why, Gaines

28

told me that they are already packing to move on. They should be gone by tomorrow."

"Mother, the circus must travel to live. And there is no way they can care for her in a caravan wagon. The jolting would be agony for her."

Katherine put down the dial with a sharp, metallic click. "Perhaps, Adam. Perhaps you are right. But Dr. Arthur tells me something else, something which disturbs me almost as much. He says that you refuse to allow him to amputate."

"That's right."

"Adam, have you no moral responsibility? What if the girl dies? Did you ever stop to think of that? If she does, her death will be on your hands. She could have lived, you know, if you had permitted Dr. Arthur to have his way."

"Lived! Like a. . . ." Perspiration sprang to Adam's forehead. He thought of the legless old man who lived at the edge of town in a log hovel. Joe Madder, a torso on wheels, who pushed himself about on a little wheeled platform. Was that what he wanted for Carisa Phillips? No! Never! The thought filled him with disgust and loathing.

"Nevertheless," he heard Katherine go on, "you *are* playing with her life."

"I don't consider it that way," Adam said slowly. "I think that I'm saving her life. She doesn't want to be a cripple, can't you understand that? She'll be grateful to me for what I've done."

Katherine made a vigorous, ugly face. "Grateful! My dear Lord, yes. I would imagine that will be the very least of her emotions. You're a very good-looking man, you know. And an eligible one. A good catch for any girl, let alone a little vagabond adventuress."

Adam turned on his heel and strode to the window. Beyond the red moreen drapes was a view of Hartshorn lawns and property, then tumbled water. Dirty clouds were banked up over the Sound.

"It's going to storm," Adam said. "Tonight, I think. We must be sure that the shutters are secured tightly."

"Adam Hartshorn, are you refusing to listen to me?"

"Yes. Yes, I am, mother. If you don't like what I've chosen to do, then I'm afraid you have only one choice. You can move out. Otherwise, I hope and expect that you will support me in my efforts to care for this girl. And that you will put all of your considerable talents to work on her behalf."

He put his arms around his mother and kissed her lightly.

"Please?" he added.

"Adam! I believe you are really serious about this, aren't you?" Katherine's hands pressed themselves tightly together in the folds of her gown. "Men!" she snorted. "What fools they can be. What deliberate, determined fools!"

She picked up her skirts and left the room.

The storm had come and burst over them with mindless ferocity, flapping at the closed shutters and ripping two of them away. But by morning it had passed, leaving the air behind it warm and limpid.

Carisa lay very still in the soft bed, its goose-feather mattress softer than anything she had ever known. Her face was turned to the wall. There was a pattern in the grain of the oak paneling that reminded her of Phoebe. It captured the very curve of Phoebe's neck, strong, elegant, graceful.

Dully she closed her eyes. Phoebe was dead. The sorrow was a huge, painful knot inside her. And she herself would never ride again. Not in the circus, at any rate. Dr. Arthur, after fixing her legs in these curious contraptions called fracture-boxes, had told her that.

He had done the best he could, he explained, but she was not to expect perfect alignment of the bones. If upon recovery she could walk reasonably well, she was to consider herself lucky. Any remaining limp would be camouflaged by long skirts and the ordinary motions of a woman's walk. But the kind of skilled muscular activity required by the equestrian act would no longer be possible.

30

Carisa, hearing this, had wanted to scream out in her pain and dismay. But somehow the screams would not come. Instead, she turned away. "It doesn't matter," she mumbled at last. "Don't you see? Phoebe is dead. And my sister."

After the legs had been set, Duddie had come to see her. By this time her wound had begun to throb. She had reached out to clasp the clown's calloused hands in hers.

"Duddie. . . ."

"A fine mess you're in, my Carisa."

She blinked back tears. "Yes. Phoebe . . . Stephie. The *Flambeaux* ruined. All of Papa's dreams . . . his plans. . . ."

Duddie looked at her. Without makeup, he seemed naked and funny. His nose was bulbous, his eyes somehow too far apart, his mouth crooked and humorous. He was less than five feet tall, not quite a dwarf, but having many of the physical characteristics of one.

He had been born in Sussex, Carisa knew, the fourth son of an Earl. From the very first his family, save for one brother, had laughed at him. The bright, misshapen boy had taken refuge from them in his riding. He had been sent away to Eton, and there they had laughed at him, too. At age 13 he had run away to the Royal Amphitheater in London, where the renowned John Astley was developing the equestrian spectacle. It was here that Duddie met John Phillips and later joined the small circus troupe.

Not only had Duddie taught Carisa to ride, he had also taught all three girls to read and to write. Carisa, the best student, he had instructed in the rudiments of Latin and French. He had also told her what it was like to live in a British country house; the flocks of servants above and below-stairs, the personal ladies' maids, the garden parties, the social life.

Carisa had listened to these tales avidly. Duddie's past years seemed to belong to another world as remote as the moon. Or *was* that world so far away? Sometimes Carisa had odd dreams that she herself was the

31

lady of such a manor. That she herself owned a great house exquisitely paneled, with Turkish rugs and fine furnishings, within sight of the sea. . . .

"Stephana was always willful," Duddie was telling her now. "But that does not excuse me. I was too proud of her, that was my error. I knew she was restless, I suspected that she had been practicing something new. And I also thought that your Papa was being over-cautious. . . ."

"And I . . ." Carisa's voice stopped. She remembered the moment when she had been about to go into the ring, when her father had spoken sharply to her. She had been hurt, and she had hesitated, and the seconds had ticked by, and it was too late.

"Duddie . . ." She squeezed convulsively at the clown's hands. "Duddie, what does Papa say?"

"He is . . . full of grief."

"Is he? Oh, Duddie, does he blame me?" The words came out in such a small whisper that the clown had to lean forward to hear her.

"Yes, Carisa. I am afraid that he does."

Carisa heard this without surprise. *Was this your fault?* Papa had said.

"Do you think that he will come to see me? Before the show leaves, I mean?" She did not have to be told that the circus would leave her here; it was customary to find a home for the severely injured performer. If he lived, he would be picked up later, when the circus came through again.

"No, Carisa, I don't think that he will."

"But . . . Oh, Duddie!" She let her hands drop life-lessly onto the smooth, luxurious linen of the bedsheets.

"He is very angry," Duddie went on. "He has been questioning everyone, and I am ashamed to say that he has hit me."

She moistened her lips. "And Anna?"

"Anna lied and told him she knew nothing of it. You know her, Carisa . . . she is easy-going and does not like to be troubled with shouting and strong emotions. And *he*, he wanted to believe her."

Duddie rose from the chair in which he had been sitting and began to walk about the room in light, springy strides. His short arms swung ludicrously at his sides. "Carisa, you must not concern yourself with what your father says or does just now. He is a grieving man, and he is angry. But later, when he has had a chance to think, and to ponder. . . ."

Carisa's eyes fastened themselves hungrily on Duddie's face. "Oh, Duddie, he must forgive me. I . . . I hope so. I couldn't bear it if Papa. . . ."

"He'll forgive you." Duddie wheeled back to her and, with a wry grimace, bowed low and produced a handful of hard candies from his sleeve. He put them firmly in Carisa's hand.

"Here, my dear. Save these and eat them in case these people don't feed you enough. And now you must concentrate on getting better at once. It will be a very sad show without you, I am afraid. We will be sorely lacking."

"I will try. . . ." Carisa's fist closed over the candy.

"You must do more than just try. You must be determined, my Carisa. You see, I've already talked with your Dr. Arthur and I know that it's going to be hard for you. But you come from a long line of brave people. Circus folk who kept going in spite of mud and rain and injuries, and who always exited with a smile and a little wave of the hand, no matter how badly they were hurt."

Duddie was smiling, that warm and gentle smile she had known since her babyhood. "You, too, Carisa. You will go on with a smile and you will not show your pain."

"Duddie . . . I don't think I can."

"Of course you can. You are Carisa Phillips, aren't you? Your mother was a strong and very beautiful lady. You will be the same."

Again she clung to him, weeping into his shirt-front. Then, gently, he pushed her away. He took her hand and pried out one of the candy-drops from the tight little mass clenched in her fist. He peeled away its paper.

"Lemon?" He popped it into her mouth. "Well, don't

let it pucker you. Taste its sweetness. *Life* is sweet, Carisa. Taste that, too."

Then, with a springy bounce, the clown was gone.

Two days had passed. Carisa lay dully in the feather-bed, staring at the whorls of a knot in the rich paneling. She had never seen such paneling before. And such soft, rich, luxurious beds! None of this seemed quite real.

Papa, she thought. Oh, Papa! And Stephana, and Phoebe, my wonderful horse whom I trained all alone. . . .

The room was full of servants coming and going. They carried basins of warm water, poultices and laden meal trays, for Dr. Arthur had ordered that she be put on an ample diet, with plenty of wine and porter, and laudanum if she wished it for the pain.

But Carisa refused the laudanum. She could bear the pain, she insisted. As for the food, she wasn't hungry.

"Not hungry? Oh, nonsense!" Katherine Hartshorn said. "Suppuration of a wound requires a full diet, and I don't plan to skimp you in that regard. I promised my son I would care for you, and that I intend to do. Whether you wish it or not, and whether or not *I* wish it."

"But, really, I'm not at all hungry."

"And what does that have to do with it? I'll tell Nelly to bring another tray, and some whipped syllabub. That should tempt your appetite."

Katherine had arrived carrying a porcelain pan filled with a noxious yellow substance, and now she set this down on the bedside table. Carisa could smell something strong and rooty, like vegetables.

"What . . ." she began.

"Oh, do stop wriggling about!" the older woman ordered, stirring the mixture. "You'll never heal if you keep twisting about like that. As for this, it's carrot poultice. Very effective, Dr. Arthur says."

Obediently Carisa sank back into the mattress.

"There, that's better. Now I'm going to sponge your wound again and put on this poultice. It's the only way

34

we are going to keep your wound from mortifying. You're already feverish and I don't want you to grow any worse. And this afternoon Dr. Arthur is coming to bleed you further."

"More bleeding?" Carisa struggled to sit up, felt an arrow of pain in both legs, and had to be content with a gesture. "Is that all he can think of to do for me? To bleed and purge, and then bleed again?"

Katherine Hartshorn stared at her. "Do you, a little circus girl taken in on what amounts to charity, dare to complain?"

"No. I . . . Of course not."

"Then lie still and let me finish this, if you please."

Carisa lay very still, trying not to cry out as Katherine's hands moved among the assorted bandages, pasteboard and tapes which bound the fracture-boxes to her legs.

"There. That's better. At least I'll grant that you have courage . . . not that it will do you much good *here*. I have advised my son of his foolishness, but he chose not to listen to me. However, I hope that you won't be so silly. You don't belong here, Miss Phillips, and the sooner you are well and out of here, the better it will be."

Carisa reddened. "My father left money for my care," she said with all the dignity she could.

Katherine's hands worked deftly. "Of course he did . . . a bare pittance. Not nearly enough to provide all that *he* has ordered for you, my dear girl."

Carisa was silent. Once her temper would have flared out at such treatment; the Phillips' were an honorable family even if they were only circus folk. But today she felt too weak to manage a biting reply, and each time Katherine moved the cloth over the wound, she had to suppress a cry of pain.

At last Katherine smoothed on the carrot poultice and bound it in place with a clean rag.

"There," she said. "Now, my son has ordered that you be brought some needlework to occupy yourself. What would you like me to bring you?"

"Needlework?"

"Bargello? Petit-point? Or perhaps you would prefer bugle or beadwork, or painting on glass?"

"I've never done any of those things."

"No, I don't suppose you had time in your *former work,* did you?"

Katherine's mouth twisted as she said this, giving the impression that Carisa might have come from life as a prostitute.

Carisa flushed. Many people, she knew, thought that women in the circus had easy morals, since they wore short costumes and traveled about the country. Because of this, John Phillips had always insisted that his daughters live lives of unmistakable virtue. They had been strictly chaperoned and never left alone with men. Thus Carisa was a virgin, and had never even had a man seriously interested in her, other than the Atlanta artist, who had only wanted to paint her.

"I'm not that kind of girl," she whispered.

"Aren't you?" Katherine took up the basin and walked to the door, her black skirts rustling. "Well, I suppose I'll have to bring you a book, then. Or don't you know how to read either?"

"I read very well, thank you," Carisa snapped. "And, yes, I would enjoy a novel or any other book. I especially like Nathaniel Hawthorne."

Katherine's eyes glinted. She left the room without replying.

Five minutes later, Carisa heard a creak of the door and looked up to see a face peering in at her. It was a boy's face—round, angelic—with a cap of tousled honey-colored hair and a mouth screwed into a ferocious pout.

"Well, hello," she said, rousing herself from her misery.

"Are your legs brokened off?" the boy asked. His voice did not match his cherubic good looks; it was rather harsh for one so young. He edged further into the room, giving her a curious and not very friendly stare.

This was Julian, Carisa knew, Adam Hartshorn's motherless son. She had heard shrieks of rage and clatterings of boots in the corridor, and had gathered that the boy's room was somewhere near her.

"They are not broken *off,*" she explained. "But the bones are broken, I'm afraid. That's why I have these fracture-boxes."

"They're ugly," he announced. "Under your skirts like that. Ugly and horrid."

He bounded into the room and raced to the window, jerking the wooden venetian blinds askew so that he could see out.

"And I don't think you should be here," he added. "Poll says that you shouldn't. Poll says you're nothing but a little circus tart, and no better than you should be."

Carisa stiffened. She could not believe that such ugly words could come from a child so handsome.

"Who is Poll?" she asked.

"Oh, Poll is my nursemaid and gov'ness. She sleeps in my room with me. Her father got drownded once in the sea," Julian announced. He pushed up one end of the antique basswood slats and let them fall with a clatter.

The door opened again. This time the face which peered in belonged to a young woman a few years older than Carisa. She had a narrow, avid face and liquid dark eyes—filled now with hostility.

This must be Poll, Carisa knew. Her wound was throbbing unpleasantly and her body ached all over. But she stared back at the other girl, surprised at the strength of the dislike she felt.

"I came to get *him,*" Poll said at last, looking away. Her well-shaped, sensual little mouth was pursed.

"The boy isn't doing any harm here," Carisa said.

The jet-dark eyes regarded Carisa coolly. Was there hatred in them? Yet no, Carisa told herself, how could there be? She had never even seen this girl before.

"Well, he doesn't like you," Poll said. "And he's got to come. It's time for his nap."

"Nap!" Julian burst out. "Aw, not a horrid old nap! I'm too big for a nap . . . I'm nine, Poll, and I hate naps. . . ."

"You'll take one if I say so." Poll touched Julian's arm in a gesture that was oddly soft and caressing. Julian seemed to settle down like a pony which has been gentled.

As they left, Carisa stared after the pair in anger and puzzlement. Surely Julian had been winding up for a tantrum. Yet this unlikely girl had been able to soothe him and get him to do as she asked.

Unease spurted through Carisa. It prodded at her like the tines of a fork. Then wearily, giving in to her pain and fever, she closed her eyes.

In late afternoon Dr. Arthur came, with his jar of leeches and the glasses he would use to prevent the creatures from escaping.

The leeches were ugly, fat, slimy things, but Carisa bore them bravely, covering her eyes so that she would not have to see the doctor smearing cream on her upper arm to attract them to that area. She had never been ill enough to require leeches before. The circus folk generally depended on their own remedies, and Duddie's pharmacopoeia had run more to strong emetics.

Just as Dr. Arthur was removing the swollen leeches from Carisa's arm, Adam Hartshorn knocked at the door and then strode into the room.

He stopped short in dismay. "Don't tell me that you are bleeding her!"

"Why, yes, I am." Dr. Arthur looked up in annoyance. "It is customary in cases of this sort."

Adam's broad-carved face twisted with anger. "How many times have you put the leeches to her?"

"Why . . . only yesterday, and just now, of course. She has taken them very well and already I see signs of improvement. She . . ."

"I don't see any signs of improvement! I think she looks paler than ever, save for those fever-red cheeks of hers. And no wonder, with all the blood she has lost. First the wound, and then you, robbing her of what strength she has left. . . ."

Dr. Arthur, with a pair of tongs, dropped the last of the sated leeches into their jar and closed the vented lid. "I thought you asked me to care for this patient."

"I did. But from now on, there is going to be no more bleeding, or purging either."

"But . . ." the man sputtered. "But what *do* you expect me to do then?"

"I expect you to cure her."

For an instant the two men stared at each other. Then Dr. Arthur bent over and picked up his black leather bag from the floor.

"Cure her!" he mumbled. "Oh, yes, I am supposed to have her well, but I am not permitted to use any of the methods commonly used to effect such a cure. Oh, yes, indeed!"

He gave a brief, angry bow to Carisa and left, still muttering.

Carisa smiled faintly. "Well, you have rescued me from the leeches, anyway. For that I am very grateful. Not to mention everything else you have done. . . ."

Adam made a dismissing gesture. "It's not necessary to thank me. Your father left money for your care."

"But. . . ."

"Just don't thank me, all right?" His voice was roughened.

"Very well, then. If that's what you wish."

Puzzled, Carisa lifted up her eyes to stare at this man, this stranger, who had taken her into his home. Adam Hartshorn was tall—well over six feet—with a broad-shouldered, rangy body with whipcord muscles honed by vigorous exercise. He wore a black broadcloth coat, a white waistcoat, and buff nankin trousers, attire which emphasized the clean, male lines of his body. His face was square, tanned from the sun and strongly carved, with a bold cleft in the chin. But its strongest feature was the eyes. These were a curious tawny shade, like the coat of a lion crouched in the breathless heat of the African bush. From the sun-browned skin they seemed to blaze out at her, to catch and hold her captive.

Carisa felt shaken as those tawny eyes examined her.

"Why?" she asked at last. "Why didn't you let them

amputate? Dr. Arthur told me that was what he wanted to do."

Abruptly Adam turned his profile to her and she saw that his nose was high-bridged and arrogant. "There is a man who lives on the outskirts of town who . . ." He stopped. "But we won't talk about that. We didn't amputate, and we're not going to do so. It would be a waste, a terrible waste of beauty."

A terrible waste of beauty. As Carisa tried to grasp the fact that he was calling her beautiful, Adam turned on his heel and began to stride toward the door.

"If you need anything, Miss Phillips, anything at all, please let me know at once. You're going to get well, and I won't hear of anything else."

That evening, while Carisa stared dully at her dinner tray, the little servant, Nelly, chatted away to her, telling her of life in this house. Nelly had been assigned to Carisa as her lady's maid.

"Oh, yes, he can be a tough man," Nelly giggled. "They *say* he once pistol-whipped a man for mistreating a horse. Granny says he has made some hard business deals, and there are a few in town who hate him. . . ."

Carisa nodded.

"As for *her*," Nelly went on, not seeming to mind that Carisa did not reply, "she runs the house with a sharp eye. Oh, Lord, there isn't a thing she doesn't see, from the kitchen to the attic, and she can be a scold, too, when she wishes to be. But I kind of like her," Nelly added. "She sends baskets of food to my granny, who's got the dropsy, and once, when I was sick with the grippe, she took care of me herself. Cosseted me and made me puddings and cordials until I felt so shamed I *had* to get out of bed!"

Nelly laughed infectiously. She was a country girl, small, slim and plain, and she did not seem to mind the homely chores of the sickroom.

"*He* is considered one of the most eligible bachelors in New London," the girl went on after a moment. "My granny and my aunts, they all laugh and say the girls are busting their corset strings to land him. But he won't look at any of 'em. It aggravates his mother no end."

Carisa could only stare at Nelly, moistening her dry lips.

"Oh! Oh, you poor little thing." Nelly was contrite. "Here I've been jabbering away and look at you, so flushed and thirsty. I'll get you some water right away. And I'll put some ice in it, from the ice-house. That should help, shouldn't it?"

That night Carisa's fever went up. Nelly, who had been told to sleep on a cot in the room with her, came over to feel Carisa's forehead. The girl's fingers were icy cold against the heat of Carisa's forehead, and she could not help moaning. Nelly gave an exclamation and then went running out of the room.

In a few minutes she was back with Katherine Hartshorn. Adam's mother wore a blue wrapper, her hair flowing over her shoulders in two thick, gray braids. Adam, in a brown silk dressing gown, was immediately behind her, holding a candle.

"It's the fever, Mrs. Hartshorn." Nelly's voice was soft with alarm. "She's got it bad. Oh, she's burning up!"

"We'd better call the doctor again, Adam," Katherine said. She moved about the room, lighting the gas fixture so that a thin yellow light flickered on the paneling.

"So he can come here with his jar of leeches and his clysters to purge her again? That's all the old fool will recommend, you know. I think we can do more for her ourselves."

"Adam!" Even in the blur of her illness, Carisa could sense Katherine's fury. "Is there no limit to your obsession with this creature? Get yourself back to bed, if you please. I've cared for many a fevered patient in my day, including yourself, and I think that I know what to do. Get out, I tell you! It's shocking, a big lummox like you hanging around the bedroom of a strange young girl!"

"Mother, you forget that this is my house." Adam's voice was cold and lashing.

"And *you* forget that you asked me to care for this

girl. And that's exactly what I intend to do, once you're gone."

"Very well. But I want you to. . . ."

"Adam, Adam, will you get out? Will you leave? Have you gone completely besotted?"

3

Later, Carisa was to have little coherent memory of that long night in which the fever consumed her body. She writhed and tossed from side to side, and finally had to be restrained to the bed with cloths, so that she would not injure herself.

The night held brief moments of lucidity. Once she struggled upward from a choked, frightening dream of the girl, Poll, only to realize that she herself was lying on the mattress, naked. Nelly was seated beside the bed, sponging her thighs and ribs with a wet cloth.

The water felt frigid, as if it had been hauled from the ice-house, and each stroke of the rag was agony. Her right leg throbbed unbearably.

"Don't . . ." Carisa moaned. "Don't . . . Oh, what are you doing?"

"I'm sponging you, Miss Carisa. *She* said I had to do it, said 'twas the only thing which might save your life." The maidservant was still in her own nightgown. Her brown hair, loosed for sleeping, hung down her back, and her eyes were red-rimmed and anxious.

"I'm not going to die," Carisa whispered. "Not yet. Not before I show Papa. . . ."

"Hush. Of course you won't die, Miss Carisa. Mr. Hartshorn said you weren't. All crazy he was. He said he'd kill me if you died. And I believe he meant it, too."

"I won't . . . won't die. . . ."

"No, Miss Carisa. Not if I can help it. And Mrs. Hartshorn, too. We won't let you."

Dreams pushed at her, cloudy, frightening ones. In one of them she was in a hotel room, desperately trying to struggle away from a man she had never seen before. In another, Papa pointed a trembling finger at her and shouted, his blue eyes mad with anger.

She twisted and struggled against the cloths which bound her.

"Papa . . ." she mumbled. "Papa, I'm sorry, I'm sorry. I was going to tell you, and then I didn't. Oh, God, I didn't. I wrecked it, didn't I? I spoiled everything . . . all your plans . . . Papa. . . ."

"She's delirious," someone said. It was a deep, male voice, husky with dismay.

Dimly, Carisa was aware that Katherine Hartshorn had pulled the bedcovers up over her body and was glaring at her son.

"Adam! What are you doing here?"

"How is she, mother? I've got to know."

"How dare you come into this room when the girl is in a state of undress? It's shocking, against all decency!"

"Mother, I asked you how she was."

"She's as well as can be expected, considering that she is in a high fever and should have had her leg amputated three days ago. And would have, too, but for your stubbornness!"

"Let me look at the wound."

"Adam!"

"Mother, I mean to look, and I will look, in spite of your prudery. I have seen Carisa's limbs before, if you'll recall. Her circus costume revealed them quite plainly."

Adam lifted a corner of the blanket which covered Carisa's nude body.

"Yes," he said. He expelled his breath in a small sigh. "Yes, perhaps the wound is better. The carbolic acid and the poultices must be helping. Certainly it is not as angry-looking as it was."

"Adam, you fool!" his mother hissed. "I can't understand what's gotten into you! To take a girl of this sort

43

into your house . . . you *know* what these circus women are like, you must! Morally corrupt. . . ."

"Enough, mother. Continue to sponge her."

The voices argued on, more blurred than before, but still clear enough.

"We'll send her away when the fever is down?"

"I don't know."

"But, Adam. . . ."

The door shut with a firm, decisive click.

By morning Carisa was weak and clammy-skinned, but resting more comfortably. Had she only imagined those quarreling voices, or Adam peering in at her yet another time, his face haggard?

"Miss Carisa? Can you take some broth?" It was Nelly with a tray. The maidservant was dressed in her sprigged muslin uniform, circles of fatigue under her eyes.

"*He* ordered Cook to get up at four o'clock to boil this," Nelly explained. "Awfully cross she was, too, but she had to do it anyway, if *he* said so."

Carisa tried to lift her head from the pillow, but dizziness assailed her. She sank back. Her leg was still throbbing, but not as strongly as before.

"I had the strangest dreams," she muttered.

"Dreams? Now, I wouldn't be surprised. You were babbling and carrying on, shouting out about your Papa and about that sister of yours, the one that died. Oh, it was eerie."

Nelly pulled up one of the carved mahogany chairs to the bed and settled herself in it. She began to spoon broth into Carisa's mouth.

" 'Course, at least I knew one thing," the servant went on cheerfully. "I knew you wouldn't die."

"You did?"

"Sure. Because I didn't see the ship. If you'd been to die, I would of seen it. Or someone would have."

"Ship?"

But just then a sudden wave of tiredness swept over Carisa, and before Nelly's small, quick hand could transfer the next spoonful of soup to her mouth, she was asleep.

However Nelly had arrived at her conclusion, she was right. Carisa did not die. Instead, with each day she grew stronger. The wound in her right leg gradually lost its redness and began to heal, although Dr. Arthur told her it would leave an ugly scar.

"Not that *that* will bother you," he added testily. "With all of the hosiery and hoop skirts and petticoats that you women wear, you could live your entire life through to the grave, and no one would ever know you were scarred."

He brushed at the bald top of his head. "You're lucky to be alive at all, young woman," he added.

"I think I'll reserve my thanks for the day when I begin to walk properly," some defiant impulse made Carisa say. She had never quite forgiven Dr. Arthur for wishing to amputate her leg. If it had not been for Adam Hartshorn, she would be mutilated now.

"Really! Will you indeed?" The doctor was irritable. "And you are quite the snippy young baggage, aren't you? Well, you can rest assured that you'll never ride with the circus again. You will have to earn your living in some other way."

His sneer was unmistakable.

"My father will come for me," she assured him.

"Oh? I heard some things about that fancy circus-man father of yours, young lady. He blames *you* for the accident, and he's dumped you here, that's all."

"You heard wrong then," she cried. "Papa *will* come back . . . he will!"

"I doubt that. No, he's deserted you like an ailing pup. And I'll wager that Mrs. Hartshorn will have you out of here on your ear in a week or two. Then just see what good your fine airs will do you. You'll have to earn your living catch as catch can."

Carisa sat as far up in the bed as her cumbersome fracture-boxes would allow her.

"Get out. Get out of this room immediately, Dr. Arthur."

"Oh, I'll go. But you just wait and see, my girl. You'll have to depend on your body to keep you . . . it's all you'll have!"

He was gone, and Carisa sank back into her pillows, closing her eyes. Dr. Arthur was right, of course. Sly and odious as he was, he had spoken the truth. Papa had *not* forgiven her, and did not seem likely to do so soon. Duddie's letters, written from on the road, had confirmed that. And it was true, also, that Katherine Hartshorn wanted to get rid of her. She was afraid that Carisa might have designs on her son, and wished to get her out of Adam's sight as quickly as possible.

Carisa bit down on her lower lip until pain lanced through it. Papa would forgive her in time, she told herself. He had to! If only there was something she could do. *Something* to make it up to him, to make him see that she still loved him, still wanted to be his daughter.

A knock on the door roused her from her thoughts. It was Adam Hartshorn, clad in a well-tailored riding habit which emphasized the narrowness of his waist and the broad swing of his shoulders. Today his face seemed darker than ever from the sun, his eyes blazing yellow. His gaze was so intent that she could feel herself begin to squirm.

"And what are you thinking of, Miss Phillips? Your face looks as if you'd just dropped fifty thousand dollars on the Stock Exchange."

"Just . . . just thinking." She could feel the color rise to her cheeks. How like him to refer to the Stock Exchange, she was thinking. Adam was casual about money, about all the wealth of fine furniture and rugs, and porcelain—even in the bedrooms—which surrounded him here at Hearts-ease. Didn't he realize that she, Carisa, had never even seen such things until she came here?

"What about?" he asked her.

"Oh . . . Nothing."

"Nothing? Surely that can't be. Is it boring for you to be shut up here, day after day? Has my mother provided you with books to read, or needlework?"

"Yes." Carisa pointed to a stack of books on the bedside table.

"Hawthorne, I see. And Mr. Melville. How do you like them?"

"I'm enjoying them very much. It was kind of you to loan them to me."

His yellow, leonine eyes regarded her, and again Carisa found herself squirming under his scrutiny. "I saw Dr. Arthur leaving here in a high state of temper," he commented at last.

She was silent.

"Has he been unkind to you, Carisa? He is a pompous little man, I must admit. Unfortunately, he is my mother's choice for a physician and we must tolerate him."

"That's all right," she said. "I don't mind."

"No, I suppose you wouldn't. You have voiced very little complaint about your treatment here. And yet, I have the feeling that you can be fiery and stubborn when you wish to be. . . ."

His eyes caught and held hers, and Carisa found that, oddly, her heart was fluttering. Then Adam strode toward a chair and sat down. Carisa glimpsed the black leather of his expensive riding boots, polished to a high patina. Boots, she noted, which were far finer than anything Papa or Rolf had ever owned.

"Do you know what sort of a man I am?"

The question was so sudden that it caught her off-guard. Her eyes flew open and she stared at him, startled. His yellow eyes met her own. There was an expression in them she could not fathom.

"I am a very lonely man," he went on. "My wife, Mary Elizabeth, died some years ago, and I have missed the company of a woman since then. I would like to change that."

"To change it?"

"I would like to marry you, Carisa. To marry you and give you a home here, at Hearts-ease."

Marriage!

To this man, this golden-eyed stranger, who came from a life so different from her own? The thought was

47

utterly alien to Carisa. To cover her dismay, she reached out for the Melville book, *Mardi,* and let her fingers touch the rough-textured edges of its cut pages.

Marry Adam Hartshorn!

His voice seemed to wash over her in a buzz. "Miss Phillips. Carisa. You must realize that you will never perform in the circus again."

"Yes."

"And you certainly can't stay here very long as you are . . . the old biddies in the town will surely gossip. I don't want them to talk about you. I don't want them to touch you with their nastiness. Marry me, Carisa. Be my wife."

She looked downward at the quilted coverlet. Her hand plucked at the careful stitching of its squares.

"I want to have children, Carisa," he said. "A large family, sons and daughters and grandchildren. Mary Elizabeth bore me only the one son, and the boy has been . . . well, not quite what I had envisioned. I want my children to be like you. With your beauty and boldness and grace. . . ."

As Adam spoke, Carisa found that her mind was roving wildly. She thought of the big house he owned, Hearts-ease, its very name a play on words. She remembered seeing it the day the circus had played, arrogant on its hills. It was a very expensive house, some imp said in her now. A house which required a large staff of servants to care for it, and a good deal of money to maintain.

Adam's voice went on, speaking of his hopes, his dreams. He is circus-struck, she thought. Struck by *her,* by the way he had seen her reclining on Phoebe on the day of the circus. She seemed magic to him. He wanted to recapture that magic, to hold it in his arms and pin it down with his body.

You'll have to depend on your body to keep you. Dr. Arthur's taunt echoed unpleasantly in her head.

"I . . . I don't love you," she heard herself say.

"It doesn't matter. Love will surely come. And in the meanwhile, Carisa, you need a home, someone to take

48

care of you and provide for your needs. I want to be the one to do that. I didn't realize how very much."

She hesitated. She had the eerie feeling that she had dreamed this entire scene before, at some time earlier in her life. Herself, frightened, yet resolute. Adam's eyes, golden, fierce with longing.

"All right," she heard herself reply. "I'll marry you, then, if that's what you want."

Adam's eyes widened. He gave a start, and then she saw triumph spread quickly over his features. He started to reach for her.

"Under one condition," she said. "Under only one condition will I marry you."

"And what is that?" He was smiling, prepared to be amused at some whim of hers.

"I will marry you if you will buy me the William deBord Circus and let me run it and do with it whatever I please."

"What?" Adam threw his head back and emitted a great peal of laughter. "You, running a circus? A girl of seventeen with both legs in splints?"

"Yes." Carisa squared her jaw and stared at him defiantly. *Papa,* she was thinking. *Oh, Papa, this way I can make it up to you. All of it. I promise.*

As if from a long distance, she heard her voice continue. "My splints will come off. I can run a circus, and I will run it. It is absolutely the only condition under which I will marry you."

There was a stunned look on Adam's face. He drew back a bit and stared at her, as if he had seen something unpleasant for the very first time.

"But why?" he asked. "Why do you want it?"

"I just want it, that's all." She did not flinch from his long, hard look. She did not lower her eyes or look away.

"It's a whim," Adam said at last, breaking the silence. "And a very strange one, I might add." His eyes gleamed at her. "And what will you do if I don't like your conditions and choose not to marry you?"

The room seemed to draw tight with silence, with tension. Carisa felt her heart begin to hammer like horses' hooves. She had gone too far. She had been too bold, and had repelled him with the force of her desire.

"Your Dr. Arthur told me there would be ways for me to make money," she said at last in a low voice. "I . . . I suppose I could find them. I'll do what I have to. And one way or another, I'll buy that show."

There was another very long silence, broken by the bark of a dog somewhere outdoors, the sound of servants laughing in the kitchen.

"You're a little witch," he said. He gave a harsh laugh. "A money-minded, hungry little witch. But I want you anyway. God help me, I want you anyway."

"Adam," Katherine Hartshorn said, "what are you going to do about that girl?"

She had braved her son in his study, to find him standing at the window, staring out at the vista of green, sloping hills and water glittering through marsh grass. The sails of a fishing boat could be seen, flashing white against blue.

Her son was silent, not even turning to indicate that he knew she was in the room. Katherine tried again. "All these years since Mary Elizabeth died, you've holed yourself up here at Hearts-ease like a . . . a. . . ." She struggled for words.

"A monk?" Adam asked dryly.

"Well, yes. I've seen to it that girls of good family were invited here, and you found fault with all of them. This one was too fat, that one too stupid, the other too silly. . . ."

"You'd rather I was like Samuel instead?"

Katherine flushed. Her younger son, Samuel, dark-haired and willful, pursued women with singleminded determination. Not even his marriage to a New London woman of good lineage stopped him.

"No, no, of course I don't." She tightened her lips. "Adam, it can't go on like this. That . . . that *girl* ensconced here in our house as she is. I have already had inquiries from the neighbors. In fact, Madeleine Kord was quite blunt about it."

Adam gave an impatient shrug.

"Oh, Adam, surely it *has* occurred to you that people would talk about this? That accident was the talk of New London. Half the town was there when it happened. And the whole town knows that you brought the girl here. And I'm sure by now they know the rest of it, too . . . that you personally attended her bedside like a doting lover, that you came into her room when she was nearly naked, that you insulted and humiliated poor Dr. Arthur to the point where he will barely speak to us."

Katherine's voice had risen harshly, and belatedly she tried to modulate it. It had been a great trial to her that middle-age had flawed her vocal cords.

"The whole town is clucking its tongues at you," she went on in a more moderate tone. "They are saying that you took a wanton circus girl into your home. That you are enthralled with her, that she has cast a spell over you, that you intend to make her your mistress under my very eye. . . ."

Adam turned suddenly to face her and Katherine saw that his face was grim.

She faltered. "I heard the servants in the kitchen, laughing at you. Servants laughing at a Hartshorn! The only thing that stopped me from dismissing them all is that they may be telling the truth."

Another silence.

"Well, son?"

"They don't know the truth."

"I think they do. They may be servants, but they are not entirely stupid. A Hartshorn, a member of a family that dates back 200 years, letting his head be turned by a little slut of a girl from a circus! A girl with no modesty whatever, showing her body to all of the rack and rabble. And riding astride, too; I've no doubt she does that and worse. I never thought I. . . ."

"Then don't."

"What?"

"Then don't think of it, mother. Remember, this won't be the first scandal the Hartshorn family has endured. A hanging, a murder and a suicide, those are enough to. . . ."

"Adam!"

"Very well, mother. I will let our skeletons rest undisturbed in their closet. But I am going to marry Carisa. We will have a very small, very private ceremony. I wish you to start preparing for it as soon as possible."

"You are going to . . . what?" Katherine found herself swaying backward in the direction of a gold brocaded chair. Her weight settled in it heavily. "Not . . . *marry her!*"

"Certainly I am."

He was a warm, generous man, Katherine thought with wild despair. An innocent man, really. A fool! Otherwise he would not be considering such insanity.

"You're not!" she cried. "You're suffering from some summer ague, and it's taken hold of your senses." She clutched at the arms of the chair, grasping its firm wooden support.

"Ague!" He gave a harsh, bitter laugh. "Really, mother. Do you think a fever would make me want to defy society in this way? No, it's much more than that."

"But you can't possibly love her. You can't! You're only enthralled by her. It would be better, so much better, if you would . . . oh, take her to Groton Heights or somewhere. Buy her a little house and pay the bills. Go to see her once a month or so, when you feel the need for it. Men do such things. . . ."

Adam's eyes darkened. "I won't make Carisa my whore. She'll be my wife, and she'll make me proud. And you as well, mother, when you learn to know her."

"I already know her," Katherine said, tight-lipped.

"Then you must know her better. Mother, I can't explain what I feel for Carisa. I just know that I want her, I need her, and I must have her. People will eventually accept her. And they will also accept the fact that. . . ."

He stopped.

"They'll accept what?" Katherine pounced.

"That I have given her permission to buy the deBord Circus and run it," Adam said in a low, tormented voice.

"Buy a circus! And run it!" Katherine felt as if she were reeling under the onslaught of shock after shock. "Why, I've never heard of such a thing. A woman doing that! And is she to travel about with the show as well, like a gypsy?"

"No. You needn't fear that she will be other than a good wife to me. I've told her that she must hire a man to manage the circus for her, that she's to do no traveling, and that it is to be an investment, nothing more. One more Hartshorn investment."

Katherine wiped damp hands on the folds of her skirt. Carisa Phillips was a girl of icy determination, who had seen opportunity waiting for her at Hearts-ease, and had seized it. Was Adam so blind that he did not know that?

"Adam, you're being a fool, such a fool. . . ."

"Perhaps. But my mind is made up, and you will not change it by telling me of my shortcomings."

"Very well," she said shortly, rising from the chair. "I see that your stubbornness is incurable. I will arrange the wedding as you suggest, and I will even defy our friends and make excuses for you. But you will never persuade me to like the girl . . . no, you won't. And I hope that someday you will not come to rue this hasty decision of yours. Regret is a very painful emotion, Adam."

And with that she swept out of the study.

"Nelly? Nelly, how do I look? Do I look quite imposing?" Carisa, sitting propped up on the bed, stared into a small hand mirror. Then she flung it to the bedcovers. "Oh, I look quite impossible! So wan and ill, as if I'd been lying here for weeks and weeks."

Nelly regarded her mistress critically. "I think it's fashionably pale you look. And quite beautiful, too. *He* will certainly think so. As for Mr. Taggart, his eyes will pop out of his head when he sees you, and no doubt about that."

"I hope so."

Rolf Taggart was due to arrive in fifteen minutes, summoned here by Adam at her request. She and Nelly had spent the past hour dressing Carisa's hair. The room was strewn with the debris of her toilette—crumpled petticoats, curl-papers, ribbons, hairbrushes. The scent of perfume was strong in the air.

The past week had been a hectic one. Adam had hired a local dressmaker, Mrs. Elvira Wiggins, to set up shop in one of the unused bedrooms in the old wing. Here, with the aid of an assistant and two of the new mechanical sewing machines made by Mr. Isaac Singer, she was frantically producing a trousseau for Carisa.

Even Katherine had to admit that the sewing machine was a modern-day miracle. This was 1854, a year of extravagance, and dresses might contain as many as twenty to twenty-five yards of cloth. Puffed out with hoops or wired petticoats, they took up enormous amounts of room in public places, and posed an actual fire hazard, for many women had burned to death with their skirts aflame.

Nonetheless, fashion was fashion, and Katherine had decreed that Carisa's wardrobe was to be impressive. She wanted none of her friends to sneer.

As a result the gown Carisa wore today—finished only this morning—was impressive. It was of blue silk, with horizontal *chiné* stripes, its matching basque fitted tightly to her narrow waist. Beneath the rich folds of silk, her body curved voluptuously, and the cumbersome fracture-boxes were invisible.

Carisa loved the dress. She had handled it reverently, and had examined with amazement the matching bead bag of crochet work. All of this—all of this wonder!—for her. How Stephana and Anna would have envied her! As circus children, they had owned few dresses. Those they did own had to be washed in village streams, and dried on bushes, or even on the wagon tops as they traveled. Once her favorite blue gown had been stolen by village ruffians. . . .

The thought took away a little of her pleasure. Well, if only Rolf liked the dress, she told herself quickly, that was all that mattered right now. She had to impress Rolf, for he was to be her tool, her vassal, her means by which she could control the circus and change it to her wishes. He must respect her.

Her thoughts were interrupted by Nelly. "It's time, Miss Carisa, it's nearly time! Jed and Bill have been waiting to carry you downstairs. . . ."

Carisa's heart jumped. This was really happening, she told herself. It was not a dream, it was real.

"Very well," she said.

"Which room do you want them to carry you to, Miss Carisa? The parlor? Or the drawing room? Oh, you've never seen anything like this house, Miss Carisa, you never have! It's all so gold and sparkly and colory, it makes you want to cry."

Carisa, in the act of touching her carefully done hair, hesitated. Which room indeed? She didn't know this house, she had been unconscious when she was brought here. She had not yet been downstairs. All she had to sustain her were the stories Duddie had told her long ago. Stories of wealth. . . .

"To the . . . to the parlor, of course," she told Nelly, forcing the nervousness out of her voice. "And tell the men to hurry. It is almost time for Mr. Taggart to arrive."

4

"Well, when our Carisa Phillips falls, she certainly falls into luxury, doesn't she?"

Rolf Taggart made a contemptuous gesture which took in the entire parlor with its furnishings.

He was a lean knife-blade of a man, with a narrow, almost wedge-shaped face. His eyes, blue and intense, seemed to mesmerize the ladies who attended the circus. Happily they would toss flowers at him, or their gloves or handkerchiefs. Village girls, eager and giggling, would seek him out after a show. Sometimes

Rolf would disappear with one of them, to return with a heavy-lidded, satisfied look.

Carisa was almost certain that he was her half-brother.

Not that anything had been said . . . not exactly. Still, Carisa felt sure that this was true. Rolf had the same intense eyes as John Phillips, the same lean body, the identical tight-muscled walk. Marta Taggart, Rolf's mother, had died two years ago in a wagon accident. But during the years when she had been alive, Carisa had overheard bits of quarrels. Marta had always wanted Papa to marry her. . . .

She could not help but think of this now, as Rolf stood looking about the parlor. His face held the same stern, judging expression that Papa's sometimes did.

"Look at this," he was saying. "Look at all of this fancy stuff! And our Carisa sitting right in the middle of it like a Queen Bee. And dressed fit to kill, I might add."

Carisa flushed. Involuntarily her eyes followed his gesture around the room. She knew exactly what he meant. This room, with its Turkish carpet done in muted shades of red and gold and black, had intimidated her, too, although she had squelched this feeling as quickly as she could. She was marrying Adam Hartshorn, wasn't she? Soon this room, this house with all of its beauty was to be hers.

And it *was* beautiful. The paneled walls had been painted gold. At one end of the room stood an imposing carved mahogany bookshelf, filled with rich leather volumes. Yellow-upholstered chairs were scattered about, and Carisa herself reclined on a red settee. There was a gaming table, a rococo gilded looking glass, and gilded ornamental brackets which hung on either side of the white marble fireplace.

"I think the parlor is very pleasant," she heard herself say.

"Pleasant! Oh, pleasant, she says! And what a great lady she thinks she is!"

Rolf scowled and began to pace about. Pausing at the gaming table, he picked up one of the ivory backgammon pieces and tossed it into the air. Deftly he caught it.

"A fancy gaming table," he sneered. "And look at that china tea set, if you please. Will you pour, madam?" He raised his voice in imitation, then made a face of disgust.

"Oh, yes, you're the great lady, all right, aren't you? Only you'd better get something straight. You're just here on sufferance, because this Hartshorn man, this towner, happens to be bug-eyed silly about circuses and that's all. Once he gets tired of you he'll kick you out of here soon enough."

"No, he won't. I'm marrying him."

"Marrying him! Marrying a . . ." Rolf's eyes narrowed. "So," he said. "That explains a lot. Yes, it does. A lot indeed."

"The wedding is planned for next week," Carisa forced herself to go on. "It will be a very small ceremony, just the family. Perhaps you would care to tell Papa, and Anna, and Duddie. . . ."

"They won't be coming. And not me, either." Rolf tossed the checker back onto the gaming table. It rolled and spun against the polished board. "Your father has disowned you, can't you get that through your head? He doesn't want to see you ever again."

Carisa swallowed hard. "I . . . I can't believe that."

"It's true, though." Rolf shrugged.

"Duddie said . . . Anna. . . ."

But Rolf, pacing about, did not wait for her to finish her sentence. "I think there's a wasp in the cream, Carisa. Do you know what's happened? The show has been sold! A man came to deBord four days ago and they were in his wagon most of the night talking. When they came out, deBord said he'd sold. The show was losing money and I think he was glad to be rid of it. How do you like that, eh? And I have the strangest feeling I know who bought it."

He stared at her.

"Do you?" Carisa said.

"Yes. I do. That Adam Hartshorn of yours. He's the

57

one who bought it, isn't he? Shelled out some of his money and took over, didn't he? Just like that."

"*I* bought it, Rolf."

"You?" Rolf stared at her, his wedge-shaped face darkening. "*You* bought it?"

"Yes, I did. I'm your new owner, Rolf."

"Well, I'll be damned. I'll just be damned." Rolf strode up to the mirror with its elaborate gilt carving, and planted one hand, palm spread, in the center of the glass. When he removed it, there was a greasy smear.

"So that's why I was called here," he said. "For you to tell me that. Well, Carisa, just what are you going to do with this wonderful little show you've bought? Rub all of our noses in it? Make us bow and scrape to your bidding?"

"Rolf, listen to me. . . ."

Rolf slammed one fist into the flat of his other hand. "Who would do what *you* said? A chit of seventeen! Not me. Certainly not me! I'll get out. I'll go to some other show. I'll go to Sands and Nathan, or one of the other river shows, Ludlow and Smith, or. . . ."

"Rolf, please listen to me! That's what I wanted to talk to you about."

"Why? Why should I listen? Why should I do anything for you? You ruined our act, Carisa."

"I didn't . . . Oh, Rolf, I. . . ."

"Besides, you're a woman. And I don't take orders from a female. And I won't take them from you."

Carisa felt her cheeks filling with color. Rolf was stubborn, like Papa. But she could control him; hadn't she known him all of her life?

"Rolf, I'm asking you to be my manager and co-owner. My gaffer."

"Your what?" Rolf threw back his head and laughed.

"My manager," Carisa said. "And I'll give you a share of the gate money. You can't lose, Rolf."

As he stopped laughing, she pressed on. "Rolf, haven't I known you ever since I was born? You know all there is to know about a circus . . . you've helped Papa, and you've helped Mr. deBord. You have a gift for it, a gift for making things work. And we need each

58

other. Where else would you get the money to buy into a show?"

Rolf flushed angrily. "I've saved something. . . ."

"Not enough for the kind of show we're going to have. Because we're not going to have just a piddling little circus with five wagons and two tigers and some dogs. We're going to be big!"

Carisa's voice had turned dreamy. "I've had hours with nothing to do but think about this, Rolf. We'll have a parade a mile long, with ten elephants . . . twenty of them! We'll play before the President, before Queen Victoria herself, the very best of society. Papa always dreamed that the Phillips name would be famous. But he dreamed only of an act, Rolf, a few separate performers. We're going to be an entire show. The Phillips Circus."

Rolf stared at her, his cheeks stained a patchy red. "You'll use the Phillips name?"

"Why not? It's Papa's dream. And I'm going to make it happen, Rolf."

For a long moment Rolf was silent. Then, slowly, his eyes began to rove about the parlor, touching on the gilt mirror and brackets, the sumptuous furniture.

She understood his look. "I have money. My husband will provide it, all that I need. Adam has promised me."

Again Rolf hesitated. At last he reached for one of the mahogany chairs and pulled it toward the settee. He straddled it, facing Carisa.

"And what's to be my share?"

"Twenty per cent," she replied instantly. "Plus a very generous salary. If the show does well, you will, too. You could become a very rich man."

"Not on twenty per cent, I won't. I want fifty per cent."

Carisa allowed her gaze to wander idly about the room. She leaned back on the soft upholstery of the settee, one hand playing with her beaded bag. Inwardly her heart was pounding. She had learned in England, as a child, to barter with shopkeepers and farmers in the small villages the caravan had rolled through. It was how the small, roving group had survived.

Now she said, "Then perhaps I'd better try to find someone else. I'll have Adam send a message to Mr. Richard Sands . . . and maybe I can hire a man from his show. Someone who isn't as greedy as you are."

As Rolf's eyes narrowed, she added, "Well, thank you for coming, Rolf. It has been good to see you, even though we couldn't come to any agreement."

"Who says we couldn't?" Rolf moistened his lips.

"Then you'll take thirty per cent?"

"I'll take thirty-five. And the freedom to manage as I see fit. I don't want to spend my life taking orders from a woman."

"If it's my show, you'll have to take orders from me, Rolf. And there will be no cheating me. Duddie will continue to be with the show and he'll tell me if you are."

Their eyes met. Carisa stared at him coldly. This was all-important, she knew. If Rolf thought she was weak—

Their glances locked and clashed. Carisa's eyes began to water, but grimly she kept them open. She refused even to blink. She was strong and capable; she could control Rolf and she meant to do so.

Rolf looked away.

"Oh, all right," he said grudgingly. "I'll take orders from you. If I have to."

That had been several weeks ago. Now it was nearly July. They had been having a week of humid, hot days, unalleviated by the fresh breezes which usually came from the Sound.

Was it the weather which had plummeted Carisa to a mood so low and depressed? Or was it the air, pressing down on her until she felt she could scarcely breathe?

She was a prisoner in the bed. She could not even get out of it to relieve her bladder, but had to call Nelly for assistance. Worst of all, she was too hot. As a circus performer she had had much more freedom of dress

60

than any New London girl could ever have imagined. But now Katherine insisted that she be fashionably dressed at all times.

This meant the tight lacing of a whalebone corset, with added layers of corset covers, drawers and wired crinoline petticoats. Ruefully she comforted herself with the knowledge that a hoop skirt was impractical for bed use—otherwise, she would have been wearing that, too. As it was, the gown added the last heavy, sticky layer.

She perspired. Her fingers grew moist on the pages of the books Adam brought her from his library. When she was not reading, she spent long hours planning the circus she would have. She made long, damp lists of things she must buy and do. Grimly she forced herself not to think of the obstacles that lay in her way—Rolf, Papa, the resistance of the circus folk, of Adam himself.

She would cope with those, she told herself, when she was out of her fracture-boxes and walking again.

She was fitted for her wedding dress. Although white was not obligatory for a bride, Adam had insisted upon this color. Mrs. Wiggins came to her room to fit her for it. Because of the heavy fracture-boxes, Nelly, who was about Carisa's size, had to act as a stand-in, so that the seamstress could pin and hem and baste.

As she did so, Nelly stood fidgeting and staring out of the window, humming to herself.

"My goodness, girl, can't you stand still just for a moment?" Mrs. Wiggins, a stout widow of fifty, would not brook any nonsense. "If this lace goes on askew, Miss Carisa will have you to blame and no one else!"

"I'm sorry," Nelly gulped. Then her face resumed its dreamy expression.

"Oh, it's all right, Mrs. Wiggins," Carisa said.

"Well, I must say she's a wriggling little thing, and if she keeps squirming around like this, I'm going to have the bodice clear up on your forehead!" Mrs. Wiggins snapped.

Ordinarily, Carisa would have laughed. But today she could only turn her face aside. Why was it that she didn't feel much joy in this marriage?

Adam Hartshorn was a striking man, in the prime of

61

his manhood. He was kind, she knew. Hadn't he fought to save her leg? Taken her in when other men would have put her in a shabby boarding home? And didn't he also have money, funds to finance the Phillips Circus which would make up to Papa for the loss of Stephana and the *Flying Flambeaux?*

So why did she now feel so small and irritable and unhappy with herself?

Worse yet, more of the strange dreams had come to plague her. She had dreamed again of the nurse-governess, Poll. This time, however, Poll was older and thinner, her eyes glittering. And she wore a black silk dressing gown sewn with jet beads. Then, in a rolling shift of images, Carisa saw Poll naked on a bed, her arms and legs languorously twisted with another nude form. . . .

She awoke from that particular nightmare in perspiring horror. Evil, she thought, her heart thumping. There had been something vile and evil about the girl. . . .

"Miss Carisa!" Nelly was shaking her, the servant's face a white blur in the darkness. Nelly still slept on a cot in Carisa's room. But tonight, because it was the night before the wedding, she had been up late, pressing Carisa's trousseau.

"Miss Carisa, you've been yelling. You must have had an ugly dream."

Carisa sat up, wiping some of the perspiration from her forehead. "It . . . it was nothing, Nelly. Go back to sleep."

"But. . . ."

"And would you please light a candle for me? I . . . I think I'll read for a while."

"You don't want the gas?"

"No, the light would disturb you. A candle would be fine."

Besides, Carisa added to herself, a candle reminded her of the simple life in the caravan wagon, before they had come to the United States. The three sisters would snuggle down on their narrow bunks within the high-sided wagon and whisper together until they fell asleep.

Speaking of things they had seen, a gypsy camp, a runaway horse, a cairn of stones said to be haunted by witches. *Stephana,* Carisa thought with a pang. *Anna.* . . .

"You do have some queer dreams, don't you, Miss Carisa?" Nelly added as she brought the lit candle, in its holder, to Carisa's bedside table. "Almost as queer as that ship they talk of—or that woman in the chair."

"What woman? What ship?"

But Nelly had already stumbled back to her cot and was snoring, her arms thrown up above her head like a sleeping child.

For a long while Carisa lay staring into the flickering yellow-orange which sent its shadows up to dance on the ceiling.

Dreams. It seemed that she had always been plagued by them: odd, distorted, sometimes frighteningly prophetic. And so many of her dreams actually came true. As a six-year-old, she had dreamed of a lightning storm in the Cotswolds which had killed two of the caravan horses. She had dreamed of the wagon accident which had killed Marta Taggart. She had dreamed of a sea voyage and then, a month later, they had taken it, coming to America to join the deBord circus. And she had even dreamed, in vivid, sickening detail, of Stephana's death.

Had her mother had these dreams, too? These strange dreams which were sometimes true and sometimes not? She knew that her mother, Benicia, had read the Tarot Cards, had also done palm-reading. Duddie had said she had been lovely and sensitive, coming originally from Ireland, where women sometimes had a "fey" quality.

Well, no matter. For some reason, Papa hated what he called her "dreams and fancies." Long ago she had learned never to mention them around him. There were times, too, when Papa had stared at her oddly, as if there were something about her he didn't understand. Or even like. Carisa wondered if this was because she was the twin born last, the baby whose death had killed their mother.

63

Or was it something else about her, something unloveable and wicked?

Whatever the reason, Carisa knew that it had been Stephana who had been Papa's favorite. Stephana, with her tall, graceful body, her talent, her boldness.

Staring at the leaping shadows cast by the taper, Carisa bit down hard on her lower lip. She bit until pain arrowed through her. There were times, in the loneliness of night, when she had begun to ask herself if she had really wanted Stephana to die. If she had hoped for her sister's death, so that Papa might love her more. . . .

Nonsense! Oh, what foolish, foolish nonsense! She had loved her twin sister. Had been close to her.

Carisa sat up awkwardly and reached for the Melville novel, *White-Jacket,* which Adam had brought her yesterday. It was a story of the brutality aboard the warships of the U.S. Navy—a topic that did not interest her very much. Nevertheless, she began to turn the pages grimly, until the print wobbled in front of her eyes and she saw nothing. At last she fell asleep.

Morning dawned hot and humid again. Carisa awoke to find that Katherine Hartshorn was standing over her bed. There was no way of knowing how long she had been there. Nelly's cot was empty.

"So. You fell asleep with a candle lit and a book in your hand, I see." Katherine's voice was cold. "And I found Nelly snoring beside you, just as foolish as you are. Didn't they ever teach you never to fall asleep with a candle burning? Do you want the house to burn down around your ears? Such an event would be most unfortunate for a girl with both legs immobilized."

"I . . . I'm sorry."

Carisa blinked her eyes, trying to clear them of sleep. Was this truly the morning on which she was to be wed? It didn't feel like it.

"Well, you should be," Katherine went on, angrily. "Once you're wife in this household I see I'll have a great deal to teach you. All I can hope is that you'll be tractable and willing to learn."

64

"I'll learn," Carisa promised, trying not to sound as defiant as she suddenly felt.

"Oh, yes, I'm quite sure. And you'll also learn to cope with an unruly child. Julian is a part of the bargain, too, and you may not find his tricks to your liking."

"I'm sure I can. . . ."

But Katherine interrupted her words. "It's not too late, you know. There's a rooming house in town, run by a respectable seaman's widow. I could pay her to take you in and care for you until your legs are healed. Then you would be free to go about your business . . . and with a sizeable payment to tuck away in your purse, too, I would see to that. You don't belong here, Miss Phillips. You're quite unsuitable for a man like Adam."

Carisa felt ice spreading through her mid-section. "Not marry Adam? But . . . But I promised him. Are you trying to *pay* me to leave here?"

Their eyes met.

A momentary look of discomfort crossed the older woman's face, then was gone.

"Yes, I suppose I am. But can you blame me? I dislike seeing my son made the prey of a fortune-hunter. As you, my dear, most certainly are."

Carisa said nothing.

"I suppose it pleases you to know that you are making the Hartshorns the butt of ugly gossip here in New London and even beyond?"

Carisa raised her chin and assumed all the dignity she could muster, even though her hair was tousled from sleep and the satin ribbon at the neck of her nightgown had come unloosed.

"Your son wants to marry me, and I wish to marry him," she said softly. "Our reasons for doing this are . . . private. As for ugly gossip, I would imagine that our wedding would tend to quell that, rather than cause it. After all, it will certainly make my presence here more acceptable."

"Well!" Two ruddy spots had appeared in Katherine's cheeks. "I doubt if anything can make *you* respectable, my dear girl. Although I can see I'm certainly going to have to try."

And with that she was gone.

By ten o'clock Nelly had managed to get Carisa into her wedding dress and was smoothing the lace and adjusting the many white velvet bows which adorned it.

It was a gorgeous gown, copied by Mrs. Wiggins from a dress which had appeared in *Godey's Lady's Book,* to which Katherine subscribed. A confection of white satin, fine net and *Valenciennes* lace, its full skirt had one deep flounce, trimmed with velvet bows. Other smaller bows were scattered about the rows of delicate lace which covered the sleeves, bodice and high throat.

Even six months ago, it had never occurred to Carisa that she might wear such a gown. Yet now that the moment was at hand, she could take little joy in it.

"Oh!" Nelly clapped her hands together as if Carisa were a goddess to be worshipped. "Oh, you're so beautiful!"

Carisa made a face. "I'm far from being that."

"But you are! Oh, *he'll* just love you," Nelly insisted. Her fingers reached up to touch her own straight brown hair, pulled back into a thick knot and covered by a maid's cap. "Oh, if I just looked like you, Miss Carisa! All that gold hair . . . I don't even have a fellow to take me walking out, did you know that?"

"I'm sure you'll find one someday, Nelly."

"I hope so." The other girl hesitated. "Do you know what I do sometimes? I pretend I'm you. I pretend I'm the one lying there in the bed, looking so pale and pretty, and it's me who Mr. Hartshorn is going to marry and sleep with . . . oh!"

She clapped a hand over her mouth.

And Carisa could feel the flush starting at her chest and blooming upward to spread over her face.

It was her wedding night.

Dressed in one of the new lace-trimmed nightgowns from her trousseau, Carisa lay stiffly in the mahogany four-poster bed and waited for Adam to come to her.

Earlier in the day, her things had been moved into the master bedchamber, which she and Adam would now share. This was a large, airy room with warm oak flooring, its paneled walls painted a rich cream. The furniture was made of mahogany, and a porcelain tea service was set out on a small table. Did they expect her and Adam to take tea tonight? Carisa wondered.

More Turkish rugs—in rich reds and blacks—covered the floor, and the entire room smelled of wax and lavender and some scent more subtle. Patchouli? The perfume of the dead Mary Elizabeth?

Quickly Carisa stifled the thought. Now, involuntarily, her thoughts went back to the wedding. It had been a stiff, almost grim, ceremony, and quickly over, with Carisa reclining on a settee throughout. In spite of what Rolf had said, one member of Carisa's "family" was there. This was Duddie.

In his broadcloth suit made rusty and wrinkled from long storage in a trunk, the little clown looked more misshapen than ever. When he had been shown in by Gaines, the butler, Katherine had eyed him with outrage. But there had been little she could do. Duddie had been invited, and Adam's eye was cold upon his mother, daring her to protest.

The other guests were pitiably few. Katherine herself was regal in purple *reps* silk, her sallow face unsmiling. Julian, dressed in a suit which was a miniature of his father's, raced wildly around the drawing room and had to be shushed by Katherine. When the champagne was served, Julian begged for a sip. After he received it, the boy made a terrible face and spat his mouthful onto the carpet, narrowly missing his grandmother's hem.

Also present was Adam's brother, Samuel Hartshorn, and his small, thin wife, Eliza, as well as a small group of distant family relatives who had come from Hartford.

"You are bringing excitement to the Hartshorn family," a lazy voice said beside her. Carisa jumped and turned.

Adam's brother was tall, his black hair unruly. His eyes were depthless and gleamed like obsidian. He had a lazy, arrogant way of lounging near her chair, like a man who knows that all of the women in the room are looking at him.

Now he gave Carisa a long, bold, frankly assessing stare.

She flushed. She had received that sort of look before—from men who had come back to the dressing tent after the performance was over.

"What excitement?" she asked coldly.

"Why, *you,* of course. English accent, pale hair and all. The Hartshorns have seen nothing like you in 200 years, as lovely and wild as an English hedge-rose. But are you as prickly?"

"Perhaps. But they will all have to get used to me," she heard herself reply. "For I am here, and I intend to stay."

Samuel made a mocking face. "Did anyone say you weren't? New blood . . . that's what the Hartshorns need. Fresh, healthy, lusty blood. Mary Elizabeth was only able to produce one son, despite years of trying. I'm sure *you'll* do better."

Adam was on the other side of the room, talking with a Hartford cousin, and Carisa gave him an appealing look, hoping that he would come and rescue her.

Samuel grinned. "What's the matter, my new Mrs. Hartshorn? Do I upset you?"

"No!" she snapped. "Of course not. It's just that. . . ."

"It's just that my wife Eliza is observing us at this moment," Samuel muttered under his breath. "Well, let her look." He gave Carisa another long, assessing look.

"Welcome to the family, Carisa. May you keep us all from being dull."

Again Carisa gave Adam a look of urgent appeal, and this time he excused himself from his cousin and made his way to her.

Samuel bowed mockingly. "Hello, dear brother. You have been neglecting your little bride . . . at least *she* seems to think so. She seemed extremely eager for you to come and join her, at any rate."

Adam's yellow, leonine eyes narrowed slightly. His jaw had hardened. "Now I am here. And I think, Samuel, that your wife wishes you at her side. Surely you should be obliging and join her?"

With a sudden, glowering scowl, Samuel turned on his heel and walked away.

Adam handed Carisa a glass of champagne, served in a crystal goblet.

"Drink this," he ordered. "Your cheeks look pale, Carisa. Are you enjoying yourself?" As Carisa did not reply, he added, "Don't mind my brother. Samuel isn't a good money manager. There's a bit of enmity between us. My father left us some ships and some other property jointly, and we often disagree as to its management. And I was given Hearts-ease as well. Samuel has never forgiven me for that."

"He gave me such a look," she faltered, sipping the bubbly wine.

"Well, he won't do it again. I'll speak to him. Perhaps you should know, Carisa, that my brother is quite a womanizer . . . when he can seize the chance. It's best just to avoid him as much as you can."

"But . . ."

Adam gave an impatient shrug. "My mother is fond of Eliza. That's why Samuel is received here. And I suppose he will continue to come here. But just be wary of him, that's all I ask."

Duddie was entertaining Julian by pulling objects such as balls, tops and candy out of his sleeves, just as he had done when Carisa was a child. The boy's squeals of

69

merriment echoed through the drawing room, drowning out the adult voices.

But at last Duddie came to Carisa, pulling up a chair to the settee where she lay, her frothy wedding dress trailing languorously. "You are going to need your husband's help," he said. "If you are really to run this circus of yours."

Carisa answered quickly, "Oh, but I'm sure I can do it. I know I can, Duddie! I have to."

"Oh?" Duddie looked quizzical. "And did you have to hire Rolf Taggart?"

"Yes. I did. Rolf is stubborn, I'll grant you that, but I can control him. And I need him, if I'm to make the show a success. He knows everything there is to know about running a circus . . . he has a genius for it, I think. I know Mr. deBord thought so. If it hadn't been for Rolf, Mr. deBord would have sold out long ago."

"Perhaps. But why couldn't you have gotten someone else to be gaffer? Someone capable but not too ambitious. Carisa, my dear, you've not hired a manager . . . you've hired yourself a hungry wolf."

Carisa laughed. "Oh, Duddie. . . ."

"No, listen to me." The little man stared into the pale effervescing liquid in his goblet. "I've known Rolf since he was eight years old. That man has something eating at him, I tell you. I think he could be dangerous."

"Rolf? Dangerous?" Carisa smiled. "Duddie, I think you're wrong. Don't forget, I've known Rolf all my life, too. I know he's ambitious, of course. But, you see, it's that very ambition which will keep him working hard for me. You just wait and see. And Papa, too. When Papa sees what I make of this show. . . ."

Duddie fell silent. He lifted his goblet and drained its contents, then set the glass down on a nearby table.

"Your father won't see," he said at last. "He's left the show. Didn't you know that, Carisa?"

"Left it?"

Carisa felt as if Duddie had just slammed his fist into the pit of her belly. But, oddly, no one else in the room seemed to notice her agitation. Katherine was deep in conversation with Eliza, and Adam was talking with his cousin again. Julian, unnoticed, lay on the floor, kicking with his heels at a chair leg.

"Where . . . where has he gone?" she asked dazedly.

"Just gone, that's all. He wouldn't say where." Duddie's face held pity. "He said he wouldn't stay in any show you owned, Carisa."

"And . . . and Anna?" Carisa whispered. "Has she gone away with Papa, too?"

"Yes, I'm afraid she has."

"Anna! I can believe it of Papa, but not . . . not Anna . . ." Carisa's voice broke miserably. She felt doubly betrayed.

"And just where do you expect your sister to go, Carisa? She is a young girl still, and your father forced her to go with him. She is fully recovered from her sprained arm now, of course. She has been rehearsing again with your father and they are trying to put together a new act."

"I . . . I wish them luck then," Carisa managed to say through stiff lips. "And you, Duddie? Will you leave, too?"

The clown touched her hand. "I taught you to ride, Carisa. I taught you everything you know. Perhaps I would like to see what you can do with that knowledge."

The rest of the small reception had passed in a blur of voices and faces. *Papa*, she had thought agonizedly. *Oh, Papa! Don't you understand? I'm doing this for you . . . for you. . . .*

But that had been hours ago. The champagne had been drunk, the wedding supper devoured. Samuel, Eliza, and the other guests had left, and a sudden, awkward silence had descended upon the house. At last the two menservants had carried Carisa back upstairs. Now she lay in the master bedroom waiting for Adam to come to her and their married life to begin.

She stirred restlessly, apprehensively. Then she heard the door knob turn and he was in the room.

In his black formal wear Adam looked taller, bigger, almost arrogant in his good looks. His tawny hair was burnished a sudden and startling gold, his eyes a deeper amber. He was a fine man, she told herself disjointedly.

71

A virile, lusty man. She could feel a flush beginning at her cheeks and moving downward to her neck and breasts.

"Well, Carisa, I thought you would have been ready for sleep by now. Haven't you had quite an exciting day for a sick girl?"

She tried to smile up at him, although her heart was hammering ridiculously.

"I'm hardly a sick girl, as you put it," she said lightly. "I merely have two broken legs. Otherwise my health is fine."

"Of course it is."

Adam moved to the bath-closet which opened off the bedroom, and began to take off his coat and waistcoat. His linen shirt was stiffly starched, and the white fabric made his shoulders look broad and bulky.

"Well, I suppose you'll have a good night's sleep," she heard him say as he hung his clothes in the mahogany wardrobe which stood against one wall of the closet. He shot her a sudden, bitter look. "You can have glowing dreams of elephants and sawdust and circus candy."

The sarcasm in his voice was plain.

"Adam . . ." she began.

"As for me, there is an empty bedroom next door, and I've taken possession of that for now. I won't disturb you there, and it will be easier for everyone."

"But . . . a separate bedroom?" Carisa heard her voice waver, and she knew that the flush on her face had grown even deeper. "I thought . . . I mean, you said you wanted children. . . ."

Her voice trailed off. He didn't want to sleep with her. He was making that very plain.

He came over to her. "Of course I want children." He bent his face toward her and suddenly he was kissing her. His lips were hard and searching. The kiss lasted for long minutes—Carisa wasn't sure how long. All she knew was that it sent a wild swirling into the pit of her belly.

"There." Adam pulled away from her. There was a curious look on his face—lust, bitterness, tenderness, all mingled together. "You little fool, can't you under-

72

stand why I've got to take that other room? Have you forgotten your two broken bones?"

"My bones?"

"Of course. Do you want me to disturb their mending?"

"Oh . . ."

Now both of them were looking away from each other. These were Victorian times, and men and women did not often speak openly of such things.

"I would have waited to marry you until your limbs were healed," Adam was saying. "But because of the gossip which might arise, I decided to do it sooner. You do understand, don't you? We will . . . resume a more normal life as soon as you are well enough."

"Yes," Carisa whispered.

"Well," he said. "I will go and tell Gaines to have Nelly's cot moved in here so that you will have someone to call in the night if you need something."

"No!" Carisa cried.

Adam looked at her. "You don't want Nelly? But surely you will need someone. . . ."

"I don't want Nelly's cot in here! If it's here, then everyone will know. . . ." She hesitated, her cheeks flaming. "Perhaps if I want something I can rap on the wall with a walking stick, or something like that. Then Nelly would hear me, and come. I . . . I would prefer that."

He stared at her for a long moment, the color rising in his face.

"Very well. Only a walking stick isn't necessary. I'll have the servants rig up a bell-pull for you."

He left the room and closed the door, leaving Carisa to lie rigid in the bed, staring up at the ceiling.

It was later that night—her wedding night—that she had the dream which was to come back again and again, haunting her for long years.

She had lain for hours, staring upward at the pale blur which was the ceiling, and had fallen asleep only at dawn.

Her sleep had been deep and uneasy. Heavily sleep-bound and tossing about in the bed, she first became aware of a strange smell. It smelled . . . *burned.* Yes, that was it. The black, oily, charred stench of something consumed by flame. And this was an odor so strong that she began to realize that it had been no ordinary stove or trash fire gone awry. Many things had burned. Canvas, rope, wood, cloth, straw.

And flesh. Yes, flesh had burned, too. Carisa could smell it, pungent and sickly. . . .

She shivered and moved restlessly in the bed, unaware that she was moaning aloud. Then, in the eerie way of dreams, she found that she was walking across a field. The blackened earth was strewn with odd, dark objects—the debris of burning. Were they bodies? she wondered in sudden horror. But she couldn't see them clearly, for the field was covered in a thin mist.

Or perhaps the objects weren't bodies at all, she thought suddenly, but stones. She stared about her. The shapes had become stones, jagged monoliths arranged in a circle and sticking up through the fog like teeth. They were old stones, redolent of antiquity, of strange, evil rites.

And—in her sleep, Carisa started. She could almost hear a woman's voice, calling out to her. Warm and low and urgent.

But then the voice faded and the stones melted away and Carisa realized that she was alone.

Alone. Never, never before in her lifetime had she ever been quite so alone. It was almost as if she had stepped onto an unknown planet and would never see another human being again.

Alone alone alone alone alone alone

Never would anyone love her again. Never hold her, or speak gently to her, or quarrel with her, or smile at her. Never again. Everything in her life that had meaning was gone, or would be soon. Everything.

Now, in the dream, a feeling of desperate urgency seized her. She found that she had lifted her skirts. She began to run, to hurry across the burned field, running faster and faster in her panic.

There was still a chance that she wouldn't be alone,

she knew in desperation. If she ran until her heart pounded out of her chest and pain stitched her ribs and her eyes streamed with tears.

"*Adam!*" she screamed. "*Adam! Adam! Oh, Adam, don't go! Please don't . . . Adam!*"

She tossed and turned on the bed, her fracture-boxes pinning her to the sheets like a butterfly to a board. Dimly she heard the shrieking voice and realized that it came from herself. Yet she could not stop.

"*Adam! Adam! Oh, God, Adam! You've got to . . . Adam. . . .*"

Someone was shaking her. Someone's hand's gripped her shoulders and pressed into her flesh. Then she felt a slap on her cheek and she was abruptly awake.

Perspiration was cold on her face, and droplets of moisture ran damply between her breasts and thighs. Her heart was pumping so fast that she could hear it in her ears.

"Carisa! What on earth is wrong with you? I could hear your screams in the next room!"

It was Adam, of course. Even in the darkness she could smell him: the faintly musky male odor, mingled with the scent of English soap and the clean sundried cotton of his nightshirt.

She clutched at his hand. "Adam! I had a dream. I. . . ."

He laughed softly. "So I gathered." She felt him touch her face, smoothing her forehead and pushing her damp hair back. "Why, you're covered in perspiration. Even your hair is wet."

"I'm sorry. I didn't mean to wake you."

"Why should you be sorry? You couldn't help it, could you?" Adam continued to stroke her forehead, as if she were a skittish horse he was trying to gentle. "I have nightmares sometimes, too. I dream of falling. What was yours about?"

"It . . . Oh, it was terrible, I was so frightened." She stopped, terror beating through her. Could the dream possibly have been one of *those* dreams? The ones that came true?

She felt her body convulse in a shudder.

"I can't talk about it, it's too awful," she muttered. She held herself rigid, away from the soft pressure of Adam's hand.

"Why can't you?"

"Because I can't. It . . . it's over now. I'll never dream it again. I'll *make* myself never dream it."

Adam laughed softly. "I tried that with my nightmare, too," he told her. "I vowed I'd never dream of falling again. And do you know what happened to me?"

"What?"

"Why, the very next night I dreamed that I was standing on the lip of Niagara Falls and I stumbled and was swept into the water and over the Falls."

Carisa gave a choked, desperate laugh. "My God, I hope that doesn't happen to me. . . ."

"It won't. Go to sleep, my darling," he whispered, so low that she was not sure she had heard him correctly. "I'll stay here until you do. If you start having the dream again, why, I'll wake you. I promise. And if you don't awaken easily, then at least I'll try to provide you with a bucket for your trip down Niagara Falls. . . ."

"Oh, Adam—"

His hand smoothed her hair in warm, strong strokes.

"Go to sleep, darling. I'll be here. I'll always be here. I'll never let anything bother you. Ever, ever. Carisa, please sleep. . . ."

She closed her eyes and gave herself up to his voice.

By morning her nightmare seemed less real. An ugly dream, she told herself. Nothing more. And certainly not prophetic—just the product of her wedding nervousness and a sleepless night.

She awoke to find that Nelly was in the room, humming as she laid out Carisa's gown for the day. The servant wore sprigged calico and a fresh white cap and apron, and she had already pulled open the slate-colored drapes to let in the day. It was probably this sound which had awakened Carisa.

"Good. You're awake," Nelly said cheerfully. "I've brought your tray up."

Carisa mumbled a sleepy reply. She rubbed at her eyes and struggled to sit up in the bed.

"Here, I'll help," Nelly said. "You'll want your extra pillows. And your breakfast. We've a good, hearty beefsteak and apple tart today. . . . Cook remembered how much you liked her tarts. *He* breakfasted about two hours ago," she added. "He said we were to let you sleep late. Now he's gone riding."

Nelly eyed Carisa curiously, and Carisa knew she was inspecting her face to see whether her nuptial experiences had left any new mark there. Did Nelly still imagine herself in Carisa's place? she wondered crossly.

Nelly busied herself with the pillows, and then blurted out, "Brigid says she saw the ghost ship last night."

"What ship?" Carisa asked. "You've mentioned that before, and I was going to ask you about it."

"Why, the phantom ship, of course. They say it's real eerie . . . all of its sails hang limp, yet it moves along anyway, without any wind to push it." Nelly's eyes danced. "They *say* it's the ghost of the schooner that the first Adam Hartshorn went down in. He capsized only ten miles from here, in the midst of a terrible December storm. And everybody says that our Mr. Adams is the spitting image of that other one."

"Oh, Nelly, surely. . . ."

"Oh, it's real, and listen, Miss Carisa, here's the best part. That ship only comes when someone's going to die! Cook saw it when poor Mrs. Hartshorn died six years ago. I wasn't here then, but Cook swears it, she swears on a stack of Bibles, and Cook never lies. So I know it's true. And now Brigid says she saw it, and you know what that means."

"It means. . . ." But with an effort, Carisa shook away the fancy. Circus people were very superstitious, but Duddie had tried to counteract this in teaching the three Phillips girls. They should be above the simple village folk before whom they played, he had always insisted.

"Of course the ship doesn't mean anything, Nelly," she went on quickly. "Cook is fanciful, that's all. Or perhaps she saw a real vessel. This *is* a harbor, you know. My husband says New London is a port almost as big as New Bedford."

Nelly snorted. "It's not fanciful! It's true! And Brigid says she saw the ship. She *swears.*"

"Well, perhaps she does, but. . . ."

"Oh, I believe her. And now all I'm wondering is this: Who's going to die?"

"Nelly! No one is going to die!"

"Oh, yes, they are. And glad I am, too, that I haven't got an ague or a quinsy, or anything wrong with me today. I'm going to be careful not to walk under any ladders, or go by the water, or step too near any carriage-horses. . . ."

"Now, Nelly, I'm sure nothing is going to happen. Why should it? I think Brigid said that just to get everyone's attention. Perhaps she was bored."

"Oh, Brigid likes attention, all right. She can be sly. But why would she lie about seeing the ship? She saw it, Miss Carisa. I know she did. And you just wait, some-one will die today."

After that dramatic pronouncement, Nelly hurried out of the room to fetch Carisa's breakfast tray. Carisa lay back on her pillows, staring idly at the dust motes dancing in a shaft of sun. With a pang, she thought of Adam riding. His body swaying effortlessly with the motion of his horse. . . .

After a while she began to write a letter to Rolf, who was still touring with the circus, telling him some of her plans.

Later that day, shortly before luncheon, Adam came upstairs to tell her that Cook had died of apoplexy in the kitchen while pounding down the dough for today's bread. Perhaps, Carisa told herself with a shiver, she had been brooding about the phantom ship.

Thus it was, with a nightmare and a death, that Carisa's married life began.

6

Winter was coming. A chilly wind plucked at the fringes of Carisa's shawl and ruffled at the tea-things.

Carisa put down her cup and looked up at the flawless blue sky with regret. It was already November first, and there was so much to be done! And here she was, still chained to the heavy fracture-boxes and the life of an invalid.

She had, however, insisted on getting outdoors today, in spite of the cold. They were having tea on the sloping back lawn of Hearts-ease, Adam in a chair, Carisa reclining on a settee which the servants had carried out for her. A blue woolen shawl was tucked about her shoulders and a blanket covered her legs. A basket of embroidery, untouched, lay at her feet.

Already Carisa loved Hearts-ease, with its view of water and harbor, its spacious lawns criss-crossed by graveled walks, its rich plantings of trees and shrubs flanked by the virgin hemlocks, which had seen the first settlers come to this area. The house itself was white and long and rambling. Its windows were shuttered in dark green, all of them rectangular in shape save for the one tall, arched window which illuminated the great stairway.

To the east, beyond a great cooper beech, was a long greenhouse. It was heated, Adam said, with an arrangement of arches and flues at the base of its heavy brick wall. When she was healed, he added, he would take her there and show her Katherine's pride, a camellia bush higher than her head, and a grapevine with a main stem as big as her fist.

"Imagine," Carisa said, impressed. "A camellia that large! I wonder how long it took to grow it."

"A lifetime." Adam smiled. "That greenhouse was built by my grandmother in 1804 . . . she was the one who planned the heating system. Each Hartshorn, it seems, adds something to the house." He looked thoughtful. "I wonder what it is that we will add."

Carisa opened her mouth and was about to tell him, but before she could do so, Adam continued. "And when you're better, Carisa, I'll also take you for a drive and you can see the town of New London. More privateers sailed from here during the Revolutionary War than from any other port in New England, and they did so much damage to British shipping that, in 1781, the British burnt the city. It was only because Hearts-ease is so isolated that it was saved."

Now, he told her with enthusiasm, the town was growing. A factory had been built to make biscuits and crackers to stock the whaling ships. There were other factories, machine shops and foundries, including a company which made pianofortes.

But the main business of New London was the sea. In 1785, ships had returned from the "Brazil banks" with 300 barrels of whale oil. The New London *Gazette* —and all of the citizenry—had crowed with delight, and the whaling craze had begun.

Now the chief concern of the town was whale oil for lamps, whalebone for corsets and hoopskirts, baleen for buggy whips, ambergris for perfume.

Adam's voice was full of warmth as he explained all of this to her.

"They whisper in the town that I look exactly like the first Adam Hartshorn," he told her. "He was a sea captain . . . the first Hartshorn to go to sea. He could be a hard man, Carisa, fierce and full of temper. He once hung seven men accused of piracy . . . and there were rumors he had killed more, as well."

Adam's laugh was short. "I cannot lay claim to such grisly fame . . . still, there are those here in New London who call me enemy. And I, too, have been fascinated by the sea. . . ."

On he talked, drawing pictures for her of the rough-and-tumble life of whaling, the breathless, heaving, dangerous fight to harpoon the great whale who thrashed beside the ship. The bloodied waters, the gut-wrenching excitement.

"It's men pitting their lives against *bigness,* Carisa . . . against the very mysteries of God and nature and the sea. It's men, too, grappling with something in themselves, and winning against it."

Adam was silent for a moment, and Carisa, staring at him, felt a kinship with him. Surely it was fear that the whaling men fought, fear of the unknown. Circus folk, too, had to fight fear. . . .

They talked quietly for a few moments longer, and then Carisa smiled at Adam. The circus, as always, was on her mind.

"Adam?"

"Yes, darling?" He had pulled his chair closer to the settee and was holding her hand, running his thumb deliciously up and down her palm.

"It . . . It's about my circus. I received a letter yesterday from Rolf Taggart. They are in Annapolis and will finish their season soon, and he wants to know what to do next. I have decided to have them come back here to New London to winter."

"Fine. I have no objection to that."

Carisa hesitated. "Nelly tells me that there is an old farm next to your property, near the field where the circus played in June. It's owned by a cousin of her father's, and he is an old man who would be willing to sell. Will you buy that farm for me?"

Adam stared at her, the November wind ruffling his tawny hair. "Buy it? But what would you want with a farm?"

"It's not the farm I want, it's just some of the land, and the houses and outbuildings. Nelly tells me that the house is old, but in good condition, and it's large enough for our needs, at least right now. And there are two good barns."

"Barns? Carisa, what *are* you talking about?"

Adam had dropped her hand. His easy, relaxed mood was gone.

"Winter quarters, of course. Did you think that a circus can just come to town and take rooms in a hotel? I need stables, to keep the horses we have now, and the ones I plan to buy. I need room for other animals, and a big, warm barn where I can build a practice ring. I need a place to store equipment, and where we can build new wagons."

"Stables! Equipment! Wagons!"

"Yes, Adam, all of those and more. I haven't had much to do besides lie in bed and think. I've been remembering all of the mud we used to encounter in England . . . sometimes it would stop us for days. *My* wagons are going to have extra-wide wheels . . . six inches, at least . . . to give us good traction over soft earth. We can travel in the spring, we'll have a longer season, Adam! And I've already found a man, Mr. Dunnett, who can make me the wagons. He's an expert carver and carpenter and he's had experience in your shipyards here."

"I know the man." Adam's eyes were fixed on her, their expression unreadable.

Carisa straightened her spine as much as she could on the soft settee, pulled the shawl about her shoulders, and narrowed her eyes at him.

"Adam! You told me I could buy this show. Had you forgotten?"

"No." Adam said it reluctantly. "No, I haven't."

"You agreed, Adam. You *agreed* to buy me this circus if I married you!"

Adam shoved back his chair, nearly knocking it over. He began to stride about on the grass. Carisa could tell by the set of his shoulders, the bullish tension of the back of his neck, just how angry he was.

"I know I agreed, Carisa." His voice rose. "For weeks you've been lying there in that bed upstairs, a lovely, fragile invalid . . . I *thought*. And now suddenly here you are, demanding that I buy you a farm. A farm, of all things!"

Carisa started to speak, and Adam made an impatient gesture. "At least tell me this, Carisa. How did you get Elias Dunnett to work for you?"

"He's Nelly's cousin."

"Oh, I see. Well, that explains it all. It seems that I was fool enough to hire as your personal maid a girl who is related to half the population of New London."

Adam's eyes glittered amber fire at her. "Well, perhaps I should fire her. I could hire someone from New York, or Boston, a girl whose relatives live too far away for you to get at them!"

"You wouldn't!"

"Oh, wouldn't I? You don't know me very well, Carisa, if you can lie there and tell me I would not dismiss my own servants if I felt they deserved it."

With a swift gesture, Carisa grabbed the embroidery hoop she had brought outdoors with her, and flung it to the grass.

"There! I hate needlework, did you know that, Adam? It's quite a chore for me. And I hate all of the other things your mother has been teaching me . . . how to make puddings and concoct perfume and conduct myself like a lady and wash nightgowns!" She was nearly panting in her anger. "Adam, you promised me this circus. I wouldn't have married you if you hadn't. And if you dare to fire Nelly Sawyer, I . . . I swear that I'll leave you!"

Silence crackled between them.

"So," Adam said at last, slowly, heavily. "You admit it then. You married me just to get your hands on that circus."

Carisa bit her lip. For some reason she could not seem to look at him. Instead she stared downward at the grass, already shriveled from a frost they had had last week, dead leaves caught in its blades.

"Adam, it . . . it wasn't altogether like that," she floundered. "There was more. I like you very much. I couldn't have married you if I didn't. And . . . and perhaps as you said, I may soon learn to love you."

Why did she feel so miserable saying those words?

"Will you?" Adam said.

Again there was that ugly tension between them, stretched as tight as a silk thread.

"Yes," Carisa whispered. "I . . . I will. I promise I'll try."

"Good," Adam said coldly. "You want a circus, and I want a loving wife and a family. We should have a very happy union."

"Adam! I told you I'd give you children. I will run your house, I'll do everything your mother has been teaching me to do, and more. But I also want the chance to build up this show." She was pleading now. "Please, Adam, you don't know what it means to me, it means everything. . . ."

There was the sudden sound of a door slamming, and then the skidding crunch of someone running on the gravel walk. Julian came racing toward them.

"Papa!" he cried out before he had even reached them. "Papa, you said you'd take me riding, you promised!"

"In a moment, son. Your mother and I have something to discuss."

"She's not my mother! She's not, she's not! I hate her!"

Adam glared at his son. "You must not speak to Carisa in that way. She is your stepmother now. She has done no harm to you."

"Oh, nonsense!" Julian piped up in an accurate imitation of his grandmother's hoarse voice. "She *has* done harm to me, Papa. She came here, didn't she? She came, and now you're always with her, and I hate her, I hate her. . . ."

Swiftly, angrily, Adam moved toward the boy and scooped him up under one arm. Julian dangled, shrieking his rage.

"I don't break promises," he told Carisa. "You'll have the farm, if you really want it. But you will do nothing without my advice. You're not of age yet, and legally I am the owner of your circus. Do you understand that?"

He took Julian and left in the direction of the stables, without looking back.

The next day, at noon, Adam came into the master bedroom to tell Carisa that Dr. Arthur would be coming later in the day to remove the fracture-boxes.

"What?" She stared at him.

"I said he's to take them off. You'll be free, girl. Isn't that what you've been longing for for six months?"

"Yes, but . . ." She licked suddenly dry lips. During

the long, dull days, Nelly had often whispered stories of those who had been left with grotesque limps. Of bones which had had to be rebroken, or had never healed properly at all.

"Now, don't worry," Adam said. "Your bones have mended well. I have already had the crutches prepared for you, and. . . ."

"Crutches?"

"Of course." Now Adam was laughing. "Good God, girl, did you expect to be walking about immediately? You will still have a long siege of invalidism. There will be pain and swelling, and you'll require months of exercise before your limbs will be anything like normal."

"Oh, no." She was near tears. "But, Adam, the circus! I'd planned to do so much! We've only one winter to rebuild the show and get it ready for next season. Do you realize just how much there is to do?"

"No, I don't. But I'll tell you this, Carisa. I'll permit you to continue with your circus . . . as I told you yesterday, I don't break promises. But you'll work with hirelings, and you will not disrupt the life of this household. Further, you will not work in secrecy."

"Secrecy!" She glared at him.

Adam shrugged. "You made plans to buy that farm without consulting me, and you hired Elias Dunnett without my knowledge. What else have you done?"

"Nothing," she said indignantly. "I've done nothing at all!"

"No more surprises for me?"

"No!" She lifted her chin. "I've told you about the farm. What other surprises could there be?"

"If I know you, you'll think of something." Adam sat down in the chair near the bed and reached out to enfold her hand in his. "Carisa, darling," he said in a low voice. "Let's not quarrel, not today. Not when Dr. Arthur is coming to set your poor limbs free so that you can be a normal human woman again."

She gazed at him, and felt a curious swooping pull at her innards. He couldn't mean . . . or could he? Yes, she thought. He did.

"The fracture-boxes are coming off," she heard herself repeat stupidly.

"Yes. And, darling Carisa, I plan to come to you tonight. God help me, I've got to. I must. I can't wait any longer."

"Adam . . ."

She clung to him, their disagreement forgotten. She could feel her breath quicken, her cheeks flush hot.

He kissed her, long and lingeringly.

When Dr. Arthur had unwrapped the bandages and splints and pried away the wood which bound both of her legs, Carisa was horrified at what she saw.

Her legs lay on the sheets like flaccid sticks, limp and pitiable and shrunken. There were bumpy marks along the bones where they had mended, and a red scar on her right lower leg where her wound had been.

"Oh . . ."

"Why don't you try putting your weight on them?" Dr. Arthur suggested, politely averting his eyes. "You'll have to do it a bit at a time, of course, each time putting on more weight until you can stand."

"Put my . . . weight on them?"

"Of course. The girl here can help you." Dr. Arthur motioned to Nelly who, white-faced and aghast, had been standing by, wringing her hands in her apron.

Obediently Carisa slid to the edge of the bed. With Nelly's help she managed to extend her feet. The moment she touched them to the floor, however, agony shot upward like sharp lancing-knives.

Carisa gave a little muffled scream and fell back on the bed.

"Well, it'll take time." Dr. Arthur bobbed his bald head as if completely satisfied at what had just happened. "And if you don't regain your strength right away, I suppose we can always leech you again."

"No leeches!" Carisa gasped. "You needn't worry about me. I'll be just fine."

He took his leave of her and went out into the corridor, where she could hear him discussing with

Adam the course of her treatment. Carisa could hardly wait until he was gone.

"Nelly," she ordered breathlessly. "Nelly, help me to slide forward again. I want to stand."

"But, Miss Carisa, are you sure. . . ."

"Yes! I'm sure. I want to walk, Nelly. I can't be helpless any more."

Again she dangled her limbs over the side of the bed. She could feel them tingle as the blood rushed into them. On an impulse, she lifted her petticoats to look at them again.

She drew in a sharp, horrified gasp.

Her limbs were no longer flaccid sticks. Something had happened to them. The blood and fluids had evidently rushed downward, for now her legs were swollen and ugly, like the bloated pigs' bladders sold in the circus as children's balloons.

"Oh, Miss Carisa!" Nelly gasped. "Oh, your limbs!"

Carisa pressed her lips together to stop their trembling, and with all her strength she forced herself not to scream.

"It . . . it's all right, Nelly," she said faintly.

"But they look terrible! Oh, Miss Carisa, they're just like my granny's legs, all full of water. She's got the dropsy so bad she can hardly walk!"

"It's . . . just natural after a person has broken a bone," Carisa managed to say, hoping that this was so. She pushed back a wild thought of the way her legs had been once, strong and vital, able to balance her body on the moving back of a horse, to do ballet steps in perfect rhythm. Once she had walked so easily that she had never thought to appreciate that miracle. Now—

"Natural? Like that?" Nelly wailed. "So swole you are, I never saw anything like it in my life! And what about your shoes? Your boots? How will you fit into them? Oh, do you think you're going to be a cripple for the rest of your days?"

"Nelly!" Carisa fought her own dismay and fright and smacked a fist into the feather softness of her pillow. "Nelly, will you please be still? Of course I won't be

87

crippled! Whyever would you say such a foolish thing, Nelly Sawyer?"

"Oh . . . Oh. . . ."

"And do stop gasping like a wounded fish. I . . . I want to rest. Please leave, and when you do come back, I don't want to hear another word about my legs. Do you hear me? I don't care if they turn purple and fall off, I refuse to hear one more word about them."

"Y-yes . . ."

So Nelly fled from the room, clutching at her long, white apron, crumpling it in her hands, and Adam came in.

"And what was all that ruckus about?" He was grinning at her.

Carisa's hands were over her face. She sobbed helplessly.

"Carisa, Carisa, whatever is wrong?"

But she couldn't stop, there was no way she could stop, she was being carried along on the tide of her own fright and hysteria.

He held her, stroking her hair with his big hands. "Go ahead and cry, then, Carisa, if it will help."

"But . . . But I don't have any shoes I can wear," she wept.

"Shoes?" He laughed. "Shoes! What do they matter? I'll have new ones made for you. The important thing is that Dr. Arthur feels that your fractures have healed very well. He's very pleased with your progress. You're going to be all right, darling. All right!"

"But my legs . . . like pigs' bladders . . ." she sobbed.

"What?" Adam's voice was incredulous. He laughed softly.

"D-Don't laugh," she choked. "My legs are s-swollen like balloons and Nelly says they . . . they look like her granny with the dropsy, and she's right, I'll never be able to walk properly again, never. . . ."

"Of course you will. The swelling will go down and you'll be beautiful. Is that why Nelly rushed out of here in such a state? What did she say to you? Damn that girl, now I *will* fire her. If she's the one who got you into this condition. . . ."

88

"No, she isn't. No, don't fire her, Adam. I got myself into this state, it didn't require Nelly's help. . . ."

They were laughing and clinging to each other, the front of Adam's shirt wet with her tears. And this was the moment Carisa was to remember most clearly hours later, when Adam held her again, in a different way, and claimed her as his wife.

"Darling?" Adam's voice was low. They lay in the darkness, their bodies naked and still moist from their lovemaking.

"Yes?"

"Carisa, was it good for you?"

Carisa was glad that Adam could not see her face in the dark. Good? Was "good" a proper word to describe that painful, startling, tender, momentous thing which had happened between them? There *was* no word to describe it. Never, in her wildest imagining, had she realized that such closeness, such personal touching, could occur between a man and a woman.

"Well, was it good?" he demanded. "Carisa, I . . . I suppose I was too rough. I tried not to be, I tried to remember your poor, pitiful legs."

"It didn't hurt much," she said shyly. "I didn't mind."

She heard him expel his breath in a long, soft sigh.

"Adam . . ." She turned to him, one hand caressing the bulk of his chest, with its springy coating of golden hair. She had never before felt a man's body. Not like this, so close that she could hear the rumble of his breathing and smell the man-smell of him.

He wrapped his arms around her, and she felt the full length of him against her, solid and muscular and hard, all the fullness of him, the maleness of him. He buried his face in her breasts. She felt his lips brush her nipples, his breath warm against her skin. He was going to make love to her again. Involuntarily, her breath quickened in excitement. She wanted him, she wanted him inside her, lifting her up to breathless release. . . .

They pressed together, each of them lost in this

close, warm world of their own making. Dimly she could hear Adam's voice, murmuring to her.

"Carisa . . . Carisa, oh, God . . . you're beautiful . . . so lovely . . . I had no idea . . . no idea . . ." A pause, punctuated by kisses, wild stirring kisses. "Carisa, do you think that one day . . . you might love me. . . ."

Had she really heard him whisper that, in a voice so low it might have been a rustling of the bed linen?

7

It was December, five days before Christmas. Outdoors, a dry wind rattled the window panes and knocked tree branches against the glass.

Inside, Adam Hartshorn stared at his wife as she pirouetted for him in front of the oval dressing table mirror, and tried to hide his dismay.

"Well, Adam, how do I look? How do I really look?"

She was gay, excited, in a party mood. Again she twirled about, and Adam knew the movements must hurt her still-swollen legs, but she did not betray her pain.

"Don't you think Mrs. Wiggins did a beautiful job on this dress?" Carisa exclaimed. "I'm sure all of our guests will be properly impressed. It's the very latest, it was in *Godey's* only this month, and Mrs. Wiggins worked so hard to accomplish the copying in time. Not to mention all of the circus sewing she's been doing for me."

Adam nodded. "She's capable, there's no doubt about it." He glanced down at his own close-fitting black coat and waistcoat, hating himself for the misgivings he felt.

He himself had approved the drawings for this gown. So this was partly his fault. But how could he have guessed that the dress which looked so simple and charming on paper would serve only to emphasize the voluptuousness of Carisa's figure?

90

In it, she was just too ripe. Yes, Adam thought, that was it. There was no other woman in New London who had a body like Carisa's, firmed by years of hard physical exercise. The plain lines of the slate-colored *mousseline* did nothing to hide her jutting breasts or her narrow waist. In fact, the fabric with its highlights seemed to call attention to these features. And the three tiered flounces, each edged in a row of diamond-shaped velvet points, made her waist look even tinier.

Pliable, swayable, kissable. . . .

Adam felt the desire begin to rise in him again.

Not now, he thought. *I can't want her now, I don't.*

Yet he knew he did. He had never been able to get enough of her, she was like a drug for him, the most fascinating woman he had ever imagined. Fascinating and infuriating. Selling herself to him for that accursed circus of hers . . . and *he,* he had been willing to take her under those conditions. . . .

He swallowed hard, hating himself.

"Well?" Carisa demanded, the slanting blue eyes sparkling. "Compliment me, Adam!"

With an effort he shrugged and smiled at her. "What do you want me to say, Carisa? You are the most beautiful woman this town has ever seen." He made a quick, impatient gesture. "But perhaps . . . well, perhaps you are just a bit too lovely. And especially in that dress. Dammit, why couldn't she have made it a bit plainer?"

"This *is* plain. There's really very little ribbon and the flounces are in good taste. Adam, haven't you any idea of what ladies are wearing these days? Your mother has been bringing me all of her magazines, and I know."

She was staring at him. The excitement in her cheeks had faded a bit, and her eyes were puzzled.

"Well, then it's plain. I'm certainly no judge of gowns. Nevertheless. . . ." He hesitated.

"What, Adam? What's bothering you? Is it that you don't want us to give this party?"

"Well . . ."

"We have to go into society sometime. Even your mother says so. I can't stay walled up here at Hearts-ease as if I didn't even exist. They've all been gossiping and wondering about me, I know they have. Now they've got to meet me. And I'd like to know them."

"Oh, I'm sure they will like you, Carisa," he said uneasily.

"Then why do you look so red-faced and bothered?"

"Dammit, I'm not 'bothered,' as you put it." He would like to shake her, he thought furiously. To lift her up by that tiny waist of hers and fling her down on the bed and strip off the gown, unlace her corset, pull it all off, everything. . . .

He smiled at her. "Anyway," he added, "what does it matter? They *will* like you. And it will be nice to have a party here at Hearts-ease again. We haven't given one in years. In fact, I think the ballroom has been closed up since before Mary Elizabeth died."

Carisa turned away from him, and, with the aid of one crutch, went to sit down at the little dressing table covered in crewel-embroidered flounces. Her back was very straight, growing out of the mass of her skirts like a stem.

"I think you protest a little too much, Adam. You don't think they'll like me, do you? Not really."

"That's not true."

"Don't lie to me, your mother has made it very plain that the entire county is gossiping about me, about the exotic circus girl you picked up and, in some moment of insanity, married."

"Now, Carisa. . . ."

"Well, it's true, isn't it? I suppose to them I do seem exotic. And now they've heard about the farm I've bought and about the circus being here, and they think I'm shocking."

Adam squared his jaw stubbornly. "Let them, then. I don't listen to gossip."

Carisa seemed to relax a fraction. She glanced down at her lap, at the two silk-gloved hands clasped together there, fingers twisting. "Perhaps it will be easier for them to accept me after I have the child," she whispered.

"Child!"

"Or . . . or children, Adam. Sometimes I think . . . I've been having odd dreams. There might be two."

"Two! What are you talking about?"

"Yes, Adam. I'm pregnant, of course. And I think I'm going to have twins. That's why I was so anxious to give this party now, while I still look my best."

"But . . . But that's wonderful!" He went to her and put his arms around her, all of his anger gone now. "My God, Carisa, we're going to be parents! You and I. We're going to have a child!"

"Two children," she said seriously. "Laugh at me all you wish, Adam, but I can feel it, I *know*. We're going to have twins. They run in my family, you know. On my mother's side."

He kissed her long and hard and felt the soft yielding of her. And for a few stolen moments he forgot the people who would be at the party, all of them staring at his wife and speculating about her.

Noises swirled about her ears—female laughter, the heartier rumble of male voices. The party had been going on for nearly an hour now, although some of the guests were still arriving.

Carisa stood trembling beside Katherine, wishing that she could turn around and flee upstairs.

They were all here, the society of New London, the men dressed in dark suits, the women impressive in heavy gowns held stiffly out by hoops and crinolines. All of them, she thought with a dull anger, enjoying the party and the spectacle of looking at *her*.

She had been snubbed. Roundly and thoroughly. Her cheeks burned at the thought of it. Oh, as each group had arrived they had nodded to her, or given her an obligatory greeting; a few men had given her pretty compliments on her British accent. With Adam standing sternly at her side, they could scarcely do anything else.

But no one had spoken to her otherwise. And now Adam had been drawn away into a conversation with some plump, hearty ship-owners, leaving her with his mother.

"You must not stand there looking so *stricken*, Carisa

Hartshorn," Katherine hissed under her breath. "Go, why don't you? Mingle with them! *Dare* them to speak to you!"

"I . . . I can't. . . ."

"Oh, yes, you can! Do you mean to tell me that a bold little miss like you can't handle herself at a simple social gathering?"

But before Carisa could open her mouth to reply (and what, anyway, could she possibly say?) Poll Henry had appeared in the drawing room and was plucking at Katherine's sleeve.

"Yes?" Katherine asked impatiently.

"It's Julian. He's having one of his temper fits again. He just won't go to sleep, and there's nothing I can do when he's in one of these stubborn moods."

Carisa could not help staring at Poll, remembering the look of naked hatred she had once seen in the girl's eyes. Tonight the girl avoided her look altogether. She looked slim and quiet in her dark maid's uniform, with a starched white cap. But instead of a uniform, Carisa had the quick thought, Poll should be in sensuous red velvet. It would become her dark, soft skin and heighten her liquid eyes.

"Didn't you try to read him a story?" Katherine asked.

Poll looked sullen. "Yes, but he says he doesn't like my voice. He gets moody sometimes."

"Oh, bother, and tonight of all nights," sighed Katherine. "What a difficult boy. You would think he did this deliberately. Well, you go to him, Carisa, and see if you can get him settled down. I must stay here and greet our guests. The Kords haven't arrived yet, and some others."

"Very well."

With a feeling of relief, Carisa hurried after the slim, dark nursemaid. *Julian,* she thought as—slowly, because of her crutch—she climbed the stairs. She had to admit that Adam's son puzzled her. She had tried so hard to make him like her.

She had read him stories until her voice cracked. She had taught him to play checkers and told him innumerable tales of the circus. She had even taken him down to the farm in which the circus had its new quarters and allowed him to ride the ring horses and play with the trick dogs.

Still, it was plain that the boy thought her an interloper. She had come here and taken away his father's attention, and he resented her as deeply as any nine-year-old could.

When they reached Julian's room, Carisa stopped short on the threshold in dismay. The bedroom was a shambles. Toys were scattered about, a set of metal toy soldiers, whistles, marbles, and a big Parlor Ball which Katherine had sewn for him out of soft cotton and net.

The quilts had been pulled off Julian's bed and wadded up on the floor. The bureau drawers were pulled out, the dresser scarf askew. And Julian himself, clad in a nightshirt, was standing on a chair at the window, where a big oak tree leaned toward the house, engaged in the act of pulling his drapes off their rod.

"Julian!" Carisa crutched herself over to him, wincing as the tendons in her legs gave their customary protest. "What in the world are you doing?"

He turned to face her. His eyes were hard and quite adult-like. "It's my room. I can do what I want in it. Poll said so."

Carisa shot an angry look at the nursemaid, who avoided her gaze. "Well, Poll certainly did not tell you that you could tear up your furnishings like a vandal!"

"I don't care." Defiantly Julian reached upward for another handful of the heavy red brocade. Balancing on her crutch, Carisa instinctively moved to stop him.

"Let go!" he panted. "Let go of me!"

He gave a vicious swipe at her crutch.

Carisa stepped backward, flushing, thankful that he had missed. "Julian." She bit at her lip. "You know that it's wrong to make a wreck of your bedroom in this way."

"It isn't. Poll said anything I do here is private. . . ."

Again Poll had turned away, her expression sullen

and malefic. *She should be dismissed,* Carisa thought. *Somehow she's bad for the boy.*

But there was no time to scold the nurse-governess now. And, anyway, what could she say?

"Well, perhaps you misunderstood what Poll said," Carisa told Julian. "Anyway, it's late, and you should be in bed now. I'll pull up the bedcovers and Poll will straighten the room. And then I'll read you a story. Which one would you like to hear? There are two new books that. . . ."

"I don't want *you* to read. Papa can read." He climbed down from the chair and flung himself on the mattress, where he began to bounce up and down.

"Your father is busy at the party, Julian. But I'm sure he. . . ."

"I said I want Papa! I don't want *you,* you silly old ugly thing. That's what you are, ugly and crippled and wicked!"

Carisa could not help recoiling. She could feel her breath come rapidly as Julian sat sprawled on the wrecked bed, his face red with fury, his eyes as shiny as two of his own agates. The baby softness of his features was quite gone.

He's only nine, she reminded herself firmly. He had also grown up without a mother, and with a father who was often very busy.

"Very well, then," she said quietly. "I'll fetch your father, then, if you promise to settle down and go straight to sleep."

His eyes glared at her.

"Get my Papa," he ordered. "Just get him."

After Adam had left to go to his son, Carisa hesitated in the door of the drawing room, wishing that someone would speak to her.

The party, she saw, was getting along very well without her. From the ballroom came the sounds of a three-piece string ensemble. In the drawing room, people stood in animated groups. Near the window Katherine held court with a group of women. Eliza, Samuel's wife, sat near the fireplace at Katherine's harp. Her fingers moved deftly over the strings, producing a soft counterpoint to the party's noise. Eliza, small, mousy, dressed in bottle green, was an odd contrast to her dashing, dark-haired husband. Yet at the harp she possessed a certain graceful elegance.

Suddenly Carisa sensed someone staring at her, and looked up to see that Samuel Hartshorn was watching her. He lounged near the fireplace, his body propped there with an easy arrogance. He had been watching her all evening, she was sure of it. His eyes were dark and insolent.

And he was not the only man, she knew, who had stared at her. Every man in the room had eyed her, had given her long, speculative looks which seemed to strip the fabric right off her back. The women had snubbed; the men had stared.

Carisa swallowed and lifted her chin higher. She felt very alone. Adam, who had provided her only protection, had gone upstairs to attend to Julian. Katherine was busy with her friends. She was at the mercy of these people who thought her a circus strumpet.

Now Katherine was coming toward her with a woman in tow.

"Carisa, I would like you to meet Madeleine Kord. She is a very dear friend of mine, and this is her first excursion after her recent lying-in. She gave birth to a fine son, Calvin."

Carisa turned, trying to smile pleasantly. Madeleine Kord was a pretty women in her late twenties, with a soft, flabby body tightly laced at the waist. She was, Carisa knew, the wife of Redlands Kord, who owned the Kord Ax Company, a local manufactory. The Kords lived three-quarters of a mile down the road from Hearts-ease.

"I'm pleased to meet you," Carisa murmured.

Madeleine's eyes gleamed with curiosity. Her glance moved from the flounces of Carisa's gown upward to her bodice with frank appraisal. "So you really are a British circus girl? A bareback rider?"

97

"Yes, I am an equestrienne," Carisa replied. "Or I was, until I had my accident. Now I am Adam's wife."

She raised her chin defiantly. *Just smile and be pleasant,* Katherine had instructed her before the party began. *If you are innocuous enough, they will accept you.* It had sounded easy enough—then. Now it was becoming difficult indeed.

"Am I to understand that you are actually housing a circus here on Adam's property?" Madeleine's voice made it sound as if Carisa had established a free love colony.

"Yes, indeed. In fact, we are very busy," Carisa heard herself reply. "We're building ten circus wagons, four of them carved with mythical figures and covered in gold leaf. I've acquired a clown band and they have been rehearsing every day. And I've bought twenty matched dapple grays for our parade. I've also bought a lithographic hand press so that we can print our own handbills and banners for next season."

Carisa heard Madeleine's gasp of shock. Katherine's cheeks had turned a dull red.

Some angry impulse made her continue. "Our sideshow next season, Mrs. Kord, will consist of Mademoiselle LaVoss, who is a bearded lady, Major Ribinson and his wife, who are midgets, and Maybelle Cameron, Queen of Snakes. And after the holidays I personally plan to travel to New York City to hire the rest of our performers."

Carisa heard Katherine give a sharp, indrawn gasp of breath. Madeleine Kord's eyes widened and her mouth fell slack. The soft, plump chin waggled.

"You are doing all that?"

"Why shouldn't I? I own the circus and I plan to run it."

Madeleine stared. "Hiring a bearded lady? A woman, doing such things! Well, you may be British and all that, but we here in New London certainly know what women in the public theater are like. And I gather that you, Mrs. Hartshorn, are no exception."

"Now, Madeleine . . ." Katherine began.

But Madeleine Kord ignored her friend. She gave

Carisa a long, hostile look. Then she turned away, the huge, circular hem of her gown dragging on the carpet.

Carisa stood stunned. She felt like a child who has been left out of a game for a reason it doesn't even know. Tears pricked at her eyes, and angrily she blinked them back. Katherine was saying something to her—something about the travel plans—but Carisa did not even hear her.

"Mrs. Kord!" Forgetting her crutch, impulsively Carisa limped after the other woman. "Please. . . ."

Madeleine turned.

"Please, I don't know why you think such ugly things about me, but I assure you they're not true. I'm a decent girl, as decent as you are. You just don't understand! I bought that show because my sister died in the accident, and my Papa . . . all his plans. . . ."

She stopped. Madeleine had turned and was talking animatedly to Nora West, the wife of Adam's whaling agent, as if Carisa were not even there. Beside them Katherine was frowning.

Carisa felt herself sway, her weak leg muscles threatening to give out. She felt the blood wash up to stain her face. It seemed to throb across her cheeks in waves. Madeleine Kord, plump, soft, vacuous Madeleine, had cut her dead. And was, in fact, enjoying every second of that accomplishment.

It was what she had come here to do. She and every other woman in the room. They hated her, because she came from a world unfamiliar to them.

She stared wildly at her mother-in-law, who had swept across the room as if she had not heard this conversation.

"You don't belong here, you know," Katherine had told her before she had married Adam. *"You're quite unsuitable as a wife for someone like Adam."*

Was she?

Carisa picked up her skirts and turned blindly. Then she began to run, limping on stiff, sore leg muscles that hurt with every step until she wanted to weep with pain. But she didn't weep, not yet, not until she had reached the haven of Adam's study and had slammed its door behind her.

"Well, and what have we here?" Samuel Hartshorn said. The party noise briefly flared, and then he closed the study door behind him with a little click. "The little lady of the household weeping away in the corner like a child who's been denied a sweet! And all because a plump ninny chose to ignore her."

"What . . . What are you doing here?" she whispered, gripping the arms of her chair. Belatedly she remembered Adam's warning.

Samuel's lips twisted in a half-smile. He lounged against the closed door.

"Very simple. I saw you rush away from that suet pudding, Madeleine Kord, and I followed you. That's all. You needn't worry, no one has noticed me. No one knows I'm here except you."

Carisa brushed at her swollen eyes and stared at this brother of Adam's. If Adam was leonine, then Samuel was a stallion, smooth, black-haired, muscular, full of nervous male energy and stamina. He was boldly handsome, and again Carisa thought of what Adam had said about him. *Womanizer.*

Samuel, Adam had explained, had married Eliza as a young man of 20, later inheriting her wealthy father's mansion on Whale Oil Row and a sizeable fortune as well. Now, although he still brooded over his loss of Hearts-ease, he seemed happy enough there. It was whispered that he kept a mistress in Groton Heights.

"I said no one knows I'm here," Samuel repeated suggestively.

"In that case, I think you'd better leave, don't you?" Carisa rose from her chair in a rustle of silk and petticoats. She felt at a disadvantage, pinned down under the amusement in those black eyes which regarded her so unwinkingly.

"And what if I don't want to leave? What if I'd prefer to stay here and comfort you, Carisa? You're very beautiful, you know."

She twisted away from him, her leg tendons pulling sharply as she did so. "I don't need comfort!"

"Don't you?"

He was standing entirely too close to her—so close that she could smell the pomade he used on his black hair, the fresh-laundered smell of his garments, the clean, male smell of his body.

"Please . . . I must get back to the party . . . Adam will be wondering where I am."

"Carisa, Carisa, what's your hurry? Your husband is still upstairs with Julian. I don't mean you any harm, I just wanted to get to know you a little better. Is there any harm in that?"

"Please . . ." Her heart was slamming. "Please move, Samuel, so that I can get out of the door. I must go to rejoin my husband and guests."

"Must you?" Slowly, deliberately, he put his arms around her. They seemed to burn across her shoulders and lower back. She felt herself tremble with her anger and her agitation and—yes—her attraction to him.

"Please . . . Samuel, you mustn't. . . ."

"Tell me, Carisa." His hands were running up and down her rib cage. "Tell me what a girl like you . . . a British girl . . . thinks of New London. Does it bother you to give up the free life you had, the men you must have known?"

"I . . . I didn't know any men!"

"Didn't you?" Now his fingers stroked slowly up and down her arm, sending thrills of sensation through her until she felt as if she could barely gasp in enough air. If he didn't stop, she knew her knees would collapse. She would sink into a heap on the rug.

With enormous effort, she wrenched away from him.

"You're just like all the rest of them, aren't you?" Her voice was high, shaky. "Those awful men in the drawing room, undressing me with their eyes! Well, let me tell you something, Mr. Hartshorn. I am a decent woman, as proper as any other woman here tonight and possibly more so than some of them. I was a virgin when I came to Adam . . . do you hear me? A virgin!"

101

He was laughing. "Come, come. You don't have to turn into a little virago. I certainly didn't mean. . . ."

"Then what *did* you mean? You waylaid me here in Adam's study, knowing that it was improper and might compromise me. Would you have done that if I'd been born and bred here in New London, if I'd been like those other women out there?"

"Well . . ." For the first time, Samuel looked uncomfortable.

"No," Carisa cried. "No, you wouldn't! You would have respected me. But because I'm different, because I come from a way of life that is foreign to you, then you think my morals are easy. Well, they're not. *I am a lady,* Samuel Hartshorn! Do you hear me? A lady!"

His lips were curved in that arrogant half-smile again. He regarded her with amusement.

"I doubt if you are truly a lady, Carisa. In fact, I don't think you are. But I will tell you one thing. I think you are going to conquer them all."

She stared at him.

"Oh, I know them, those people out there. Today they don't like you and that circus of yours . . . you stick in their craw. But one day you, my hot-tempered little Carisa, are going to shove your ring horses and your clown band right in their . . . faces. And when your show is a success, they'll accept it, all right. And they'll accept you, too. They understand success."

She could scarcely believe what she had just heard. "But . . ."

Samuel laughed. "It's boldness that counts in this world," he told her. "Boldness and drive. You've got those. You and I, Carisa, we're a good deal alike in some ways. I'm not a gentleman and you're not a lady. And we like it that way."

"How dare you . . ." she began faintly.

"I dare. And what's more, I dare this."

He scooped her forward and kissed her, his mouth covering hers boldly. Searching, demanding, conquering her struggles and holding her quite captive.

* * *

"Carisa?" Adam said out of the dark.

"Yes, Adam?"

"Was that party difficult for you? My mother told me that Madeleine Kord was quite rude to you."

And you were equally rude back, she knew he meant. Or did he?

"It . . . it was hard," she admitted. "But I survived it." She thought of Samuel, his mouth crushed against hers, and felt her cheeks color painfully. Thank God, she thought, that Adam couldn't see her face now. Or know what had happened. She would never let herself be placed in such a position again, of course. She would put Samuel Hartshorn completely out of her mind.

"I'm sorry I took so long with Julian or I could have spared you some of that," Adam told her easily. "But I'm sure they'll soon come to accept you. After all, we are Hartshorns. They won't snub us for long. They can't afford to. I'm on too many railroad boards and own too much property. And I have too many enemies who dare not offend me."

He gave a soft, rueful laugh into the darkness.

"I hope so, Adam."

"Don't worry, I'm right." Adam paused. "You were the most beautiful woman there. They all knew it. Your hair was like a candle flame. And that gown . . . that delicious scandalously plain gown. . . ."

His hands were at the neck of her nightgown, pulling at the ribbons. Then he was lifting it, pulling it over her head with hands that were gentle, yet strong. Hands that followed the curves of her body, savoring them, *all* of them.

"Darling," he murmured. "God help me, I want you. . . ."

His lips were on hers, tender, searching. Languorously Carisa gave herself up to his caresses, to the warmth that flamed between them. Gasping, pleasuring, seeking . . .

In a few moments she forgot the party, she forgot Samuel, she forgot everything except that she was in Adam's arms.

103

8

"Pull the carriage blanket around your knees," Adam ordered. "And watch it . . . there's a very nasty chuckhole just ahead."

They had gone for a drive, jogging along behind the superb team of matched grays, while the horses' hooves clop-clopped and bridles jingled.

Adam, in one of his rare good moods (he had been moody lately, although Carisa was not sure just why), was showing her the town of New London.

The town, he told her proudly, had been built on one of the best natural harbors in the country. It was sheltered by Fisher's Island from the storms which raged in the "devil's belt," as the first settlers here had called Long Island Sound. The town had been known by several names—Naumeaug, Pequot, and Fair Harbor—and it was not until 1658, when John Winthrop was governor, that it was finally named New London.

"So, naturally, we had to change the name of our river, too," Adam told her with a smile. "Mohegan just didn't seem to fit any more. And what better river could there be for a town named New London than the Thames?"

The town had begun along a three-mile, crescent-shaped slice of waterfront curved between the needle-shaped inlet of Winthrop's Cove and Shaw's Cove. Now, with the booming of the whaling industry, it had started to move outward.

In fact, the sea *was* New London, Adam informed her with pride. And as they neared the docks, Carisa could see why. The wharves teemed with confusion. Ships of all sizes, from fishing boats to whalers and barks, crowded the jetties, or were in the skeletal stages of construction.

Barrels of whale and sperm oil were stacked by the thousands wherever room could be found for them.

These added their own smells to the tang of seawater, rotting fish, rope and tar.

Carisa wrinkled her nose, too, as they drove past large, whitened heaps of whalebone. Stacks of other supplies were being loaded into wagons and one-horse drays which shuttled back and forth, being directed by shouting, perspiring men. More men on foot roamed about. A small, thatch-haired boy darted across the road, and Jim, their driver, had to pull up sharply to avoid hitting him.

"Busy, isn't it?" Adam's eyes were sparkling. He made a wide gesture which took in the entire scene. "But I confess I love it. All the excitement, the hustle, the color and the smells—I never seem to get enough of it. As a mater of fact, my shipping office isn't far from here."

They were now passing a saloon from which a drunken sailor staggered, to be noisily sick in the muddy snow of the road. Carisa hastily averted her eyes.

"Look, Carisa!" Adam had not even noticed. "There's the coopers . . . they make barrels to hold our oil. And next to it is the ships' chandlery which I own. We make almost everything we need for the sea right here in New London, you know. Biscuits and crackers for provisions, casks to hold the oil, sails to propel the ships, ropes to rig them and even . . ." Adam laughed. ". . . even dentifrice so that the sailors can brush their teeth, assuming that they're inclined to do so, which many aren't."

They passed hotels, warehouses, fish markets, more warehouses, and still more saloons. It seemed that the section of town known as Water Street was where the sailors went, to throng in and out of the drinking halls, gaming houses, brothels and saloons which were crammed into this small area.

"Oh, it *is* wonderful!" Carisa cried at last, caught up in the lusty vitality of it all.

"Yes." For an instant a frown crossed Adam's face. "Although whaling has fallen off a bit since gold was discovered in California. It seems that gold is a pretty

105

powerful lure, Carisa, much stronger than sperm oil or ambergris."

"But surely that shouldn't affect New London!"

"I hope not. But I can't count how many captains and seamen we've lost to the gold lust, not to mention the ships we've had to divert to take them to California. But of course," Adam added, "this setback is only temporary. The whole world craves whale oil. And as long as people need oil for their lamps, the city of New London will boom."

And booming it certainly seemed to be, Carisa thought, as they passed more shipyards, the Brown Cotton Gin Works, hotels, banks and churches.

In contrast to this grandeur, however, the streets themselves were crooked, dusty, and overrun with chickens and pigs. Private carriages jostled the public hacks and omnibusses, and all of them threatened to overrun the store delivery boys with their laden wheelbarrows, who had to use the roads because there were no walks.

"Now," Adam said reluctantly. "Let's go and pay a call on Samuel and Eliza. There is some business which I must discuss with my brother. And while I do, you can chat with Eliza."

Samuel and his wife lived on Huntington Street, near a row of imposing Greek Revival homes, each of which had tall white columns in front and looked absurdly like its neighbors. The street, Adam told her, was called "Whale Oil Row," because of all the wealthy whaling agents and owners who had built these homes and lived in them.

They were shown inside by a tall, stiff, very proper butler. When Samuel came sauntering into Eliza's ornate drawing room, Carisa's heart jumped. She found that her hands were clenched over the embroidered bead bag she carried, until the sharp little beads cut into her flesh.

"Well, hello, both of you." Samuel's eyes raked boldly over Carisa, and she was sure that there was a gleam of amusement in them. "Come to pay a call, have you? My wife will be right down. I think she is fussing with her hair."

"Just some business to discuss," Adam said sharply. "A contract for you to look over and co-sign, that's all."

Samuel scowled. "And if I don't wish to sign it?"

"You will. If the signing is to your advantage."

Samuel's mouth twisted. "Business!" he said to Carisa. "Never own property jointly with anyone, Carisa. It causes quarrels."

"Any quarrels we have ever had, Samuel, have been because you wanted them," Adam said carefully. Carisa could sense the anger he was holding back.

"Well, here is my wife," Samuel said. He motioned in the direction of the entering Eliza without warmth. "Why don't we go into my office, Adam, and get this little ceremony over with? Eliza can entertain Carisa."

"And what do you think of New London, Carisa?" Eliza asked after they had been served tea and small cakes, and Carisa had admired the lovely gold-leafed harp which occupied a place of distinction in the parlor.

"I like it. The city seems very much alive, as if something is always happening here."

Eliza coughed, then made a *moue* of disgust. "Oh, yes. Too much happens, if you want my opinion. Sailors brawling about the streets . . . and now we have a circus here to titillate them and stir up the rabble."

Carisa, who had been sipping tea, put her cup down. "And why should my show cause trouble? Circus people are among the finest, most moral people in the world. . . ."

"Oh?" Eliza smiled sweetly. "My husband tells me that circuses are also famous for their gambling and pickpockets and confidence men who cheat the innocent country people. We certainly don't need that sort of thing in New London."

"My show isn't like that! My show is absolutely honest!"

"Is it? There have already been rumors, my dear Carisa, that certain of your employees have been seen in the gambling houses in town, and that they are *very* sharp with cards."

"Rumors can be wrong, then."

Eliza looked quizzical, had another paroxysm of

107

coughing, and changed the subject. Carisa sat fuming. She was relieved when Adam finally came out of Samuel's office and they could leave.

"It's not fair!" she burst out on the way home. "Eliza implied that my show is going to drag the city of New London into the muck. That we are all cheaters and liars and confidence men. . . ."

As the carriage jounced them together, Adam took Carisa's gloved hand and patted it.

"Don't listen to her. Eliza has her ways, and after a while you'll get used to them."

"I hope so. Why on earth did he ever marry her, Adam?" she asked impulsively.

"Why did who marry who?"

"Why, Samuel, of course, and Eliza. Why did he marry her, of all people? She— She seems so very dull and spiteful and old."

"Perhaps she is, Carisa. But she's had reason to become that way. She lost three children in stillbirths, and during her last confinement she nearly died. Then, too, her lungs are weak, and Dr. Arthur is constantly urging her to seek a warmer and drier climate. But Eliza knows that Samuel's life is here in New London and she will not leave."

"Oh . . ." Carisa caught her breath, remembering what Adam had said about his brother before, that Samuel was a womanizer, and had a mistress in Groton Heights. And still, she thought, Eliza loved her husband and wanted to be with him.

As Adam helped her out of the carriage and into the house, Carisa felt her cheeks sting, and knew that she had been rebuked.

The January thaw had left the roads frozen into hard, deep ruts. Some days later Adam was able to put away his cutter and switch to a wheeled carriage again.

Carisa's legs were now well enough for her to take the path through the rock-strewn hemlocks to the field where the circus was quartered. One small barn had been turned into a workshop, and here labored the four

108

Italian workmen whom Elias Dunnett had hired to carve out the fantastic designs of the parade wagons.

Curved, elaborate dragons, painted green and standing out in sharp contrast to fanciful carvings covered in gold leaf. Gods, goddesses, unicorns, chariots—Carisa thought the wagons were beautiful. And she never tired of watching the men smooth on the gold leaf, which came in small books, each page rolled out to a tissue-thin sheet. It was painstaking work, done with a knife, a "tip," and a "cushion," and Carisa was sure that she herself would never have the patience to do it.

She and Rolf had already begun to plan their parade, for no proper circus was ever without a parade, that glorious free spectacle when every wagon, animal and circus employee marched through the streets of a town, generating giddy excitement among children and adults alike, and making everyone want to attend the show itself.

At least, Carisa told herself, that was the way it *should* be. And her show, she vowed, would be as colorful and exciting as she could possibly manage.

But there were many details to see to. There were dozens of costumes to be sewn. Equipment must be made or purchased, and the intricate details of routing planned. Fortunately, she had recently been able to purchase in its entirety another small show like deBord's which had foundered near Bridgeport. This had doubled their own stock of canvas, supplies and equipment, and had given them the beginnings of a good side-show.

"I really believe you're going to do it, Carisa, my girl," Duddie told her one morning when it seemed their plans had struck a snag and nothing was going right. "You're a natural-born organizer. Perhaps that's been your real talent all along."

Carisa gave him a rather strained smile. "Tell that to Adam. Sometimes I think he is very angry with me for doing this, Duddie, although he tries very hard to conceal it."

"Carisa." Duddie said it gently. "Are you sure you're doing the right thing? Wouldn't it be better, perhaps, to sell? To settle down to being a wife as your husband wishes?"

"No!" Carisa whirled about to face the little clown angrily. "No, I won't quit, Duddie, and I'm surprised that you would even suggest such a thing!"

They were in the "ring" barn, and now Duddie walked up to the white Percheron mare, Sugar, whom he was training to pace about the ring, and patted her gleaming flank.

"Under other circumstances . . . But I think perhaps you did your husband an injustice, marrying him as you did, Carisa."

"So?" Defiantly she tossed her head. "Adam understood all that when I married him. And he accepted it. We made a bargain, Duddie. I would be his wife in exchange for a circus. Many marriages are built on such arrangements, you know that. *We* are both happy enough with it."

The ring horse whickered and Duddie spoke to it soothingly.

"Are both of you that happy?"

"Of course we are!" Anger pelted through her, as she thrust back the memory of Adam's recent moodiness, the sudden flaring quarrels they had had recently. Of course Adam was happy! All she had to do was think of the passion he showed her in bed to know that.

"And from now on, Duddie," she heard herself say. "I'll thank you to keep your personal opinions to yourself. I've made you boss of ring stock, and you've plenty to keep you busy, haven't you?"

Duddie gave Sugar another pat. There was hurt on his face.

"Oh, Duddie!" Carisa gave him an impulsive hug, tears springing to her eyes. "Please, please, don't be angry with me. I couldn't stand that. You're all I have now, really, from the old show, save for Rolf, and he doesn't count as a friend. I need you, Duddie. Please forgive me!"

It was now eight months since the disastrous accident which had killed Stephana and broken Carisa's legs. The

110

Phillips Circus had begun to impose new patterns on the town of New London. Strange, pungent smells drifted townward from the circus barns. The townspeople had already begun to complain about the noise. The roars of Herod and Barabas frightened them, nor did they like the exotic assortment of trumpeting, barks and cries which floated in their direction.

The two elephants for which Carisa had paid an exorbitant price were a startling sight as they ambled across the fields. Twice teams of new "baggage," or work horses, ran away and had to be brought back amid great shouting and excitement. One more event, Carisa thought defiantly, to disturb the composure of people like Eliza Hartshorn and Madeleine Kord.

The old farm house had begun to fill up with circus people. When they went into town to shop or to attend church, they caused consternation.

"The town just can't get used to it," Katherine said in her dry, husky voice. "And I can't blame them. That bearded lady of yours, with that awful, scraggly blonde beard . . . why, she's enough to scare a person silly. As for those two midgets . . . why, the whole thing is shocking."

"They are just people," Carisa retorted. "People like you and me."

"*I* haven't got a beard," Katherine said. "At least I didn't have one the last time I looked in the mirror. And I haven't got three legs, either. I suppose that's the next monstrosity you'll bring in."

"If I can find one," Carisa heard herself retort pertly.

She had received two anonymous notes, one accusing her of being a "disciple of Beelzebub," and the other informing her that she was "a wanton, immoral woman who'd ought to be hanged."

Carisa tore both up with a feeling of revulsion. Little more than a generation ago, in a remote Pennsylvania town, circus folk had actually been stoned, for being "disciples of the devil." Traces of this feeling still lingered. For this reason, and because of the churches, shows were careful never to perform on Sunday.

111

Problems! Carisa thought in dismay. As soon as she had solved one, another rose to grin and rattle at her.

One Tuesday morning when she went down to the circus compound, Duddie greeted her, saying that he had received a letter from her father. Quickly Carisa took it from him and scanned its rather tortuous scrawl.

John Phillips, she read, was now in New York and unable to work because of a twisted knee—that most feared of injuries—which he had received while rehearsing a new stunt in the ring. This had happened some weeks ago. Now he had been left behind by the small family show he had joined. Only Anna was with him, taking in sewing and piecework in order to feed them both.

"They must be on the verge of starving," Duddie told her. "Otherwise he wouldn't have written to me at all."

Her father had not even mentioned her own name in the letter, Carisa remembered with an indrawn breath.

"Well, we'll just have to have them come here, then," she said quickly. "I'll give them something to do in my new show."

Duddie looked at her pityingly. "I don't think he'll come, Carisa."

"Oh, but he must! Besides, this show bears his name . . . why shouldn't he come? It's his show, really. He is the reason I'm doing all of this. He belongs here."

"Does he? Never make a gift to someone who won't appreciate it, Carisa."

Cheeks flushed, feeling more upset than she wanted to admit, Carisa walked back to the house and sat down to write a letter inviting her father and Anna to join the Phillips Circus. Later that day, Adam mailed it in town.

But it was Rolf Taggart who proved to be her biggest problem. He resented her ideas, objected to any suggestions she made, and hired employees without her advice or consent. There were days in which he barely spoke to her, and she knew the situation would soon come to a head.

One February morning she walked out to the barn, where Rolf was directing some workmen in the repair of a farm wagon they had just bought. A sense of urgency had begun to pervade the circus complex. Spring was almost here, and in a short while the new season would begin.

After observing the wagon work for a moment, Carisa made a suggestion.

Rolf looked up with annoyance. "Carisa, if we do it your way, we'll add at least forty pounds of extra weight. Don't you know that dead weight is the death-knell of a circus?"

"But I just suggested that. . . ."

"Do you want to mire us in mud to the tops of our wheels? Why don't you go back to your fine husband and your big house and let me handle this? It's what you're paying me for."

Carisa met his eyes. She made a gesture to dismiss the workmen temporarily.

"In case you've forgotten it, Rolf, *I* own this show. I have the controlling shares and things have to be done my way if there's any disagreement."

Rolf threw down his tools and jumped to his feet. His handsome, wedge-shaped face was flushed.

"I don't like taking orders from a woman."

"I understand that, Rolf. But you can see, can't you, that in order to make this show succeed we're going to have to cooperate."

"Cooperate!" Rolf spat on the ground. "What if I decide I want to get out? Then what?"

"Then I'll hire someone else." She looked him straight in the eye, hoping he would not notice that her hands were trembling.

"Hey, now. Wait a minute. I never said that I. . . ."

"Didn't you? I thought I heard you telling me that you won't work for me. That you don't like my ideas and won't listen to them."

Rolf looked away.

"Well?"

He looked again at her and she could see the dislike in his eyes. "I was saying . . . oh, all right, Carisa. Look. I've been managing a show since I was twelve years old. I helped deBord for five years. I *know* every detail, from ticket-selling to layout to getaway day, and everything in between. Whereas what did *you* do? You were an equestrienne, and that was all. You rode bareback, while someone else did all the planning for you."

She felt stung. "That's not fair!"

"It's true, though. Hear me out, Carisa. I can run this show for you, and I can do it better than anyone else. I'll make money for you, too, more money than you'll know how to spend."

Rolf gave a kick at the iron wheel of the farm wagon. "So, if you want me to stay, here's how it's going to be. You provide the money and the long-range planning. *I* do the details."

Carisa looked at him. Perhaps he was right, she began to think slowly. She *had* been trying to interfere in the daily details of circus life, things she knew little about technically, whereas Rolf knew a great deal about them. That, after all, was why she had hired him.

"Very well," she said. "But just one thing, Rolf. *I* hire the featured acts. I'm going to New York in a week or so and do it myself. In fact, I've already placed ads in the papers there."

Rolf's eyes flashed, but he nodded. "All right then. But remember, the rest of it is my job." He tightened his lips, giving her a stony look that reminded Carisa uncannily of her father.

"And don't interfere with me," he added. "Do you hear? I'll do things my way, or I won't do them at all."

On an afternoon in early March, Carisa set at her desk, breathing in the soft, moist air which almost seemed to smell of melting snow and crocuses. She was in the room which she had named her "office." This was an unused bedroom which she had converted for her own use, furnishing it lavishly with an Axminster carpet, a desk, settee, bookshelves and chairs.

Adam had objected to this step—as he objected to so much she did nowadays. But she had been defiant.

"*You* have your study," she had retorted angrily. "You go there every day to write, and to handle your business affairs. I need a place to work, too."

Adam's mouth had twisted. "Evidently when, in a

114

moment of foolishness, I promised you a circus, I also promised you a farm and barns and elephants and wagons and canvas and tents and an office."

"Adam . . ." She sidled up to him to throw her arms around his neck. "All these things are part of a show, you know that."

Adam pulled away from her slightly. "The women in my family have always been strong, Carisa. And I see that you are no exception. Still . . ." He was silent a long time, and she could see the emotions fleeting across his face—anger, yearning, sorrow, something else she could not name.

"Never mind," he said at last, heavily. "Go on . . . have your office if you wish it. I won't stop you from having your circus."

Now there was a knock at the door, interrupting and scattering her thoughts.

"Yes?"

"It's me, Mrs. Hartshorn. Poll."

"Very well. Come in then."

Julian's nursemaid entered the room. As usual, Poll was dressed in fresh white sprigged muslin, a choice which only served to emphasize the odd, witch-like quality of the girl. Again Carisa had the thought that velvet would suit Poll far better. Rich, sumptuous, luxurious. . . .

Last week, she and Adam had quarreled about the girl. She was sullen, Carisa had insisted, and was not a very good influence on Julian. Hesitantly she mentioned the condition in which she had found the room the night of the party they had given. And the odd, disturbing dreams she had had of the girl.

"Dreams!" Adam had only laughed. "Oh, come now, Carisa! Don't be silly. Poll's father was a Hartshorn captain, and he went down with the *Betsy* ten years ago. The family . . . there are four girls . . . has had a hard time getting along, and I feel responsible for them. Poll is a good nursemaid and she has done very adequately at teaching Julian his letters and numbers."

"But . . . Oh, I can't explain it. I think there's something . . . well, wrong about her. You may laugh at me all you wish, but I still feel it."

Adam's expression seemed to harden, as if a mask had dropped over his face. "We'll drop the subject, Carisa. Poll Henry is one of my employees, and I have no intention of dismissing her because of some foolish dreams and imaginings on your part."

"But . . ."

"I said we'll drop the topic, Carisa. And that's that!"

Now, thinking of this, Carisa listened as Poll explained that Gaines had asked her to bring a letter up to Carisa.

"Thank you, Poll," Carisa said, taking the letter. "And now you may get back to Julian. I heard you laughing a while ago. What were you playing? Checkers?"

Poll nodded, her avid, liquid-dark eyes evasive. "Yes. He's tired of that now, though. Now he wants me to tell him a story. That child can't get enough of stories and he throws a temper fit when he doesn't get them."

Abruptly she thrust out her left arm and rolled up the sleeve. Carisa saw a slender arm, marred by a set of half-moon scars.

"Look," Poll said. "See those? That's where he bit me, when I first came here. Such a pretty boy he was, so bonny and fair. . . ."

But Carisa had heard only the first words. "He bit you!"

"Oh, yes, he was only two then, but that didn't stop him. The wound swelled up and I thought it was going to fester, but it didn't. Cook put a carrot paste on it and it got better."

"Well . . ." An uneasy feeling was flowing over Carisa —a light raising of the hairs on her neck and back. "Well, he certainly doesn't do such things now, does he?"

"No. He doesn't bite me now." Poll's face was expressionless, although her eyes gleamed.

Carisa nodded and dismissed her, and was relieved when the girl glided out of the office, her long skirts rustling. What *was* it about her? Why did Poll fill her

116

with such unease? And yes, she thought, the malevolence was still there in Poll's eyes, lurking behind that expressionless, polite mask. For whatever reason, whatever cause, Poll still hated her.

Carisa sighed, and looked down at the letter Poll had brought her. Instantly her heart jumped. It was written in the careful, labored handwriting of her sister, Anna.

With trembling hands, Carisa ripped it open.

My dearist sister. I would like to thank you for your generus offer to have us join you and I would but Papa —Here something was crossed out in a huge, spraying black blot. Anna had had little time, as a circus child, to practice her penmanship.

But Papa sed we could not impose on you this way so now he is better and I have found a job with the Wixom show it is a very small family show but we are used to that. And Papa is hired too he—

There was more, but Carisa did not read it. She let the letter fall to the desk, where it mingled with the clutter of other papers there. A strange, twisting ache had taken possession of her heart. Papa was not coming to join the Phillips Circus. Neither was Anna.

Was this your fault? Papa had said.

Carisa put her head down on the cluttered desk and let the sobs come.

At last the ugly, silent, wracking tears were over. Carisa sat up and fumbled in the desk drawer for the lace-trimmed handkerchief she kept there. She blew her nose and patted her face dry and tried to put her hair into order.

No one—especially Adam—must know that she had cried. If Adam knew how much her father had hurt her, he would refuse to help Papa. And that was what must be done, of course. She must send Anna some money and tell her to use it as she thought best. Even though Papa and Anna had jobs now, still, things could happen. Family shows were precarious at best, and there might be some illness, some accident or disaster—

Wiping away the last traces of her tears, Carisa jumped out of her chair, wincing as a muscle spasm reminded her of her injured legs, which still often troubled her, although the swelling was much diminished now.

She would go downstairs and find Adam and see to this at once, she decided.

In the hallway she stood drawing a deep breath. Laughter and giggles drifted to her from the far end of the corridor, where a padded window seat had been built in. Here sat Poll and Julian, both of them turned in order to stare out of the window.

Idly Carisa wondered what they were looking at. A gull? A squirrel on the lawn?

Suddenly Julian laughed. It was a high, avid, childish laugh, but it had a quality that made Carisa shiver. No child should laugh like that, she thought involuntarily.

Instead of continuing downstairs, something made Carisa hesitate. Again Julian laughed.

"Look! Look at that!" Poll had unconsciously raised her voice. "There she goes. Ugly little Nelly. She doesn't know that *we* see her, does she, Julian? I think we'll make her give us a half-dollar for this . . . ah . . . look where she's going, to the greenhouse. It must be Jed, the gardener. Ha! She's a fool if she thinks that *he*. . . ."

Poll's voice went lower and became inaudible. Carisa stood where she was, frozen and dismayed. That Nelly was meeting Jed was disturbing; Carisa liked Nelly and did not wish her heartbreak. But that Poll should blackmail Nelly! And, worse, that she should discuss this with Julian—

She was just about to speak and make her presence known when Poll's voice began again, low and gloating. "Well, Julian, at least we gave silly old Nelly a start yesterday, didn't we, telling her about the woman in the chair?"

"Which chair?" Julian's voice piped up.

"You know which one, little ninny! That one in the parlor. I've told you about it, haven't I? *She* sat there once, rocking and rocking, and thinking about killing her baby. Now she's dead, but her spirit still sits there."

"Sits!" she heard Julian chortle. "Why does she sit there, Poll?"

"Why, because she's dead, silly. And because she's a murderess. She killed her baby. Haven't you ever gone down to the parlor at night and seen that chair rocking back and forth all by itself? Well, I have. And I've smelled the smell, too."

"Smell?"

"Oh, yes, the smell of evil. It reeks so strong and thick, Julian, that it seems to fill up the whole room. And no one knows any place it could come from except . . . her."

"What's it smell of?"

"Oh, the grave, of course. Dead things. And blood and rot and corruption."

Carisa had heard enough—too much. She picked up her skirts and angrily marched down the hall toward the window seat. The two turned and saw her. Julian cowered against his governess' skirt, while Poll looked defiant.

"Julian, please go to your room," Carisa said. "As for you, Poll, would you please come into my office? I want to talk with you."

"Everyone knows there's ghosts here at Hearts-ease," Poll insisted sullenly. "A hanging ghost, that ship, that chair in the parlor, everyone in the house knows. Everyone."

"Perhaps. But to tell such wild tales to an impressionable small boy. . . ."

"If I didn't, then someone else would have."

The girl's eyes were narrowed and glittering, and again Carisa had the feeling of unease, as if a cold hand had touched her.

"Perhaps. But I don't want you telling him. And I don't want the boy made a party to your blackmailing of Nelly!"

"You heard that, too?" Now the other girl had dropped all pretense of being a servant. Her face twisted insolently as she gave a quick little shrug. "Well, who cares? What does it matter what *you* think? We all know what girls from the circus are like."

Carisa felt color pouring into her face. "I'm going to

119

tell my husband about you," she said as evenly as she could.

"Are you?"

"Yes, I am. And I. . . ."

But Carisa could not finish her sentence, for Poll had flounced out of the office in a swirl of skirts, slamming the door behind her.

That night, after their dinner taken in the small, elegant dining room which was virtually a display cabinet for the fine English silver and porcelain which the Hartshorns had picked up on their travels, Carisa followed Adam to his study.

He offered her a chair and then leaned back in his own chair, gazing at the blue smoke which curled delicately upward from his Havana cigar.

"Why, Carisa?" he asked her. "Why should we dismiss Poll?"

"She just . . . isn't suitable."

"And why not?"

Carisa's hands tensed on the arm of the wing chair as she remembered Poll's defiance, the odd *frisson* of alarm which had shivered through her, not once but several times.

Quickly she told Adam of the scene in the window seat, the blackmailing of Nelly, and of her own confrontation with Poll afterward. "She was rude to me, Adam! It's bad enough that she encouraged a child to connive in blackmail. But to fill that little boy's head with stories of wicked women who rock in chairs and murder their babies. . . ."

Adam stubbed out his cigar in a heavy, fluted silver ashtray. He was frowning. "I'm afraid, Carisa, that Eugenia Hartshorn was quite real."

"Real!"

"Not that we are proud of her, of course. But she certainly did exist. She was the first wife of Adam Hartshorn's son, Samuel, and was thirty years old when she married him. One night she was raped by a drunken seaman. She had been very strictly brought up, in a convent, and she loathed the thought of giving birth

120

to a 'devil's whelp,' as she called it. All during the pregnancy she sat in that chair and rocked.

"Eugenia's time came early, and it happened that she was alone in the house at the time. Everyone was at a christening, and even the servants had been dismissed. She gave birth to the child all by herself, in the parlor, of all places. Then, still weak, she crawled over to the desk . . . that one . . . and she pulled out a letter opener. First she used it to cut the cord. Then she stabbed the baby. She finished by stabbing herself four times in the belly, God knows how she managed it."

"Oh . . ." Nausea twisted in Carisa's belly.

"When Samuel came home from the christening, he found them like that. The parlor rug, I understand, had to be burned. The blood stains never could be removed."

"Adam . . . Why, that's a terrible story!"

"Perhaps. But you'll notice that Poll gave Julian a very mild version of it. And she's right . . . he *was* bound to hear it sometime."

"But to tell a young child such things at all . . . Adam, don't you care about your son?"

Adam stiffened. "Of course I do."

"Then I think you had better get rid of Poll. She's a bad influence on the boy, Adam, I feel it, I *know* it. . . ."

Adam rose. He strode toward the door which opened onto the garden, his back to her. Carisa knew by the rigid set of his shoulders just how angry he was.

"I want you to understand something, Carisa. I am a Hartshorn, and like it or not, I've assumed all of the burdens which go with that name. And one of them is the family of Poll Henry. Her father, Lebanon, died in *my ship.*"

Carisa's head had begun to throb with the start of a headache. She spread her hands helplessly. "But . . . Adam . . . Can't you just pay Poll's family some money and tell them you don't need her services any more?"

Adam turned. His eyes held an oddly tormented expression. "We don't do things that way here in New London, Carisa. People here are proud. They do not

121

accept charity. If Poll were not allowed to work for her money, then her mother wouldn't accept it."

"But . . ."

"The subject is finished." Adam sank into his desk-chair and pulled a stack of papers toward him. "And I suggest that you leave my study now. I have some work to do. Why don't you go upstairs to your new office? You can sit there and plan the circus you black-mailed me into buying for you."

"Adam!"

"Well? And isn't that how you managed to acquire it? Through a very pretty form of bargaining and witch-ery? So please don't tell me that our Poll Henry is blackmailing another servant for a half-dollar. You, Carisa, have done much the same thing. Only you set your sights a little higher, that's all."

She had never seen him so angry.

9

Why? Carisa kept wondering. Why was Adam so very angry with her? And why did that fury somehow have to do with Poll Henry?

During the next three days it rained, and Carisa, caught up in a mood as gray and ugly as the water which spattered the roof of Hearts-ease, pondered these thoughts and could come to no conclusion.

Water—it seemed to be everywhere, gray, cold, in-terminable. It flooded the lawn and turned the dirt roads into quagmires, effectively trapping them here in the house. And she could not even walk down to the circus quarters, for the path was full of sucking soft mud. Even their trip to New York had to be postponed.

Never had Carisa felt more restless, more thwarted. After her quarrel with Adam, she shut herself in her office and worked there until she was trembling with weariness. Later she read stories to Julian and helped him to build a fort for his lead soldiers. She paced about the house, wincing on her still-sore legs and gazing out of each window in turn, staring at the rain. Rain—which could bring ugly and uncomfortable thoughts. . . .

To complicate matters, Samuel's wife, Eliza, had come to stay with them for a few days while Samuel was in New Haven on business.

Now it was the afternoon of a moist day. Rain drummed interminably on the roof. Carisa, resting on her bed for the afternoon on Katherine's orders, sighed and pulled at the lace-trimmed, low shoulders of the "Nonpareil garment," in which she had been napping. This was a one-piece creation combining camisole and underdrawers, made for her by the enterprising Mrs. Wiggins, who had seen it in *Godey's*.

"Should be more cozy for you, honey, now that you're in a delicate way," the seamstress had remarked as she measured her for it.

Thinking of her pregnancy, Carisa sighed. She was in her third month now. According to Katherine, she was lucky. Her nausea was easily placated by a few nibbled bits of rusk and dry bread. But her figure, of which she had been so proud, was already beginning to change. Her breasts were fuller, her nipples larger and darker. Her waist was as slim as ever—if Nelly laced it tightly—but Carisa knew that would not last long. Within a few months she would be large and cumbersome. Then Adam would insist she stay in seclusion, as "ladies" did.

That, of course, meant that she had only a few more months to travel, to see that the Phillips Circus was properly launched.

Which meant that the rain had to stop so that she and Adam could go to New York.

Again Carisa sighed and stirred restlessly on the bed. She closed her eyes, letting her thoughts, as gloomy as the rain, seep over her.

The circus, she had to admit, was not her only problem. All was not well between Adam and herself.

True, their quarrel over Poll had seemed to be over, settled within hours by lovemaking. They had apolo-

123

gized, they had held each other and caressed, and at last had fallen on this very bed to sate their bodies with each other.

And yet—

"Damn you, and damn your witchery," Adam had muttered as he had buried his face in her breast. "And damn the bargain we made, Carisa. It's like a poison, it's going to burn its way into everything we have. . . ."

"Adam?" she had questioned.

But then he was kissing her again, and there was no time for questions, or for anything other than savoring the contact of his body with hers.

But now, lying on the bed they had shared, Carisa wondered miserably if Adam wished that he had taken Katherine's advice and put her in a boarding house to recover. Did he wish—oh, awful thought—that he had taken her for his mistress rather than for his wife?

Nelly's knock on the door scattered her thoughts, and with relief Carisa called for the servant to enter.

Nelly hurried in, looking cheerful. "Do you want to dress now, Miss Carisa? The other ladies, they're up now, and Miss Eliza has called for hot bath water. Rain!" she added. "Have you ever seen anything like it? Do you think it'll ever stop?"

"I hope it will," Carisa said. "I'm afraid I'll go quite mad if it doesn't, thinking of all the things I should be doing, and can't."

"Me, too," said Nelly.

Carisa could not help smiling. Nelly's romance with Jed had foundered. To Carisa's relief, the big, ungainly gardener had found a scullery girl on whom to lavish his attentions. But Nelly seemed undaunted. As she explained to Carisa, "I didn't care that much for ugly old Jed anyway. I just wanted to know I could have a man after me if I wanted one. And I found out that I could."

Now Nelly moved toward the large wardrobe where Carisa's gowns were hung, carefully stuffed with tissue paper to keep them from creasing. Helping Carisa to dress was one of Nelly's main duties. The boned corsets required help in lacing, and the heavy dresses, with their yards of fabric and back buttons and loops, were difficult to put on unaided.

And Carisa secretly enjoyed such attentions. Never had there been anyone—other than her sisters—to help her dress. And never had there been such an array of sumptuous clothing to put on. She supposed that she liked new gowns *too* well, she often told herself luxuriously. She was sure that Papa would consider her love of finery a vice.

But, she consoled herself, if it was a vice, at least it was a pleasant one, and did harm to no one else.

"A pretty one, this is," Nelly said, taking a pale green day-gown out of the wardrobe and pulling away its protective tissue.

"Oh, yes," Carisa agreed.

"It goes well with your eyes, that it does. *You'll* look nice today, even if it is raining."

Nelly took out a clean corset and laced Carisa into it. Next came a frilly corset cover and the crinolines, wired and stiff. But she had barely settled the green gown over Carisa's shoulders when they heard a loud, blood-freezing shriek.

Nelly jumped, and Carisa's heart gave a great leap as she caught at the gown and pressed it loosely to her breast.

The scream came again, high, angry and hysterical. This time it was mingled with unintelligible words. It came, Carisa was sure, from the bedroom which Eliza had been given.

The two girls looked at each other. Then they both turned and ran toward the door, Nelly, whose legs were strong from running up and down stairs, in the lead. Behind her stumbled Carisa, nearly tripping on the sagging flounces of the unfastened gown.

Nelly reached the door of Eliza's bedroom first and jerked it open. Carisa, still trying to manage the trailing gown, was right behind her, and could not suppress her shocked gasp.

They were greeted by an extraordinary sight. Eliza Hartshorn stood in the center of the room, clutching the tie-dyed bedcover to her flat, bony breast. Beneath

125

that fabric she was obviously nude, for her bare legs, thin and unappealing, protruded from beneath the jumbled folds of the spread.

On the floor, his head thrust from beneath the lower flounces of the bed, was Julian.

"Look!" Eliza pointed a bony finger downward at the boy. "That child is a monster! A filthy little animal full of mischief and deviltry!"

Carisa, bewildered, took a step forward, forgetting about her own unfastened gown. The scene was so wild that she could not seem to take in its meaning. Why was Julian under Eliza's bed? Why was Eliza wrapped in a bedspread? And why was she so livid with anger?

"I don't understand . . ." she began.

Eliza's mouth fluttered open like a fish's. "Oh, don't you? *Look,* you foolish girl. Look with your eyes, will you? Do you know what that evil creature did?"

"No, I . . ."

Eliza bent over, grasped Julian by the scruff of his neck, and dragged him out from under the bed as if he had been a dog.

"He spied on me, that's what he did! He spied. . . ."

"What's all this screaming? What did Julian do?" It was Katherine, up from her own nap and fully clad in a black bombazine daydress. A "chatelaine," complete with scissors, keys, thimble and other necessaries, swung from her waist by a chain.

"I'll tell you what he did!" Eliza screamed. "Oh, I'll tell you, all right!" She gave Julian a shove in the direction of his grandmother.

Julian bent his head, darted past Katherine, and was gone. They could hear his running footsteps, clattering on the stairs.

Katherine advanced toward her other daughter-in-law. "And to what do we owe this excitement, Eliza?"

Eliza, faced with the iron in Katherine's gaze, took a step backward. "I told you, he spied on me! I was just washing myself, washing my . . . my most private parts, when he . . . when I saw a movement and heard a noise under the bed. I lifted up the flounce and there he was, the little beast! *Looking at me!*"

"Well, now, Eliza, he is only a boy. Boys do get into mischief sometimes, and I'm sure that no harm was done. I'll talk to Adam and see that he is properly punished."

Eliza stiffened. The folds of the bedspread flapped dangerously, revealing a sallow, flat breast.

"Oh, he's small enough in size, I'll grant you that. But he's no innocent child. Oh, no, he's far from that. He was *spying on an unclothed woman.*"

"Eliza, you are overwrought. I would suggest that you lock your door and finish your toilette. You will feel much better when you. . . ."

Eliza's face went beet-red. "You don't understand! He is a monster, I tell you! Do you know what he was doing when I found him? Do you?"

Katherine paled. "No."

"He was . . . oh, I don't even know how to say it . . . he was abusing himself! I know he was! *Abusing* himself while he watched me naked!"

Carisa and Nelly stole a horrified glance at each other.

Katherine's lips pressed themselves into a thin line. "You don't know what you're talking about, Eliza. How could you have known what that child was doing? He was well concealed by the bed-flounces! The only part of him visible was his head!"

"I tell you that I do know." Eliza's face had turned even darker. "He is a monster, and always has been, ever since he was an infant. I knew it then, and I know it now. He . . ."

"Be so kind, Eliza, as to keep still and finish getting dressed." Katherine's voice was a whip-crack. She turned sharply to Carisa and Nelly. "Well? What are you two foolish girls doing here, staring and giggling? Carisa, I suggest that you get back to your room and get yourself buttoned into that gown. You are in a shameful state of dishabille. As for you, Nelly, if you have nothing better to do than to hang about other people's bedchambers, then I'll find some work for you. There is plenty of ironing to do. . . ."

Carisa and Nelly found themselves standing in the

hallway, looking at the closed door of the oak bedroom, from behind which came Katherine's voice as she began the considerable job of trying to soothe Eliza.

"I wonder where Julian went," Carisa said.

"Oh, he's hiding, I've no doubt. That boy is good at creeping off when he's done something wrong."

"And Poll?" Carisa asked. "Where was she when all of this was going on?"

Nelly looked uncomfortable. "It's her day off. Sometimes . . . sometimes Poll goes out of the house. They say she has a man in the town. Or men. . . ."

A shiver semed to skitter across the back of Carisa's shoulders. *Poll again,* she thought. She was sure that in some ugly, hidden way, the servant was at the root of this.

"Julian?"

Carisa bent over the boy's bed. It was past seven o'clock, and the rain had lightened to a fine, misty spray. Julian had been missing most of the day, and a frantic search had finally disclosed him, wet and muddy to the waist, hiding in one of the circus barns. To amuse himself during his exile, he had found one of the little books of gold leaf, and had carefully ripped it to shreds.

The Italian workmen had been furious with him for ruining the expensive leaf. Adam was angry because Julian had run away from his punishment. And Katherine was angry because, in addition to the above, he had also put himself in danger of catching pneumonia. The boy had been spanked by Adam and sent to bed without supper.

"Julian?" Carisa repeated now. "I came to say goodnight."

He wriggled, poked his head out from beneath the covers, and gave her a stony stare.

"Julian, I know you weren't given supper, and it was right that you be punished. But I thought you should at least have a glass of milk."

"All right."

He squirmed to a sitting position, reached for the

128

tray she had brought, and greedily began to stuff himself with cold biscuits and milk.

Carisa watched him as he ate. What a beautiful boy he was, she found herself thinking for the hundredth time. His features had a natural symmetry, and his eyes were large and almost disconcertingly blue. If only his mouth was not quite so full and stubborn!

And these days she rarely heard Julian laugh with the carefree joy of childhood. He was a very private boy, she had decided. And as far as she could see, he loved only two people, Adam and his nursemaid-governess, Poll.

"Julian," she began, as he munched on a chunk of biscuit. "Why did you do such a wicked thing? To steal into your aunt's bedroom and hide yourself there. . . ."

The boy lifted his eyes to stare at her. His eyes were large and blue and quite unchildlike.

"I wanted to."

"But, Julian, why? To upset your poor Aunt Eliza. . . ."

"I liked it. She screamed funny, didn't she?"

"Julian!"

"Well, she did. And she looked funny without anything on. Not like. . . ." Abruptly the full-lipped little mouth closed. Julian chewed hard on a mouthful of biscuit.

The words of scolding died on Carisa's lips. The boy was still a child, she told herself firmly. A boy who had been without a mother, as she herself had been.

"Eat your fill, son," she told him gently. "And then you must go to sleep."

That night, as they were preparing for bed, Adam brushed off her suggestion that Julian was, perhaps, too adult for his age.

"Nonsense," he told her. "All boys get into scrapes. When I was eleven, I can remember climbing a tree and spying on the maidservants as they were having their monthly bath. As I recall, I got whipped for it."

Carisa settled her nightgown about her and began to

fasten the small, pearl buttons at its lacy yoke. "I suppose . . . still, Adam, the way he spoke of it afterward. . . ."

"He is a boy," Adam said impatiently. "And a bit spoiled, if the truth were known. Perhaps I should start sending him to the school in town, instead of having a governess as we've been doing. It's time. And the company of schoolboys his own age should help."

"And Poll?" Carisa dared to say.

Adam's look was suddenly cold. "Perhaps Julian has outgrown the need for a nursemaid . . . I'll admit that . . . but she'll still be in my employ."

Carisa swallowed. "Nelly told me that Poll has been . . . leaving the house to go to town. She has a man there, or men, Nelly said."

"It's difficult to control what a servant does with her time off. I don't want to hear any more about it, Carisa. Anyway, what had Poll to do with Julian's behavior today? She certainly didn't tell him to spy on his aunt."

For Adam the subject was obviously closed. He stirred the embers in the fireplace grate, extinguished the gas, and climbed into bed. Darkness settled in the room like a heavy cloak.

"Well? Come to bed, Carisa. Don't just stand there in the dark, dreaming. My darling, I can think of better things to do than that."

And so he could. For an hour or so, Carisa forgot Poll Henry, and the problem of Julian, and the rain. Adam held her and whispered muffled, intimate things to her, and then joined his body with hers. And there was room for nothing else in Carisa's mind.

There was only Adam, and herself, and the current which ran between them, as strong as a river.

Two days later she was completing her preparations for her trip to New York. She planned to travel by steamer, a mode of transportation which was becoming increasingly fashionable. The original plan had been for Adam to come with her. But a crisis had come up in the management of the New London, Willimantic and Palmer Railroad Company, of which Adam was a trustee, and he did not feel that he could leave.

"Let your trip wait," he told her. "I should be free to travel in a few weeks, perhaps a bit longer."

His hands brushed her arms, caressed them. In spite of herself, Carisa felt a swift rush of pleasure. Adam's touch could always do that to her: make her feel as lazily feminine as a she-cat stretching. She pushed aside a thought of herself and Adam, locked in each other's arms in a hotel room bed. Adam was a satisfying lover, all that she had ever dreamed of in a man, and more. . . .

"Adam!" she heard herself cry out. "This trip can't wait a few weeks. I must go now, it's already getting very late. No one has ever heard of the Phillips Circus and it's going to be hard to get good acts."

"No," he said. "A woman traveling alone. . . ."

"Please?" She flung her arms around his neck. "I'll be perfectly safe, I promise you! I'll take Nelly with me as my chaperone, if that will make you any happier."

Adam scowled. "Nelly, a chaperone? Don't be ridiculous, Carisa. Besides, you're expecting a child."

Carisa reddened, releasing her arms from around his neck. "I'm *not* being ridiculous! You forget, Adam, that I've been traveling with the circus for most of my life. I know how to take care of myself. As for my pregnancy, my mother performed in the ring when she was six months along . . . Duddie told me. I'll be all right, I tell you!"

There was a long silence, while Adam stared out of the window at a solitary gull, wheeling and mewing in the sky.

"Very well," he said at last. "I made you a promise and I'll keep it, even if I didn't bargain for your traveling alone like this. But you'll take Gaines with you, too. And you'll stay at Mrs. Adair's. It's a very respectable hotel with special accommodations for women traveling alone, and my mother uses the place frequently when she goes to New York.

"Nelly *and* Gaines?" Carisa burst out. "Do you mean that I'll have to take them both? Why, Adam, I'll have

131

to spend all of my time shepherding them about instead of tending to my business!"

Adam's mouth hardened. "You'll travel as I suggest, Carisa, or you won't travel at all. Like it or not, you are my wife now, and I happen to want to keep my wife safe."

"I *will* be safe! Adam, you're being entirely. . . ."

"Enough, Carisa. Count yourself lucky that you're going at all."

Carisa did. She suppressed her annoyance at being forced to travel with a retinue of two, and she did her best to listen to Katherine's advice on traveling alone. She started her packing with a wild sense of elation. After all these months spent cooped up here at Heartsease, at last she was going somewhere!

As for Adam's objections to her traveling, she told herself firmly, she would prove to him just how safe it all was. Because in order to run the Phillips Circus properly, she *was* going to have to do some traveling. And Adam would have to get used to that fact.

Now it was past eleven on a Monday night, and Carisa was completing the last hurried details of her packing, for she planned to leave early the next morning. Katherine had insisted that she wear a black *moiré* traveling dress on the steamer, as it would not show dust or cinders.

But she was also packing a handsome gown of gold *poult de soie* and a mantle of green mantua silk, trimmed lavishly with silk fringe and ruches of satin ribbon. This last was much more to Carisa's taste— she hated plain black—and she brushed off Adam's suggestion that she was being too extravagant.

"If I want to hire the top performers for my show," she told him airily, "I'm going to have to impress them. Otherwise, they won't have any faith in my ability to pay their salaries."

Now the master bedroom was a scene of disarray. Clothes, trunks and portmanteaus were scattered about, along with stacks of underwear and petticoats. Nelly had gone downstairs to press the full, puffed flounces of the gold gown, a task which might take her several painstaking hours. Adam was out of the house, attending a late meeting of the troubled railroad board.

Carisa searched unsuccessfully among the scattered garments for her gold bead bag. She was fond of it, it was the first such ornate bag she had ever owned, and she wanted to take it to wear with her gold dress.

Sighing in annoyance, she decided to go downstairs to ask Nelly if she had seen it. She was halfway down the upstairs hall when she heard an odd laugh coming from behind the closed door of Julian's room.

It was low, sensual and throaty.

Carisa paused, her hands pressed against her skirts. Then she heard it again.

Poll Henry! The laugh belonged to the servant. Carisa's heart gave a little skipping beat. It was late; Julian should have been asleep for hours. As for Poll, she slept in the servants' area over the new wing. She should not be in the boy's room now.

The laugh pealed a third time, wanton, eerie. It drew Carisa swiftly toward Julian's closed door, and she stood leaning against the heavy wood, aware that eavesdropping was shameful, but unable to stop herself.

Pressing her ear to the wood, Carisa heard a soft, muffled sound coming from Julian. A cry? A laugh? She didn't know what it was. But she could stand it no more. She grasped the brass door knob and thrust the door open.

For a moment she stood frozen, staring into the room without comprehending what she saw. The fire in Julian's grate had started to smoulder fitfully. Two candles had been left to burn in their holders on the dresser.

But beneath the odor of melted wax, Carisa thought she could smell something else. A muskiness. An odor fecund and pungent and sexual.

She drew in her breath quickly and turned her eyes to the narrow little bed. The candles, sputtering, had cast huge, jagged shadows to leap and dance up the walls. Nevertheless, there was still enough illumination

133

for Carisa to see that Poll and Julian were lying on Julian's little spool bed, wrapped in each other's arms.

They were quite naked.

Carisa did not know how long she had stood there, unable to move or to speak. But, although it seemed a lifetime, it could not have been more than a few seconds, for Poll's eyes—like dark puddles—had begun to widen.

In a swift, animal-like gesture, the girl grasped the sheets and yanked them up to cover her own body and Julian's. In some inconsequential corner of her mind, Carisa noted that there was a little heap of white on the floor where Julian's nightclothes lay, and a larger white circle which was Poll's plain cotton nightdress.

"Poll!" Carisa's voice emerged hoarsely.

Their eyes stared at her. She felt as if she had surprised some foxes in their den. Poll was the vixen, Julian the cub; she could almost smell the acrid, animal scent of fear coming from them now.

"Poll," she repeated. "Please get dressed and come to my office at once."

Poll drew a deep breath, and all at once the foxy look left her eyes. They seemed to widen and grow more luminous.

"No."

"What? Did you say no?" Carisa drew herself up. She was trembling with her shock and outrage. "You'll get out of that boy's bed, and you'll get out now. First you will come to my office and you will explain all of this to me, and then you'll pack your things and you'll leave. Quietly, and at once. I don't want to find you here in the morning."

Carisa knew that it was midnight, that Poll would have nowhere to go for the night. Yet, savagely, she didn't care. She didn't care whether Poll had to go and lie in the stables, or in the roadbed. She didn't care whether a carriage ran over her.

A grown woman, debauching a child in this way . . . for surely there could be no other explanation. The thought filled her with sick horror. Surely Julian—

how——? Wildly she veered away from a thought she could not face.

Julian was still staring at her, his face white. Carisa had the strong feeling that this was not the first time such an incident had happened to him. Poll, she remembered, had been the boy's nursemaid since he was two years old.

Two years old. *Dear God,* she thought, licking her dry lips.

"Get out," she heard herself whisper savagely. "Poll, I want you up and out of this bed immediately. I'm going to tell my husband about you, and you'd just better pray that he doesn't kill you!"

With disbelief she heard her voice rave on, pouring out all her shock and fury. And all the while she was plucking the naked Julian out of the bed and settling his nightshirt about his shoulders. The boy's skin was cold, and he trembled against her. His fingers were in his ears, as if to stop himself from hearing the torrent of Carisa's accusations.

But Poll remained in the bed, her eyes glittering at Carisa.

"Oh, who are you to talk to me? You, a little circus slut! Oh, yes, they're all saying it, below-stairs, all of them! I've heard them, I know. You're nothing but a cheap little tent floozy, I knew it the minute I saw you!"

"I am Mrs. Adam Hartshorn, and whether you like it or not, I am mistress of this house. And now I ask you to get out of this bed and dress yourself and leave. If you don't, I . . . I'll get my husband's pistol and drive you out!"

"Would you, now?"

Poll's mouth twisted. Slowly, deliberately, she threw back the sheets, revealing the full length of her nude body, the small, hard breasts, the bumps and hollows of her rib cage, the flat, narrow belly, the surprisingly large triangle of pubic hair.

She was like a lithe, bony cat, Carisa thought, feeling sick. It was a good thing she did not have Adam's pistol in her hand just now, for surely she would use it.

135

Poll slid out of bed.

"No," she said. "You won't shoot me." With a quick movement which revealed long, curved lines of hip and thigh and leg, she reached down and picked up her nightgown. When she stood up, her eyes seemed to suck at Carisa's. Julian, huddled now by the door, could have been invisible.

"No, Mrs. Hartshorn, you won't shoot me, and neither will your fine husband. You see, he and I have been lovers. Oh, yes! Not just once, but many, many times. When his wife died I came here and he liked me . . . oh, yes!"

The shock hit Carisa with physical impact, as if Poll had actually shoved her in the belly.

"No . . ." she whispered. "It's not true . . . you're lying!"

"Am I? Go and ask him, you little circus whore. As for me, I'll leave this house, all right. Why would I want to stay here and work for the likes of you, with your airs and your graces and your 'Adam darling' this and 'Adam dear' that?"

Poll gave a cracked, grotesque imitation of Carisa's tone. "Oh, I satisfied him, I did. More than you ever could. I made him moan and writhe with pleasure. . . ."

"Get out!"

"I'll leave. I'll go." Poll had flung the nightgown over herself. "But not before I say something. I hope God curses you, Carisa Hartshorn!"

With each word, Poll's voice grew lower, more malevolent. "I hope God takes away your husband and your circus and every other goddamned thing that you love, and I hope that someday you'll die lonely. Lonely, do you hear me? Lonely and old and *forsaken!*"

It was the meaningless curse of a fired servant, of course—in the rational part of her mind Carisa knew this. She also knew that she was being foolish to listen to such ravings. But at this moment the rational part of her mind was not in control.

From somewhere she found the strength to speak.

"I'm leaving this room, Poll, and I'm taking Julian

136

with me. When I come back in half an hour I expect to find you gone."

As she pulled the boy out of the room, she heard a low, hoarse laugh coming from Poll. Carisa shuddered, and shut the door behind her.

Ten minutes later she had settled Julian on the small settee in her office. She felt numbed and empty, as if it were some other woman who put Julian to bed, covered him with a blanket.

For once, to her relief, Julian was amenable to her attentions. He said little, but meekly accepted the blanket and the hot chocolate she brought him. When he had finished it, there was a brown mustache on his upper lip.

"Oh, Julian!" Carisa whispered, somehow touched at this homely evidence of childishness. Surely Julian had not asked for this to happen to him. Because of his beautifully appealing face, he had been used. That was all it had been.

"Julian," she whispered, hugging him. "Julian, it's going to be all right. Truly it is, I promise you."

But he pulled away from her.

"Just . . . just go to sleep, son. You'll be all right here. You . . . didn't know you were doing anything wrong."

Or did he? some mad little voice in her mind whispered.

She tucked the blanket up around Julian's chin, saw that his eyes were drooping shut, and quietly left the room.

In the corridor she leaned against the wall, feeling drained of all strength. The door of Julian's bedroom was standing open, and she knew that Poll had left it, was probably in the servants' quarters now, packing. In a few minutes, she would be gone.

"You see, he and I have been lovers. . . ."

The small oil portrait of the first Adam Hartshorn stared down at her, his yellow eyes fixed and grim.

137

10

Somehow Carisa managed the explanations, the things which must be done to cover Poll Henry's departure from Hearts-ease. The girl had stolen, she told Katherine, staring the older woman in the eye and daring her to contradict this story.

"Oh? What did she steal?" Katherine began testily.

"A brooch and a pin which Adam gave me when we were married," Carisa replied. "I insisted that she leave, and she has already done so."

"Without even waiting to consult with your husband?" But Katherine's protests were only token, and as she turned aside, she gave Carisa a long, knowing look. *Did her mother-in-law know about Poll and Adam?* The thought crept into Carisa and lingered there, like a bad smell.

By 12:30 Adam was home, climbing upstairs to their bedroom with vigorous steps, even though she knew he must be weary. Carisa waited for him, wearing a green silk dressing gown which showed off the proud lines of her body.

Adam's tawny hair was tousled, his eyes reddened with fatigue. He had been to an emergency meeting of the railroad board, which had been in financial trouble for some time. The line, built by the whaling merchants of New London in order to bring in more business, had been having trouble meeting payments on the short-term note to which it had had to resort. Adam had been attempting to lift the group out of disaster.

"The railroad is in trouble and they all know it," he sighed now, tossing aside his coat and loosening his wilted collar. "And I'm afraid only ruthlessness will get us out of it now. Now we must be wolves, and begin to gnaw the flanks of our rivals. . . ."

He removed his tie, and tossed it onto a chair. Then,

as if for the first time, he seemed to notice Carisa's frozen silence.

"Why aren't you in bed? I thought you had to get up early in the morning and go to New York." He glanced at the packed trunks which Carisa had dragged to one corner of the room.

She said nothing. *Poll and Adam,* she was thinking. *Poll's arms, flung about my husband. . . .*

"Carisa? You're so very pale and silent. Is anything wrong?" Adam stripped off his shirt and undershirt, revealing the broad, muscular chest with its curly mat of golden hair which Carisa loved to touch.

"Yes. There is something wrong," she said reluctantly.

"Then what? Tell me." He crossed the room to her, clad only in his trousers.

"It . . . It's Poll Henry."

"Poll?" She could actually see the tensing of Adam's chest muscles. He took a quick step toward her and gripped her shoulders. "What about Polly? What is it, Carisa?"

She jerked back from her husband as if he had touched a lighted match to her flesh.

"So you call her Polly? Is that the name you whispered to her, Adam, as you slept with her? Did you call her Polly in your most *intimate* moments?"

Adam released her with a rough little push. He turned and began to hang up his coat in the closet wardrobe, his back to her. "That was a long time ago. Before you and I even met."

A pang pressed at her chest, tight, hurtful.

"Oh?"

"Of course it was."

"*Was* it, Adam? Poll said. . . ."

"Dammit, I don't care what the girl said. Yes, I did sleep with her after Mary Elizabeth died. I was lonely, Carisa, lonely and dead inside. I'd lost my wife, I was bereft. Poll had just come to the house. She was very young, Carisa, but she had a way about her. . . . I didn't love her, I didn't even really like her. To this day I still can't explain just how it happened, but it did."

He slammed the door of the wardrobe shut. "Well, you needn't worry about her now, Carisa. It's over. It's been over since I first saw you."

"Oh," Carisa whispered. "So that's why she's always hated me. I saw such hatred in her eyes, such dislike. I took you away from her, didn't I?"

"Perhaps." Adam stripped off his trousers, moving unselfconsciously. Now he stood before her nude, his body filled with a tight-muscled, arrogant grace.

"Poll is a very strange girl," he went on after a moment. "I will grant you that, Carisa. She told me once that her mother has gypsy blood. Fey blood. Perhaps that's it."

Involuntarily Carisa shivered. "Adam, I am afraid that she was not a good choice for a nursemaid for your son."

"What do you mean?"

In two steps he had reached her, and she felt overwhelmed by the nearness of him, the clean, perspiring male scent. Suddenly her anger faded, and she had no heart for what she was about to say. Naked, Adam seemed so vulnerable. And what she had to say was going to hurt very much.

"Adam," she whispered. "I . . . I wish you would put on your dressing gown. Or at least your nightshirt."

"Why? You never objected to looking at my body before. In fact I rather thought you enjoyed it."

"I do. I have something to tell you, that's all."

"Then tell me." Instead of reaching for the dressing gown, he reached for her. She couldn't help it; her hands went out to touch him, to savor the silky texture of his skin.

She swallowed hard, forcing herself to go on. "I was packing. It was after . . . after eleven, I think. I was in the corridor on my way downstairs when I . . . I heard a noise coming from Julian's room."

"Yes?"

Carisa found that she had to swallow again, convulsively. "I . . . something made me push open the door and go in. I saw them. In bed, the two of them."

"In bed! What two? What are you talking about?"

He was shaking her, until her head ached and she wanted to sink to the floor with the burden of her anger and fear. Bile had risen at the back of her throat. It tasted hot and tinny.

"Poll and Julian," she managed to croak. "They were naked. *Poll was in bed with your son.* In bed . . . that way. And she has been his nursemaid for six years, Adam. Six years. God only knows what else she has done to him."

She saw the color recede from Adam's face, turning his skin a pasty white.

Dawn had tinted the sky a translucent pink. It would be a sunny day. Adam Hartshorn sat alone at the breakfast table, his bacon and eggs untouched, and thought about murder.

It was a week later. Carisa had at last left for New York, and reluctantly Adam had decided not to accompany her. She would be well chaperoned by Nelly and Gaines, and her hotel was respectable. Besides, he had things to do here, things which could not wait.

Poll. Even now, after seven days, he felt a swooping sickness in his belly whenever he thought of her, and of the unspeakable acts she had done with Julian. A child, a boy of nine—and that small, moist tongue, busily licking. Those slender hands, avid—

Adam swallowed. What did it matter if Julian was not yet a man, with a man's lust? The boy would have been a passive object. It would have been Poll who did all the work. . . .

Adam shoved his coffee cup away so violently that half the liquid spilled.

He had made Carisa swear to tell no one else in the house the truth about this, not even Katherine. The story of Poll stealing the brooch and ring would have to satisfy his mother. And he had at last decided to send Julian to the Grammar School in town, where he would be with other boys his own age.

Adam had made another decision, too. Poll Henry must be got rid of, gotten out of town, bribed if necessary. He had spent the last week looking for her, searching at the home of her mother, who was ill with a tumor, and at the homes of various others. None had seen her. Poll's young sister, a slatternly girl of fourteen, had even dared to snicker at him.

"She ain't here. And don't know when she will be, either."

He had stared at the girl who carried Poll's blood. Strange, he hadn't remembered the family as slatterns. In his mind they had been the honorable people of an honorable man who had gone down with the whaler *Betsy*. Yet now he saw that the girls were sluttish, the mother unkempt and bitter.

"I wish to speak with her," he went on, hiding his fury. "I have her severance pay to give her . . . four full months. Surely she'll show up for that?"

The girl had licked her lips. "She . . . she might."

"Here." Adam thrust a handful of bills at the girl. "Take these. All you have to do is send me a message if Poll comes by the house."

The girl had nodded, her fingers closing over the money. "She might. She hasn't picked up all her clothes yet. She's got business, she says."

"Well, she'll come back at the smell of money. And when she does, I want to know about it, do you hear me? Send me a message."

Now all he had to do was wait. Adam was not sure what he would do when he did find Poll—he would like to hit her, to smash her nose into red, bloody pulp. He supposed he would know what to do when he saw her.

"Adam? Good heavens, are you awake so early again? Why, it's just past dawn. I can't see why you have to get up before the birds are even properly awake."

It was Katherine, sweeping into the room in a rustle of skirts and the jingling of the chatelaine which dangled from her waist.

"I like getting up early," he replied shortly.

"Oh? I think your getting up early is only an excuse to eat breakfast alone and avoid the rest of us. Is that the case, Adam? If it is, I think you're quite shameless!"

She was smiling, and meant only to tease him. Ordinarily he would have grinned and said something pleasant. But today she irritated him. Everything did. He flung his napkin to the table and got up, his chair scraping.

"Perhaps I am shameless," he heard himself say.

Katherine's eyes widened. "You are sharp today, aren't you, Adam? But never mind, I've brought you a letter. Someone came 'round first thing this morning and delivered it. A pretty young hussy by the looks of her. Are you trafficking with street girls these days, Adam?"

"What letter?" He felt his heart jumping. "Give it to me, please."

"Certainly. My goodness, are you so eager to read the scribble of a little girl? And why on earth would she. . . ."

But Adam did not hear his mother's question. He was already gone.

Mrs. Lebanon Henry lived in a dilapidated section of town not far from the Brown Cotton Gin Works. Here the roads were muddy, and scrawny livestock wandered to and fro. Groups of men, glum-faced and sleepy, walked toward the mill or in the direction of the wharves, on their way to work. A pair of little boys were playing a game with stones in the mud.

Adam debarked from his carriage, told Jim to wait, and skirted a sizeable pile of horse droppings before approaching the Henry home. The house, of unpainted wood frame, needed new shingles and a coat of whitewash. Its front stoop had begun to sag noticeably to the left. Scraps of wood and rags and old metal littered the tiny front yard, and yesterday's wash still flapped dismally from a line strung at the side of the house.

Just as Adam started up the little path to the door, Poll came out of the house. She looked tired, her face sallow. Her worn calico dress was too tight for her, its fabric strained over her small, hard breasts. In her left hand she carried an old carpet bag.

143

"Poll!" Adam hurried up to her and caught the girl's arm before she could twist away from him.

"What do you want?"

"Where have you been this past week? I've looked high and low for you."

She cocked her head at him, her eyes so black that their pupils seemed almost invisible. "I've been around. Here and there. I slept in your greenhouse one night, if you really want to know. But why should you care? What business is it of yours?"

"Why should I care! After what you did to my son! Debauching him, turning him into your whores' plaything. . . ."

Poll made a face. She glanced across the narrow street to where a man lounged by a cart, spitting streams of tobacco juice into the mud.

"Remember," she said. "We're on the street." She moved closer to him, smiling a soft, curving, seductive smile which showed her teeth. Those teeth—Nausea pushed at Adam's throat and he thought he would be sick.

"Poll . . . I have to talk with you. . . ."

"Fine, Adam." She put down the carpet bag, her hips swaying beneath the calico dress. He could smell her body odor, female and slightly sour. "All right, then. Let's talk. Tell me, Adam, what is it that you would like to say to me? We never did spend much time *talking* before, did we?"

Was she laughing at him? By God, she was. Adam felt the rage well up in him, pounding at his veins. With enormous effort, he pushed it back down, the violent thoughts. Murder was something for the imagination, he told himself quickly. Not for the reality of this narrow little street near the cotton gin works, with children playing nearby and a curious cart driver watching them.

"I want you to leave this town," he heard himself say in a strange, distant voice. "You can't stay here in New London any more, for Julian's sake. You must go."

"Leave! And just where is it that you'd like me to go?"

He shook his head. "I don't know. Far away from

144

here, that's all. California. Michigan. Anywhere. Just so that we never have to see your face here in this town again. Ever. Do you understand?"

She took a step backward and regarded him, her hands on her hips.

"Oh, I was thinking of leaving, all right. My Ma's sick, and the house is too small. It stinks of that tumor of hers, too, it stinks of death. But I was thinking more of Groton Heights. I have a friend there, a good friend who might keep me for a while." She gazed at Adam calculatingly. "I can't afford to go any farther."

Adam stared at her. Then he thrust his hand into his pocket and pulled out his leather wallet.

"Here," he said. "Take this, then. To be blunt, it's a bribe, nearly five thousand dollars to keep away from here. See that you do. And give a bit of it to your mother to ease her . . . there's enough for that, too. I don't want her to suffer. I owe your father that much, at least."

Poll's slim hand extended and she took the money. Her fingers brushed his.

"That's very kind of you, sir," she said mockingly. "Your bribe and all, I mean. But I think my Ma can get along. She always has." Her eyes seemed to glisten at him, full of amusement. "As for me, I'll find very good use for this. Indeed I will."

"You'll leave town. You'll go, and we'll never hear of you again here in New London," he warned.

She bent and picked up the carpet bag. "Oh, you needn't worry," she said lightly. "I won't squander this."

Then she whirled on her heel and trotted across the mud of the street to where the driver of the cart lounged. She said something to him, jumped into the cart, and they drove off. Adam, staring after them, saw that the driver's hand was on Poll's knee.

Carisa stayed in New York for five days. Their boat trip, complicated by the winds and gales of March, was uncomfortable. Nelly was seasick and Carisa, too, felt queasy, haunted by thoughts of Julian and Poll Henry, of Adam and Poll. Only the tall, thin Gaines, at thirty

145

as dignified as a man of fifty, seemed unaffected by the choppy rocking of the boat.

But even Nelly dragged herself on deck to watch as they approached the island of Manhattan with its waterfront lined with wharves and bristling with the tall masts of ships.

"Look at that, Miss Carisa! Oh, just look!" Nelly kept exclaiming as they came close enough to see the ranged rows of four- and five-story buildings, some smaller ones even built on the piers themselves.

Carisa, too, felt excited. This was New York! Nearly a million people lived here, with more arriving every day. And out of those million there should be some performers for the Phillips Circus, she told herself firmly.

Her hand slid down to the waistline of her gown. Beneath it, next to her skin on a stout leather cord, hung a small bag containing more than four thousand dollars. Adam had been reluctant to give her this much, but Carisa had stubbornly insisted. Without money she could not stage a circus. And without funds, she had added angrily, she might as well stay home in New London and learn how to knit.

Their hotel was a small brownstone building on Broadway near City Hall, run by a woman named Mrs. Adair, a person (Katherine said) of iron respectability. Her food would be palatable and free from the threat of typhoid or dysentery. Then too, she kept a ladies' parlor and a separate ladies' entrance, so that women traveling alone might feel comfortable.

To Carisa's consternation, Katherine had spent at least an hour advising her on her proper behavior there. She was never to go out of her hotel unescorted, and was to avoid loitering in the halls, or standing alone at her bedroom window. If she were asked to play the piano or sing, she should refuse.

Carisa had laughed. "Unfortunately, I don't play the piano. As for singing, I'm afraid my voice resembles a frog's. You forget, Mother Hartshorn, that I've stayed in so many hotels and boarding houses that I've lost track of them. The deBord show never slept in wagons,

146

but always boarded in the towns we played. And sometimes our accommodations were a bit primitive!"

"Still, you're living the life of a lady now," Katherine had replied tartly. "And a true lady works hard to avoid giving the impression that she is . . . available for masculine attention."

Carisa had tossed her head. "Circus background or not, I am as respectable as anyone!"

"If you were, then you would stay at home and forget all this circus nonsense," Katherine had responded, having the last word.

Nelly and Gaines, being servants, were given rooms at the back of the third floor, which meant an extra flight of stairs for them. Carisa's room, however, was on the second floor. It had a spool bed and a set of faded gold brocade draperies at the window. Opposite the bed stood a modern washstand cabinet, which provided a mirror at its top, along with space for two drinking glasses and two lamps. Protruding at the center was a washbasin, and in the bottom cabinet was space for a chamber pot.

It was a room similar to many she had shared with her sisters, and Carisa did no more than give it a glance. As soon as she had tipped the porter, she rushed to the window and peered out.

Broadway! The brick buildings, tall and narrow, with equally narrow windows, were imposing. Some of them were five and even six stories high. Many had big canvas awnings at their entrances which extended over the sidewalk.

The wide street itself was crammed with traffic. Fighting each other for space were horse-drawn drays, vans loaded with boxes and barrels from the city's many manufactories, ice wagons, carriages, carts. Horse-drawn omnibusses, bearing signs like "Red Birds" and "Original Broadways," stopped to disgorge passengers, then swayed again into the thick of the traffic.

And all of these vehicles, Carisa noted, seemed to proceed down the street exactly as they pleased, with no apparent order. There were constant confrontations and jam-ups. Pedestrians, adding to the confusion, darted and dodged between carriages, or simply strolled in the street at random.

A small boy of ten was hawking matches, waving energetically to passers-by. A stray dog ran after a brewery horse, nipping at its hooves, while the driver cursed at it. A policeman with a nightstick leaned against a lamp post and surveyed all of this calmly.

With effort, Carisa managed to yank the window up. Then, heedless of Katherine's advice to act decorously, she leaned out as far as she could. Noise assaulted her— the clatter of iron wheels and horseshoes on cobblestone, the shouts of the dray drivers, the monotonous cry of an old man selling apples.

There were smells, too, of soot and cinders and horse dung. Of the city's burgeoning iron works and printing presses and tobacco factories and twine manufactories, paper box makers and a thousand others.

She heard a knock at her door. Carisa jumped, startled, then reluctantly drew inward and closed the window.

"Miss Carisa? Is there anything you might wish?"

It was Nelly, her plain sallow cheeks bright with excitement. The servant was wearing the new bonnet and blue bombazine dress which Carisa had asked Mrs. Wiggins to sew for her, and she had carefully brushed off all signs of soot and travel from them.

"I don't think so, Nelly," Carisa said.

"Oh . . ." the girl burst out. "Isn't it wonderful! I never saw so many people before in my life! And the shops! The yard goods and the silversmiths and the millinery! And a man to carry our trunks! And I saw a four-wheeled cab in front of the hotel and I think if we paid him he would take us anywhere we wanted to go!"

Carisa smiled. The other girl's enthusiasm was infectious. "Would you like me to engage a cab, Nelly? We still have nearly two hours before we can order our dinner."

"Oh! Could we? Oh!"

They drove about, accompanied by Gaines, who, away from the constraining influence of Katherine, did

148

not seem so formidable, and even allowed himself to gawk as openly as Nelly.

"Goodness! Oh, good gracious! Oh, look!" Nelly kept exclaiming as they drove past the impressive, columned City Hall, Franconi's Hippodrome, the extravagant new Crystal Palace. This last was a stunning edifice made of cast-iron framework supporting huge frames of glass. The Industrial Exhibition had been held here in 1851.

Hotels—splendid blocks of stone and marble—drew squeals of delight from Nelly, as did the array of shops, banks, churches and theaters. Their cab driver, caught up in Nelly's delight and undoubtedly thinking of the tip he would receive, then drove them to P. T. Barnum's American Museum. This was a five-story structure sandwiched between other buildings, with Barnum's name spelled out in flamboyantly large letters. A crowd was gathered about its entrance.

"Can we go inside?" Nelly begged.

"Why not? We'll have the driver wait for us."

Barnum's wonders held them enthralled for an hour —the albinos, trained fleas, jugglers, automatons, dioramas, flying fish. When they emerged from the museum it had grown dark. Calcium lights were shining from the roof of the museum, illuminating the entire area and drawing Nelly's awed exclamations. Even Gaines, who had grunted in surprise on viewing Barnum's "ornithorhincus," gazed upward. New York, it seemed, was a city of lights and wonder and magic.

As she urged the two servants back toward the waiting cab, Carisa's mind surged with plans. Tomorrow morning, she decided, she would go back to Franconi's Hippodrome, where circus, pageants, spectaculars and gladiatorial contests were held. Surely, for a fee, they would allow her to use the facilities in order to audition the scanty number of circus performers who had answered her ad.

She awoke the next morning with her stomach in a tight knot from tension. Nelly arrived promptly at seven to dress her. Carisa struggled into her corset and told the girl to lace it tightly, for she must not look pregnant. And, at all costs, she must not appear hesitant or nervous, although she was growing more so with each passing second.

It was one thing, she told herself, to make her plans from the security of Hearts-ease. It was quite another to be here, in New York, faced with the actual necessity of building her show.

What if she could not find talented performers? What would she do then?

She allowed Nelly to fasten her into the gold gown, and then sat impatiently while the girl arranged her hair and added a lace-trimmed bonnet, draped with a little garland of artificial leaves and spring flowers.

At last she examined herself in the small, square mirror of the dressing-stand. She looked . . . yes, impressive. Her hair showed prettily from beneath the bonnet, and her cheeks were flushed high with color.

She told Nelly to find Gaines and give him his orders for the day: he was to hire another cab and deliver some messages to the performers who had answered the ads. Meanwhile, Nelly herself was to stay here at the hotel, pressing Carisa's other two gowns.

"But . . ." Nelly stared at Carisa, her eyes gone suddenly round. "But that means you'll be going out alone!"

"That's right."

"But *she* said we were to stay with you every moment and never let you out of our sight. It isn't proper for a lady to travel without escort, and not without at least her ladies' maid. . . ."

"Nelly. Mother Hartshorn isn't here now, is she? And I don't consider myself a lady alone, but a businesswoman, a circus owner. And I can transact my business much more effectively if I am not trailed about by two servants!"

"Oh, but . . ."

Carisa was annoyed. "I tell you I'll be all right. I'll hire a cab and pay the man to wait for me all day. That will be escort enough. Now, please go and find Gaines and tell him what I wish him to do. And I don't want you to say one word of this to Mrs. Hartshorn or to my husband. Not one word! If you do, or if Gaines does, I . . . I swear I'll have you both dismissed!"

For emphasis she narrowed her eyes and glared at Nelly.

Fear and doubt wavered on Nelly's face—should she believe Carisa's threat? Then slowly her eyes regained their sparkle.

"Very well, Miss Carisa," she agreed. "Do you think I'd tell? And I'll see that Gaines keeps silent, too. He likes me, you know. He said so last night. He said I was sweet. Imagine!"

Then, with a giggle, Nelly picked up her skirts and hurried out of the room, leaving Carisa to struggle with her amusement and her apprehension.

Franconi's Hippodrome was a monstrosity of a building located on Madison Square at the northwest corner of Broadway and 23rd Street. Shortly it was scheduled to be torn down for a new hotel. Meanwhile it squatted on its corner like a grotesque combination of a fort and a tent, with its brick walls and billowing canvas roof, complete with peaks and dozens of flying flags.

To her relief, Carisa saw that the Sands and Nathan circus was playing here, advertised in banners pasted on the brick walls and by three sandwich men who, with circus posters strapped to their backs, sauntered about the entrances.

No one stopped her as she made her way toward one of the entrances, a tower-like structure flying with more flags, and resembling a medieval keep.

She had barely stepped inside when a young woman with glossy black hair pulled to the nape of her neck in a bun came slamming out of a door and nearly collided with Carisa.

Carisa gave a little gasp and reeled backward, catching her balance with the ease born of years of circus training.

"Oh!" the girl exclaimed. "Oh! Sorry! I did not mean. . . . Oh, but he makes me so very angry . . . I could take hees neck in my hands and tweest it like a . . . how you say . . . chicken or a geese."

The young woman was in her twenties, lithe and

pretty, and to Carisa she had the unmistakable look of a circus performer.

"Who?" she heard herself ask. "Whose neck would you like to twist?"

"Oh, *hees*, that Richard Sands. . . ." And here the girl uttered something in gutter French. "I ask for top billing when he hire me and he agree to it and now he tell me that he cannot do it, I am not that important. . . ." She was nearly gasping in her fury.

"Of course you are important," Carisa soothed, taking the girl's arm and walking with her back out to the entrance. "I myself read your name on the posters outside," she lied. "And of course it's true that you should have top billing. It's a crime that you do not."

"A crime," the girl agreed. "Marcella Duquesne to be billed exactly the same as a singing clown . . . Pfah!" Emphatically she spat onto the dusty walk. "I am more than clown, I am great wire-walker known all over France and Germany . . . How dare he? . . ."

"Is it, then, Richard Sands who hired you?" Carisa asked thoughtfully.

"Yes, it is he, the dog!" More rapid-fire streams of gutter French poured out. "He think heemself so special . . . he dare to insult me, Marcella Duquesne! . . ."

"Mr. Sands is still in his office, then?"

"Oh, yes . . ." Marcella Duquesne had recovered from her anger long enough to give Carisa a curious stare. "But why you ask? If you are looking for job, too, it won't do any good. Thees place closing soon . . . they build big hotel here . . ." Marcella's arms gestured widely to suggest a structure of palatial proportions.

"Then where will you go, Marcella, after the Hippodrome is torn down?"

"Oh . . ." The girl gave a Gallic shrug. "With the circus, where else? With *heem,* I suppose. . . ."

"Must you go with him? Why couldn't you come with me? I'd give you the top billing you deserve. If he made you promises when you signed on, and then didn't fulfill them, perhaps we can break your contract. At any rate, we can surely try."

Marcella Duquesne's eyes narrowed, all of her anger

152

abruptly gone now. She pursed her red little mouth in a business-like way.

"You tell me," she said. "Tell me who you are and maybe I will come with you. If I like you. . . ."

By the time Carisa sat in Richard Sands' office, she was flushed with the triumph of having met Marcella Duquesne, and at the same time horrified at what she had done. Pirating away a performer from under Sands' very eyes—if he knew what she had done, if *any* circus man knew, he would surely have thrown her out of his office.

Yet, she reminded herself quickly, the circus world was rampant with such intrigue. Scheming, betrayal, rivalry. . . .

The male secretary had not wanted to let her in.

"Mr. Sands is very busy and he hasn't time to be disturbed," he told her. "Unless . . ." A frown flickered across the man's face. "You're not here about those new equestrian costumes, are you?"

"Well, I . . ." Carisa began.

"They've been on order and they're a rush job, and Mr. Sands is very angry that they're so late. He has an act waiting to use them."

"Yes," she heard herself say. "I'm from the seamstress."

She was terrified that the secretary would ask her for some identification, or even for the seamstress' name, but he did not.

"Come this way," he said hurriedly. "Mr. Sands can give you just five minutes, no more. Then he's got other fish to fry. So you'd better have all of your excuses on the tip of your tongue, Miss, as he does not relish being disappointed."

Richard Sands was sitting at a huge, pigeon-hole desk which dominated his cluttered office. He looked up irritably as she entered and the secretary clicked the door shut behind her.

"Well?"

Carisa's eyes traveled rapidly over the circus man. Richard Sands was only in his early thirties, but he was already well known in the United States and in the British Isles, where he had had many successful showings and command performances before royalty. Despite his large and skilled company, Sands himself was also a gifted performer, and had perfected the upside-down ceiling walk, an act which called for much skill. Today he wore a well-cut suit of dark wool cheviot, which accented the athletic lines of his body.

His face, however, twitched with irritation. Four fingers drummed on a splash of color on his desk. Involuntarily, Carisa's eyes followed them.

"Well?" he repeated. "What are you staring at, girl? What do you find so fascinating?"

"Why . . . Why, it's the posters," she managed. "I've never seen circus paper in color before. They're stunning!"

It was true. The circus bills had been lithographed in fantastic full-color inks—tigers jumping through hoops, equestrians balanced on snow-white horses, acrobats whirling through the air. Until this time, circus posters had always been done in block letters, and in black and white. Carisa had never seen anything like these.

Rag bond, she told herself, rapidly taking them in. But the cost—

Quickly Richard Sands had gathered up the top posters and pulled a stack of newspapers over them so that their hues were hidden.

"Thank you," he said dryly. "Although no one is to see these yet. But as long as you're only a seamstress, I suppose it doesn't matter very much."

"I . . . I'm not a seamstress."

His eyes narrowed. "You're not? Then who are you?"

"I'm Carisa Hartshorn, and I. . . ."

He rose, slamming his fist on the desk top, so that the papers, and a stray coffee cup, rattled perilously.

"Carisa Hartshorn? Who the hell is that? Dammit, girl, do you think I have time to sit here and have idle conversation with you? I have a show to put on. I have performers throwing tantrums and rebellions, costumes delayed, two sick horses, and a gaffer out on a whiskey

154

binge and seeing little green bugs. How the hell did you get past my secretary?"

As he spoke, Sands moved from behind his desk and clamped both hands onto her shoulders, firmly propelling her toward the door.

"But . . . please. . . ."

"Is it a job you're after? Well, I'm not hiring now, not unless that little primadonna, Marcella Duquesne, chooses to quit, and frankly I doubt we could be that lucky. So I'd suggest that you get your pretty self out of here just as fast as. . . ."

Angrily Carisa dug her heels into the oak flooring, bracing herself so that he could not push her further.

"I am not looking for a job!" she gasped through angry tears. "And if I were, I certainly wouldn't accept it from a man as high-handed and arrogant as you are!"

Abruptly he released her. He walked back to the desk again and flung himself down in the chair, lounging back lazily. "Arrogant I may be . . . I've been told that before. But high-handed I'm not; I can't afford to be. No circus owner can."

"I know," she said steadily. "I'm an owner, too."

"You? You own a show?"

"Yes. Why not?" She walked to a second chair which was shoved against one wall. She lifted off an untidy pile of papers, dropped them on the floor, and sat down. Calmly she adjusted her skirts.

"I've just bought the William deBord show," she told him. "And I'm being amply financed by my husband, Adam Hartshorn, of New London. I've come to ask your help, Mr. Sands."

"*My* help?" Richard Sands threw back his head and laughed. "And what do you expect me to do for you? Loan you my elephants?"

"No." Carisa stiffened in the chair, holding her back very erect. "And please don't laugh at me, Mr. Sands. I assure you that this is a very serious matter for me. You see, I'm a member of the *Flying Flambeaux,* or I was, until we had the accident. My father, John Phillips. . . ."

"John Phillips! He and his daughter are with our

155

show now, in a small capacity. They hired on a few weeks ago. He is a has-been, but his daughter possesses modest talent. In fact, it is Anna for whom those damned costumes are being sewn . . . Do you mean to say that you are John Phillips' daughter?"

"Yes, I am."

Carisa felt herself begin to relax. At least Richard Sands had not kicked her out of his office—not yet, at any rate. His eyes were fixed on her with interest, and she found herself telling him all about her accident, Stephana's death, Papa's anger. She also told him of the efforts she had made thus far in order to build the Phillips Circus.

"I see." He was nodding. "I must say you haven't done too badly thus far. There is no faster way for a circus to grow than to absorb other, smaller ones . . ." His eyes blazed with sudden suspicion. "But why are you here, then? Surely you don't plan, as your next step, to annex *my* show?"

Carisa tried to laugh. "Hardly." She hesitated, drew a deep breath, and then blurted out the rest. "But I do have a confession to make. I have been very bold, and I have sent messages to the performers who answered my ads, telling them that I will audition them here, at the Hippodrome. I am staying in a small hotel and I have nowhere else to see them. I will make every effort not to inconvenience you, of course, and I will pay you well . . ."

Her voice trailed off.

"Auditions, here?" Richard Sands was staring at her, incredulous. His eyes were dark with anger.

"Yes, I . . . I had nowhere else to take them, and I thought. . . ."

"*Your* auditions here in *my* hippodrome?" There was a brief, tense silence. Then again Sands threw back his head and roared with laughter. "Good God, girl, it's bold you are, all right! But I like that. You know what you want and you go out and grab it."

Carisa thought she would sag with her relief. "Then do you mean? . . ."

"Yes, why not? You can borrow our ring for an hour

or so, and I won't even charge you. I'll even throw in some tickets for our matinee this afternoon if you'd like to attend. But as for my own performers and top acts. . . ."

Carisa gazed at him levelly, hoping that her thoughts did not show on her face. "Yes?"

"You are not to touch them, do you hear, you little minx? They are mine, they belong to me, and I intend to keep them."

"Even if I can pay them more?" she heard herself say.

"Pay them more!" Richard Sands banged his fist down on his desk so violently that the discarded coffee cup spattered brown liquid all over the papers. "You *are* audacious, girl! Well, let me tell you something. My show is world-renowned. We've played at Balmoral before Queen Victoria. See this diamond stick-pin?" He thrust out his chest. "She gave it to me, as a token. I tell you, my show has a reputation. But what does yours have? Nothing. A dream or two, and a woman owner."

"That's not fair! I . . ."

"Mrs. Hartshorn, you're a fool if you think you can make a success out of that show, not the way you're planning it. Why, you've told me yourself that you can't even travel with it, but will have to rely on a manager."

She faced him. "That doesn't matter. My show *will* be a success, I'll make it be!"

Sands grimaced. "How? By staying at home and having babies, while your manager is free to steal from you, or to sit around on his hindquarters and let your show go to ruin?"

Carisa reddened, for these were worries she also had thought of. And could Sands possibly guess her pregnancy?

"Rolf won't ruin me," she insisted. "He's a real circus man and he'd be too proud to let the show fail. As for him stealing from me . . ." She hesitated. "I suppose he will do that to some extent. But Duddie will be there to see he doesn't grow too blatant. And I have promised Rolf a free hand, you see, so that. . . ."

Sands nodded. "He'll resort to grift, then, and to

gambling, to make what he can on the side, as many shows do."

"My show will be honest."

"Perhaps." Richard Sands looked dubious. Abruptly he unfolded himself from his chair. "Well, it's your funeral, Mrs. Hartshorn . . . and your husband's money. If you lose it for him, what concern is it of mine?"

His eyes lingered warmly on the lines of her bodice. "However, maybe you would like to have luncheon with me after you have auditioned your performers. I know a very quiet little place just off Broadway where they serve Basque cooking. . . ."

"I don't know. . . ."

He grinned at her. "I assure you my intentions are quite honorable, even if you are a little would-be thief."

"I'm not a thief! I mean, I . . ." Her hands were perspiring inside the elegant silk gloves she wore.

He gave her a mocking bow. "If you're a circus owner, then you're probably a thief . . . in one way or another. And the matter is settled. Lunch it is. I'll meet you inside the Hippodrome at noon."

The interior of the Hippodrome—built for ten thousand —was eerily empty, save for a dozen people sitting uneasily in a front row of seats. Above Carisa's head the shabby canvas roof, stained with hundreds of water leaks, flapped precariously in the wind. No wonder they planned to tear the place down, she thought. It was amazing that it had lasted this long in the rigors of New York weather.

It was cold here, too, and Carisa sat huddled under her mantle in one of the higher seats, trying to ignore the three workmen who, with push-brooms and canvas sacks, were sweeping the aisles of debris.

"Damme, a woman, would you look at that? Bossin' 'em around just as pretty as you please," one of them whispered loudly to a companion.

Carisa flushed and ignored them. She stared downward to the regulation circus ring, set within the larger "hippodrome track" used for pageants. There a tall, thin clown was going through his routine with five

158

trained poodles. The dogs yipped, and jumped through hoops—or refused to jump, depending on their mood. When they refused, the thin man cried out at them in exasperation, and smacked them on the rump with his hand.

"Very well," Carisa called out, when the last dog had jumped and yapped. "You may go now. Thank you very much, and I'll send you a message later, when I've decided."

The man, in white-face makeup, looked up at her, discouraged.

"Thank you," Carisa repeated. "Next! The Rigioris, isn't it?"

The auditions droned on. More clowns, acrobats. A stilt-walker. A man with a trained horse which could answer simple questions by touching a painted board with its right hoof.

With a growing sense of despair, Carisa watched the acts and then dismissed each. These were capable people, she knew. Most had worked small family or medicine shows, had been circus folk all of their lives. But none were stars, none had the sparkling extra shimmer of talent which would make people gasp in wonderment and awe. And it was this which Carisa needed—flash, magic, wonder—in order to get the Phillips Circus talked about.

She thought again of Marcella Duquesne. Marcella might have that something "extra." And Marcella had also promised to talk to friends of hers, others who were with the Sands show. Carisa would see them all perform at the matinee this afternoon.

Someone slid into the seat beside her, interrupting her thoughts. He smelled of cigar smoke and—more faintly—of Cuban rum.

"Well?" It was Richard Sands, of course, come to meet her for their luncheon engagement. "And how is it coming? Have you found any great stars yet?"

"No," she said, suddenly irritated. "You didn't expect that I would, did you?"

"Frankly, no. You would have done better to have your manager place those ads. Rumors get about.

159

People don't want to work under a woman, you know. It rankles them."

"Oh?" Carisa reddened. "Well, they are just going to have to rankle, then, because I don't plan to quit."

Sands nodded. He changed position in his seat, his hands brushing her knee as if by accident. Her face burning, she edged away.

"No," he said slowly. "I can see that you won't quit. Or you think you won't."

"That's a very strange thing to say!"

"It's true, though. You, my pretty, are going to have to want that show very badly if you are to succeed at it. You'll have to ache for it badly enough to defy your husband, your manager, and everyone else who tries to stop you. You'll have to keep one thought in your mind and one only . . . the show. You'll have to live it, eat it, sleep it, and immerse yourself in it. And give up for it, too, perhaps things you didn't intend. Are you strong enough to do all that?"

Carisa pressed her lips together. "Yes. Yes, I think I am."

Richard Sands gave her a long, searching look, the pupils of his eyes alive with highlights and color.

"I wonder. I really wonder. When the time comes, Mrs. Hartshorn, I'd be very interested to know. Just what *are* you willing to give up . . . and what aren't you?"

Carisa could only stare at him, an odd prickle of misgiving running through her.

11

No one was seasick on the way home. Carisa stood at the rail of the steamer *J. N. Harris,* staring downward at the ship's tumbled, frothy wake. The waves were flat today, and docile. The sun hung brilliantly overhead, reflecting in great splashes of light off the water. In less than an hour, the captain had promised, they would be back in New London.

She gazed down at the water, where a waterlogged chunk of driftwood bobbed, and sighed. She should have been returning to New London in a state of giddy triumph. After all, hadn't she managed to snatch not one but *three* acts from under Richard Sands' very nose? One was, of course, Marcella Duquesne, whose elegant toe-dancing and ballet posturings on the high wire would surely make her the talk of every town in which she played. Carisa had also secured a skilled animal trainer who wore sequins and glitter and billed himself as the "Great Rudolph." Lastly, there was a team of German acrobats whose lithe bodies flew through the air like cannonballs.

More than this, she had come home with ideas—for colored posters, a new kind of band arrangement, a more secure animal cage. Richard Sands, relaxing expansively over lunch and a bottle of Bordeaux at the little Basque restaurant, had obviously not considered her much of a threat, for he had spent the entire meal talking circus. He had even dropped hints of a newly invented "steam piano," which, it was rumored, could play louder in the open air than any known band.

At the time, she remembered guiltily, Sands had not yet known of her triumph in hiring away Marcella and the two other acts, although there had been a moment near the end of the meal when he had stared at her suspiciously.

"Perhaps you are a sly one, Carisa Hartshorn, eh?" The man's eyes had gleamed at her.

"Sly?" She had felt her heart sink. "Whatever do you mean, Mr. Sands?"

He had grinned at her, poured himself some more wine, and the moment had passed. But now she frowned at the swirling water. Well, she asked herself, wasn't the circus world a competitive one? Circuses struggled to best their rivals. Besides, hadn't Sands himself told her to defy anyone who tried to stop her?

She pushed away the thought. There was more than just Richard Sands on her mind at this moment.

161

There was her father. . . .

On her third day in New York, she had gone to the address which Richard Sands had given her for her father and Anna.

It had been a blustery morning, the strong wind full of cinders and factory smells. Her father, she found, had taken a suite of rooms in a brownstone near Canal Street, a shabby-genteel establishment run by a widow who catered to show people.

She had been shown into a small parlor fitted with tall, narrow windows and bristling with small tables, peacock feathers, seashells and knick-knacks. The room was filled with an old-woman stench of perspiration and unwashed garments. Here Carisa had to wait for nearly half an hour, fidgeting with her gloves and bead bag, and staring at the stern daguerreotype of the widow's late husband.

But at last Anna came running into the room. She was as pretty as ever, Carisa saw, her eyes a deep blue, her brown hair becomingly curled in soft ringlets. She looked like an illustration in *Godey's Lady's Book*, soft and plump and perfect.

"Carisa!" Anna burst out. "Oh, sister, I am so glad to see you! *So* glad!"

The two sisters embraced. As she felt Anna's perfumed closeness, Carisa found herself thinking, *Anna lied*.

But Anna seemed to be unaware of her thoughts, and she hugged Carisa again. "Oh! How ruddy and healthy you look, Carisa! I declare I never thought you would walk again, not like this! And now look at you!"

"Yes." Carisa said it flatly. "I can walk. The doctor is pleased with my recovery, although he says I'll never perform again." She bit her lip. "But, Anna, where is Papa? Is he ill?"

Anna hesitated. "No, not ill."

"Then isn't he at home today?"

"Yes, he's here, although we leave in an hour for the Hippodrome." Anna's eyes looked away. "But he refused to come down to the parlor to see you. That's what took me so long. I was arguing with him, trying to persuade him."

Carisa stared at her sister. "But why? Why won't he see me? Surely he can't still be angry. . . ."

"He is."

"But . . . he can't be!" Carisa heard herself repeat helplessly. She blinked back tears. "But he can't refuse to see me!"

Anna made a restless movement. "Carisa, you have to understand something. Since the accident, Papa has changed. I don't know, he just seems much older. He's not the same."

"But I thought surely, after all this time. . . ."

Anna moved to the parlor window and stood staring out at the street through the narrow slit in the lace underdraperies.

"Carisa, it hasn't been easy, living all these months with Papa. I think he knows that I lied to him about Stephana. But he won't admit it to himself. It's you he blames, when he should be angry at me as well. I should be sharing that blame. . . ."

Anna's voice cracked. "I haven't been able to stop thinking about it, the way I lied. I don't know what you must think of me. Papa has been so upset . . . it hasn't been easy to be around him. You know how I hate raised voices and fusses and quarrels. . . ." Her eyes appealed.

"Yes, Anna. I know that."

"He . . . he needed someone, sister! Don't you see? If I . . . if I admitted that I lied, then he would have no one to take care of him. And he has been quite ill. First he hurt his knee and then he had pneumonia which left him quite debilitated. Did I write you about that?"

"No. I don't think you did."

"Well, he was sick. Your money . . . I don't know what we would have done without it. Carisa . . ." Again Anna's eyes were filled with that naked begging. ". . . I suppose I'm very weak. Despicable. I . . . I didn't want ugliness. I didn't want to hear him shouting at me . . . or slapping me. . . ."

163

There was a long silence while Carisa's fingers played with the lace edging on her gloves.

At last she said, "I had a long time to lie in bed and think about that, Anna. At first I was very angry with you. But after a while . . . I guess I can understand why you did it."

"Oh, Carisa!" Anna gave a little skip which made her crinolines rustle. She hugged Carisa, looking suddenly very young and pretty. Her eyes were glistening.

"Oh, Carisa, I'm *so* glad you think of it that way. I couldn't bear it if you. . . ." She let the sentence fade away. "And now I suppose you had better go. Papa is waiting upstairs for you to leave."

"To leave?"

"Why, yes." The glow faded from Anna's face. "He is quite implacable, you know. He says that your new show will never mean anything to him. He thinks you are a fool for attempting it."

A pounding had begun in Carisa's forehead. Her fingers pressed into the beadwork of her bag. "Then why can't he tell me that himself?"

"You don't understand. Papa has been ill. . . ."

Carisa lifted her skirts and marched toward the door of the small, ill-smelling parlor. "I don't care. Ill or not, I'm going to see him. Tell me which rooms you have. I'm going upstairs and talk to him."

"But the landlady. . . ."

"I don't care about the landlady! I want to see Papa! I have a right to see him. I'll *make* him understand!"

Full of anger and resolve, Carisa brushed past her sister and out into the empty, drafty entrance hall. "Which room?" she demanded.

"Upstairs and to your right. He's in the back room. But, Carisa, you really shouldn't be doing this. You haven't seen him recently. You don't know. . . ."

The room was small and frayed and painfully neat, filled with too many pieces of dark, battered furniture. A bed was covered with a patchwork quilt. Piles of the New York *Tribune* were neatly stacked on a dressing table. An old trunk which Carisa remembered from her

164

childhood sat at the foot of the bed. Once that trunk had been stuffed full of costumes. Bright red and blue cloth sewn with spangles and lengths of golden ribbon. . . .

She paused on the threshold, opening her mouth to breathe and feeling as if she could not get enough oxygen.

"Papa?"

He sat in a chair beside the bed, clad in a black wool suit which was at least ten years old, scrupulously clean and pressed. But the flamboyant, imposing John Phillips was gone. In his place was a man whose suit seemed gathered loosely over his bones. Even his face had shrunk, so that the blue eyes seemed sunk in behind a web of wrinkles. The flowing shock of hair had turned gray-white.

"Papa . . ."

"What are *you* doing here?" Papa's voice, harsh and resonant, was still the same.

"Papa, I came to beg you and Anna to come back to New London with me. My husband has agreed to finance my show, and I need both of you. It would be a job, a good job, and . . . and I would really like to have you with me."

The blue eyes stared at her. "The Sands circus is one of the greatest in the country. Even if the part we play there is very small."

"Papa," she stumbled on, "my show, too, will one day be great. The Phillips Circus . . . I named it after you. Please come."

"What could Anna and I do in *your* show?" The eyes blazed at her. Yet Carisa had the odd feeling that they did not really see her at all. "The *Flying Flambeaux* are dead. You killed them, Carisa. You betrayed me and you killed your sister."

"Papa! I didn't! Papa, it was Stephana who. . . ."

"Get out, girl. What do I want with you? I only have one daughter now. Just one daughter."

"But, Papa . . ." She fought back tears. She felt like a little girl again, ready to sob in humiliation. Papa had used to beat her ankles with a stick when she had failed to practice. Strange, that she should remember that now—

"Papa," she repeated. "I know that you hurt your knee. Anna wrote me about it. And she told me today that you'd been ill, too. But that doesn't mean that you can't perform, that you can't be useful. . . ."

"The *Flambeaux* are gone, I tell you. Dead as old dust. Dead."

"Papa . . ."

"Dead, I say! Dead!" His voice rose, patriarchal, magnificent, shaking. "Killed by a worthless slut who should never have been born. Dead . . . yes, I remember the pool of blood that day. I was walking in it. And then I pulled the damned babe out, the babe that killed her. . . ."

"Papa!" Carisa was unaware that she was screaming at him. "Papa, you can't say those things. . . ."

The blue eyes burned at her. Then, as if it came from another world, she felt Anna's hand plucking at her sleeve.

"Carisa, you must come away now. You're upsetting him terribly. He hasn't been this bad in a long time."

She pulled Carisa out into the corridor. Helplessly Carisa allowed herself to be led. She heard the door click behind them. Her throat ached. She wished she could sit down and put her head in her hands. She wanted to pound something with her fists.

"How long has he been like this?" she asked dully.

"Oh, months. He keeps talking about the day you and Stephana were born. How he had to walk in Mama's blood . . . and he keeps talking about stones, some strange stones he says they saw that day. And then he says how you betrayed him. Carisa, I've tried to talk with him. Really I have. . . ."

Carisa walked downstairs with her sister. She managed to lift her chin, to stifle the terrible sobs ready to burst in her. "He . . . he has been ill, of course," she whispered. "That's it. When he's better . . ."

"I don't think he's going to get any better."

"But of course he will. He must!" she cried, ignoring Anna's look of pity.

166

She had hurried back to her hotel room and packed for home, abruptly anxious to be back. Hearts-ease waited, and Adam, and the circus. . . .

"Miss Carisa!" Nelly's voice said now. The steamer's engine was loud, and smelled of oil and cinders. "Miss Carisa, I swear you're a hundred miles away. I asked you three times if you'd anything more for me to do before we dock. And you didn't even answer me."

Carisa jumped. She turned to see Nelly, bright and cheerful in her traveling dress.

"Oh! Nelly . . ."

"Yes, ma'am, and do you have anything more I should be doing, before we get to New London? I've your luggage all in order, and I've counted it twice . . . heaven help me if I should forget something! And then Gaines and I were just having a bit of a stroll to the back of the boat . . . the day is so fine. . . ."

Nelly looked flushed, her plain face almost pretty.

"No, Nelly. I have nothing else for you to do now."

The servant eyed her. "Is something wrong, then? You look bad, your face is so long and melancholy. Is the voyage disagreeing with you?"

"No, of course not."

"Well, then . . ." Still Nelly hesitated. "Anyway, at least it's a fine day, and you'll soon be home again. *He* will be so happy to see you. . . ."

Adam. Who had, as Poll Henry had boasted, writhed with pleasure in her arms. . . .

Carisa could feel the color spreading up from her neck to stain her cheeks. It was all coming back to her —Adam, Julian, Poll Henry—the new set of problems she would have to face as soon as she arrived back at Hearts-ease.

"I . . . I'll be all right, Nelly, I promise you. So why don't you take another walk around the deck and enjoy it while you can?"

Nelly disappeared in the direction of the small, bare lounge which some of the servants traveling on the steamer had taken for their own. Carisa resumed her vigil at the rail, frowning out at the sunglare on the water.

167

Adam, she thought. *Oh, Adam . . .*

To her dismay, there was no one at the wharf to meet them when they docked. Finally Gaines had to hail a public hack. Carisa rode the miles back to Heartsease in a state of vague uneasiness. Had Adam forgotten that this was the day she was to return home? It seemed unlikely.

When they finally drove through the grove of ancient hemlocks and down the long, curving driveway of Hearts-ease, Carisa grew even more uneasy. A black surrey sat in front of the carriage house, its pair of well-matched chestnuts being rubbed down by one of the young grooms. The animals looked familiar to Carisa and she stared at them with a growing sense of alarm.

"Those are Dr. Arthur's team," Nelly said.

"Dr. Arthur!" Panic swept through her.

"That's right. I saw those horses often enough when you were sick, Miss Carisa. I should know them by now."

Carisa barely waited until the hack had pulled to a halt before she had scrambled out of it. She went hurrying up the graveled walk, her crinolines swaying awkwardly.

The house smelled odd, was her first wild thought. Like kerosene, pungent and choking. And there was some other odor, too, equally strong.

In the front hall she met Katherine, who was coming down the staircase, wearing a day dress which was untidy and stained with water. Her face was gray with fatigue, her eyes sunken, as if she had gone several nights without sleep.

At the sight of her, Carisa felt an ugly lurch of fear.

"Who is sick?" she demanded. "It isn't . . . Adam?"

Katherine regarded Carisa with blank, weary eyes. "No, it's Julian. Diphtheria has been going around at the Grammar School . . . six have already died . . . and now Julian has caught it. Dr. Arthur has tried to be reassuring, but . . ." Katherine's shrug was eloquent.

"Diphtheria!" Carisa's hand had gone to her breast. She was ashamed of the wild rush of relief she felt.

Adam was well. It was Julian who was ill, not her husband.

"That's right, my girl. It's diphtheria. And you were far away from your responsibility. Gallivanting to New York, instead of staying here at Hearts-ease as any proper wife should do."

It was an unfair thing to say, but Carisa did not stop to argue. Instead she rushed upstairs past her mother-in-law, the tendons of her right leg pounding with pain and fatigue.

Diphtheria, she was thinking as she ran. This was one of the most dreaded of childhood diseases, and when it struck, it gripped a community in the throes of terror. Wildly infectious, it could carry off entire families of children. A child victim, fevered and delirious, would struggle to breathe against the strangling membrane which grew in his throat. As his windpipe clogged, he would be too busy trying to breathe even to cry. His face would turn dusky as his struggles grew more intense. And then. . . .

No! She choked off the thought. Difficult as Julian could be, he was Adam's son and she could not wish him ill.

She reached the door of Julian's bedroom, her eyes taking in the scene. The room was strewn with the clutter of illness: towels and wet rags and basins. A small can of kerosene sat on the dresser, its fumes permeating the air. Mingling with it was the even stronger stench of sulphur. Both substances, Carisa knew, were considered effective in fighting the disease.

Seated at the side of the little spool bed was Dr. Arthur, his bald head glistening in the shaft of sunlight which streamed in through the window. He was in the act of picking a leech out of an earthenware jar with a small pair of tongs.

Adam was there, too, on the other side of the bed, his face wearing a look of ashen desperation. He looked, Carisa saw numbly, as if he had not changed his clothes or shaved in days.

And in the bed itself was Julian. But—Carisa caught her breath—how childish and innocent he looked now.

169

He lay under a light quilt, his form so slight that it barely caused the quilt to mound. His curly hair was a damp mass, his skin flushed, his cheeks a fiery red. There was a rag poultice on his neck, and the sounds of his labored breathing were loud.

"Adam, how is he?"

Adam looked up. "He has had it for four days now, Carisa. He caught it at the Grammar School. The Medford boys are both dead, and it has spread like wildfire. Dr. Arthur insisted that they close the school at once, and thank God they have done so. But it's still too late for our Julian. He has caught it."

"But . . . how is he?"

Adam gestured toward the bed, where Julian twisted and moaned and tried to pluck away the poultice.

"You see how he is. At first he seemed dumpy and listless. Spiked a bit of a fever. My mother thought he was coming down with a touch of the grippe, and she dosed him well with an emetic. But it didn't help . . ." For the first time Adam's eyes seemed to focus sharply on her. "Why didn't you come back earlier? Didn't you get my message? I sent it out by Captain Trevill on the *Elisha Scott*. It should have reached you."

"Message?" Carisa could only stare at him. "No, I received no message, Adam. I left my hotel early; perhaps that is why. But what does that matter now? It's Julian who is important! How bad is he, and what is Dr. Arthur doing for him?"

Before Adam could speak the doctor interrupted, smiling bleakly. "He's better than some of the others. But the membrane is beginning to extend into the nasal passages, and I'm afraid that is not a good sign. I've been combating the disease with bleeding and emetics. Also insufflations of sulphur and kerosene. Perhaps that will help him . . . I cannot say."

Adam managed a small, ashen smile. "Brigid, from the kitchen, has also been here, urging us to try one of her grandmother's remedies, a gravy made by baking live green frogs in a roaster with butter."

"Frogs!"

"Brigid swears her grandmother has used this in past epidemics and has effected cures with it. Or we could try mashed snails and earthworms in water. That is another common remedy." Adam's face twisted bitterly.

"Old wives' tales," muttered the doctor, turning to fish in his leather bag for something.

"Well?" Carisa's voice was tart. "Frogs are certainly every bit as sensible as trying sulphur and kerosene, and certainly the odor would be less overpowering." She frowned, trying to think. Marta Taggart . . . Surely there was something, something from her childhood . . . but the thought would not come.

"Come out into the corridor for a moment, Carisa," Adam said. "I want to talk to you."

They left the sickroom, closing the door behind them. In the hall, the family portraits stared down.

Adam threw out his hands in a gesture of helpless anger. "I don't know. I just don't know. Why is it that such cruel diseases come to take little children? A boy not even ten!"

"Adam, Adam." She moved into his arms and for a long moment they clung to each other.

"I cursed that boy, Carisa," Adam whispered, his voice so low that she could barely hear it. "I damned him. In my mind I called him a devil's blow-by. I hated him for what he did with Poll. I blamed him. . . ."

Carisa could feel the shaking of Adam's chest against her own. "I wished him dead," her husband went on. "And now he will be. God, dear God, Carisa, I've struck my own son dead with my wish. . . ."

A shiver ran through Carisa, a little drift of thoughts eddying in her head. Pictures in her mind. A young man with blue, haunted eyes. . . .

"No." She said it abruptly. "No, you haven't struck Julian dead with your wish. He isn't going to die."

Adam lifted his chin. The moment of closeness, of shared grief, was gone. "And how can you possibly know that? Dr. Arthur has been here for hours and he can do nothing. Do you plan to cook up a witches' brew of dead frogs? Or perhaps a decoction of worms?"

171

"No. I don't know! I'm not sure. I only know he won't die."

She left Adam and went into the bedroom again. Impulsively she went to the bedside and knelt down, so that her face was close to Julian's. He stirred and mumbled, his eyes fever-bright.

"Poll . . ." he muttered. "Poll . . . Polly. . . ."

Carisa walked slowly downstairs, barely conscious that she did so. Diphtheria . . . hadn't Stephana suffered from it once, long ago in England? Dimly she remembered it. She herself had been ill as well. Hadn't Marta Taggart, Rolf's half-wild mother, done something to cure them somehow? Or had it all been only a fever-dream, half-remembered?

She met Katherine in the lower hall, carrying a tray of warm tea and broth.

"Where are you going, Carisa?"

Again Carisa shivered. Again the thoughts skittered through her mind and were gone.

"I . . . I don't know. I've got to go somewhere and think."

The dishes on the tray rattled as Katherine gave a hoarse, bitter laugh. "Think? About what? About Julian dying like the others? Or about the husband and home you've been neglecting for that foolish circus of yours?"

Carisa's cheeks reddened. She bit off a sharp reply and fled out of the front door, barely realizing where she was going. It had rained the previous night, and the path which led to the circus quarters was muddy. Carisa slipped and slid, staining the hem of her traveling dress with muck.

But she hurried blindly on, heedless of the mud, or of the aching pains which still shot through her legs.

Duddie was just emerging from the front door of the old farmhouse which they had converted into circus housing. With him was a small, brindled dog, Boxo, which Duddie hoped to train for use in the equestrian act.

"Duddie!" Carisa picked up her skirts and hurried,

172

her feet skidding in the mud. The clown waited for her, looking small and ludicrously misshapen in his everyday clothes. But Carisa had known him for so many years that she did not see his defects at all. She only saw that his face was round and kind, his eyes now filled with concern.

"Carisa! What are you doing here today? And in the mud! You've been running, is anything amiss?"

"You mean you don't know?"

"Know what?" Duddie made a wry little face. "We here at the circus are not exactly in the confidence of those at the house, Carisa. Especially when you are away. I think Mrs. Hartshorn would be very pleased to see all of us disappear forever without a trace. As for your husband. . . ."

"It's diphtheria, Duddie! Julian is very ill with it, and he could die if we don't stop it somehow. Duddie, you've got to tell me. Didn't Stephie and I have diphtheria when we were very small? I think I can almost remember it. And didn't Marta Taggart help us somehow?"

"Ah, Carisa, that was long ago."

"But, Duddie, you were there! You must remember something!"

"Carisa, it was 14 years ago. I was only a boy myself, young and feckless. Then, too, Marta did not like me much."

"Duddie, you must help me! You must remember!"

"Very well. Come into the ring barn with me, then, Carisa. I think best when I am riding."

"But what did Marta *do,* Duddie?" Carisa demanded. "What did she do?"

The clown frowned. "Do? Why, one of the things she did was to brush out your throat and Stephana's with an odd sort of narrow little brush. Then . . ." Duddie frowned. "I can't think of it, Carisa. I'm sorry. It was so many years ago, and I was busy that day, we had a performance to put on. There was always the show, even if someone was dying. . . ."

Carisa gripped the little clown's arms urgently. The

ring horse, Sugar, whickered at them and nudged Duddie, too, with her nose.

Absently Duddie fed her a handful of sugar.

"Carisa, if I could remember, I'd tell you. You know that. But . . ."

"Think, Duddie," she urged. "It's all still there in your mind, I know it is, if only you could bring it out again. Please."

"Very well." Duddie leaned against Sugar's glossy sides and covered his face with his hands. There was silence in the ring barn, broken only by the soft, snuffly breathing of the horse, and by a sudden, coughing roar from one of the jungle cats who was caged in the neighboring barn.

"A brush," Duddie said. "A soft, very narrow brush. And there was . . . yes, I think there was a reed, too. A hollow reed, that was it, Carisa! And something to drink. Something a noxious brown color, like thin gruel . . . oh, it looked awful, I remember that."

Duddie frowned, his eyes distant. "I remember watching her fuss in that basket of hers. She slapped at me and scolded me, pulling things out, and then she made me get some water, some honey and whiskey. Then she asked for. . . ."

"For what?" Carisa demanded breathlessly.

"Why, for . . . for moldy bread." Duddie stared at her. "Does that make sense, Carisa? Moldy bread? Yet I'm almost sure. . . ."

The little clown hesitated so long that Carisa lost patience with him. "Oh, Duddie! Please! Remember!"

"There was a little verse she chanted, I suppose it must have been a formula of some kind, or an incantation." Duddie threw out his hands. "But what does it matter, Carisa? I can't remember, and even if I could, I could never duplicate the brew she made."

"But the reed!" Carisa persisted. "Surely we could get one of those. And make a brush. . . ."

The look the clown gave her was pitying. "I suppose I could try. It's better than sitting by and doing nothing. But don't set your hopes on it, girl. If God wants to

174

take away Julian, then he's going to do just that. And nothing you or I can do will stop him."

An hour passed with agonizing slowness. Carisa told Dr. Arthur of the brush and the reed, and the doctor's face turned sullen. But Adam insisted that the physician remain. He alone was familiar with the anatomical structure of the throat, and his services would yet be needed.

They waited tensely by the bedside. Adam was very still, saying nothing, his face a frozen mask. Katherine sat in a chair compulsively doing needlepoint, her needle flashing through the canvas. And Carisa sat pleating the fabric of her traveling dress into accordion folds, trying not to listen to the stertorous gasping that came from the bed as Julian struggled to breathe.

Once they were interrupted by Nelly, who came to say that Eliza and Samuel were downstairs, asking how Julian was. Adam left the room, and returned five minutes later. Silently he settled in his chair again to resume his vigil.

"What did they say?" Carisa asked, more to break the silence than from any real desire to know.

"Why, all that Eliza can remember is that the boy spied on her," was Adam's brusque reply.

Darkness had fallen, creeping toward the house from the hemlocks, when Duddie finally came. He was shown upstairs by a frightened Gaines.

"This Mr. Dudley wishes to see you," Gaines muttered.

Katherine started to rise indignantly. "What on earth. . . ."

"It's the brush," Carisa said quickly. "And the reed for Julian's throat."

To Carisa's surprise, Katherine nodded. "I've heard of such things used before. I'll help."

The slow minutes passed. Katherine, Duddie, and Dr. Arthur bent over the struggling child. The sick boy gagged and cried out, his arms and legs thrashing beneath the coverlet. His spine was arched, his voice a wordless shriek.

"Adam . . ." Perspiration was running down Carisa's face. She grasped at Adam's arm, nausea pushing through her. "Adam, this is hurting him!"

"Hush, Carisa. You were the one who wished this done, were you not? If you can't bear to listen, then leave the room."

"No . . . No, I'll stay."

Adam squeezed her arm. "Have courage, Carisa. With luck, the boy is so ill he won't remember this later."

There was more gagging, another hoarse cry, and it was done. Julian lay limp beneath the coverlet, his breathing more normal.

"It's finished," Dr. Arthur said tiredly. The physician's face dripped perspiration. "For better or for ill. I think we got most of the membrane, and we certainly relieved his breathing. But whether or not all of this will cure the child's disease, I haven't the faintest notion."

Julian fell into a heavy slumber. Katherine volunteered to sit with him, and to call if there was the slightest change. Wearily Carisa and Adam left the sickroom.

"Adam, you must eat something," Carisa said. "You look exhausted."

"No, I'm not hungry. And I'm not tired either."

"But you must be. You . . ."

"Oh, all right. Carisa. Come down to my study with me. I don't want food but I could use some brandy. And you need some as well. Your face is as white as a linen shroud."

"Oh, I hope not so white as that!" she exclaimed, shivering.

Downstairs they found the study dark, smelling faintly of cigar smoke and old leather book bindings—a very masculine smell which Carisa supposed she would always associate with her husband.

Adam lit the lamps and then poured himself a glass of brandy. He filled a smaller one for Carisa.

"There," he said. "Drink that."

Obediently, Carisa sipped. The brandy, full of rich fumes, seemed to flood her senses.

"Julian is going to live, Adam," she said at last. "I know he is, I feel sure of it."

"You said that before. How can you know it?"

"I don't *know* it. I . . . I just feel it, that's all."

"Feelings! Dreams! Is that all you can speak of, Carisa?"

Carisa's eyes filled.

"I'm sorry." His hand touched hers. "But you'll have to pardon my bitterness. I spent today sitting at Julian's bedside listening to that fool Arthur tell of all the cases he has treated which seemed to be improving and then suddenly died. And of the cases he's had where the toxins of the diphtheria produced paralysis. And then when she came, my dear sister-in-law, Eliza, made sure that she repeated to me the entire list of the dead here in New London. . . ."

"Adam." Carisa said it softly, feeling her heart twist.

He went on as if he had not heard her. "All of the time he lay there, he called out for Poll. Did you know that, Carisa? Poll! Over and over he'd say her name. My mother or I would try to talk to him, and he would push us away. It was Poll Henry he wanted. Damn her!"

Carisa thought of Adam, bearing all of this alone, and felt her mouth go dry. "I'm sorry," she whispered. "I just didn't know. I left my hotel so quickly that I didn't get your message. I wouldn't have gone to New York if I'd known that Julian was going to be sick."

"But you did go, didn't you?"

"Adam, I . . . You gave me permission to travel! You even gave me the funds to transact my business."

"I know I did." Adam's eyes were burning at her, golden, leonine, inaccessible. Then suddenly he reached for her. She found herself pressed so close to him that she could feel the frantic pounding of his heart—or was it her own?

"Carisa . . . I needed you, God, how I needed you . . . and you were in New York instead of where you belonged. . . ."

His hand had slid down her back, to the heavy hoops and bustle. "Take off those damned things," he whispered hoarsely. "I don't want to feel whalebone . . . I want to feel you. Warm, living flesh. . . ."

His mouth was on hers, forcing her lips apart. His tongue searched her mouth with urgency. "Carisa . . . My Carisa . . . God help me, God help both of us. . . ."

12

June, 1855. It arrived sumptuously, cloaked in the vibrant greens of early summer in Connecticut. Carisa, walking on the graveled paths of Hearts-ease, or pausing at a window to gaze at birds winging against a flawless sky, felt as if she had somehow wandered into the wrong month. June should not be so beautiful. Not when she herself felt so suspended, so adrift in time.

Julian, recovered now from his diphtheria, rode his pony along the paths of Hearts-ease at breakneck speed, until Katherine fretted and Adam threatened to take the animal away.

A letter had arrived from Richard Sands. *Do you really think, Mrs. Hartshorn, that you can keep my performers whom you so boldly stole? However, I must compliment you on the adroitness of your thievery. . . .*

The Phillips Circus left on its first season's tour, departing with a purposeful bustle, an air of sadness and excitement. Carisa had hated to see it go. She had watched the caravan rolling down the dirt road until the last cloud of dust had settled, a knot in her throat as unwieldy and dry as hemp rope. If it had not been for her accident, she, too, might be traveling with those wagons. . . .

You'll have to keep one thought in your mind, and one only—your show. Richard Sands' words mocked her. *You'll have to live it, eat it, sleep it, and immerse yourself in it. And give up for it, too. . . .*

178

Give up being with the show itself? The thought was a hurtful one. Yet she knew that this was the way it was to be.

The spring itself had been a grim one. Carisa had been so uncomfortable with her pregnancy that she seldom could ride in the carriage, and Dr. Arthur had cautiously confirmed her prediction: he believed she was indeed to bear twins. There had been fighting and killing in Kansas over the issue of slavery—the newspapers wrote of "Bleeding Kansas," and, in late May, of the murders of five proslavers, committed by a fanatic named John Brown.

Adam had to make a trip to New York on railroad business, and during his three-week stay there he also called upon Carisa's father, to deliver yet another invitation for John Phillips to come to New London.

"I'm sorry to tell you that he refused me," Adam told her when he returned. He had arrived home in an oddly taciturn mood.

"Refused," Carisa repeated dully. They were eating breakfast and now she prodded with a fork at her plateful of eggs and creamed cod on toast. "I had hoped . . . if you yourself talked with him, you could get him to see reason."

"Reason!" Adam gave a short laugh. "If the infamous John Brown is a fanatic, I suppose your father is cut out of the same bolt of cloth. He, too, has determination which is unshakable."

"Yes. I know." Carisa toyed with her fork, poking it at the sunny yellow of her eggs. Silence drifted between them. "Is your agent coming this morning?" she asked at last.

"Oh, I suppose so," Adam sighed. "There is much work piled up. We are hiring on two new crews this week, and a third ship, the *Gypsy*, is ready to be launched."

Carisa nodded. "Why didn't you ever go to sea, Adam?" something made her ask.

Adam regarded her, his eyes focused on her as if he were seeing her for the first time this morning. Golden lights, she noticed, sparkled in their depths.

179

"I did go to sea."

"You did?" She dropped her fork and stared at him, startled. "But you never said. . . ."

"I suppose I didn't." Abruptly Adam's eyes had darkened, and he pushed away his coffee cup. "At eighteen I ran away against my mother's wishes, for she had made me promise I would never go. My father died at sea, you know, as did an elder brother, whom you never met."

"Oh . . . I'm sorry. . . ."

"He lived as he wanted to live, Carisa. As for myself, I enjoyed it . . . for a year . . . the whales, the danger, the excitement. Until one day a friend of mine, Elihu Scott, a man in the crew whom I'd grown to like, was killed when the whale we were trying to harpoon smacked its flukes against the side of the boat. Elihu was crushed to death. I . . . I was angry. Angry at a fate which could have done that to a man I looked up to. And one day we were in port, in Reykjavik, Iceland, at a saloon there."

Adam fell silent for so long that she thought he had forgotten the story he was telling.

"And then?" she prompted.

"There was a fight," Adam said reluctantly. "A man died. I suppose it wasn't totally my fault. There were many men besides me involved, and we all had had too much to drink. But he had said something ugly about Elihu and I . . ." Adam's voice broke.

"Afterward, he lay there on the floor of that squalid little drinking place, his mouth open and his dead eyes still open, too, still watching me. I had done it, I had helped to cause his death. I and my anger and the sea . . . I suppose it's hard to understand. But I came home after that, Carisa. I never went to sea again."

Carisa stared into her coffee, as if she could see there the kind of young man Adam must have been, full of the Hartshorn passion and temper and idealism.

There was a knock at the door, interrupting her thoughts. Nelly had brought the mail, a small stack of letters for Adam and two letters for Carisa.

One, she saw, was from Rolf, and the other was in

the carefully rounded handwriting of Anna. She tore open Rolf's letter first and skimmed it rapidly. The Phillips Circus, he told her, was doing well. In several cities they had had to turn away customers. In a small town near Hartford they had been "in donaker," with a poor location. (Carisa smiled as she read this: in circus parlance, donaker meant "toilets.") Two horses, he wrote, had suffered from quarter-crack, but had been reshod to take care of the problem. There had been mud to mire down the wagons, but Rolf had managed to hire a farmer and his oxen to help pull them out.

The entire tone of the letter was one of barely concealed arrogance. Rolf wished to make it very clear to her that he was doing splendidly and wished no interference on her part.

She tried to quell her irritation, and finished the letter. The last paragraph reminded her that the show would be playing in late August, if all went well, in a village called Cherry Valley, in upstate New York. Did she wish to come and see it there? See for herself just how well it was doing? If so, at that time she could also view her sister Anna in the new equestrian act. For Anna Phillips, it seemed, had telegraphed him in Hartford that she wished to join the show.

Anna? Joining the Phillips Show? Carisa nearly dropped the letter in her astonishment. Adam had not told her—

Quickly she tore open Anna's letter. Phrases leaped up at her as she skimmed it. *Dear Carisa. I knew you would not mind if I decided to join your show . . . changing my mind at the last minit . . . as I write this late at night, Papa and I have had a falling out . . . am glad to be going away, glad! . . . Papa, of course, will not come and I don't know what he will do now . . . suppose you can continue to send him money . . . must hurry as the last packet boat leaves soon . . .*

"Adam?" Carisa felt her fingers begin to perspire on the letter. "Adam, did you know that my sister Anna has left the Hippodrome? When did that happen? Were you not aware of this when you were in New York talking to Papa?"

181

Adam looked uncomfortable. "She was not there when I visited your father. I supposed she was at the Hippodrome, rehearsing. I didn't really ask. Anyway, what does it matter, Carisa? I should think you would be glad. You've written to invite your sister to join the show often enough and now she has done so."

"I *am* glad," Carisa said, wondering why she wasn't. "It's just that . . ." She hesitated.

Adam laughed. "Carisa, Carisa, can't you ever let go of that circus? You hired Rolf Taggart as your manager and gave him full authority on the road. Now he's hired Anna, which you wanted him to do, and you've got a face like a thundercloud. Surely you don't object to your own sister being hired?"

"No. I . . . Oh, you don't understand, Adam!"

She was not sure she understood, herself. Adam would never know how hard it had been for her to see the long string of circus wagons disappearing down the Mohegan Road, going away without her. Duddie had been in the next-to-last wagon, waving at her. And Carisa had waved back, unashamedly sobbing as the form of the misshapen little clown grew smaller and smaller with distance.

Yes, she had given Rolf authority. And, yes, she loved Anna. Still—Why couldn't Rolf have consulted her first? Why couldn't Anna? Why did she have to find it out this way, in a letter, after the thing was already done?

"Come, come, Carisa. Smooth that outraged look off your face and call Nelly to help you dress. We'll take a stroll out to the greenhouse before Mr. Rush arrives."

"I don't want to go to the greenhouse," she said sullenly.

"Then I will go alone." Adam rose, putting his napkin aside.

"No! Adam, I . . . I didn't mean that!" She rushed up to him, awkward because of her size, and flung her arms around him. "I'm sorry I'm cross. It's just that you were away for so very long, and the days have been warm, and I'm so huge and uncomfortable, and . . . and I miss the circus . . ."

182

Adam smiled, the distant look in his eyes nearly gone now, and then he kissed her, his lips soft and searching. Carisa gave herself up to it, letting all her thoughts dissolve like sugar in cream.

"Darling," he whispered into her ear. "You are still beautiful . . . even as you are, enormously pregnant . . . Why didn't I remember it?"

"Why didn't you indeed?" she whispered back playfully. She stood on her tip-toes and blew in the direction of his ear. "Adam?"

"Yes?"

"Adam, Rolf said that the show would play in upper New York near the end of summer. The babies will be born by then . . . I'm sure they will. We could take a steamer to New York City, and then I do believe we could get a train, and then a stage. . . ."

Adam drew back. "My God, Carisa, what are you thinking of? Not travel to New York State! Why, your lying-in will scarcely be over by then. You'll have new-born infants on your hands."

She had set her mouth stubbornly. "I don't care. I want to go, I must! Anna will be there. And the show, I must see how it can be improved, spot any rough areas. . . ."

"I tell you I won't consent to it."

She slid her arms up over the bulk of Adam's shoulders, knowing that the lace-trimmed *écru* silk dressing gown she wore fell back provocatively from the white flesh of her arm. She gave him her most appealing smile.

"Please, darling? For my sake? I promise you it won't harm the babies. We'll hire wet-nurses and they'll have the very best of care while we're gone. Besides, your mother will be here with them."

"No."

"But, Adam . . ." She was twisting inside with a strange, angry, stubborn feeling which could not be quelled.

"I said no, Carisa, and I meant it. You haven't even given birth yet, and here you are already thinking of

183

leaving your children. Is that the sort of mother you're going to be?"

She slapped him. The sound of her palm cracking against flesh was loud in the room, and already there was a red mark on Adam's face. Almost instantly he leaped toward her and pinioned her arms behind her.

"Never do that again, Carisa. Never. Or I won't answer for myself. I never hit a woman before and I don't wish to. But you tempt me. . . ."

"Hit me back, then. Go ahead!" she defied him. Her eyes blazed at him. "But I'll tell you this, Adam. Babies or not, you let me buy that circus and now you have got to let me run it. One or two trips a season is surely not too much to ask. And I do ask it. I intend to go to New York State, do you hear me? You may accompany me or not, as you wish. *But I'm going.*"

He stared at her for a moment. Then he released her and slammed out of the room, the door banging behind him. Carisa sank into a chair, trembling. For an instant she had thought she heard Richard Sands' laughter, mocking.

"I'm sorry," she whispered to Adam as they went in to luncheon. "I shouldn't have done it. Slapped you, I mean. But I still want to go to New York and I'm not going to apologize for that."

Adam touched her lightly. Quick to anger, he was also quick to make up, and their quarrels seldom lasted even a few hours.

"I'm sorry, too." He hesitated. "You're going to be a good mother, Carisa. You're very warm-hearted, and even Julian is beginning to like you, I think. I should never have said what I did."

He was apologizing. Abruptly Carisa felt her eyes moisten, her heart begin to leap with sudden happiness.

"I . . . I love you, Adam," she whispered.

"What?" He stared down at her, his eyes filled with an odd, stunned look of disbelief.

"I said that I love you," she repeated, surprised herself at these words which had popped out of her.

"Do you, Carisa?" His voice was suddenly cold. His

184

expression withdrawn, he took her arm and led her into the dining room, holding her with formal care, as if she had been a stranger.

After the noon meal, Adam was again closeted with his agent, Mr. Rush, and Katherine announced that she intended to pay a call on Eliza, who was in bed with a summer lung complaint.

"Then I think I will take the small surrey," Carisa said. "I want to go into town and see what sort of lace I can find. I've had an idea for a new equestrienne costume for next year, and. . . ."

"What?" Katherine was horrified. "Go into town in your condition? Jounced and bounced around in the surrey? I thought you were so uncomfortable."

"I am." Carisa hesitated, flushing. Then she thought of Adam's cold face when she had told him she loved him, and felt quite sullen and rebellious. "But the ride won't be long, and I . . . I really want to get out," she added lamely. "I have to."

"Well, you shouldn't. It's disgraceful, to flaunt your belly about the city as if you were a common seaman's wife! People will surely talk."

Carisa reddened further. "Let them! I hate being imprisoned here. That's what I feel like . . . as if I were in jail."

"Nonsense. Hate it or not, all women of our station stay at home when they are in their last few months of pregnancy. I knew I should not have countenanced your trip to New York . . . it gave you ideas. Perhaps you circus folk have the habit of indulging in such flagrant displays, but decent people most certainly do not."

"I don't care. I'm strong, I'm healthy, and if I wear my hoops high and adjust my mantle properly, no one will know."

"*I* will know." Katherine gave Carisa the firmest of looks. "You are to spend this afternoon quietly. Taking a nap, as any sensible woman should."

Seething inwardly, Carisa saw her mother-in-law to the door. Then she went upstairs to her office to look through her correspondence. In ten minutes she had dashed off two letters and read two more.

Then she tossed her pen to the desk. She would go! Katherine—and, yes, Adam, too—expected her to sit here at Hearts-ease like an enormous placid cow, content in her breeding. Well, it wasn't in her personality to be placid. She needed activity, she needed hard work, the sight of a face which did not belong to Katherine or Nelly or one of the other servants.

The afternoon was hot and humid, and Carisa was soon perspiring under the heavy layers of clothing, and the added mantle. But she didn't care. She felt like a child which has escaped some onerous chore. She had even left Nelly behind. Only Jim, the driver, was with her, and thankfully he was the taciturn sort.

The day, she decided, was lovely even if it was hot. And, as they rattled into the town of New London itself, she caught glimpses of water through trees and buildings, sudden vistas of shipyards, mills and warehouses across the glittering expanse of Winthrop Cove. Oh, it was a beautiful day.

And even the sight of a blind beggar sitting with his cup under a tree, his face hideously scarred from some accident, could not spoil her sense of runaway pleasure. She bade Jim stop the surrey and gave the man two dollars in coins. She was rewarded by his delighted face as he bit the silver to see if it were real.

Happily, forgetting all of her problems for once, Carisa strolled in and out of the stores. In an importers' shop she bought a fine large Khorasan rug for their bedroom because its gay, mingled colors appealed to her. She ordered it to be delivered later.

In a small shop run by a seaman's widow she examined lace and at last bought twenty yards of assorted trim, to be experimented with on the filmy costume she had in mind. She also chose a selection of buttons—glass, pearl, horn, ivory—which could be used for costumes.

Lastly she bought a bolt of expensive lavender silk for herself. Let Adam call her extravagant! She was so, she supposed, but today she didn't even care. If she had seen other bolts of fabric she would have bought them too.

It was as she was emerging from the widow's shop that she bumped into another woman on her way in. Carisa stepped backward—the impact had tilted up her hoop awkwardly—and then shock pounded through her as she saw who the woman was.

"Poll Henry!"

Poll's eyes flew open for an instant as wide as Carisa's own, but quickly a film seemed to close down over them, and she gazed at her former mistress defiantly.

Carisa could only stare back at her. In servant's garb, Poll had possessed a wild, thin beauty. But today she had a vivid flamboyance which made her stand out like a carnation in a patch of grass. Her gown was red— brilliant bloom-red—with a tight bodice which revealed a jutting bustline. A bosom, Carisa noted quickly, which surely must be padded out with ruffles, for Poll had certainly never possessed such curves before.

The dress, she saw further, had been expensive, and was lavishly trimmed with rows of flounces and lace insertions. Where, she wondered, could Poll possibly have gotten the money to buy such a creation?

And then she remembered. The money Adam said he had given the girl to leave New London.

She could feel the angry color rising in her cheeks. But, sensing the widow's curiosity, she stepped out of the doorway of the shop, pulling Poll with her to the shade of a big oak which spread its branches over the dusty road. Anyone who looked at them would merely see two well-dressed women out for a stroll, she thought grimly.

"Poll, what are you doing here?" she demanded as soon as they were safely under the concealment of the wide branches. "I thought you were to leave town."

"Was I?"

Poll tilted her face back, her eyes slitted with amusement. *Oh, I satisfied him. I pleased him more than you ever could. I made him moan and writhe with pleasure* . . . The memory of that taunting voice slithered into Carisa's mind. She felt as if she would be sick.

187

"Yes, you were to leave! Adam . . . my husband gave you sufficient funds to take you far away from here, and you assured him that you would go!"

"I did not assure him of anything, other than that I would use his money well. And so I have."

Carisa eyed the carnation-red gown. "Yes, I certainly do see *that*."

Poll's fingers smoothed the shiny fabric. "You've got no call to be so sarcastic and high with me. You're no better than me. Not one whit better."

"You accepted my husband's money. You promised to leave New London. Now I must insist that you do so at once, today. For Julian's sake."

"I don't have to."

"Why . . . why, you certainly do. If you don't I. . . ."

"You'll what?" Poll laughed. "You can't tell me what to do any more, Mrs. Adam Hartshorn. I don't work for you now. If your husband was fool enough to give me that money, it's his problem."

"But you must leave this town!"

"And I tell you I won't. I bought a house, do you hear me? A good, solid house, and I'm furnishing it up real splendid. Perhaps you'd like to come and visit me sometime!"

Again Poll laughed, tilting back her head and pealing out greats gusts of sound.

Carisa stepped backward in dismay. A house furnished splendidly? And why was Poll laughing so raucously, as if she had played an enormous joke?

"Oh . . . Oh . . ." Poll gasped at last, as Carisa did not speak. "I'm getting my sisters to work with me there . . . Ma's died, so they might as well . . . and maybe I can get you, too. Oh, yes, once you drop that brat, you might come to town and work for me. You'd be a fine one, you would, with that yellow hair of yours. And maybe you know some special circus tricks."

Now, at last, Carisa understood. She stood stock-still, the blood pounding through her veins.

"Don't you ever say such a thing to me again! Don't you dare!"

188

"I will if I want." Poll's face had reddened with fury. "You little circus harlot!"

But Carisa, her distended belly bobbing painfully, had already whirled about and fled in the direction of the parked surrey, waiting near a hitching post a half-block away. And all the while she ran, she could hear Poll's curses, trailing after her.

Carisa had arrived home, to face Katherine's scolding and Adam's displeasure with defiance. On the following day, Adam Hartshorn went to see Poll Henry. He had little trouble in locating her; a former neighbor was happy to inform him where the troublesome young Henry girls had gone.

The woman shook her head, double chins wobbling. "If you ask me, them girls are up to no good. They've barely laid their Ma in her grave and already they're up and out of here without so much as a good-bye."

She gave him garrulous directions, then ducked her head when Adam thrust a coin into her hand. "Yep," she told him. "Like I say, that young Poll, she's the worst of 'em. The others, they're pretty enough but mostly simple. But Poll, she's smarter than any of 'em. Buying a big house like she was gentry! Well, I got my ideas why she did that. And it ain't for living like the quality, neither."

Adam found the house with little trouble, and was struck by the fact of its apparent isolation. About forty years old, it had been built on a hill in the midst of a small but dense grove of trees; one day the city would claim this area for its own, but that had not happened yet. The house, brick, square, solid, also boasted a large carriage barn immediately behind it. A large, unkempt forsythia hedge added the last touch of privacy. A dozen patrons could be accommodated here with little visibility, Adam thought, especially if they arrived and left after dark.

He had driven the small surrey himself, and now he fastened the chestnut gelding to the hitching post conveniently provided. He proceeded up the bricked walk, which was overgrown with weeds. From inside the

189

house came the staccato sounds of a hammer. As Adam neared the front door, a glazier's wagon pulled up behind his own surrey. Two men began unloading large sheets of glass, each swaddled in burlap for protection.

Adam knocked. Almost instantly the door was pulled open by the girl he recognized as Poll's younger sister, Dora.

"Go to the back, whyn't you, you darned fool . . ." She stopped, her mouth dropping open, as she realized that Adam was not the glazier.

"I wish to talk with your sister," he said.

Dora's fourteen-year-old face turned sullen. "She's in the other room. She's busy."

"Then tell her to come out."

"Don't know if she'd want to."

"I think she will." Adam's voice rasped out the words, and he narrowed his eyes at the girl.

Dora shot out her lower lip. She shoved back a strand of lank hair from her forehead, and then strolled insolently toward a door which opened off the large entrance hall to Adam's right. She opened it and slammed it behind her.

Adam waited. The house was obviously in the midst of redecorating, for a number of large, ornate pieces of furniture had been shoved into a corner of the big hall. Four rolled-up rugs were stacked nearby, and a bolt of red velvet had been flung on top, spilling out heavy color. Jammed in with these things was a new pianoforte, of a type made in New London itself.

The door to the right flung open. Adam glimpsed a room stripped down to bare walls and floor, and then Poll herself emerged. She wore black, her gown smudged with dust and her hair piled carelessly on her head. She looked thin and imperious and oddly foreign.

"Well? How do you like it?" Her eyes mocked him. "I'm sorry that you had to come so soon, before everything is finished. It's going to be very elegant."

"I thought you promised to leave town," he said coldly. He had to jam his fists into his pockets in order to restrain himself from plunging forward and shaking the girl until her teeth chattered.

190

"Did I? Did I tell you that, Adam?" Poll's smile flashed at him. "I don't think I did. Come." She approached him with a rustle of flounces and taffeta, a smell of some musky perfume. He found that she had grasped his arm and was pulling him through the door and into the bare room. "Come and see what I am going to do in here, Adam."

With one movement of his arm, he could have pushed her away. But he did not. Instead, he followed her, the exotic smell of her strong in his nostrils.

"This parlor," she said, gesturing, "is going to be the talk of New London. It's going to be completely lined in mirrors, each one encased in the finest birds-eye maple. See?" She pointed to the floor, where long lengths of wood were stacked. "The maple is already here, it came yesterday. Gentlemen such as yourself will come here to disport themselves in the most discreet of atmospheres. I have a ballroom at the rear . . . aren't I lucky, the chairs were already in the house? . . . and I plan to provide good food, conversation, music, and, of course, other things as well. . . ."

"I want you out of here."

"Do you?" Her eyes danced at him; he had never noticed how dark they were, like boot-buttons, like nubs of coal, without highlights.

"Yes, damn you. *I want you out.*"

"And I tell you, Adam, that I'm not going. No one can make me, no one, not even that harlot wife of yours. I'll admit you gave me the money to buy this place . . . more fool you. But I'll give you a percent of my proceeds, if you'd like." Poll threw back her head and laughed. "How would that be? Mr. Adam Hartshorn, taking a share of the proceeds from a place like this. . . ."

Adam took a step toward her. Blood was pounding in his forehead until his head ached. This did not even seem real, he thought dully. It was like some fantastic whiskey dream. Like that night in the saloon in Reykjavik so many years ago.

"I don't want any of your money," he heard his voice grate.

"You'll have it if I give it to you . . . or would you rather I paid it to your son? I'll wager young Julian might appreciate it when he's old enough. . . ."

Adam sprang toward her so rapidly that she had no time to evade him. His fingers clenched themselves around her neck, the soft, cloying flesh of her.

"Leave my son out of this, you little bitch!" He could feel her struggling under his grasp like a wild vixen. Dimly he was aware that her fingernails were clawing him, that the sounds of hammering in the background had stopped, that someone—the sister?—was peering at them from around a corner.

His hands did not seem to belong to him.

"Let . . . go . . ." Poll gasped. Her mouth opened and closed, sucking in harsh air. Her face was darkening, the tongue pushed forward. Her nails dug frantically at him.

Adam felt perspiration soak his body as thoroughly as if he had stepped under a bucket of water. His fingers released themselves, one by one. He took a step backward, sickened at what he had almost done.

He had almost killed her. By God, he had almost murdered her, and in front of a witness. He swallowed hard, choking back hot, metallic-tasting bile. He had almost strangled this woman.

Poll staggered away from him, half-tripping on the lengths of maple, and caught onto the jamb of the door for support.

"Get out of here," she said thickly. "And don't come back. If you ever do, if you ever try to close me down, I'm going to tell the whole world about that little devil of a son of yours. And about what *you* did."

"You wouldn't . . . Not Julian, he's not. . . ." Adam could barely talk. He stared at her, at the dark, wild, frightened face, and felt the cold sweat running down his ribs and back.

"You don't know that boy very well, do you, Adam? Well, let me tell you something." Poll's voice was low and thick; Adam had to force back another wave of nausea. "Beautiful he is, like an angel in a painting,

192

almost too beautiful to be real. But he is a devil. Do you hear that? *He is one.*"

"If he is, you made him that way!"

Her eyes were so black that he could see no pupils in them. "Perhaps. And perhaps not. All I do know is this, Adam. You tried to kill me. And my sister was a witness. And if you don't let me alone, I'm going to talk. Just imagine all the things I could say. And do you know who'd listen? All of those fancy people, the Coits and the Kords and those. Oh, Lord, would they listen!"

Adam took a step backward. Then another one. Dreamlike, he was aware that a door had banged somewhere at the rear of the house. A cheerful whistle told him that the glazier had arrived with his first load of glass.

The man would have been a second witness, he told himself sickly. If—Dear God. He felt as if his clothes and undergarments had been drenched in moisture.

"Very well." Was that his own voice, so hoarse and harsh and strange? "Very well. Stay then, stay here and ply your trade. If you can. But leave me and my family out of it. Don't send me any of your money, and don't ever dare to mention my son's name again . . . ever. If you do, I'll come back here, and I will kill you."

Poll's face had attained its normal sallow color again. She wiped her palms on the shiny black fabric of her skirts. "You won't," she said. "You won't kill me, Adam. You haven't it in you."

"Don't ever test me."

The glazier pushed his way into the reception hall from the back, maneuvering the awkward section of mirror glass. He gave Adam an incurious look.

"Say, Miss, where'd you want this here stuff to go?"

"There." Poll pointed to the empty room, the parlor-to-be.

Adam left.

13

It had been months since Carisa had had one of the prophetic dreams. Thus, she was unprepared for the one which came suddenly one hot night in June.

This dream was of the circus. In it, Carisa found herself seated in a large brick barn, watching an equestrienne rehearsal—a solo act. The performer was a tall, lithe girl of 16, poised effortlessly on her horse, her bare arms lifted to reveal their clean, young lines. Around and around the ring they went, the girl pirouetting and swaying with the rhythm of the horse.

Carisa found herself leaning forward, straining to see who the girl was. She had something of Stephana's bold beauty. Yet Carisa was certain that she was not Stephana.

Then who was she? Each time the girl passed the wooden bench where Carisa sat, she changed her pose, averting her face so that Carisa could not see it.

Carisa awoke to find that her heart was hammering, her body covered with perspiration. Adam breathed softly beside her, deep in sleep.

She lay staring into the darkness, conscious of a vague feeling of discomfort. Her back ached, that was it. She twisted about and tried to rub it, only to find that the ache was stronger than ever, and that it had moved down now, to include her pelvic area.

Grimly she tensed herself against the cramps, and tried to think of something else. The circus . . . next year she would see to it that they built more parade wagons. Elias Dunnett would have to hire more workmen, or else they would have to patronize a skilled wagonmaker in New York.

And costumes . . . she clenched her jaws together to avoid crying out as another cramp gripped her, stronger than the last one. Costumes, color, glitter, display . . . how important these were in the circus, where so much depended on illusion. Thank heavens that Mrs. Wiggins was so skilled with her sewing machine. She could copy anything, and invent her own patterns, even for something as exotic as a ballet skirt or a pair of tights. . . .

Pain pushed at her. It felt as if a tent stake were being driven into her vitals. Involuntarily Carisa twisted about on the mattress, moaning.

"Carisa?" Adam stirred. "Darling? What is it? Are you all right?"

"I . . . I don't know . . . I think this is it, Adam. I think the babies are coming."

"Babies . . ." His voice was fuzzy, blurred with sleep. Then suddenly he flung back the covers and sat up. "My God . . . I'd better get Dr. Arthur!"

Adam left in a clatter of hastily-donned boots.

Carisa tossed and turned on the bed, letting the contractions pick her up and shake her in their iron claws. Soon Katherine bustled in to take charge, gray hair braided for the night, black dressing gown cinched tightly about her waist.

"First babies usually take a long time to be born, but I don't think these are going to," her mother-in-law announced crisply. She was sorting through bed linens. "Indeed, these are going to come fast. I might have expected a circus girl to have a baby as a cow drops a calf!"

Carisa managed to gasp a reply. "When it comes to giving birth, I don't believe *any* woman is a lady. Even you, Mother Hartshorn!"

"Hmmm!" Katherine snorted. But she busied herself about the bedroom, preparing for the birth, and said no more.

An hour later, the twins were born. They were delivered by a sleepy Dr. Arthur, who was annoyed because he had been roused from his sleep and further irritated because the cup of coffee offered him by Katherine upon his arrival had cooled before he had had a chance to drink it.

They were a boy and a girl, fraternal twins who arrived without problem. The boy howled lustily, his face empurpled, his little fists clenched. The girl gave a few mewling cries, and then lay quietly, her eyes gazing about her as if she could already see.

"Well, they're a month early, and they're small, but they're well formed, and they should do," Dr. Arthur told her. "As for you, Mrs. Hartshorn," he added tartly. "At your next confinement you'd better call me at the first pain, or you'll have to give birth as best you can."

Dawn had begun to lighten the sky outside the bedroom window, and somewhere Carisa could hear the excited morning twitter of birds. On the dirt road wheels squeaked, and horses' hooves clopped; the milk wagon was making deliveries. As Carisa lay exhausted, Katherine and Nelly bustled about the room, washing the babies and sponging Carisa's face. They also changed the bedsheets, so that when Adam came into the room, he would not have to view any of the untidiness of birth. Dr. Arthur, who felt himself above such activity, had already gone downstairs to have his breakfast.

"There," Katherine said, her harsh voice softer than usual. "The babies are all washed and wrapped in flannel, ready to be seen."

Carisa gave a pale, tired smile. "Good. I want to hold them, please. And . . . and to look at them."

Carefully, almost reverently, she peeled back the flannel wrapped around the infants, to reveal tiny, red limbs, arms, genitals. She swallowed tightly, forcing back sudden tears. How beautiful they were. How small and perfect and beautiful.

Adam came striding into the room and came directly to the bed. His tawny hair was tousled, his eyes redrimmed from lack of sleep. Carisa had just finished rewrapping the babies in their flannel and now held one in the crook of each arm.

"Carisa! Carisa, my God, are you all right?"

"I'm fine," she whispered, touched by his concern.

She stared up at his face, strong, rugged, seeing the fierce golden eyes, the tawny hair.

"I can't count the men I know here in New London who've lost at least one wife to childbirth," Adam whispered. "Thank God it didn't happen to you."

Katherine and Nelly had tactfully withdrawn from the

room, and now Adam knelt beside the bed, to take her cold hands in his warm ones.

Carisa's voice was low. "What do you think of them, Adam? Our children!"

He looked down at the babies. With a forefinger he reached out to touch one tiny infant hand. "They're beautiful, of course." His voice was husky. "Like their mother."

Carisa looked at her husband, his features curved and tender now with emotion. She loved his face, the thought came to her suddenly. Loved the lines of it, the goodness in it, the gracious mouth which could laugh so easily, or flare just as quickly into temper.

A pang pierced her, as she thought of herself, lying in the bedroom after she had arrived here, solemnly telling Adam that she did not love him. What had been wrong with her? She *had* loved him then; or had been beginning to.

"Adam . . ." she began. "Adam, there is something I must tell you. . . ."

"Yes, Carisa?" Adam had reached out and taken the little girl in his arms, and now held and rocked her, his face bent to the infant's as if he saw an ineffable vision there. Then the girl started to whimper and the boy began to cry, in huge, lusty, demanding sobs.

As if this were a cue, Katherine bustled back into the room. "You're going to have to leave now, Adam, while your wife takes a much-needed rest. And I've got to go and have the wet-nurses brought up. This little fellow here is furious with hunger!"

"Already?" Adam was laughing. He bent down and gave Carisa a kiss on the forehead, his lips brushing hers as softly as moth's wings. "Two fine children! And if you can produce two more the next time, why, we'll be well on our way to having a huge family!"

"Two more!" Carisa exclaimed in horror. Then, as she saw that he was joking, she gave a weak laugh. And so the moment passed. And the words of love she had been going to speak were not said.

They decided to name the girl Victoria Katherine, after the queen and her grandmother. The boy they named Matthew, after Adam's father. Two wet-nurses had been hired, both of them women from New London who had recently given birth and still had milk in their breasts. One, Persis Gibbon, had lost her infant, and the other, fat Emily Fletch, planned to bring her own baby with her and feed both.

Carisa defied Katherine's admonitions, and was up and walking about on the second day. By the eighth day she was working in her office and taking short walks outdoors, thankful for the fact that her legs had mended sufficiently for her to do so. She would never be swift and lithe as she had been before the accident, but she was no cripple either. And now the running of a circus and the care of two infants was going to require all of her strength.

"I never saw such a thing!" Katherine cried one morning when she discovered Carisa bent over a letter she was writing to Rolf. "I lay in bed a full two months with each of my boys. And Madeleine Kord was abed even longer with her Calvin."

Carisa put down her quill pen and smiled at her mother-in-law. "But I feel fine. Why should I stay in bed when I don't need to? Besides," she added, "Mother Hartshorn, the women of the circus can't afford to pamper themselves. They give birth to their children and then, just as soon as they are able, they're back in the ring again, performing."

You are not in the circus now, Katherine would have retorted six months ago. Now, to Carisa's surprise, she hesitated and then nodded.

"Perhaps you are right," she said slowly. "I can remember how I chafed at being kept in my bed after Adam was born. It was October, and so lovely. I wanted to go for a ride in the carriage and see the colored leaves, and I wasn't permitted."

Katherine settled a small household matter, and then withdrew from Carisa's office, the chatelaine around her waist jingling on its chain exactly as ever. But after she had gone, Carisa sat staring down at her half-written letter. Katherine had altered. In a small way, perhaps, but it *was* a change. It seemed that no one, not even the middle-aged, remained the same.

Carisa felt oddly shaken, as if she had learned a new truth.

The babies quickly developed personalities. Putting aside her office work, Carisa spent a good part of each day with them. She insisted on bathing them herself, and would sit for hours rocking the girl, Vicki, who was colicky and fussy, and cried often.

She was already regretting her decision not to nurse them herself, especially when she saw the dreamy, pleasured expression on Persis Gibbons' face as she fed Vicki. But, as Katherine had pointed out, Carisa could hardly be expected to nourish two, and if they had to hire one wet-nurse, they might as well engage a pair. Besides, Carisa admitted to herself privately, she did relish the thought of the freedom she would have. She was still determined to go to New York in August.

When she was not fussing, the girl, Vicki, was a rather pale and quiet baby. She had a little soft, fuzzy head in which a pulse could be seen, plainly beating away. Her wide, grayish eyes stared at Carisa like those of a little bird.

Matt, on the other hand, was lusty and loud in everything that he did. He bellowed for his food, and as soon as the nipple of the wet-nurse was offered him, he would clamp down on it like a voracious leech. He was very active, waving his hands and feet in vigorous flings. Yet when Carisa rocked him, he could fell asleep, instantly and completely.

There were two flaws to mar her joy in her children these days. One of them was the knowledge that Poll Henry, established now in her big brick house, awaited customers there as a lithe young spider might await flies. The very thought that Poll was still here in New London made Carisa feel soiled. That mocking, raucous voice, those taunts, drifting toward her on the dusty air. . . .

The other flaw was Julian.

Julian, out of school now for the summer, and at

199

home with Miss Best, the governess Adam had recently hired for him, had grown thin and sullen. He disliked the babies, and had been caught once by Miss Best peering over Matt's bassinet with a handful of gravel in his fist. He had been intending, the woman accused shrilly, to drop the stones into the baby's mouth.

Carisa scolded Julian and tried to stifle her horror. Surely Julian was only jealous of the babies? This was a normal enough emotion, she knew, felt by hundreds of small children at the birth of a brother or a sister. Yet somehow, the thought did not comfort.

One day when the babies were three weeks old, Carisa approached Julian with the intent of reading a story to him. She was rewarded with a savage kick in the knee. The attack was sudden, and the hard leather toe of Julian's boot sent waves of agony rocketing through Carisa's leg.

"Go away!" he shrilled at her as she staggered backward, gasping from pain. "Go away, ugly Carisa! I hate you! You took my Poll away and I hate you!"

"Julian!" Carisa stared at him, at the young boy grown suddenly lanky and sinewy. She tried to push back her own anger, to calm herself.

"You said Poll was bad and you took her away and I hate you!" Julian's eyes were two blazing blue stones.

"But, Julian, it was only for your own good. Don't you see? She . . ." But her voice faltered. What could she possibly say to those hard, adult-like, hating eyes? And, she thought bitterly, she and Adam had actually thought him safely through the crisis of losing his nursemaid!

Without waiting for her to finish her sentence, Julian stalked away outdoors. Carisa, peering through the parlor window, could see him stumping toward the carriage house and stables, his head down, his face in a scowl, boots kicking at gravel.

He would ride his pony, she knew, push it at breakneck pace through the riding paths which bisected the hemlock forest, jumping the forbidden, mossy stone fence which cut across the circus path. Twice he had been punished by Adam for doing this: the pony was too light, and untrained for jumping. But Carisa knew that Julian did it anyway. Twice, on her way back from the circus quarters, she had seen him.

Three days later, on a muggy, humid July morning in 1855, Carisa came downstairs to the parlor and found Julian sitting in Eugenie Hartshorn's chair.

Ever since Adam had told her the grisly story of the woman who had stabbed her infant, Carisa had been meaning to put the chair in the attic. She discounted most of Poll's tale as nonsense, of course—the "evil smell" Poll had spoken of was probably nothing more than the peculiar sharp, moldy smell which old furniture often gets. Still, the story had chilled her.

The days, however, had passed, and she had forgotten about the chair. Thus she was quite unprepared for the moment when she walked into the parlor to find Julian sitting in it, rocking furiously, his hands gripping the worn, wooden arms.

Carisa paused, forgetting the book she had to fetch. There was something wrong about the way the boy rocked. He did it so grimly, so intensely. And his head was cocked to one side, as if he were listening to something that Carisa could not hear.

Listening? Oh, nonsense, Carisa told herself quickly. But she felt a light shiver go over her shoulder blades, and as she stepped into the room, she thought she could smell an odd odor.

Not mold. Not old furniture. But . . . something. It was, she thought rapidly, like nothing she had ever smelled before. *Oh, the grave, of course. Dead things. And blood and corruption and rot. Horrid things like that* . . . She could almost hear Poll's voice, full of relish.

"Julian!" Without stopping to think, Carisa darted forward and grasped at the boy's forearm. "Julian, you must stop rocking like that."

He looked at her coldly and braced his body against her. His fingers were clenched hard around the chair arms, his boots hooked around one of the rungs.

"No. I won't."

201

"Julian, you must! That chair . . . it isn't good for you to sit in," she finished lamely.

A smile curved his lips, bringing back, for an instant, the old, angelic beauty of his face. "Why not? Because of the ghost? Are you afraid of the ghost, Carisa?"

Carisa felt something pulling in her, something tense and tight like a thread of yarn stretched between two nails.

"Yes, Julian," she said quietly. "I am afraid. Now, please get out of that chair at once."

"I tell you I won't! And you'd better not make me." He pouted. "Now you've come in and spoiled it all."

"Spoiled it?"

"I was listening to *her*. I heard her crying. She was talking and telling me things. How she killed her baby. She stabbed it, you know. Poll told me. She stabbed it right in its belly . . . whack! whack!" Julian made slashing motions, his eyes fixed downward as if a bleeding baby really did lie in his lap.

Carisa suppressed a shiver of dread. "Julian . . ."

"Oh, be still, will you, Carisa? I don't like you."

Something—was it the boy's dislike, or her own fear? —something made Carisa kick out at the rocker, so that the boy was thrown off balance. As he started to tilt forward, she grasped him by the arm and pulled him away.

The chair rocked for a moment by itself.

"You did it!" Julian screamed. "You took me away! Carisa, I hate you! I hate you, hate you, hate you!"

She was shaking all over, but she forced her voice to remain even. "I don't hate you, Julian, I like you very much. And I'm sorry I had to pull you out of that chair, but it was necessary. I hope someday when you're older you'll understand just why I had to."

For a moment their glances locked, and then the congested, furious red of Julian's face slowly faded to normal.

"It doesn't matter," he said in an ordinary voice. "She's gone now. You made her go, Carisa. You'll be sorry."

She was frightened by his certainty, but she forced her own tone to remain calm and pleasant.

"Julian, I think you're letting your imagination run away with you. There was no woman in that chair . . . nothing but you and your own make-believe. Come upstairs now, and I'll find Miss Best for you. It's time for your lessons, I would think."

Julian followed her willingly enough, and after he was safely turned over to the middle-aged governess, Carisa found Gaines and told him to have the chair taken out to the kitchen garden, chopped into pieces with an axe, and burned.

They were going to go to New York. In a frenzy of excitement, Carisa packed and made her plans. Not only had she persuaded Adam to accompany them, but they would also tour with the show for a full week, joining it at a village called Cherry Valley, and then continuing with the show on its southward swing.

"Adam, you won't regret it, I promise you," she babbled, over-talkative in her joy, for she had not really expected him to accede. "There is nothing like a circus . . . absolutely nothing like it in the world. And once I see the show in actual performance, I'll be able to assess it better. I'll know what changes to make, and what further plans to start for next year. I'm going to enlarge, you know. In a few years, the Phillips Circus is going to be impressive indeed!"

"I am already impressed by it, Carisa," Adam said dryly. "And even more impressed by your determination in getting all of us there to see it. Don't you realize just what a long, difficult trip it is going to be? Especially for a woman recovering from childbirth?"

"I don't care," she said gaily. "I'd endure anything just to be with my show for a week. Oh, Adam . . ." She threw her arms around him and kissed him on the mouth. "Oh, Adam, I'm *so* happy that you're really letting me do this. And you're coming with me! That makes it even better!"

"If I don't accompany you, you'd probably hop on a

circus wagon and keep right on going, wouldn't you, Carisa?"

Carisa looked away, stifling a feeling of guilt, for when the circus had left, she had had to stifle the wild urge to do just that.

"Why, no," she said. "Adam, how can you think that! Didn't I promise you when we were married that I would stay at home and be a wife to you? And am I not doing just that?"

"Yes, Carisa. You're doing it. You have kept your share of the bargain reasonably well. And I have kept mine. Neither of us should be discontented."

He turned away, then, leaving Carisa to stare after him, her eyes prickling with absurd, unshed tears. Angrily she dabbed at them. Then she busied herself with the packing again. Of course Adam was contented, she assured herself. Surely he had not meant to sound as if he was not. And yet—

Julian, she found, had grown out of all his clothes. Mrs. Wiggins' help had to be enlisted in sewing him more, for Carisa had decided to take him with them. It would be a special treat for him, she reasoned. What boy would not be delighted to be a part of the circus for one full week? Perhaps, she planned, Duddie could be persuaded to rig Julian up in clown costume and let him cavort around the ring in the "clown walk" with the other clowns.

She was also having fittings for a new gown for herself. This was a sand-colored serge traveling dress made with deep flounces, trimmed in black lace which she hoped would withstand the dust of traveling. She was all at once filled with a wild exuberance. Suddenly her life here at home, playing with the babies and writing countless letters in her office, seemed dull, stale. She wanted to go, to move, to travel! To be a real part of the circus! And perhaps, she dreamed, she would even don a costume and ride in some small way in the equestrian act. She hadn't forgotten how.

Adam scotched that notion at once.

"Carisa, remember what you promised me?" His eyes held pity. "You're my wife now, not a performer. Besides, there are your limbs. Thank God you're walking properly now, and I pray that you'll continue to do so. But Dr. Arthur has told me that the tendons in your knees are not very stable and you could have real trouble if you abuse them."

So the subject was closed. Still, when she took her long walks on the circus path or in the nearby hemlock forest, Carisa persisted in her daydreaming. She, Carisa Phillips Hartshorn, dressed in a filmy costume, reclining on the back of a large, muscular, curved-neck horse such as Phoebe had been. . . .

But now she knew that was all it was to be—a fantasy. She would never ride professionally again, not in the circus. She would have to accept her life as it was. But she did have the circus, she consoled herself. That would be her dream now. And it was a dream she would make come true. She knew she could do it— if she just worked hard enough.

One morning, on her way to the unused bedroom which Mrs. Wiggins and her two helpers used for their work space, Carisa paused at the children's nursery to look in on the babies. She found a homey domestic scene.

The fat wet-nurse, Emily Fletch, was asleep in a rocker, snoring heavily. Vicki was still at her breast, her small nose nearly stopped up by the pillowy flesh. Mrs. Fletch's own infant, a chubby boy of six months, lay gurgling in a basket at his mother's feet, and Matt's cradle was by the window.

Carisa went in, thinking to scold the nurse for sleeping. But as she did so the woman, evidently hearing the rustle of Carisa's skirts, awoke herself.

"Oh . . . Oh, me! Here I fell asleep! Poor little Vicki, did she get her fill? Oh, my poor baby."

But the "poor baby" was sound asleep, her pale eyelids fluttering, and an indignant Carisa was about to take her from the nurse when a small noise came from the direction of Matt's cradle. The noise was a hiccup.

Carisa froze. Surely the sound had not been made by Matt, who slept in the cradle, with its skirted flounce, as deeply and fully as he did everything else. Nor did it come from Mrs. Fletch's Timmie, now inspecting his toes with great interest.

There was another hiccup. Then, as Carisa and Mrs. Fletch watched, the bassinet ruffle began to move and sway perilously. Mrs. Fletch let out a little scream.

Carisa rushed forward and snatched up the skirts of the cradle. Beneath it crouched Julian, his short black wool trousers smudged with dust. In his hands he clutched his father's brass letter-opener.

Wildly she remembered the day when she had found Julian in Eugenie Hartshorn's chair. She remembered, too, the stabbing motions he had made, as if a real, bleeding baby were on his lap.

"Julian!" Carisa's voice was high. Anger and horror poured through her. "What are you doing with that?"

"Nothing." He was sullen.

"Well, I'll be," began Mrs. Fletch.

"Please leave the room, Mrs. Fletch, and go to my office. Fetch Persis Gibbons and have her go there, too. And take all the babies with you."

Carisa said this sharply. She waited until the wet-nurse had done as she asked, then, in a low, even voice, she ordered Julian to come out from under the cradle.

Unwillingly, he did so.

"Give that opener to me, please. You know better than to take things from your father's study."

"I didn't take it," he mumbled, his eyes looking their hatred at her.

She slid the opener into her bodice, shivering as she touched its cold metal. Then she gazed at her step-son, at his defiant blue eyes.

"Oh, Julian, Julian, why?" she whispered at last. "Why must you be like this? Why must you hate so?"

He strained away from her, his back stiff, his shoulder blades two hard little points. Where had the baby chubbiness gone? she wondered with a sense of despair. In the past year, Julian's childhood had gone—if, in fact, he had ever had one.

"Don't ever harm my children!" she heard herself say in a shaking voice that she did not recognize as her

206

own. "Don't *ever* hurt them, Julian, because if you do. . . ."

His eyes defied her, and for a moment their glances locked. Julian was a stranger, a hating stranger. Then, abruptly, he looked away, became a boy again, the Julian she knew.

Gloomily she escorted him to his own room and left him in the charge of Miss Best. Then she returned to her office to confront the two frightened wet-nurses.

She issued new and strict orders. The babies were never to be left alone, not even for a moment. Someone was to be with each infant at all times. She herself would see to it that someone was with Julian, as well. And once school started, it would all be easier.

She fixed the blowsy Emily Fletch with a hard look. "And if I ever find you sleeping again when you are with the babies, you'll be dismissed at once, and without reference. Or if you ever leave them alone again, even to visit the privy. Do you understand me?"

"Y-Yes, ma'am." Emily Fletch was ashen.

"Do you understand me, Persis?"

"Oh, yes. Yes, Mrs. Hartshorn."

That night, when they were alone in their bedroom, she told Adam what had happened. As she related this, she could see the angry color wash into his face.

"By God!" He slammed a balled-up fist onto the small table which held their Chelsea porcelain tea service, causing the cups to rattle. "By God, I'm going to get rid of that boy!"

"Get rid of him?" Carisa was ashamed of the rush of relief she felt. "What do you mean, Adam?"

Adam's voice was savage. "I'm going to send him away to school. There's a boys' boarding school in New York—Huddleston's, on Houston Street. I've been asking about it. It's small, but strict."

He went on to explain that, although Julian was young, the school had agreed to take him and to provide the necessary discipline. "What's more, we can enroll him when we go through the city on our way to

207

Cherry Valley to see the circus. We'll combine the two trips."

She was torn with pity and relief. "But, Adam, a boy of ten! No matter what he has done, surely he doesn't deserve to be sent away so young. . . ."

"I must send him, Carisa." She had never seen Adam's face more grim. "He is a clever, wily child, more than a match for any number of wet-nurses or governesses, or even for his own parents. My God, do you think I like doing this? But I haven't any other choice. Unless, of course, you relish the idea of walking into the nursery someday and finding your baby son or daughter lying in her cradle disemboweled."

"Oh. . . !" She recoiled.

"Well might you react with horror. This can be a very ugly and evil world, Carisa. There is a tenement district in New York known as Five Points . . . bad things have happened there. Terrible things. Children killing and being killed. Stabbings. Torturings. And my son . . ." Adam's mouth twisted. "And my son seems cut from the same evil cloth. I want him away from here."

Carisa bit down on her lower lip until her flesh stung.

"Carisa, will you stop looking at me like that? I had hopes for that boy . . . oh, go away, will you? Take a walk or something. Leave me be."

"But, Adam . . ." She put her arms around him.

Savagely he shook her off. "Tonight is one night when I do not want your wifely comforts, pleasant as they are. Get out of here, will you? Go! Just go!"

"Very well."

She grabbed a wool mantle to pull over her shoulders and stumbled out of the room, and outdoors to the darkened greenhouse, there to sit among Katherine's flowers in the moist, earthy darkness. In their bedroom, she knew, Adam was in torment.

Numbly, grimly, her joyous mood completely fled, she completed the last of the travel preparations and dealt with Katherine's protests. The boy didn't need to be sent away to school, his grandmother insisted. A good whipping in the carriage house would soon take care of any notions he might have of attacking the babies.

"New York is not the end of the world, Mother Hartshorn," Carisa said dully. "We can visit him as often as we wish. And Adam insists that he go."

"My son is only going to make things worse by doing this."

"I've tried to tell him. . . ."

"But he won't listen. I know. Adam can be a very stubborn man when he wishes. But this time he is asking for disaster. And I am so afraid that he is going to get it."

Julian himself received the news with a set, blank face. In spite of her resolve, Carisa's heart constricted with pity. She reached out in an attempt to comfort him.

He jerked away from her. "Go away, Carisa. I hate you and I hate Papa and I hate everything here at Hearts-ease. I'll always hate them and you can't stop me."

"Julian . . ."

"Carisa, leave the boy alone," Adam snapped. His eyes were red-rimmed and haunted. "If he wishes to be rude to his step-mother, then surely you shouldn't spare any affection for him. A year or so at school should calm him down a bit. Then we'll think about bringing him back."

Julian was silent.

"Go to your room, son," Adam said. "Go there and think about what you tried to do to your baby brother. Think about it. And try to pray, why don't you? If you can."

The boy whirled about. He fled out of the study and up the staircase. Carisa thought she heard a burst of muffled sobbing at the top, and then there was the clatter of Julian's boots on the upstairs carpet and the slam of his door.

Ten years old, she thought, feeling sick. A little boy.

"Adam," she began. "This is all wrong. We can't do this."

He grasped her arm, his face darkened with anger. "We *must* do it. We can't have him here, you know that.

And for once I don't want to hear any of your pitying and your feeling sorry. I tell you, we can't have the little devil here. He's got to be taught."

Carisa smiled sadly. "I'm afraid, Adam, that he will be."

14

The date set for their departure coincided with the first of an August heat wave. The temperature was in the nineties, the air humid and sticky, the sky porcelain white. Carisa thought she would faint in the heavy serge of the traveling dress Mrs. Wiggins had hurried to sew. Even Nelly looked pale, and Gaines, who would also travel with them, went about with a constant shiny film of perspiration on his forehead.

Julian, too, suffered from the heat. On the morning they left, he went into a rage when Nelly attempted to dress him in his new navy serge suit. He was too hot, he shouted at her. He didn't want to wear his new suit and tie. He wanted to go about in only shirt and pants, like a farm boy he had seen. He hated this trip. He hated school. He hated everything.

They stayed overnight in New York, this time in the splendid St. Nicholas Hotel, with its row of elegant shops and bazaars at street level, its velvet pile carpets, embroidered mosquito nettings, and air of opulent luxury quite different from Mrs. Adair's. The next morning they went to enroll Julian in the school.

This was a three-story building made of white stone, situated on a street which held several other such schools. The structure, rectangular and graceless, was shaped rather like a barn, Carisa thought unkindly.

The master, Mr. Ephraim Huddleston, turned out to be a short, mustached man who walked with a slight limp. His eyes were cold as he gazed at Julian assessingly.

"You needn't worry," he assured Adam. "The boy won't be a problem. We'll see to him."

He took them through the school, and they viewed the dormitory where the boys slept in two even rows of beds; the room, filled with long tables, where they ate; the classrooms, study rooms, small library and games room. It was all very clean, and there were yards, enclosed by high brick fences, where the boys could play games.

As they inspected the largest yard, bare and well-raked, Carisa could hear giggles and laughter wafting over the bricks from a place three buildings away called "The Institution of Messrs. Abbott, for the Education of Young Ladies."

They sipped tea in the headmaster's study while Julian was taken to meet his classmates.

"It's so *bleak*," Carisa whispered to Adam when they had been left alone for a moment. "Oh, Adam, do you think we are doing the right thing?"

Adam looked at her grimly. "Have you forgotten what that little devil tried to do to our babies? Do you forget what he has put us through?"

She hesitated. "No. I haven't forgotten. Still, we should have taken him to see the circus before we left him at the school. All children love the circus, and. . . ."

Adam put down his teacup with a rattle. His hands gripped both of her shoulders, his fingers cutting into her flesh. "I am not a deliberately cruel man, Carisa, no matter what you may think. I believe that this school is the best thing for Julian. It is you who are too soft on the boy. A circus, indeed, after the unspeakable things he has done!"

She flushed. "But . . ."

"I wish to hear no more about it. Julian will receive the discipline he needs here, and he'll be far away from the twins and any harm he can do them. Let that be enough."

Father and son said good-bye stiffly, their faces grim, and in this moment, oddly identical. Fierce amber eyes met equally fierce blue ones.

211

"Julian," Carisa began. "We'll write you letters, we'll come to see you as often as we can. . . ."

But Julian had already turned away, turning toward the playyard where the voices of boys could already be heard.

They took the train north to Albany, then disembarked and boarded a four-horse stagecoach for the fifty-two-mile trip to Cherry Valley. The heat wave continued, baking them within the close confines of the coach. Road dust blew chokingly in the windows, until they swallowed it and could feel it gritty between their teeth. The black lace of Carisa's traveling gown had gone gray.

The coach wound up and down hill along a narrow, dusty, rutted turnpike which, their driver informed them, had been laid along the old Seneca Indian trail. At periodic spots were pull-out places, rutted semi-circles so that coaches could pass slower carts or wagons. Small taverns were situated every mile or so. Several times a day the stagecoach would stop at one of them, for the passengers' comfort (if any was to be found, Carisa thought wryly), and to change to new horses.

It was rolling, idyllic country, scattered about with tiny settlements, forests, stone fences, cleared fields. Carisa had seen such areas many times before—rural scenes were all very familiar to her—yet still she enjoyed it. And she found that her spirits were beginning to lift. Soon she would be with the circus again. She could talk with Rolf and Duddie, assess the performers, check receipts and expenses.

Adam had telegraphed ahead, and they were to lodge in a small boarding house in the village. When they finally reached Prospect Hill House, a tavern three miles east of Cherry Valley, the coach pulled up, and they all got out to stretch their legs. Before them was stretched out a vista of folded hills and valleys in a hundred muted shades of blues and greens, made even more misty and faded by the heat.

"Oh!" Nelly gasped. "Oh, look! You can see forever, almost!"

But Carisa was not looking at the view. Her heart had slammed into her throat at the sight of a Phillips Circus poster tacked to a tree near the inn. *Stupendous show,* it screamed out in huge, black letters. *Marcella Duquesne, famed cord dancer. The Great Rudolph, death-defying animal trainer. Maybelle Cameron, Queen of Snakes. And many others. None like it.*

She herself had written those words. And now, on this hot afternoon they still had the power to weaken her knees and set her heart to pounding. The Phillips Circus! Her own show!

They proceeded downhill to the little town nestled toylike in its green masses of oaks and elms. In a cloud of road dust, they entered the village itself. The wide dirt street was lined with trees, their branches nearly meeting overhead to give a shady, almost cave-like atmosphere.

On the edge of town they had passed a tannery, with its unmistakably pungent stench of curing hides, lime, and rotting heaps of offal. There were other smells, too, Carisa noted now. A cabinet shop gave out its whiff of sawdust and varnish. There was a brass foundry, a marble works, a brewery, a truss works. And, as always, the usual smells of human habitation— horse dung, dust, household slops, and cooking food, all of it made even stronger by the heat of the day.

But the village itself was pleasant, reminding Carisa of many she had seen in her travels. Hitching posts were provided at intervals, and planks were laid across an occasional ditch for pedestrians. More Phillips posters were emblazoned on a livery stable, a feed store, and various trees.

They proceeded at a brisk pace, the driver cracking his whip as they neared another tavern, Tryon House. Down a side street Carisa glimpsed private residences, Victorian wood frame homes sleeping in the heat.

"Well," Adam said. "We'll have the driver take us to our boarding house and then we'll unpack. And we'll all have baths. God knows we deserve them after

213

this long drive. I wonder if we can get anything edible in this town."

"Oh, there are always the taverns," Carisa told him. "Or our landlady. She'll be willing to cook for us, too. The food will be simple, but I don't think you'll object to it."

This was her element, she thought suddenly; this anonymous village identical to so many others she had stayed in over the years.

Adam grimaced and wiped dust from his face, his good humor suddenly returned. "Driver!" he shouted, leaning precariously out of the window. "Take us to Mrs. Allison's, if you please. We'd like to begin scraping off our first layer of dust."

The show had arrived at dawn, and was now set up in a vacant lot at the outskirts of town. Carisa, alighting from the small buggy she had hired that morning at a local livery stable, felt her heart lift up with a pleasure so intense that she had to blink back tears.

She was *home*. Yes, that was what it really was, for everything seemed so familiar that she could weep. The huge field, its grass already trampled by animals and wheels, dotted here and there with horse dung. The big top, its canvas billowing in the breeze, flags flying from its main and quarter poles. The smaller "menagerie top," "cook top" and other utility tents. The string of wagons lined up in parade order. The tiger cage, pungent with the jungle stench of cat, being goggled at by four awe-struck town boys. The canvas water troughs for the horses, the "red wagon," or ticket office, waiting for the first customers to arrive.

The only discordant note was the group of flashily dressed men who lounged in the shade of a wagon playing cards. They were too well-dressed to be roustabouts, and Carisa did not remember hiring them as show employees. Well, she told herself quickly, perhaps Rolf had hired them. She would ask him later.

Meanwhile, among the array of scattered tents people were walking about, moving equipment or intent on errands. Carisa, looking about for Rolf or Duddie, was surprised by a shriek coming from behind her.

"Carisa! Oh, Carisa, you're here!"

It was Anna, racing toward her, clad in a loose-fitting white practice dress, the little dog, Boxo, yapping behind her. Anna, Carisa noted, looked as pretty as ever, her skin clear and creamy, her cheeks flushed. Her brown hair, pulled back from her face, was curling in the heat.

"Carisa, it's so good to see you!" Anna threw her arms around her sister. "And to think that I am an aunt now! Twins! How did you ever manage it? I can't believe it. Oh, Carisa, aren't you lucky?"

Did Anna's face seem momentarily to cloud?

"Yes, I am very lucky," Carisa said. "And they're beautiful babies," she added proudly. "I wish I could have brought them for you to see, except that they never could have endured our hot journey. And we couldn't have managed having them plus two wet-nurses crammed into the stagecoach with us. I think we all would have suffocated!"

Anna laughed. "Where's Adam?" she asked. "Surely he didn't let you travel here all alone."

"No, he's here, and so are Nelly and Gaines, our butler. But they are all still in town yet, at the boarding house. I hired this buggy from the livery stable. I'll drive back into town later to watch the parade with them. But I couldn't wait any longer," Carisa confessed. "I had to come out here to the lot as soon as I could."

Anna nodded. She went on to tell Carisa of the new act which Rolf had devised for her. She was being billed as "Anna Phillips, the Golden Lady," and would wear a short-skirted yellow costume with golden spangles.

"Gold spangles?" Carisa asked. "Where did you get this costume? And your routine, is it something new, or is it merely left over from one of your old acts? I really wish that Rolf had. . . ."

"Come, Carisa," Anna said, tugging at her hand. "We can talk about that later, after you've seen the show. Right now I just want to see *you*. Come into the dress-

215

ing tent, and we'll talk. There's so much I have to tell you . . . oh, it'll be strictly like old times. Only Stephana isn't here, of course."

Again Anna's face clouded, and Carisa had the sudden feeling that all of her gaiety was being forced.

A long tent had been divided with canvas down the center for use by men and women as a dressing area, and it was here, to the women's half, that Anna took her. The floor of the tent was green trampled grass, the sides rolled up to let in air and light. Ropes had been strung up for clothes to hang over, and a kitten with a chain fastened about its neck snoozed on a wooden chair. At the far end of the tent Marcella Duquesne, in costume, lounged on the grass, knitting. Her dark, pretty face was bent over the yarn with as much concentration as she gave to her rope-dancing. She nodded and smiled at Carisa, then looked down at her work again.

"Over here," Anna whispered. "Where we can be private."

They sat down on the lid of a large, black trunk, and looked at each other. Again Carisa had the swift impression of Anna's tension—her hands opening and closing, her laughter a little too fast and loud.

Words poured out of Anna in a rush. She described her efforts to track down the Phillips Circus on its route, her telegram to Rolf, her subsequent journey—with her rosin-back horse, Jupiter—to join them. She bubbled on with news: of sellout crowds, a roustabout with a broken leg, a trained pig with worms, a dog which had inadvertently been left behind at a town, which had had to run to catch up with the wagons.

"And Papa?" Carisa asked at last. "It seems that I have heard news of everyone and everything but Papa."

"Papa? Oh, he . . . he's the same. You know." Anna frowned and began to play with the folds of her dress.

"But you wrote me that you and he quarreled."

"Yes, and so we did."

"But what about, Anna?" Carisa pressed.

"Oh . . . Well, it was about a man I'd met at the Hippodrome, actually." Anna looked uncomfortable.

"You see, he came to see one of the shows, and afterward, he came back to meet me."

"Anna." Carisa said it gently. "We three always had men coming back to ask about us, don't you remember? All circus women do. It's simply a part of show life, and certainly nothing unusual. Surely you and Papa didn't quarrel about that?"

Anna would not look at her. "It was more than that," she muttered at last.

"More?"

Now Anna's whole face seemed to droop. Restlessly she reached out, scooped up the sleeping kitten, still on its chain, and cradled it on her lap.

"Well, you see, Carisa, he came the first night only to admire me, to tell me how much he enjoyed the performance. We talked for a while, for a very long while, really. He seemed very lonely. And when he asked to take me to supper, I felt sorry for him, and I said yes. The second night he was back. He had hired a beautiful carriage, so lovely, its appointments all red velvet and brass . . . oh, you've never seen anything like it."

"I'm sure I haven't."

"And then . . . he took me to the German Winter-Garden. I'd always wanted to go there, I was the one who suggested it. It's a beer hall on Bowery Street, Carisa, quite as splendid as a cathedral, with wonderful music and balconies and arches. . . ."

Anna's forefinger stroked the kitten under its chin. Its purr was loud and rattling.

"He seduced me, dear sister," she whispered at last. "Or perhaps I seduced him, I don't really know. We . . . we went to a hotel and registered as husband and wife. I— I quite lost my head. I stayed with him all night, and part of the next day, too."

Anna was weeping now, her tears falling onto the soft white fur of the kitten.

Carisa pushed back her shock. She stared at her sister, at the sweet oval face, the flushed cheeks. *Anna, the prettiest*, she thought. And it was true. Her sister was soft and warm and lovely. Perfect prey for a rich idler who thought he could go backstage and pick up a circus girl, she thought furiously.

"Anna! How could you!" she began.

"Don't you start that too, Carisa. I couldn't stand it if you did. I came home hours late," Anna added dully. "Papa called me a . . . a whore and a harlot and a lot of other things. He said that I didn't deserve to be his daughter. That I didn't deserve to be a member of the *Fl-Flambeaux*. . . ."

She began to sob. Marcella Duquesne, on the other side of the dressing tent, glanced in their direction, picked up her knitting, and walked away.

"Don't cry about it. Please, Anna, don't." Carisa touched her sister's arm. "It's all over now. You're here, aren't you? And everything's fine. You can start all over again."

"No, I can't," Anna wept. "It's not all right. I'm going to have a baby."

"A baby?" Carisa repeated stupidly.

"I'm pregnant, Carisa, and it's so hot, and I'm so tired, and I just wish I could die. I just want to die, die, die!"

Somehow Carisa managed to soothe her sister, to pat her shoulder and assure her that everything would be all right. She, Carisa, would see to it that Anna had sufficient money to bear her child in comfort. Everything would be provided for.

"Everything but a f-father . . ." Anna wept. "For my b-baby. . . ."

"Perhaps you can travel back to New York with us and seek the man out and tell him of your problem," Carisa said after a hesitation. "If he knew, maybe he would. . . ."

"I don't want him to know!" Anna screamed. "He was rich, and married, and he . . . he was only trifling with me! He said I was pretty, he said I was alluring, he said wonderful things to me. Oh, God," she sobbed. "I won't force myself on him, I couldn't. I'd rather die first. He'll never know, never!"

218

The man was married, then, Carisa thought with a sensation of unreality. "But, Anna . . ." she began.

"Promise me one thing, Carisa. Just one thing, that's all I'll ever ask of you." Anna let the cat slide from her lap, and clutched at Carisa's hands. Abruptly she looked far older than her years, her prettiness washed away in a stream of tears.

"And what is that?"

"Carisa, promise me that if anything ever happens to me, you'll take my baby and give her a good home. I . . . I couldn't bear it if she went to an orphanage. There was one down the street from where Papa and I lived. Oh, it was horrid, all the poor, thin little girls and boys going for walks in two double lines, in their ragged brown clothes with chilblains on their hands . . . ugh!"

"Don't be silly. Nothing is going to happen to you."

"I tell you I don't want my baby to be an orphan. I want her to have love. And I want her to be in the circus." Anna's voice rose. "We've been circus folk for hundreds of years, Carisa, on both sides of the family. I don't want that to change. She *must* have her heritage, at least, even if she can't have a father."

"But, Anna." Carisa tried to laugh. "How do you know it's going to be a girl? And you're not going to die! Why should you? You look as healthy as a farm wife. You've grown plumper since I saw you last and your eyes are very bright. No doubt you'll have an easy delivery as I did, and everything will be fine."

Anna's fingers squeezed Carisa's, pressing her flesh. "Mama died in childbirth. Just promise, Carisa. Promise me! It's all I ask."

"All right. I promise. Now, let's go and find Duddie."

"I . . . I don't want to, Carisa. You go and find him. He loves you so. He'll want to see you."

Anna would not be persuaded to accompany her, so Carisa went herself, locating the little clown near the cook-tent.

"Hello, Carisa." Duddie grinned and pulled a small piece of hard candy from his sleeve. With a flourish, he

219

presented it to her. It was a gesture she remembered well from her childhood.

"Duddie, Duddie," Carisa laughed. "Oh, I'm *so* glad to see you! You'll never change, will you? The world may crumble, Kansas may bleed and slavery be fought over, but you'll always have a candy up your sleeve."

Duddie grinned again at her, tossed another sweet into the air and caught it deftly. Then his face—devoid of makeup although he wore his tri-color costume—grew suddenly serious.

"I may be the same, Carisa. But this show is not."

"What do you mean?"

They began to walk together, around the periphery of the circus with its orderly clutter. Slowly they passed the sideshow tent, with its huge painted canvas banners advertising inside attractions. A big color panel showed Maybelle Cameron, with six fat snakes wrapped about her body and an expression of ecstasy on her face.

"I mean," Duddie said, "that Rolf has turned this show into a grifter's paradise."

"What?"

Carisa felt her heart sink. Of course! So that was who those gaudily dressed men had been—gamblers or "short changers" who traveled about with a show or trailed along behind it, working the crowds with con games and crooked gambling.

"William deBord," Duddie went on, "for all of his faults, did keep an honest show. Sure, he was in the minority, and he could have made a lot more money than he did. But we were honest, and I liked it that way."

Carisa felt shaken. "But I don't understand. Surely Rolf wouldn't. . . ."

"Rolf would, and he is. He's getting a cut in their dirty business, you can bank on that. Oh, I've kept him honest enough in the gate money . . . I've had your interests at heart, and I've counted every cent of the take, and I've seen to it that your share was put into the safe. And, by the way, your share has been considerable, for Rolf has already made his expenses. The

220

show's good, Carisa. And Rolf is good, too. I have to grant him that."

"Oh . . . I'm grateful to you, Duddie, for helping me. I've counted on you."

"And I won't let you down if I can help it. But it's this I worry about now. We're short changing people, Carisa. Rolf is running dishonest concessions, too. As for the gamblers, they're everywhere with their three-card monte and their shell games. Back in Hartford we nearly got into a nasty fight with the townies over it . . . it made for an ugly thing."

Carisa nodded. She did not need to be told what such fights could mean. Brawls between circus men and town toughs were common, especially when the townsmen were angered by cheating practices. In one such bloody confrontation, ten men had been killed.

"I'll talk to Rolf about it," she said, swallowing.

"You'd better. And while you're doing it, ask him about the other stunts he's pulled. Why, the Ezra Stevens show went through this area two weeks ago, and Rolf nearly ruined them. He changed our routing to cut ahead of them, and he tore down all of their paper. He cut our prices nearly in half, and even chopped down a tree over the road so their wagons couldn't get through."

Carisa nodded. These were common tactics used in the cut-throat wars sometimes staged between rival circuses.

"I . . . I'll talk to him right away," she whispered. "I'll tell him what he is to do. I can't have him ruining Papa's show."

She found Rolf kneeling beside one of the parade wagons, carefully repairing a nick in its gold leaf, brushing at his work with a soft cloth and then standing back to examine the effect. So absorbed was he that he was not yet aware of her presence.

For a moment Carisa hesitated. Her first instinct had been to storm up to him and confront him with what she had learned. But that, she told herself, was what he would expect of her. No, she would not behave like any man's idea of a hysterical female, who acted before she had all the facts. She would consider everything before she spoke.

Rolf brushed the cloth over the gold leaf again, then turned his attention to another nicked area, on the carved nose of a Grecian goddess. He whistled softly between his teeth as he gave careful attention to this delicate work.

Rolf was good at his job, Carisa knew. More than good—he was superb. Management of a show on the road took the skill of a juggler and the ingenuity of a magician. There were thousands of important details. Routing, planning, avoidance or containment of disasters such as mud, high winds, tornados, rains, grasshoppers, small fires, injuries and illness. There were employees, too, to badger and cajole: not just performers, but the whole spectrum of circus workers. Twenty-four-hour men, hostlers, ducket-grabbers, joeys, layout men, cooks, canvas men, chandeliers, kid workers—dozens of people, many with titles incomprehensible to the layman, but without whom the show could not function.

She had seen Rolf in action, and he was indefatigible. If something broke, he knew of a way to fix it, and could make the repair in ten minutes. He could doctor animals. He could deal with irate town councilmen, hand them free passes and humor them into providing whatever the show needed. He could (and she had seen him do this) persuade a woman acrobat that she did not want to marry a farmer and leave the show. He could break up fights. He could convince six hundred people sitting on wooden bleachers in a hot tent to move up and squeeze together to make room for more paying patrons.

Where else was she to find a man like Rolf, a man who, moreover, was willing to run her show instead of his own.

"Hello, Rolf," she said.

Rolf dropped the rag and rose easily. His eyes gleamed at her out of his wedge-shaped, handsome face.

"Hello, Carisa. Did Duddie tell you that we cleared

222

our expenses last month? We're on velvet now, and the profits are going to keep right on rolling in."

"Yes," she said. "Duddie told me."

"I'm going to make you a rich woman, Carisa. One of these days soon." His eyes challenged her, and she knew that he was waiting for her to say something about the men she had seen.

"I'm happy about that, Rolf," she said at last. "Except that it isn't really my show, not entirely. It's Papa's. The Phillips Circus. And I want. . . ."

Rolf gave a sudden kick at the rag he had been using, sending it sailing into a clump of flattened grass. "Phillips," he muttered. "That name should have been mine."

Had she heard him correctly? The family had never spoken directly of Rolf's parentage, and now Carisa did not know what to say.

"Those men I saw," she said, changing the subject. "The men who were playing cards. Are they our employees, Rolf? Did you hire them?"

"In a way."

"Oh? They're your hired gamblers, aren't they? Do they pay you to allow them to travel with the show?"

Rolf stared at her defiantly. "Enough to satisfy me. And to satisfy you, too."

"And the concessions, Rolf. You're short-changing customers, not to mention what you did to the Ezra Stevens show. And I don't like it. I don't want that kind of cut-throat activity associated with the Phillips Circus."

"Oh, *you* don't want it, eh? *You,* the great female show owner?"

"Don't mock me!" she retorted furiously. "You knew perfectly well that I wouldn't approve of those things, didn't you? Yet you did them anyway. Underhanded methods . . . dishonesty . . . driving out the competition . . . it's dirty, and I don't like it."

Rolf pressed his lips together. Then he took her arm and pulled her in the direction of one of the wagons, the "silver wagon," painted in silver gilt, as was circus custom, and painted with the name of the Phillips Circus.

"Come in here, Carisa. I want to show you something."

"But . . ."

"I said come here. There's something you should see."

It was the manager's wagon, of course, its interior carefully filled with built-in cupboard and desk space and a small cot for Rolf to sleep. Inside one of the cabinets was the safe, and it was this which Rolf opened now, twirling the combination so quickly that the numerals seemed to flash in front of Carisa's eyes.

Then the door swung open to reveal bills and coins— a great, crowded mass of them.

"Look," Rolf said, breathing quickly. "Just look at that. Money, hundreds of dollars of it! And all of it is your share. Yours, do you hear me? And most of it was earned," he added, "by the very same methods you are questioning."

She stared at the bulging mass of bills, the coins cascading from beneath them.

"Rolf. I'm glad to see that the show is making a profit, of course. It means that we are on the way up. But . . ."

"But what?" Rolf slammed the door of the safe shut. "You still don't understand, do you? You're just like a female, so concerned with being pure and holy that you can't see the reality."

"What reality?" she demanded.

"Why, this, dear Carisa. Without the underhanded methods and the gambling money, we would have had very little to put in that safe. How do you think that some of the big circuses managed to get where they are? By beating out the competition, that's how! And by a few friendly monte games and shell games for those who wish to indulge."

They were standing in the crowded center of the wagon now, their heads nearly bumping the wooden roof. As Carisa started to object, Rolf went on. "The circus world is a rough world, a *man's* world," his voice grated. "If we don't push to get ahead of our competi-

224

tion, why, they'll cut our throats without even a twinge of conscience. That's the way it is, Carisa."

"Perhaps," Carisa said, remembering Richard Sands' remark about most circus owners being thieves. "But, still, Rolf, the gambling, the short-changing . . . it dirties us, don't you see that? It sullies the Phillips name."

For an instant a dark, angry expression flicked across Rolf's face. Then it was gone, and he shrugged.

"I happen to know your father wasn't above a bit of gambling and short-changing when he wished. Besides, it'll sully the Phillips name even worse if we fail. People like to gamble, you little fool. They expect that sort of thing from a show. My crew couldn't get along if there weren't people willing to play, to cooperate with them, to let themselves be taken. Don't you see, Carisa? One hand washes the other. That's the way it is in the circus, and always will be."

"*Always?* I wonder." A feeling of nausea was pushing its way up from her belly. She would lose Rolf if she didn't let him do things his way . . . the implication was clear. And if she lost him, she would lose her show, for there was no one to take his place.

Carisa swallowed hard, against the knot of bile which rose to choke her.

"Rolf," she heard herself say. "The short-changing is the most despicable thing of all. To cheat innocent folks . . . poor people, children . . . out of their money. I won't have it."

Their eyes locked in challenge. After a moment Rolf looked away and nodded. "Very well. I'll stop the short-changing then." Rolf hesitated. "But do you want to rise, Carisa? Do you want this show to be a great one, *really* great?"

"Yes," she whispered.

"Then you'll do as I say. I keep my men, and I continue to deal with the competition in the way I think best."

He stepped toward the opened door of the wagon, and gave a gesture which included the scattered array of tents, the village children gawking at the cat cages, the tethered baggage horses.

"If you won't let me, Carisa, then *this* is all we'll ever be. A little family show traveling about the country and playing in one-horse towns such as this one. A dog and pony show, the lowest!"

As if for emphasis, Rolf spat contemptuously onto the floor of the wagon.

Numbly, Carisa drove the mile back to the center of town, barely seeing the farmhouses and placid fields which she passed. The Phillips Circus, dirtied by gambling? By ugly, cut-throat competition?

Yet—she swallowed hard. The William deBord show may have been honest, as Duddie had pointed out. Yet hadn't Papa himself, long ago in England, taught Rolf and Duddie how to manipulate the shells for the shell game? Well, hadn't he? And hadn't she once glimpsed Papa ripping down a banner posted by some other circus? More than once, if the truth were known.

Well, she would think about all of this later, she decided quickly. When she had time to ponder, to mull it over in her mind. For now there was the parade to watch—it was due to begin at any minute. And she had promised Adam that she would be in town to see it with him.

As she pulled up to the boarding house, Nelly came running out onto the porch, followed by Gaines. She was flushed with excitement.

"Miss Carisa!" Nelly shouted, as if she were still a child herself. "Can't you hear it? The parade! It's coming! I hear the band, I hear it!"

Carisa tried to smile. "Yes, I hear it too. Where is Mr. Hartshorn?"

"Coming!" Adam emerged from the boarding house still adjusting his tie. He looked cheerful and rested as he gave instructions for Gaines to take Carisa's buggy back to the livery stable and order them something large enough for four.

"It's a gorgeous day for a circus," he said, smiling. His eyes this morning looked like chips of gold in the summer sun. He pressed Carisa's arm warmly, and she could not help squeezing back. They had slept in each other's arms last night, entwined like two nestled spoons in the way Carisa loved best. When Adam held her in his arms, it seemed to Carisa as if her life were complete. . . .

"Let's go," urged Nelly. "Oh, let's hurry to Main Street and not miss any of it."

Already people were pouring out of houses and walking the one block to Main Street. Small boys ran and pushed. Little girls giggled in excited trios and fives. Matrons and grandmothers admonished, and hurried faster themselves. Dogs yipped, and buggies rumbled over the rutted dirt road, swirling up clouds of brown dust. No one, it seemed, was going to miss the excitement of a free parade.

When they reached the main street, they saw that it had been transformed. Yesterday the street had been somnolent, deserted, baking in the heat. Today all of that had changed. Carriages, wagons, phaetons and buggies jammed the sides of the road, using every available hitching post. Buggies were stacked up three deep in front of the livery stable and at the stone horse-trough located at the other end of the street.

Seemingly from nowhere, vendors had appeared—a man hawking fresh hot roasted chestnuts, a red-faced woman selling pies, a woman with gingerbread, two boys with lemonade.

Children ran back and forth. People were everywhere, leaning from upper-story windows, swarming under the trees, perched in a row on the roof of the livery stable. Life in a small town, Carisa knew, could be of a deadly sameness, one day blending into another. But today would be different. Today there would be the circus.

They found themselves standing in front of the local bank. The tinny sounds of the clown band, thinned by the moist, hot air, grew louder.

In spite of herself, Carisa felt her heart squeeze with the familiar pang of grief and regret. If it had not been

227

for her accident, she, too, might have been a part of this parade . . .

Then it came, sweeping toward them in a surge of brassy music and color. First was the clown bandwagon, its gold leaf, carved in fantastic shapes of gods, goddesses and flowers, gleaming and reflecting in the sun. It was pulled by a six-horse hitch, matched snow-white animals wearing ostrich plumes which bobbed in the air.

Then came the five German acrobats Carisa had hired, smiling and waving at the crowd. They rode regally, their saddle-blankets red velvet with sequins and gold ribbing sewn on to gleam in the sun.

On and on they came—all of the panoply and splendor and costumery that Rolf and Carisa had been able to devise over the long winter. Nearly every employee of the circus—from roustabout to cook to clown—had been decked in costume and used in some capacity. There were two tableaux wagons and a Persian float. There were ten marching Hindus, exotic in brightly colored robes and turbans. Anna Phillips reclined on her horse, Jupiter, looking soft and pale and remote.

There was a bell-wagon, ringing with sound, which Carisa had bought from the small circus which had foundered. There were clowns. Elephants, huge, gray, ponderous, tusk-less, robed in gorgeous green velvet covered with spangles.

There were sounds: the brassy rhythm of the band, the deep knocks and squeaks of the wagon wheels, the sandpapery shuffle of elephant feet, the rattle of chains, the clop-clopping of horses' hooves. And smells, of perfume and perspiration and horses. The jungle-like cat stench, the dense odor of the elephants, unlike anything else.

Carisa watched it all with a squeezing, thrumming feeling at the base of her throat. She was totally caught up in the spectacle of it. *My show,* she thought, exulting. The Phillips Circus.

She felt Adam nudge her. His eyes, too, were gleaming with suppressed excitement.

228

"So, Carisa. Now I can see why you and Rolf Taggart were so busy this past winter."

"Do you like it, Adam? Oh, but this is nothing, nothing compared to what it will be like in ten years. Someday we're going to have a parade that is more than a mile long. We'll have two hundred horses and 15 elephants, we'll be the best show in the world. Adam, I'm going to do it. Someday! I know I can."

"Will you, Carisa? Those are very fine ambitions, but. . . ."

"Of course I will!" She caught at his hand and squeezed it, feeling the power and energy flow through her, until she hardly knew how to contain them. "Oh, Adam, we're going to be the very best!"

"The best," he repeated.

Carisa, straining now to see which wagon was to bring up the rear of the parade, was unaware of the shadow which had crossed her husband's face.

-❧ 1861 ❧-

15

Time, Carisa thought dreamily. It passed on wagon wheels, was measured in sequins sewn and horses purchased, posters printed and letters written. It passed so quickly that it seemed there was never enough of it to do all the things she wished to do, never enough hours to be filled with hard work and planning.

Six years of time. And the circus had grown. They had ten elephants now, all females, for these were safer. They had a calliope, the fantastic "steam piano" which Richard Sands had hinted at, its infectious music so blaring and compelling that it called people from miles around. They now used colored posters, elaborate lithographed works of art which emblazoned the show and fired the imagination. And they had also hired a new family of six French aerialists, followers of the famed Mr. Jules Léotard, who was electrifying Europe with his fabulous flying aerial feats. The Molyneaus wore a new type of costume—daring tights named after Mr. Léotard himself.

On an April afternoon in 1861, Carisa sat on the stone veranda of the cottage Katherine had bought three years previously at the seaside resort of Newport, Rhode Island, going over some circus correspondence and listening to the voices of the children as they played indoors, in the parlor.

At the end of the long lawn, tinged with spring's

230

first green, surf tumbled against rocks and gulls swooped and dived for food. It had been raining earlier; now the air was full of tiny wet droplets.

A sudden gust of damp wind rattled her papers and blew childish voices in Carisa's direction.

"Matt, you little beast! You nearly knocked that battledore on Grandmama's new shepherdess!"

The voice was full of horror and a certain little-girl rectitude. It belonged to Vicki Hartshorn, at six a pale child with large, solemn gray eyes.

"I have better aim than that," Matt said scornfully. "It was Neecie who 'frew it. Neecie, not me!"

"No, it weren't me," Benicia's voice said. She was Anna's daughter, at five already ravishing, with her perfect oval face, her cap of blonde curls, her flashing dimples. Anna had died the previous year in Baton Rouge of yellow fever (strange, Carisa often thought, how her fears of childbirth had never materialized, and yet she had died young anyway). The little girl had been shipped north to Carisa so that she could fulfill the promise she had made on that August morning in 1855.

"It were, too," Matt shouted.

"It were not!" Benicia came rocketing onto the veranda, her skirts flying. The little feather shuttlecock the children had been playing with was clutched in her fist.

"Carisa, Carisa, they say I 'frew the battledore and I didn't. It didn't even hit, and the silly old shepherdess just stayed where she was all the time. So Grandmama can't scold, can she? She won't!"

"No, Grandmama won't scold," Carisa said, unable to resist a smile. "Almost doing a thing isn't the same as doing it, you know."

"That's what I told 'um," Benicia said.

"Come on, Neecie! Neecie, come and play," Matt called. His voice rose with excitement. "Nelly says we can go out in the garden and catch worms. They're all coming up on account of the rain. Millions of 'em!"

The little girl glanced warily at Carisa; it was a well-known fact that grown ladies shuddered with revulsion at squirming objects like snakes and insects and toads.

231

"Well . . ." Carisa hesitated. "Well, you'll have to change your clothes, then, before your grandmother gets back. She's having tea at Vaucluse."

"Oh, we will, we will!" Neecie bubbled.

"Then all right."

"Matt! Matt! Carisa says we can go! She doesn't mind! She likes worms!"

Carisa suppressed another smile as the child skidded off, her boots slipping on the cocoa matting which had been carried out to carpet the veranda. Sometimes she wished Anna could be here to see what a beauty Benicia had turned out to be.

But then, she supposed, Anna had already known. Before her death, Anna had been training her daughter as an equestrienne. The child's balance and timing were superb, Anna had written Carisa excitedly. Even at three, the child was a natural.

Of course, all of that had had to be dropped when Benicia arrived one morning at Hearts-ease, wearing a coat too big for her, having already charmed the minister's wife who had accompanied her on the journey.

Adam fell under Neecie's spell at once.

"Are you going to be my papa now?" the child asked, extending her arms to Adam.

"Do you know how to ride a horse?" she demanded. "Will you take me riding with you? I c'd show you how to ride bareback."

Adam had suppressed a smile. He bent down to the child's level. "Could you now? Well, if you will teach me that, perhaps I can take you down to the wharves and show you a whaling ship. Would that be a fair exchange?"

"Yup. Good." The little girl had nestled into Adam's arms at once, taking his love of her for granted.

"She's beautiful, Carisa," Adam told her later, after Benicia had been fed and put to bed in a room next to Vicki's. "She makes me think of you, as you might have been when you were a child. Except for the dimples. Those are entirely her own, and devilish, too, I might add."

He kissed Carisa lightly.

"Oh, Adam," Carisa had breathed. "Then you don't mind? Rearing her, I mean. It meant so much to Anna that her baby not be an orphan . . . she lived in dread of that happening."

"Mind?" Adam gazed at her, his expression curiously intense. "How could I possibly mind? The child is of your blood, isn't she? Perhaps I'll even adopt her. Would you like that?"

"Adopt her?" For an instant Carisa was startled. She had prayed that Adam would accept Anna's child, never expecting that it would be all this easy. Yet Benicia *was* a lovely, appealing little girl. And she would be a good companion for Vicki, who was very quiet and needed someone to make her more lively.

"Why, yes, Adam," she told him. "That would be wonderful, if you would adopt her."

So it was done. The only flaw had been that Adam did not wish to have the child trained as a circus performer. There was no possibility of such a young child traveling about the country with a show, leaving her family behind at Hearts-ease.

"It's a pity, but it's best not to encourage her, Carisa. She'll soon forget the few tricks she's learned. She'll always be able to ride for her own pleasure, of course. But we'll have to rear her as any other New London girl of good family."

Carisa nodded grimly. This meant that Neecie would learn, as other girls did, to sew and play the piano and speak French. At the proper time she would make her debut and then marry into one of the town's shipping or manufacturing families.

All of her protests had been to no avail. And Katherine had backed up Adam.

"Surely, my dear Carisa, you don't expect to transplant that child out of the circus like a clump of violets or poppies? Do you intend to let her travel with the wagons at her age? Of course not! Then why train her at all, and especially in a pastime that will ruin her reputation as a proper young lady?"

"Circus women can be as proper as anyone!" Carisa

233

flared. "Besides, I promised my sister that I would see to her child's future."

"Well, surely you see that marriage *is* the best possible future for her. She is pretty and she has spirit. She should have no trouble finding a good husband here in New London. And when she does, you'll have fulfilled your obligation to her."

"And what of my obligation to Anna?"

"It would seem," Katherine said tartly, "that when a woman gives birth to a child without benefit of husband, she should be grateful enough that her child is provided for at all."

So the circus training had stopped—officially, anyway. But Benicia was inseparable from Duddie when the show was in winter quarters. And Duddie, Carisa was aware, allowed the child to ride the horses in the ring barn, the "mechanic," a canvas safety device, strapped about her middle.

Carisa knew full well that she should stop this—after all, it was against Adam's wishes—but she did not.

"She's fearless," Duddie told Carisa one afternoon. "She was born to ride."

"I know. I know that, Duddie. But what can I do? My husband says. . . ."

Duddie looked thoughtful. "Perhaps he will change his mind later, who knows? In the meanwhile, let the child practice. Let her ride, let her have the fun of it. Your husband doesn't have to know. And perhaps someday . . ."

"Someday," Carisa repeated. She gazed for a long moment at the misshapen little clown who had been her own teacher and mentor. A sudden, piercing ache possessed her throat. Once there had been a "someday" for herself as well. With difficulty she pushed away the thought. "But do you think that she can keep a secret? She's such a baby, only four."

Duddie grinned. "She'll keep this to herself. She's a Phillips, isn't she? She'll do anything she has to."

Now the shouts of the three children grew louder as they rushed, boots clattering, out of the side door which led to the garden. How noisy they were! Several days of rain and Katherine's intense housekeeping had made them hilarious.

As Carisa continued to work, the childish voices changed pitch. They were beside the cottage now, digging with shovels and spades. Carisa could hear them clearly; Matt bossing the work in his high-pitched little shout, Benicia digging furiously and talking non-stop. And Vicki, always the quiet one, did the bidding of the other two, shrieking once as Matt tossed a worm at her. Two generals and one soldier, Carisa thought, half-smiling.

She let the quill pen slide from her fingers and stared at the vista formed by grayed April sky and gunbarrel water, accented by flying birds like double commas. It was a scene which matched her mood. Pensive. Heavy-hearted.

Usually Newport seemed a retreat—as indeed it was. But today Carisa's thoughts kept ranging to the world which lay beyond, with its enmities and harsh emotions, its fanaticism over the issue of slavery. Secession, the seizing by South Carolina troops of the U.S. Arsenal at Charleston. The ugly tension at Fort Sumter, the gaunt, mournful face of the new president, Mr. Lincoln.

And her own marriage, too, reflecting some of this same divisiveness.

Yes, they had had good times. Warm times, happy times. Days spent walking the beach near Hearts-ease, exploring what the sea washed up as if they were two children, instead of husband and wife.

Nights spent locked in each other's arms, joined in the intimate sharing which was a part of every marriage, or should be.

"Carisa," Adam would whisper. "Oh, God, Carisa, how I love you. More than any man should love a woman. There are times when I burn for you, when I'm obsessed by you. . . ."

Then she could only turn to him, giving up her body to him, her very self, existing with him in the special world they had created together, that world where there

235

was no time, no children to cry or demand, only each other.

And yet—

Problems. It seemed that their marriage was not without its share of those.

Part of their difficulties, Carisa realized, were due to Katherine. It was her mother-in-law who had insisted that they buy this cottage here at Newport, even though Adam had objected that he could not afford it.

"She can, though, can't she?" Mother Hartshorn had snapped in Carisa's hearing. "Haven't we money piling in from that circus of your wife's? More money than we know what to do with? If my friends are going to be looking down their noses at me—and they do, Adam, they do—then the least I can expect is some compensation for that."

So it had been blackmail—of a sort. And reluctantly Carisa had made available the funds, knowing that this was money wasted, money that she would not be able to plow back into her circus enterprise.

And now they were saddled with a stone monstrosity, a "cottage" in name only, for it possessed ten rooms and an array of towers, cupolas, carved wooden decorations and mock railings. Pillars and balconies bristled out in odd places, like afterthoughts.

After the purchase papers had been signed, and he and Carisa were alone in their hotel room at the Ocean House, Adam shook his head. "Hideous as the place is, Carisa, Katherine *is* my mother, and she has had much grief in her life. Losing my father and my older brother was very hard on her, and she was also very fond of my first wife, Mary Elizabeth, and tried valiantly to save her. Perhaps if this house will make her happy. . . ."

"But I need the money to invest!" Carisa had cried.

Adam put his arms around her and pulled her to him, so that, as always, she found herself helpless against the physical allure of him, the crisp way his tawny hair curled about his ears, the clean, male smell of him, the taut feel of his muscles.

"There will be more money, Carisa, your Rolf Taggart will see to that. And I have made my mother

236

promise to live very simply while she is here. That should help."

"Simply!" Carisa had suppressed a laugh. "Does anyone ever do anything simply at Newport? Especially someone like your mother?"

Adam had laughed, too. "Perhaps not. But there is one thing to be said for Newport. You and I will be able to come here, too, to relax and enjoy ourselves. Do you realize just how hard you have been working, Carisa? How little time you are willing to take just to sit and relax?"

For some reason she felt uncomfortable. "But the circus . . . it does require so much work. . . ."

"Yes. Well, perhaps things will change now that we have this cottage. The life here can be very pleasant and leisurely. There are picnics and beach parties and garden parties, and everyone goes driving on Bellevue Avenue, bowing to each other, seeing and being seen. And the clambakes, Carisa . . . everyone stuffs themselves to bursting on clams and chowder and lobster and sausage and corn. It's quite a life."

"You know I'm not that sort of person, Adam," she said stiffly. "I'm not a socialite and I never will be."

He smiled at her, teasingly. Then, easily, he picked her up and carried her toward the bed. "Perhaps you could be. My God, Carisa, do you realize that with your beauty, you could rule Newport? August Belmont, Ward McAllister, all of them, you could make them all worship you as I do. . . ."

Slowly, deliberately, he was stripping off her gown. "But it doesn't matter. Just so you and I can come here occasionally by ourselves. We'll dismiss all the servants and cook for ourselves and just stay locked in our bedroom all day . . . not even dress if we don't wish to. . . ."

"Adam . . . it sounds wonderful. . . ."

She had helped him, then, with her dress, wrapping her arms around him and arching her body to his in the sheer joy of being near him. He had caressed her breasts, drawing from her nipples a sweet fire. She loved him . . . she loved him. . . .

237

Unfortunately, they had not gotten to Newport as often as they had planned. Summer, the time when the resort's social season was at its most brilliant, was also the time when Carisa was most deeply involved with her circus.

"It's always one crisis after another, isn't it?" Adam had exploded angrily one June morning as they breakfasted at the small table in their room. She had had to refuse a trip to Newport due to an epidemic of dysentery in the circus. Six clowns had quickly to be replaced, and she must make a trip to New York immediately.

"Oh, Adam . . ." She rose from the breakfast table to fling her arms around him. "I'm sorry, really I am! It's just the dysentery . . . the circus must have been given some bad water, and many of them have been sick. . . ."

"There is always a good reason for your trips, my dear." Adam said it sharply. "Did you know that the weather has been lovely this week? It will be beautiful at Newport. We can swim in the ocean, have a clambake on the beach, ride in the carriage, or simply lie in bed all day. . . ."

Adam's golden eyes were gleaming at her, and Carisa could feel an answering throb of desire in herself.

"Adam," she whispered. "You know I would like to go."

"Then do it."

"But you *know* I can't. You know the circus needs me! Adam, I must go to New York to hire those clowns. Rolf cannot hire them all, much as he would like to do so."

"Carisa . . ."

She had put one hand to his lips. "Please, Adam. You know how much my show means to me. I promise. We'll go to Newport later in the summer. We'll do everything, everything you said, and more."

Yet they had not. The trip to New York—and later to Boston, to Philadelphia—had been pressingly urgent. Adam had not said anything more, nor had he reproached her. But no longer, either, did he suggest that they escape to Newport alone. . . .

Five days previously, they had had their latest quarrel. It had begun ordinarily enough, with Katherine in a fever to get to the Newport cottage in order to house-clean it before the season began. Since the Phillips Circus would be touring near that area, Carisa had decided to visit it to solve a problem there, then join her mother-in-law at the Newport cottage. She had begged Adam to come with her. If he did, she pointed out, they would have the pleasure of staying for several nights in fine hotels without the distraction of the family. . . .

"No." He had said it sharply. "Not this time, Carisa."

"But, Adam! You've always traveled with me when you could. You've insisted on it."

They were in their bedroom dressing for dinner, for Katherine had invited the Kords to dine with them. Carisa was already gowned in apple green, her favorite color and one which emphasized the sea-blue of her eyes, the delicate shadowed contours of her cheekbones.

Adam, nude from waist up, was shaving. Half-clad, he looked very lithe and male. Carisa longed to reach out and caress the springy crisp mat of hair on his chest, but did not dare.

"This is one time, darling, when you can manage to travel without me," he was saying. "I have things to do. And you'll have your show to occupy you, won't you? After all, isn't that the purpose of this little jaunt? Surely Newport itself was only an afterthought."

He was right, of course. Still, it hurt to have it stated so baldly, and Carisa felt her eyes fill with moisture.

"But, Adam . . ." She began.

"Besides, you won't need me," he said lightly. "If my mother plans to do her spring cleaning, then she'll be loaded down with a retinue of servants bigger than Queen Victoria's. There'll be nothing to amuse us but the sound of carpets being beaten and the sight of dust flying through the air."

She moved to the window, the double-tiered silk

flounces of her gown rustling. "Perhaps I won't *need* you. But I'll want you, Adam. I want to show you the new act I've just hired. There are *manege* horses, eight of them, and their trainer has taught them to. . . ."

"I don't care about trained horses, Carisa. Not this time. I've things to do, I told you that."

"What things?" she asked sullenly.

Deliberately Adam moved the razor over his face, shaving the deep cleft in his chin with care. "The *Marie Galante* is in dry dock with repairs. I must see to that, among other things."

"Oh, that. A ship. But, Adam, you can do that any time. And anyway, isn't that why you keep your agent, Mr. West? To care for business such as that?"

Adam's eyes met hers, gleaming with a hard, golden light. "I'm a whaling man, Carisa, a man of the sea. But at present there is something else which is equally important to me."

She was impatient. "I'm sure there is. But the show is vital, too, and surely you'll want to see what I've done. I've already told Rolf and Duddie that you'll be coming with me. . . ."

"Then tell them I'm not."

"But, Adam . . ."

"Carisa, is there anything else you can think of besides that circus of yours?"

"Of course there is. Don't be so silly."

His smile was fleeting, almost sad. "Such as what, Carisa? What else do you think of?"

"Well . . ." Absurdly, humiliatingly, she was floundering. "Well, there are the children, of course. I love them, I love to be with them. . . ."

"When the circus doesn't interfere," he pointed out. "My dear, you are either closeted in your study working, or you are telling the children stories about the circus when you were a child. The way you learned to ride, the time you got caught in a mud slide, the way you used to barter like a little gypsy for food."

"Adam . . ."

"Or," he went on inexorably, "you are taking them down to the ring barn itself, putting them on the horses or helping them into clown suits or teaching them to turn somersaults. Neecie sleeps, eats and dreams circus, Carisa, and a large part of that is due to you."

She was growing angry. He made her sound as if she wasn't a good mother. Of course she was! She always made time in her day for her children. She loved them dearly, she always would. How dare he imply that she didn't?

"Adam, you're not being fair to me," she said slowly. "The circus, whether you like it or not, is their heritage, all three of them. My mother's family were circus folk in Ireland for two hundred years. And my father's family in England for perhaps even longer. And besides," she added, "that show means something to me, and it means something to *us* as well."

"To us?"

"Certainly. It is bringing in good, healthy profits, and at this time we need all the money we can get. Especially since your mother saddled us with that house at Newport. . . ."

Adam's face seemed to freeze. He wiped the shaving lather from his face with a towel and pulled on his cotton undershirt, his chest muscles rippling. To her annoyance, Carisa found that her eyes were drawn to him, to the arrogant masculinity of him. Even when they were quarreling, her eyes could not seem to stop wishing to look at him, her hands from aching to touch him, to caress him. . . .

"My mother was extravagant, of course," he said quietly. "And spiteful. I tried to speak to her about it privately, but it did little good. She seemed to feel that we owed her that house, Carisa." He gave a short laugh. "I'm afraid she would not be dissuaded from that feeling. I'm afraid that my mother, like all Hartshorns, can be very stubborn when she wishes to be."

"Yes." Carisa hesitated. "The truth is, Adam," she heard herself go on in a voice that she hated but seemed powerless to stop. "The truth is that our expenses have been very heavy indeed, and we *depend* on this circus you taunt me with. You've had some bad luck . . . two of your ships went down this year and another needs

241

extensive repairs. And that new oil, the oil made from petroleum, is cutting into the whaling business."

"Carisa . . ." Adam's eyes flashed with a warning of anger.

But she pushed on. "And then, of course, there is Julian's school. His *third* school. He has been expelled from two of them now, and it seems the only way they'll keep him is if you donate handsomely to the building projects. And of course, there's also. . . ."

"Enough, Carisa. Enough!" Adam reached for his starched shirt, his collar and tie and shrugged into them. Then he pulled on his waistcoat, his suit coat. In one violent motion he had started for the door.

"Adam!" Carisa ran after him. "Where are you going?"

"I don't know. Downstairs. To my study. Until our guests arrive."

"Adam!" She threw her arms around him. "Oh, Adam, I'm sorry. I don't know what makes me talk that way, I was just so disappointed that you didn't want to come to Newport with me. We could have enjoyed ourselves so much. . . ."

He stood rigidly, his body not giving when she attempted to embrace him.

"No," he said. "No, Carisa, I'm sorry, but I can't accompany you to Newport this time. I've other things to do."

"But what?"

"Didn't I just tell you? *Business*, Carisa. The same excuse you have given me so often."

He was gone, striding out of the room, his boots clicking on the carpet.

Business. The same excuse you have given me so often.

Now, at Newport, the words seemed to whirl uncomfortably in Carisa's brain, accusing her.

But couldn't Adam see how important the circus was to her? How very much it meant to her? She had to make it succeed . . . she *had to*.

Now, restlessly, Carisa rose from her chair and paced toward the railing overlooking the gray Atlantic. Her thoughts were interrupted by the clattering of horses' hooves. She watched as a phaeton, with Katherine in it, pulled up the curving drive to the front of the cottage's verandah and stopped.

Katherine alighted with dignity, and with the help of the coachman, who tactfully looked aside as his mistress' full hoop skirt billowed upward. The past years had aged Katherine. Her skin had grown more sallow, her facial bones more harsh. Her voice, too, had grown even deeper, and now held a gravelly, mannish timber which was her greatest humiliation.

But, in spite of the issue of the Newport cottage, an odd truce had sprung up between the two women. There were times when Carisa was actually almost fond of the crusty older woman.

"Rain!" sputtered Katherine now. She opened her black umbrella and hurried around the corner to the carriage house. "How dare it rain just when I planned to get all the housekeeping done so that we wouldn't have to worry about it later in the season?"

"It is very damp," Carisa admitted, hearing a boisterous shout and thinking with dismay of the children and their worm hunt, of which her mother-in-law would certainly not approve.

But she saw that Katherine's thoughts were not on the children, or on the rain either. There was a white line about her lips, and her gloved fingers played with the umbrella distractedly.

"You should have come along to tea with me, Carisa. And Adam should have been here too," Katherine went on, her face still holding that quenched, gray look. "He's been working himself too hard. And now . . ."

"He . . . he said he had business. Whaling business." Carisa faltered. "Otherwise I am sure he would have come to Newport with us."

Katherine's lips tightened. "Business? Adam has always left his agent in charge of that when he traveled, and surely he could have done the same now. If he weren't so very stubborn, . . ."

Carisa nodded. She knew there was something else that Katherine wished to say.

243

"Carisa," Katherine went on after a moment. "Something has happened. I could hardly sit there . . . Carisa, the women at Vaucluse were saying something very disturbing. They said that General Beauregard has opened fire on Fort Sumter and that they have fired on it for 34 hours. It has fallen."

The voices of the children in the side garden rose suddenly loud and raucous, but Carisa scarcely heard them.

"What?" she said stupidly. She could do nothing but stare at her mother-in-law.

"Do you know, Carisa, Fort Sumter is in Charleston Harbor. Eulalia Weston lives in Charleston, she was a very dear girlhood friend of mine." Katherine's fingers plucked at the ivory handle of her umbrella, as if she did not know what she was doing.

"But . . . Fort Sumter," Carisa repeated. "Then that means. . . ."

"Yes. It means war. I believe that war is certain now. Have you been so wrapped up in your circus that you haven't read the papers, my dear? And there is something else, too. I didn't want to tell you this before, Adam told me not to. But now I think that you should know."

This was nightmare, Carisa had the rapid thought. Katherine's face looking so old and drained, her eyes fixed on Carisa—yes—so pityingly.

"Tell me," Carisa whispered. "Please."

Katherine laid the umbrella against the verandah railing, shaking the moisture carefully out of it. Then she came to seat herself in the wicker chair next to Carisa's.

"Why, if there is war, then Adam is planning to enlist. He has told me so."

Carisa felt as if the verandah were whirling about her. She clutched at the woven arms of her chair. "But . . . he can't be! Mother Hartshorn, surely that's nonsense. He can't enlist, there's going to be a *war,* you've just told me. They've fired on Fort Sumter. . . ."

"I know, Carisa."

"Then . . ."

Carisa jumped out of her chair, her skirts rustling

244

almost as urgently as her thoughts. *Business,* Adam had said. She could feel the color flooding up into her face.

She must go home . . . she must go back to Heartsease at once. She must talk him out of this. . . .

Much as she wished to, however, she could not travel that night but had to wait until the following morning. She dispatched Nelly to the telegraph office in Newport with a frantic telegram for Adam—he was to do nothing without consulting her first, nothing at all.

"You needn't be in such a hurry, Carisa," Katherine said, giving her another of those pitying looks. "These things take time, he won't have gone anywhere in the week we've been gone."

Carisa pressed her hands to her throbbing temples. "I know, I know, Mother Hartshorn, but I still have to go back. I'd go today, right now if I could."

"But as you can't, you'll have to wait until tomorrow morning. And I have to wait until the day after," Katherine remarked with a touch of her old, dominating ways. "Thanks to the children's being allowed outdoors in the damp and the mist, I do believe that Vicki is catching a cold. I'll have to stay here and wait to see how she does."

That night Carisa dreamed, tossing and turning on the linen sheets of the bed which seemed, as always, so empty without Adam.

As before, the smell came first. Carisa moaned in her dream, moaned and tried to burrow away from it. But still it was there, the stench of burning, greasy, fat-bubbling, charred. And other objects, too, had burned: cloth, leather, wood, rope, straw.

Carisa tossed her head from side to side and uttered a desolate little scream of protest.

And then she found that she was walking, across what seemed to be a bare field, and she knew with gut-cramping fright that she had been here before. It had all happened before, this smell, this field, this feeling of utter, devastating loneliness.

She stumbled on desperately. Thank God a mist had come up, a gray, sodden fog which blurred the outlines of the things scattered about. Mounded, dark, hideous objects lying so very still. *What were they?*

But she dared not look, she dared not do anything except hurry past them, consumed by her terror and by her desperate loneliness.

Alone.

Never, ever, had she been so solitary, so bereft, so heart-stoppingly alone.

Never would a man love her again. Never would he touch her gently, or hold her, or strain his body against her own in passion, or thrust hard, tumid maleness into her. Never . . .

Her chest felt as if a long, glittering shard of glass were twisted in it. And then, slowly, a feeling of urgency seized her. She must run, she knew this with a wild, plunging relief. If she did, if she ran as hard as she could, there was still a chance—

"Adam!" She awoke screaming. *"Adam, Adam, don't go! Oh, God, Adam, you mustn't go! You mustn't!"*

The noise of her screaming echoed in the big, sea-damp bedroom at Newport. Then it faded away. Carisa lay very still in the bed, feeling as if some heavy weight had been placed on her body, pinning her to the mattress. Perspiration was running off her face and body, dampening the sheet. Yet her hands and feet were icy cold. Her skin felt clammy and sick.

Adam—Her thoughts were wild. *Oh, Adam*—She stirred in the bed, gave a little sobbing gasp, and sat up. She reached for the lace handkerchief she kept on her bedside table, and wiped the moisture from her face.

Reality began to seep back. She became aware of the swift pumping of her heart. She looked about her, at the thick, unfamiliar darkness. Dim light glimmered on the handle of a ewer, and she realized that she was not at Hearts-ease. She was still at Newport, in the large bedroom there which she and Adam had often shared.

"Miss Carisa! Miss Carisa!" Nelly came running into the room, her nightgown a swirl of white. "What's wrong? You were screaming! Oh, it gave me such a turn!"

In her long cotton nightgown, her hair pulled back

into a knobby braid, Nelly looked no older than the 18-year-old country girl who had first been assigned to Carisa.

"It . . . it was nothing, Nelly. I had a nightmare, that's all."

"Another one?"

"Yes." Carisa reached for the little tin box which held matches, and drew one out with fingers that trembled violently. Once, after such a dream, she was remembering, Adam had held her to him and stroked her hair as if she were a child. . . .

"I'll light the lamp," Nelly said. "You're shaking like a leaf, it must have been a bad one, eh?" She took the matches from Carisa and deftly manipulated the lamp. Sudden light flared into the room. "Would you like me to fix you some hot milk? They say it does wonders for night upsets."

"Oh, all right. I don't care." Carisa sank back weakly onto the soft mattress, trying to quell the feeling of apprehension that still wriggled in her like an insect.

In a few moments Nelly was back with the tray containing a small pot of hot milk and some scones left over from afternoon tea.

"I found these," she announced. "For once Brigid managed not to eat them first."

She set down the tray, rearranged the scones on their plate, and stood back until Carisa had taken her first sip of milk.

"I never heard of anyone having dreams like yours before," Nelly said after a moment. "Scary ones that make you scream like that. My Granny, she says you're a diviner, a foreboder. You see the future, don't you?"

Carisa said nothing.

"Granny, she says it's rare for folks to see the future like that," Nelly went on with relish. "She says hardly anyone ever does it, and if they do, it only happens to them once. Once she dreamed my Grandpa shouldn't go on the *Elisha Smith,* that was a whaler owned by Mr. Samuel Hartshorn. So she told him to stay home and he did. Later that ship went down off Greenland with all hands lost."

Carisa took another uneasy sip of milk. She wished that Nelly would stop talking and go back to bed.

"But you dream a lot, don't you, Miss Carisa?" In the lamplight Nelly's eyes were eager. "My Granny she says it prob'ly runs in your family."

"My mother used to read palms and do the Tarot Cards," Carisa admitted.

"See?" Nelly was triumphant. "Can you read the future, too?"

"Nelly, it's the middle of the night. And I think I can rest now. I'm finished with the milk, so if you could just take away the tray. . . ."

"But you could try," the girl urged. "Oh, I know you could, if you wanted to. All I want to know is maybe the next five or ten years of my life. See, Gaines, he wants me to marry him. He's been askin' me for six months now, and I don't know what to tell him."

"Do what you think best, Nelly." Carisa said it wearily. "If you would like to marry, then go ahead. You will have a job here at Hearts-ease as long as you wish it. I'll see to that."

"Thank you, oh, thank you! But I don't know. See, the war's coming on, and they're talking about getting up volunteer companies. *He* said if Mr. Hartshorn enlisted, he might want to go and do it, too. . . ."

"Gaines! Enlist!"

"Well, of course, he's a bit old, he's not a boy, but he figures they might have him, and he could always lie about his age. His hair's not hardly gray at all. . . ."

Carisa put both hands to her temples and massaged them. Abruptly her head ached, her temples were pounding, and she couldn't stand any more of this. *Adam,* she wanted to cry out. *Adam, Adam, if you ever loved me at all, even a tiny bit, if you ever, ever loved me*—

". . . So, if you could just tell my fortune, Miss Carisa, I know I haven't any right to ask, and I swear I won't ever ask it of you again. . . ."

"Nelly, I can't. My mother died when I was born, as you know, and I never learned to read palms. As for my dreams, they . . . they're not reliable . . ."

"Oh," Nelly's voice indicated hurt. She picked up the tray and started toward the door. "Well, you get a good night's sleep, and then you'll have good traveling in the morning. I'm sure of it."

"Yes," Carisa said. "And . . . thank you for the milk, Nelly."

"You're welcome, ma'am."

But after the servant left, Carisa could not go to sleep. She lay unmoving in her bed, staring toward the tall rectangle of window just beginning to gray with light. She lay there watching until the square of sky beyond the glass had turned pearly with morning.

Earlier in the day it had been misty but now it was clearing. The water of Winthrop's Cove gleamed through the trees, giving glimpses of mills and wharves and stacks of barrels.

The farm wagon, with its rickety slatted sides filled to capacity with chickens, ground to a stop. Julian Hartshorn climbed out of the back. Feathers had flown into his face for the past five miles, mingled with the hot stench of droppings. He was relieved that his trip was finally, after five days, over.

"This here where you're stopping, boy?" The farmer, a red-faced man in his thirties, sent a long brown stream of tobacco juice spurting into the dust.

"Yes."

Julian dug into his pocket and extracted a coin from the horde he had managed to steal from ugly old Roe, the master at his last school. Horrid Roe, he wished he had killed him. For eight months he had dreamed of doing just that.

"Here," he told the man. "Take this."

The man looked at the coin. "Now, you've no call to be paying me a thing, son. Didn't want to say it, but you look like a runaway to me, and I prob'ly warn't doing you no favor taking you further from home. By the looks of you, skinny and half-starved, you won't last long. You need all the money you can hang on to."

Julian stared at him without gratitude. "All right," he

said. He picked up his bundle from the cart bed and started to walk away.

"Boy?" yelled the farmer. "Boy, you'd better go home to your Pa. Ain't no good runnin' away like this. Better to go home and take your licking like a man and get it over."

Julian made a rude gesture. The farmer slapped the reins and the wagon, amid squeak of wheels and protest of chickens, began to roll again.

Julian stood looking about him, drawing in deep breaths of New London air. He was on Main Street, looking toward town and an array of buildings, stores, livery stables, wharves and mills.

It was really an ugly town, he thought with a sudden rush of anger toward it. Not like New York, which had been huge, row upon row of streets and manufactories and houses, going on forever. He had liked New York, with its traffic and vitality and its din of street vendors shouting out their wares—peanuts and hot corn and hot chestnuts and pies. Even the Hale School had been—he stopped the thought.

Damn old Roe's ugly, pimpled face anyway, he had no call to beat Julian as he had done, no call at all. *Hands reaching, towels snapping, something jabbing, unspeakable pain . . . the boys, all of them, looking at him naked, jeering, laughing . . .*

Julian swallowed back bile. He drew in another, shallower breath, breathing in the odor of ammonia and horse as the wind blew smells from a livery stable in his direction. Billows of white steam rose from a chimney somewhere to stain the sky.

Ugly, Julian thought. Ugly, dirty, horrid, this town and all of the people in it. All of them! Except Poll, of course. She alone was not horrid. She alone . . .

He began to walk toward the center of town, stuffing his small cloth bundle into the blouse of his shirt so that it wouldn't show. He had long ago thrown away the ugly black coat and waistcoat of his school uniform. Now his shirt was filthy, his pants clay-colored from road dust and chicken droppings and the daubs of mud he had deliberately wiped on them. Now he looked like any street boy, any farm or horseboy. Ragged, tough, carefree . . .

A little girl came scuffing up the road, the hem of her skirt brown with dust. She was rolling a hoop with a stick. She had a little pushed-in face and small, tired blue eyes. She was about eight, he decided, looking at her boldly.

He sauntered up to her and kicked with his boot toe at her hoop. It wobbled, fell over into the dust, and lay still.

"Listen," he said. "Where's Poll Henry's place? Do you know where her house is?"

"Who?" The little girl made no effort to pick up her hoop. Her eyes regarded him warily. She must have brothers, Julian thought disgustedly. She must be used to kicking and pushing and gibes. He was disappointed. He had wanted to make her cry.

"I said Poll Henry, you little idiot! Do you know where she lives?"

"No."

"You don't know anything, do you?"

"No."

"Aw, go on, will you?" Julian gave a savage kick at the hoop and watched it skitter in the dust. Abruptly he was tired of this. "Go on, I said! Get out of here, you little pig!"

Stupid, he thought as she snatched at her hoop and ran. He continued on down the road to where a red and white pole indicated a barber shop. A flag was flying in front of the barber shop, too. Had someone died? Were they celebrating something?

Like a shiver coming over him, he thought back to school, to the moment when he had heard the masters joshing each other. They hadn't known Julian was crouched there under the stairs: if they had, they would probably have beaten him.

One of them had come from New London. He was telling the others about a woman named Poll Henry, about the big house she kept where the pianoforte played all night long. Hers was a mighty popular place to be, the man had boasted. There was a mirror room, too, four walls of glass and glass on the ceiling, too, each square of it framed in birds-eye maple. It was the talk of New London—in some circles, at least. And reflected in those mirrors were some of the prettiest girls in the East—

Poll Henry. Julian, crouched down low so that no one would see him, had frozen. He had thought his heart would pound itself right out through his clothes.

Poll. He had thought her gone, gone forever out West, as his father had told him once, gone to make her fortune in gold. How he had hated her for leaving him.

But now it seemed that she hadn't gone at all. She was right in New London. And he could remember so clearly the soft feel of her, her hands on him, gently urging, the husky whisper. No one else had loved him as Poll had, or ever would again. He knew this, and now he was going to find her.

Boldly he approached the barber shop, stared for a moment at the flag, and then walked in. Inside it was cool, dim, soap-fragrant. Two barbers were bent over towel-draped customers, shaving them while a third man waited. One wall was lined with dark separated shelves, which held shaving mugs—fifty or sixty of them—belonging to regular patrons. Was his father's mug there? Julian wondered fleetingly.

An ornate sideboard held five mirrors all framed in carved mahogany and gleaming with bottles. Signs nailed to the wall advertised dandruff cures and hair tonics. Looking downward to the floor, Julian saw wads of cut hair—black, gray, blond, brown—and damp places near the spittoon where someone's aim had been less than perfect.

The barber in the first chair looked up. He had been deep in discussion with his customer over someplace called Fort Sumter, and some meeting which some people were having to raise money. It was clear that he found Julian an interruption.

"You want a shave, son?" He grinned, revealing a missing front tooth. "Though from the looks of you, it's a bath you need more'n anything else."

All five men guffawed loudly. The waiting customer hawked and spat a gob of saliva into the spittoon.

Julian flushed. "I shaved this morning," he lied. "What I do need to know is where Poll Henry is. I have a message for her."

"A message! Poll Henry!" Again all the men laughed. "And what would a young sprout like you be needing with the likes of Poll?"

"I just want to see her."

Julian was scowling. He didn't like these men, he didn't like anything about them. Men in barber shops were like the boys at school, or even the masters at their leisure. Secret societies which you couldn't get into, and you never knew why not, all you knew was that you were out, forever out.

"You?" The second barber's teeth were very white under his black handlebar mustache. "You haven't got a dong big enough to ring a bell, never mind what it takes to ring Miss Poll's bell."

Again they all laughed.

Julian could feel his heart begin to thud. His saliva felt sticky in his throat. He advanced on the second barber and narrowed his eyes at him.

"I didn't ask you to laugh," he said thickly. "I asked you to tell me where she is."

He kept on narrowing his eyes at the mustached barber and he put hate into his look, all the hate he had stored in him waiting to come out.

"Oh, all right, kid. Just joshing you, eh?" The barber glanced uneasily at his companions. "She lives up on the hill. You know, up and off the cove in that there woods . . . kind of private, you know. Anyone can go back there and no one would know, see. . . ."

"Where? Which street is it?" Julian demanded.

The man told him, the barber shop fallen oddly silent as he did so. When he had finished, Julian turned and left without thanking him. He could hear the buzz of their talk as he left the shop, and he felt the anger whir in him like insects.

Well, he didn't care. Let them die. Let them all die.

253

He was never going to go back to that barber shop anyway.

The big house where the barber had said Poll lived lay quiet in its grove of trees. Its bricks had been painted white and its windows were shuttered with dark green, giving the place a cool look behind its trees. A little wooden picket fence enclosed the small front yard and behind the forsythia hedge Julian glimpsed a large carriage barn still in its original red brick. A stable man snoozed in a doorway.

He trudged up the driveway, still thinking of the barbers with hate. He would like to come back with a match sometime and set that ugly old barber shop on fire. Burn up all those shaving mugs, especially his father's.

A sleepy-eyed girl came to the door. She wore black silk and a fine white lawn apron pinned to her dress.

"Who're you?" she asked him, yawning in his face.

He gave her the narrow-eyed look. "I want to see Miss Poll Henry."

"Hell, I know you do, you just said so. And I just asked who you was. *She* says I got to." The girl laughed happily. She hadn't even noticed his glare.

"I'm Julian Hartshorn. She knows who I am. And I said I want to see her."

"Oh. Well . . ." She shrugged and ushered him into a big entrance hall, which had a parquet floor polished to mirror brightness, not a heel scuff on it. Curved stairs with a mahogany bannister led upstairs. Three dark paneled doors opened off the hall, but they were all closed. Julian wondered which one belonged to the room with the mirrors.

"Julian!" Poll came partly downstairs and then paused, a bottle-green wrapper pulled about her thin body. Her eyes were puffy, as if she had just waked up. "Julian, that isn't you, is it?"

"Yes. It's me." He stood stiffly, hands jammed into his pockets.

"Julian. Little Julian. I'd never have recognized you. God, you used to look like a little angel in a painting once. And now you're nearly a man grown . . . your voice is changed and all, so deep. Your hair's the only thing about you that's the same. It's still as curly as ever. I used to comb your hair, did you know that? No one ever had such soft hair as yours."

He stared at her, his heart squeezing with some odd pain he hadn't felt in years. Why didn't she come down?

"Poll . . ." he began.

"But what on earth are you doing here, Julian?" he heard her ask. "*Here* of all places."

"I ran away from school."

"Well, you've no call to be here. My God, do you realize what your father would do if he ever caught me having you here at my house? He'd kill me, you little fool. Or try to."

"I ran away from school," he repeated. "I heard you were here. Some of the masters, they were talking. About your mirror room."

"Ah, yes, my famous mirror room." Poll made a face. She advanced six more steps down, her dressing gown rustling. He caught a whiff of her—stale perfume and sleep and feminine body. It was a smell out of his childhood.

"I want to see it," he said.

She threw back her head and laughed. "Why? You want to see my mirror room? Imagine what your dear father would think if he knew."

Her eyes gleamed at him and the cords in her neck worked, as if she were silently laughing at some private joke of her own.

"He doesn't know. And I hate your laughing at me. Come downstairs, Poll, all the way down. Show me that room. I want to see it."

She gazed at him for a long moment. Her eyes were deeper and darker than he remembered them, with a new look that hadn't been in them before. Like the eyes of that little girl he had seen on the street, he thought suddenly. Yes, that was it. As if Poll already had brothers and didn't care what anyone did to her any more.

"All right," she said huskily. "Come on, then, you

255

little brute. Come on and see my mirrors. Why the hell should I care? But then you'll have to go. I'm not running a boys' school, for God's sake. Not me, not Poll. Jesus, just the opposite. And if you think I want you here for very long. . . ."

She came down the remaining steps. She reached him and touched him and he drank in the familiar smell of her and then sobs started to rip through him.

16

Three years previously, Duddie had received a package from England, from a favorite brother, Ledyard, the only member of his family with whom he still kept in touch. In it was a letter and a photograph, carefully wrapped in oilcloth to withstand the rigors of the Atlantic crossing.

Later Duddie, tears in his eyes, had shown the picture to Carisa. Taken in 1856, it showed a handsome young British officer seated wearing his great-coat and the hat of the Grenadier Guards, one arm held tightly about a pensive little girl, who leaned toward her father with one finger in her mouth. The officer, too, looked pensive, his eyes piercing and sad.

At first glance the picture seemed ordinary enough, and Carisa was about to give it back to Duddie, when suddenly she noticed that the officer had no left arm. The left sleeve of his great-coat trailed across his lap, empty. And, she saw with growing horror, the man's left pant leg had been folded up as well. He was missing both an arm and a leg.

"He has only one arm to put around his daughter now," Duddie told her in a low, muffled voice. "Balaclava did that to him, Carisa."

The photograph, coming as it did so soon after her own leg injuries, had made a deep impression on her. Now, curiously, it was this of which she was thinking as she arrived back in New London the following afternoon. The beautiful, mutilated man. . . .

To her dismay, she found that the city was flying with flags because of the news of Fort Sumter. More flags waved from the vessels in the harbor, as if this were a holiday instead of the beginning of war. Men rushed excitedly up and down the wharves, and small boys played with sticks of wood as muskets. A woman was jubilantly hawking hot muffins, and somewhere a string of firecrackers went off.

How dare they? Carisa wondered, feeling sick. How could anyone laugh and play at war? She thought again of the picture, the piercing, sad eyes of the man who had looked out at her from it. Only six years ago the British had lost tens of thousands of men in the Crimean War, Duddie had told her. They had died of wounds, of cholera, malaria, dysentery, cold, starvation.

Could such a terrible thing happen here in the United States? Could—but quickly she pushed away the thought.

She averted her eyes and hurried past the waving flags and the excited men. She hailed the first public hack she saw and sat numbly in the shabby conveyance as it jolted its way over the ruts of the road to Hearts-ease. Her thoughts were in a turmoil. Why hadn't Adam confided in her? Why hadn't he told her what he planned to do? And why, she wondered furiously, did he have to enlist at all!

A cold wind had sprung up, and afternoon shadows were beginning to creep out of the grove of hemlocks. Hearts-ease lay among its lawns and trees, silent and seemingly deserted. The hack pulled up by the carriage house and as she paid the man Carisa noticed that the brougham was gone. Evidently Adam was elsewhere.

The hack rattled off down the drive, its horse weary and sway-backed, as were the animals who pulled most public conveyances. On an impulse, Carisa picked up her skirts and went into the carriage house.

Tim Kelly, the new stableboy, was polishing some brass harness fittings. The smell of dung, of ammonia and straw, was strong in the air.

"Mrs. Hartshorn." He ducked his head in surprise. "Mr. Hartshorn is out. He left an hour ago in the brougham."

"So I see," Carisa said.

"And Master Julian took out Thunder," the boy added.

Carisa stared at him. "Julian? Did you say Julian?"

"Yes, ma'am." Blue eyes regarded her. Tim Kelly, roughly Julian's age, was the orphaned son of an Irish immigrant who had died shortly after reaching the United States. The boy's mother and young sister had died, as well, of influenza. The boy had come to Hearts-ease begging for work, and Adam had hired him, although usually he did not hire youngsters as young as this one. But, as Adam had told Carisa privately, the boy could not be allowed to roam the streets like some of the "street arabs" in New York City. Besides, he seemed willing to work, and thus far had done his job without complaint.

"But when did Julian get back?" Carisa asked the boy now.

"About an hour ago, I guess. He came in here and asked was his father at home, and then he went in the house. After a while Mr. Hartshorn came out and went away and then Mr. Julian came out and asked for his horse. He's out riding Thunder now. Down that path, I think. The path that leads to the circus barns."

"Yes," Carisa said. "Yes, I see. Thank you, Tim."

The boy nodded soberly. "Yes, ma'am."

She hurried into the house, redolent with its familiar smells of beeswax and wood and old furniture. Today, however, the house was silent; Katherine had taken most of the servants with her to Newport and would not be returning with them and the children until the following day. Now tiny motes of dust floated in the bar of sunlight which streamed in through the tall, oval window by the staircase.

Carisa drew in a quick breath. She could visualize what had happened. Adam had probably given Julian a

258

severe scolding for running away from school, then had left the house in one of his quick angers.

She stood for a moment, indecisively. If only she knew where Adam had gone, she would follow him and have this out with him at once. But she didn't know—he could have gone to town, to one of his friends', to his shipping office, anywhere.

Abruptly she turned and rushed upstairs, throwing off her bonnet and mantle as she went. Within a few minutes she had struggled into her riding habit, of dark blue pelisse cloth, and was back at the stables. She asked Tim to give her Judge, her favorite bay gelding. If she could not talk to Adam, at least she could find his son.

For several years now she had been riding, thankful that her legs had healed sufficiently for her to sit upon a saddle. She would never perform again, of course, nor could she take unnecessary risks. Nor could any saddle horse ever be like Phoebe, so intelligent and responsive. Still, the riding had been a pleasure, and she did it as often as she could.

Now she wheeled Judge forward and spurred him to a gallop, her skirts flying to reveal the discreet trousers which were a part of every riding costume. For an instant she gave herself up to the sheer animal pleasure of the ride, the motion of the animal's body, the answering sway of her own.

In a few moments she had rounded the corner of the path and was approaching the large, octagonal brick building which she had built for the Phillips Circus to practice in during the winter months. It contained one circus ring and seating for 100. A spur drive had been constructed off the plank road to the right so that carriages could reach the building.

But today the octagonal building was deserted, its entrance hidden in deep, late-afternoon shadow.

A shadow that moved, Carisa noted as she rode closer.

"Julian! Julian, is that you?" She brought Judge to a quivering, restless stop. He champed skittishly at the bit.

She dismounted. "Oh, do be calm, Judge," she said, patting the animal's flank. "Julian, what on earth are you doing home? Surely your school term isn't up yet, is it?"

"No." The boy sat glumly on a carriage stone, his cheeks cupped in his hands, staring into the distance.

"Then you've run away again, haven't you?"

"Yes."

She gazed at him more closely. At this moment Adam's son looked more like a stableboy than a student. His shirt was ragged and grimy, and she saw no evidence of a hat, coat, or waistcoat. His trousers were covered with yellow dust, and there was a hole in the toe of his boot. She saw, too, that there was a fresh, lacerated bruise on the side of his face, and another one on the palm of his right hand.

"Julian!" she heard herself cry. "Not again! Your third school. Why do you keep running away? Don't you like school?"

"No! I hate it. I hate it, I tell you. The masters, they hit you with their stick if you make the slightest mistake. And . . ." Julian stopped. A shudder ran through his body, and a curious expression crossed his face, as if he had seen something unspeakably ugly.

"Julian, would you tell me about it?"

His eyes lifted to hers, and now she saw how very blue they were, how hard and piercing and direct. Unsettling eyes to belong to a boy not yet sixteen.

"Did your father punish you for running away from school?" she asked gently.

The boy did not answer.

"Well, then, I can guess. You argued with him, and then you came to the stables and decided to go riding." She glanced about her. "But, Julian, where is Thunder? Where is your horse?"

The boy's eyes lowered, and with one dusty boot he traced a semi-circle in the dirt. "He's . . . down the path. Toward the woods."

"Down the path?" Carisa found that her mouth was suddenly, uncomfortably dry. She stared at her step-son.

How pale he looked, she thought abruptly. And where had he gotten the abrasions on his face and hands?

Suddenly she knew. A sick feeling flooded through her.

"Oh, Julian. Julian, you didn't. Not that jump . . . the fence you always used to jump with your pony?"

"Yes."

Carisa took a step backward, involuntarily touching the warm, heaving flank of Judge, as if to assure herself of his existence. "But . . . Thunder? Is he all right?" she heard herself ask. "Did you lame him?"

"He threw me and broke his right foreleg and I had to come back to the stable and get the pistol. That Tim Kelly didn't even know."

Nor did Adam, Carisa felt sure. Not yet. Shock catapulted through her.

"Don't look at me like that," Julian said. "It wasn't my fault."

"But it was your fault, Julian! Don't you see? You abused that animal, running him breakneck, you were careless with him. . . ."

Julian's eyes, suddenly raised to hers, blazed desolation at her. "I'm never going back to school again, Carisa. I don't care what Papa does to me, he can kill me if he likes, I don't care. But I'm not going back. I'm never going back there again. And I don't care what happened to that stupid old horse, do you hear me? I don't care."

"Why on earth did you send me that telegram, Carisa?" Adam's laugh was bitter. "Did you think that I planned to leave for the War tomorrow morning? It takes weeks to organize a regiment. Didn't you know that?"

It was four hours later. Adam had only just now subsided from his rage on learning that Julian had destroyed his horse. He had whipped his son and the youth was now sullenly confined to his bedroom, supperless and forbidden to ride again for a year.

Carisa and Adam had dined on shad and boiled potatoes prepared by Elsie, assistant cook to Brigid, whose culinary abilities left much to be desired. They

261

had spoken little, for Carisa did not wish the servant girl to hear their conversation, and preferred to wait until they had more privacy.

But now their talk could be delayed no longer. They were in their bedroom, preparing for bed. Wind rattled and shook at the window panes; it had begun to rain. Adam paced restlessly back and forth across the carpet, stopping with each circuit to gaze at the moisture running down the outside of the glass.

It was as if, Carisa thought bleakly, he wished himself elsewhere, even in this rain.

She herself had unlaced her corset and pulled on a loose, beige silk dressing gown. Now she sat at her little dressing table staring blindly at her own reflection in the mirror.

"It sickens me," Adam said suddenly. "To think of a good animal being wantonly destroyed like that. There are times when I cannot believe that Julian is my son, that he came from my loins even as Matt did."

He was silent for a long moment. "Even at six, Matt is more of a son to me than Julian will ever be," he added heavily. "God help me, God help us all, but it's true."

Silence—except for the sound of the rain—again settled on the room while Carisa tried to gather her thoughts. Julian—Fort Sumter, the coming War—what would happen to them all?

She realized that Adam was speaking to her again, this time about the War.

"I'd have thought that you, Carisa, of all people, would have the stuff in you to be calm," he said. "Especially when it seems that the whole city of New London has gone wild with the news of Fort Sumter."

"Yes. I saw the flags."

"I think it's going to be a very fast war," Adam went on. "The Southerners have fire and courage . . . I'll grant them that . . . but we here in the North are the ones with the factories and the railroads. We control the sea, and with the quantities of food we can grow to send abroad, we'll be able to buy all the munitions we need.

262

I'll give them six months, possibly less. Then they'll come crawling back, ready to rejoin the Union."

Carisa sat while Adam, his voice waxing enthusiastic, went on to talk of the war, and of the North's chances of winning it. His cousin, Henry Holburn, who lived in Hartford, already had a commission in the Army. Holburn, Adam said, was a good man, both loyal and honest, and if he were to form a regiment there, Adam wished to join him. Of course, if a regiment were to be formed here in New London itself—

Carisa wasn't listening. All she could see was Adam's face, alight with the desire to leave his wife and children to go to war. As he talked, she watched him. A handsome man in the prime of his manhood, whenever Adam entered a room, women were aware of him. Of the arrogantly broad shoulders, of the rangy body which moved with such authority. The tawny hair, the boldly clefted chin, the yellow eyes which could blaze out with anger and which, it was said, resembled almost exactly the eyes of the first Adam Hartshorn.

And yet tonight, in the flickering lamplight, she could see the tiny sun-wrinkles fanning out from Adam's eyes as he talked. Adam was 42 years old, she remembered. Didn't he realize that war was for younger men— for youths in their teens and twenties?

"Adam . . ." She swallowed hard, forcing her voice to remain steady. "Adam, why? Why are you doing this foolish thing? You don't have to; you're needed here, in New London. There will be ships to build, whale oil needed for the Army, money to raise."

Adam made a derisive gesture. "The life of an old man, Carisa."

"But . . . you're *needed* here!" She was fuming. "Adam, *I* need you here!"

"Do you? I'm a man, Carisa. A Hartshorn. And these days it seems that you are the person of affairs in this household, while I merely sit in my study and indulge in endless conferences with my whaling agent. Or take your money," he added bitterly.

"So that's it!" Carisa threw down the pins she had been taking out of her hair, and jumped out of her

263

low chair. She flung herself at Adam, throwing her arms around him. He stood rigid, his body pulling away from hers.

"Adam, you're talking nonsense. Why shouldn't I give you whatever money I can? After all, don't I owe it to you? Haven't you financed the Phillips Circus right from the very beginning? Without you, without your backing, we would be nothing."

"I realize that."

"Then what is wrong with you?" she demanded furiously. "With us? We . . . we haven't really talked in months! We quarreled when I left for Newport. Now we're quarreling again. You act as if there is a barrier between us. A barrier you don't even want to cross any more. Is it the circus?" she demanded. "Is it my show which is doing this to us?"

"I don't know."

He had pulled away from her to stand at the window, his back to her. She felt the flood of her helpless anger and fear. He was slipping away from her—further and further, it seemed, with every word they uttered. He *wanted* to leave her. Wanted to go to war to escape her. That was it, she was sure of it.

"Adam, haven't I fulfilled every part of the promise I made to you when we were married? I bore you two children, and. . . ."

"It would have been three children, Carisa."

She caught her breath. Her miscarriage in 1859 had been a deep issue between them, for it had happened on one of her circus trips. Adam could not accompany her, and had requested that she remain at home until he could. However, she had refused to do so. The show needed her, she insisted, its problems could not wait. She had slammed out of the house with only Nelly to accompany her. Ignominiously, the belly cramps had struck her almost as soon as she had boarded the steamer; she had had to suffer the miscarriage with only a frightened Nelly and another woman traveler to help.

If she lived to be ninety, she would never forget the

ashen look on Adam's face when she had been brought hastily back home. Or the words he had grated at her: *"In a way you killed our child, Carisa. Even if you didn't wish to. You and your damned obsession with that circus."*

And even later, after she had wept in his arms and he had comforted her and kissed her and told her he hadn't meant what he had said, still she had known that Adam would never forget the small son who had been lost to them.

"It is the circus, isn't it?" she asked now, dully. "Somehow I think you've always hated it."

"No." Adam slowly turned and she saw the expression of pain on his face, the bitter twist of his mouth. "No, Carisa, I've never hated the circus. If I had. . . ." He was silent for so long that the empty air of the room seemed to beat between them.

At last he went on. "Do you remember that day when the deBord show came, and the *Flying Flambeaux* performed? God, but you were beautiful. You were a naiad, a nymph, a girl from another, more golden, more perfect world."

Her heart squeezed painfully inside her. She stumbled over to the dressing table and sat down again. She felt her hands pick up her hairbrush and begin to pull it through her long hair. Stroke after stroke, tugging at her scalp, the hairs soft and fine and crackling with electricity.

"I think I loved you that first moment I saw you," Adam went on in that terrible voice which would not let her near him. "You were reclining on the back of that wonderful horse you had then, all huge curved neck and muscular flanks and intelligence . . . what a beautiful animal. And then, later, you looked so helpless. So pitiable, like a fallen bird. . . ."

He paused. "I couldn't help myself. I had to have you, at whatever the cost. Even if the price was buying a circus for you."

"And now you're sorry you paid that price." Her hands continued to brush without her volition. In the mirror she could see Adam's face.

"Yes." He said it heavily. "I suppose I am. You see, Carisa, I deluded myself. I thought that the circus was . . . oh, I don't know, a toy. Something to give you in place of what you'd lost. I thought that after your legs were healed you'd tire of it and settle down. After all, you were so young. How was I to know that you'd turn out like this, so singlemindedly intent on building a monument to your father? A monument," Adam's mouth twisted bitterly, "constructed out of canvas and spangles!"

"Adam . . ."

"I suppose it's shameful of me, but in a way I almost wish that your first season's tour had been a failure, Carisa. Then it would have folded and all of this would have been over."

"No!" she cried out involuntarily.

"You see? You can't stand to think of it failing, can you? Oh, we both know why you married me. And it wasn't out of love, although you may pretend that to yourself now. Nor was it even from a shabby desire for security or for children . . . any of the usual reasons women marry. No, you wanted me for one reason only. You wanted that circus, and I was the one single avenue through which you could get it."

"Adam . . ." The brush seemed to float down from her fingers, to land on the floor. She barely noticed it fall. "No . . . Adam, it's not like that, I swear it isn't . . . I do love you, truly I do. . . ."

She was weeping. Unashamedly begging. Stretching out her hands to him.

Adam took a step toward the bedroom door, his body moving with easy grace.

"Well, Carisa, we have kept our bargain, haven't we? And now you have your show, your immensely successful circus which keeps on growing every year. Your gorgeous show which your father spurns, which he's never once been to see, and which he'll probably go down to his grave without viewing."

"Adam!" She screamed it out. She jumped to her feet, the dressing gown rustling frantically about her.

266

But his hand was already on the doorknob. "Don't follow me, Carisa, don't come with me."

"Adam?" she whispered. "Adam, where . . . where are you going at this hour of the night? It's raining."

"I don't know." Did she see a glitter of moisture in her husband's eyes? Or was it only the lamplight reflected there? "Perhaps I'll ride, Carisa. I just want to be out in the clean night air, I want to think."

And he was gone.

17

That night Carisa lay alone in the big four-poster bed, listening to the tick of the ormolu clock and thinking feverishly of the daguerreotype of Duddie's brother. The handsome, sad-eyed man with only one arm to put around his child. She tossed and turned restlessly, dropping off to sleep, then almost immediately awakening again.

At some point she became aware that it had begun to rain harder. Thunder rumbled, and finally it cracked outside the house, so loudly that she was sure it would explode the ceiling and floor apart.

She sat bolt upright, her heart pounding, to discover that Adam was in the room. She could hear the small sounds he made as he undressed and then slid into the bed beside her. He smelled of ozone and rain, and she knew he must have been riding all of these hours.

"Are you wet?" she mumbled sleepily. "Your clothes . . ."

"I took them off. Don't worry about me, Carisa. Go back to sleep, if you can in this storm."

"But I don't want to sleep."

Thunder crashed. Eerie yellow-white light filled the room, illuminating Adam's face, every line of it known to her as well as she knew her own, and yet with the power to stir her.

Something made her fumble at the high yoke of her nightgown, tearing away ribbons and pearl buttons. "Adam . . . please . . . I don't want to sleep . . . not yet. . . ."

She had never known that her fingers could move so fast, be so heedless of ribbon and cloth. Some strange urgency drove her. In a few seconds she was naked. When the lightning cracked again she knew that Adam was looking at her, at the pale pearly color of her skin, the curves.

Yet he did not move toward her.

"Adam!" She said it desperately. She moved across the bed toward him and began to unbutton his nightshirt. Thunder boomed outside their bedroom as if they had been transported to the center of some giant cataclysm. Yellowish light flared again, revealing Adam's face, angry and yearning and full of passion.

"Adam? Please?" she whispered.

"Oh, God damn you, girl . . . damn you. . . ." He pulled her to him. She felt his body press against hers, so tightly that she could not tell where his flesh left off and hers began.

"Carisa . . . oh, my love, my little love. . . ."

His hands, his mouth, his lips, taking fierce possession of her.

Their climax came as another bolt of thunder, fiercer and more magnificent than the rest, boomed in elemental fury. Carisa, clinging to Adam and rocketing with him in the sudden, sweet explosion, had no time for thought. She was mindless, a part of the thunder and the rain and the stormy wind.

They slept in each other's arms. When Carisa awoke the next morning the rain had stopped, the windows were dry and clear, and the bed beside her was empty.

Two days later Katherine and the children were back from Newport. Vicki, although still pale, had recovered from her fever, and Matt and Neecie, filling the house with their chatter and noise, were in their usual ruddy good health. Matt and his father had gone for long rides together, the small boy attempting to sit his horse exactly as Adam did, his eyes, so like Adam's, alight with hero-worship.

Julian, however, had refused to go back to school.

"I hate it there," the boy told Carisa. "I won't go back, and if you try to make me, I'll only run away again. I'll run away and join the Army."

"You'll do no such thing," Carisa snapped. She stared at the blue, defiant eyes. She had never been able to reach the boy. She did not know if anyone could. But certainly the boarding schools had done him little good.

She hesitated. "Very well," she said at last. "If you wish, Julian, I'll speak with your father."

"Yes," Julian muttered.

Adam, going over some correspondence in his study, looked up when Carisa knocked. Quickly she entered and told him what his son had said.

"So perhaps the influence of a father is what he needs now," she finished reluctantly.

Adam put down his pen. "If only Julian were more like Matt . . ." he stopped. "Very well. He can stay home until the fall term. But he has to go back then, I insist upon it. In spite of his failures, Julian is a bright boy, perhaps even a brilliant one. He must at least have his education."

"Then let him go to a different school. I don't think they were very kind to him there."

"Kind! Of course they were. He's made that claim about every school to which we've sent him. It's not the schools, Carisa, it's Julian himself, the ugliness in his mind. That's why he doesn't fit in and why they don't like him."

"Ugliness," Carisa said slowly. "Yes, it's as if he carried a taint, a curse about with him wherever he goes. Oh, I think it's pitiable, Adam."

"Yes." Adam suddenly shoved at the stack of letters. Two of them fluttered to the floor. With a quick, cat-like motion, he rose from his chair and went to stare out of the door which opened onto the side garden.

"God knows I know that, Carisa. Don't you think I haven't thought about it a thousand times? I've asked

269

myself why. Was it something in the Hartshorn blood? Why did this have to happen to *my* son?" He hesitated. "There's a devil in him, Carisa."

"Adam! What a thing to say about your own son!"

"Is it? If you don't believe me, Carisa, just gaze into those eyes of his sometime. And see what looks back at you."

So the days passed, and Julian remained at home—quiet, withdrawn, moody. There were long afternoons when the boy disappeared, and no one, not even the servants, knew where he was. And when he was not on one of his mysterious errands, he was teasing the younger children. Twice he had cuffed Matt to tears, and one morning Carisa discovered Vicki locked into the upstairs linen closet, a pool of vomit on the floor.

"Vicki! Darling, darling, how ever did you get in here? Who locked you in?"

The wide gray eyes, swimming in tears, so old-looking for a child of six, looked up at her.

"Was it Julian, darling? Did Julian do this to you?"

The child's lips were trembling convulsively.

"Darling, it *was* Julian, wasn't it? It had to have been. Oh, you can tell me, you can tell your mother. Whatever happened, it wasn't your fault. And I promise you won't be punished."

But Vicki would not—or could not—say a word, and Carisa, trembling with helpless rage, had finally gone to Julian anyway.

"You've been tormenting Matt. Now you've frightened Vicki," she stormed at him. "You are to leave them alone, do you hear? Especially Vicki. She is so quiet and sensitive, she can't stand teasing."

"I hear." His eyes had blazed at her. Then he had turned and run from the room, boots clattering, and they did not see him again for the rest of the day.

"Adam," Carisa said one morning, "Julian and Matt squabble constantly, why, it's as if Julian actually hates the boy. Vicki is so frightened of him that she cries whenever he appears. As for Neecie, even she is quiet when he is around. If we were to allow him to ride his horse again—"

"Ride! After he killed one animal, you want me to give him leave to damage the rest of the horses in the stable? No, I've told him no riding for a year, and one year it will be."

Adam's chin had hardened. "I fear that the boy takes after Jonathan Hartshorn. He was the first Adam's elder brother. He was hanged for murder when he was twenty-one years old."

"Why, Adam!" She stared at him. "You never told me such a horrid thing!"

"Do you blame me?" Adam's smile was fleeting. "There is already enough scandal in the Hartshorn family without spreading this particular story about. Can you imagine what the servants would make of such a tale? Not that some of them don't already know." He touched her arm gently. "Don't fret so about the boy, Carisa. He doesn't deserve your worrying, or anyone's. Some seeds, when they are planted in the ground, come up awry. I fear that Julian is one of them."

"That boy is not a seed!" she snapped.

"Oh? Tell that to all of the schools he's caused havoc in. Meanwhile, I suggest that you tell Persis Gibbon to stay with the younger children at all times. And, as I've said, we'll engage a tutor for Julian, a good, strong fellow who'll put up with no nonsense. That should take care of young Mr. Julian Hartshorn!"

The days passed like wooden beads on the children's play-string. The city of New London was full of war excitement. Volunteer regiments were in the process of forming up for a ninety-day enlistment period. A meeting had been held at the courthouse to raise money for these regiments, amassing the grand sum of ten thousand dollars. Adam himself gave one thousand to the cause. And people were starting to urge that the United States Engineers develop nearby Fort Trumbull and Fort Griswold into proper defense forts.

Carisa, going into town to shop for dress material, could look about her and think how much New London had changed since she had first seen it. The harbor now

271

was filled with ships, many of them flaunting United States flags. The streets, gas-lighted now, were thronged with carriages, and there were horse-drawn omnibusses to carry people about. Business was booming, and companies like the New London Horse Nail Company, on Canal Street, were already operating day and night to produce goods for war.

Emerging one afternoon from W. P. Benjamin's Long Store, Carisa was startled to look upward and see a familiar face peering at her from a new, shiny black buggy.

It was Poll Henry, clad in an elegant wine-red silk, which highlighted the curious dark voluptuousness of her skin. No longer the young girl who had shrieked such fearsome curses at Carisa, Poll was a woman now, with a hard, knowing look about her mouth.

The color mounted to Carisa's face. She had tried to ignore Poll Henry these years, to pretend she did not exist. As all of the other decent women in the town did. . . .

"Afraid of me, Mrs. Hartshorn? Afraid I might sully your fine skirts if I get too close to you?" Poll's laughter bubbled. "Well, say, I still have a job for you, if you dare to take it. And for young Julian, too, if he wants it. Oh, yes, I've seen him . . . every afternoon he's at my house, hiding by the hedge and spying on us! And a lot of nights, too!"

Her laughter echoed maliciously.

Carisa hurried away, her cheeks flaming. She climbed into the surrey and told Tim to head for home, her voice shaking. As the iron carriage wheels jolted over the hardened ruts in the road, she fought back revulsion and dismay. So that was where Julian disappeared to for such long hours—Poll Henry's! And at night, too. Spying on the company, on the men who came and went from that house. . . .

She suppressed a shudder. The big, white-painted brick house was already notorious in the town. According to Nelly, who loved to whisper of such things, it boasted a parlor entirely lined with mirrors. It also had a ballroom where a pianoforte played and young girls lounged about in abbreviated evening costumes. Among those girls, gossip whispered, were Poll's own sisters.

Carisa felt herself shiver again, as she thought of Julian, drawn back like a pitiable moth to the woman who had taken sexual liberties with him as a child . . . Oh, the very thought made her sick. She must do something about this at once.

But what? It would be impossible to tell this to Adam, it would only lend fresh fuel to his rage with his son. As for discussing this with Julian himself, that would be impossible, too. Julian did not listen to her, he did not listen to his father, he did not listen to anyone.

The right front carriage wheel hit a pot-hole, and Carisa had to clutch for support as the surrey swayed wildly. No, there was only one thing she could do, of course. She must speak to Poll herself. . . .

At the end of May, Carisa gave one of her rare dinner parties, to which the people of New London came because she was Mrs. Adam Hartshorn, and they dared not refuse her. This was to be a farewell party for both Adam and Samuel, both of whom had volunteered for a locally formed regiment, for an enlistment period of ninety days.

She still had not been able to bring herself to visit Poll, although the days had merged into weeks, and still Julian disappeared for long hours each day, eluding his tutor. If Adam ever learned where his son was at these times—But he must not know. While he was away, he must have nothing to worry him. She would see to it that he did not. . . .

Numbly, feeling as if she were moving in a dream, she planned the dinner menu, decided which flowers were to be cut from the greenhouse and gardens, which guests were to be included.

Nothing she could say would dissuade Adam from enlisting. The war would be a short one, he insisted. Wasn't his enlistment only for 90 days? He wanted to see some action before it was all over. She, Carisa, was being a timid mouse, a fact all the more surprising in a

273

bold woman like herself. And her fretting was all for nothing. He would be home by August!

The night of the dinner party was one of those spring nights when the air is soft and dreamy, full of the scent of growing things. Carisa dressed for it carefully. Her gown was of light blue silk, a flowing, elegant fabric which caught and held the light. The skirt had three deep flounces, and the collar was turned back at the throat, revealing a delicate, lacy insert. The entire dress was trimmed with matching satin ribbon.

The effect, Carisa told herself, turning in front of the bedroom mirror, was one of restrained elegance. If Adam did have to go to war, at least he would take with him the memory of her as she was this night.

She slapped at her cheeks to put color in them, and forced her lips into a smile. She would let no one see her fear and hurt, her terror at letting him go.

The truth was, she admitted to herself bleakly, Adam wanted to go to war. He actually looked forward to it with zest. And she was sure that a part of his eagerness was simply a desire to get away from her, from what their marriage had become. Adam simply could not believe that she really loved him. In spite of all their lovemaking, in spite of all her persuasions. . . .

"Carisa? Are you quite ready?" The knock on her door proved to be Katherine, come to check on last-minute details for the dinner party.

"Yes . . . I guess so."

"We must go down and see that the flowers are right." Katherine's eyes inspected her daughter-in-law, as if not quite sure she approved. "It's always a mistake to leave such things for the servants."

"Yes . . ." Carisa's lips trembled.

Katherine patted her arm. "Go downstairs, Carisa, and hold your head high. Don't let them see your fear. I'll guarantee you that every woman there will have her own private worries, and will not wish to be reminded of them."

"Yes . . . I suppose you're right. He *wants* to go, Mother Hartshorn. That's what I can't understand. He *wants* this war, he's actually looking forward to it."

"And so is Samuel. So are they all. They're men, and they are all immortal . . . or at least they feel that way. We women know that they are not. . . ." She gave Carisa a firm push. "Now, you must carry your head high and pretend that this is any ordinary party."

"Yes . . . I'll try."

A trace of Katherine's old asperity had returned. "And do be courteous to Madeleine Kord, won't you, Carisa? She has grown plump and disagreeable since the birth of her last child, and even I find her a trial at times. But she is still our neighbor."

"Very well." Obediently Carisa straightened her spine and drew a long breath.

"That's better. Try to look and act like a lady. That can carry you through anything."

Katherine had taken Carisa's arm and was urging her toward the stairs. Numbly Carisa allowed herself to be led. Whether she liked it or not, the party had begun.

Tomorrow, Adam would leave for the war.

Later her memories of this night were to be blurred— Samuel Hartshorn's eyes inspecting her coolly, taking in every aspect of her new gown and the way it clung to her breasts. Eliza, seeing this and bridling, inserting her arm possessively through her husband's. Adam, talking too much, as if this were his last chance to savor good conversation.

At dinner the talk was entirely of the war. Over the baked bluefish Samuel Hartshorn and Redlands Kord argued loudly about naval strategy, even though this was a topic which would ordinarily have been reserved until after the ladies had retired.

But tonight was different, and even the ladies were murmuring to each other of the blockade President Lincoln had ordered of the southern ports, and of the fact that North Carolina had, on May 20, seceded from the Union, with Tennessee sure to follow.

"It's all such a shame," Eliza said, coughing. Two red spots on her cheeks made her look almost feverish. "Did you hear that the troops of the Sixth Massachusetts were *stoned* in Baltimore? Can you imagine it? People stoning other people as if we were all nothing but savages?"

There were nods of agreement.

"And what's going to happen to your famous circus, Mrs. Hartshorn?" Madeleine Kord asked as the ladies finally withdrew to the drawing room, leaving the men to brandy, cigars, and more war talk.

"What do you mean?"

"Well, now that the country is all agog with war."

"Why . . ." Carisa flushed. "I imagine that we'll go on just as before. Or try to."

"But with fighting going on? If it does?"

"Well, as a matter of fact," Carisa admitted unhappily, "we've already had to change our summer tour plans. I received a telegram yesterday from my manager saying that he is coming back to New London. He feels that it is best."

She did not add the full import of Rolf's grim message: that employees were deserting the show in large numbers in order to volunteer; that they were already being hampered by soldiers; that he was afraid their horses and wagons might be requisitioned if they happened to encounter troops on the move.

"Well, perhaps it *is* all for the best," Madeleine said with a certain acid satisfaction. "Certainly it will mean enforced retirement for you, my dear. I've always thought it very improper for a woman to run a circus. It's entirely masculine and certainly not attractive at all. I wonder that Adam lets you do it."

Carisa felt angry color flood her cheeks. She narrowed her eyes at the plump woman. "He lets me do it because he promised me that he would. As for the war, my show is not going to close. I . . . I'll think of something."

"Oh?" Madeleine gave a sidelong look at Eliza and tittered gaily. "Well, my dear, I don't suppose you have anything to say about it, do you? Not now. I'd say that decision is now up to the United States Army . . . and the Confederate States, of course."

It was true. The fate of her circus depended on the

caprice of men caught up in the war lust. Carisa stood frozen, hearing the voices of the men disagreeing in the dining room, a thump as someone banged a table to emphasize a point.

"Oh, bother them!" she exclaimed. "Damn men and their foolish wars! Listen to them now . . . talking and arguing as if this were merely a game instead of a real war where real people are going to be killed and real businesses destroyed."

Everyone was looking at her, all of the women, from Eliza to little Betsy Martingdale, a cousin of Madeleine's, whose husband was also leaving.

"Carisa . . ." Katherine's voice was a warning. "Don't you think it is time we changed the subject? War is hardly a pleasant after-dinner topic."

Betsy Martingdale caught her breath and then conversation began again, and the moment was over. Eliza sat down at the harp and began to play. Women moved gracefully about the drawing room, and the scent of their musky perfume filled the air, making Carisa think of the exotic flowers these women really were. What would they do, she wondered angrily, if their husbands came home from the war mutilated, as Duddie's brother had been? Or if the war destroyed their family's livelihood?

She stood alone, not listening to their talk. *Adam, oh, Adam.* The words were a cry in her.

They said good-bye within the confines of their bedroom, for Adam said he did not wish her or the family to come to town to see him off. It was a cool, sunny morning. A crisp breeze blew from off the Sound, and the sky arched itself overhead like a blue pottery bowl. The perfect day seemed in ironic contrast to the desolation within Carisa. She still could not believe that all of this was really happening.

"Adam . . ." She pressed up against him and wept shamefully into the front of his newly-tailored uniform. Her own chest ached, as if knitting needles had twisted themselves there.

"What? Are you crying?" Adam lifted her chin with

one finger and stared into her eyes. With his square, clefted chin and his yellow eyes, he looked like a medieval painting of a warrior ready to do battle. Or perhaps, she thought wildly, like a privateer, as the first Adam had been. . . .

"No . . . I . . . of course I'm not . . ." She dabbed at the tears, feeling foolish and childish. Eliza Hartshorn, she felt sure, was not crying as she took her leave of Samuel. Nor would Katherine, who was giving two sons to the war, and who had already lost a husband and another son. No, Katherine would not cry.

"You, of all people," Adam said. "Don't you know that wives are supposed to be brave?" His voice caught. "It's part of the unwritten law of wartime, if there could ever be said to be such a thing."

Abruptly he pulled her to him, crushing her breasts against the hard buttons of his uniform. She was aware of the smells of soap, wool, starch and leather. Masculine smells, exciting her, filling her with a wild, painful grief.

"Take care of the children for me, Carisa," Adam was saying. "Use a firm hand with young Matt, he's grown much too strong-willed. You'll have to curb Neecie a bit, too, and get her more interested in dolls and feminine things . . . she's becoming quite a hoyden. As for Vicki, perhaps you can get her to be less fearful. Those nightmares of hers . . . and certainly she must not have a lamp burning in her bedroom any longer. She must begin to grow up."

"And Julian?" This was a matter they had discussed before.

"Just leave him to his tutor. As I instructed you, you'll have to get him to his school if I'm not back by fall. The Cabot School are strong disciplinarians, and I have been assured they can handle a boy like Julian."

"But Adam, I'm not sure that a school. . . ."

Is what he needs, she had been going to say. But she clamped off the words and did not utter them. Surely she was not going to argue with her husband on what might be the last occasion she would ever see him!

"School, Carisa, will at least keep him away from

278

Hearts-ease, and at present we'll have to settle for that." Adam's jaw had squared, and firmly he put her away from him. "Well, I suppose I had better go now. My mother is waiting to say good-bye to me, and so are the children. And Nelly, of course, wishes to say good-bye to Gaines." He smiled faintly. Gaines had also enlisted, and would be Adam's *aide-de-camp*.

"Adam . . . Oh, Adam . . ." She couldn't let him go like this, so matter-of-fact and full of family business. She had to reach out and cling to him again. Her throat was aching.

"Adam, I had a dream last night. Such a frightening one. You were in it, and you. . . ."

"A dream?" Adam's shrug dismissed it. "No, Carisa, you know this won't be for very long. I'll be back in ninety days, probably less, and undoubtedly little the worse for wear. As for you, I think you had better tell Rolf Taggart when he arrives that you want him to disband the circus. I see no other choice."

She froze. "I won't break up my show."

"But you must. Where are you going to get your roustabouts, your tent men, even your performers? They are all eager to enlist, or, if conscription comes, they will be drafted. As for your horses, they are likely to be requisitioned."

She stared at him. He was already edging restlessly toward the door, eager to be away, dismissing her circus as easily as he had dismissed the household business.

"Very well, Adam," she heard herself say. Her voice seemed to come from some stranger, to have no connection with herself. "Go then to war, if you must. You didn't ask my permission to enlist, and now I don't plan to ask for your permission in deciding what to do about my show. I'm of age now, as you know. I can do as I wish."

Silence seemed to beat between them.

"Very well, Carisa." Adam's eyes glittered at her. "I'll leave, just as you suggest."

He turned then, and opened the door, leaving the bedroom with firm steps. Going away from her.

"Adam . . ." She ran after him. "Adam . . ."

But he was already descending the stairs, and now he was surrounded by a group that included Katherine, the children, Nelly, Gaines, Mrs. Wiggins and the other servants. Matt tugged at his sleeve and Adam's hand tousled the boy's hair roughly.

"Papa, Papa!" Neecie cried out in her soft, high voice. Adam bent down to pick her up. His eyes glistened, and for an instant his mouth twisted. He crushed the child to him.

Carisa was without shame. She lifted her skirts and ran down the stairs so quickly that she nearly fell. She ran up to Adam, and, as he at last put Benicia down, threw herself into her husband's arms.

To her relief, he held her close, his face buried in her hair, and she could feel the trembling of his body beneath the stiff woolen uniform.

"Carisa," he whispered.

"Adam, you know that I . . . I didn't mean. . . ."

But before she could finish, there was a banging at the door. Samuel's voice, heavy with joviality, called out that the cart was ready, they had better go, and what was keeping Adam so long? They had a war to fight!

Abruptly Adam released her, and the moment was over, fleeting past in the flurry of seeing Adam and Gaines to the door, of loading their kits onto the wagon. She had to discipline Matt, who wanted to climb onto the wagon, too; and comfort Vicki, who was sobbing wildly. Benicia stared at Adam with round, excited eyes.

Horses' hooves clattered, iron wheels creaked, and somewhere a dog barked hysterically. Then they were gone, the wagon rumbling in a cloud of dust down the gravel drive and out of sight behind the hemlocks.

Carisa felt suddenly weary, tired beyond all endurance, as if she had been laboring to haul canvas for eighteen hours. Vickie's sobs had subsided, and she gave her a hug, and sent all three children to Nelly.

"I think I will go upstairs and rest," she told Katherine heavily. "Rolf and the circus are due here later today. I'm going to have to think what to do about them."

"Yes." Katherine's face looked sallow and old. Her eyes were puffy. True to Carisa's surmise, she had not cried upon seeing her sons off, but it looked as if she would do so soon.

"You had better rest, too, Mother Hartshorn. You look exhausted."

"I have a headache coming on," Katherine said bleakly.

Feeling as if her legs had grown suddenly ancient, Carisa climbed the stairs. On her way down the corridor toward the master bedroom, she heard an odd sound coming from within Julian's room.

Julian. In the excitement, no one had noticed that he was not there to see his father off.

A pang pushed through Carisa. She knocked, then opened the door of the boy's room and entered.

Julian was crouched by the window, staring downward through the branches of the tree which leaned near the house at the cloud of yellow dust left by the wagon.

How old he looked, Carisa had time to think. Sixteen: nearly a grown man, in size at least. Only the cap of honey-colored curls remained to remind her of the small boy she had met when she had first come to Hearts-ease.

"Julian," she began in pity. "Why didn't you come downstairs with the rest of us?"

"Go away, Carisa. Just leave me alone. That's all I want."

His eyes, fierce blue, full of pride and hatred, warned her away.

18

"I tell you, Rolf, we're not going to disband the show! I refuse to hear of such a thing!"

"And I say that we're going to have to. You have no other choice, you little fool." Rolf's voice was harsh. And his face looked tired and defeated.

Only half an hour ago the long string of brightly painted wagons had turned off the plank road and into the circus compound. Now the barns and surrounding fields were a scene of confusion, as animals were fed and watered and staked out, wagons unhitched and tents pitched. An elephant trumpeted, and Herod, the aging Bengal tiger, gave an irritable roar. Duddie, his facial muscles drawn tight with weariness, busied himself hauling water, a job usually reserved for roustabouts, or for "kid workers."

They were short of help, disastrously so, Rolf said. En route they had lost thirty employees, who had deserted to join the Army. Even Major Ribinson, the midget, had announced his desire to fight, if any regiment would have him.

Major Ribinson, a soldier? Oh, Carisa thought, this was ridiculous, pathetic and maddening. What was she going to do?

"Why?" she demanded now of Rolf. "Why do I have to close it? My father wouldn't ever have given up so easily. And this is his show, it bears his name."

"Yes, the Phillips name." Again Rolf's face twisted with that resentful, glowering expression. "But even the great John Phillips couldn't keep a show open in the face of a war like this one's going to be."

"He could. I tell you he could, Rolf. I know him. He's my father, and he. . . ."

"Your father, dear Carisa, is a tired, half-mad old man now, and when will you get that through your head? He couldn't help you even if he wanted to, which he doesn't. He hates you because you ruined his chances to be famous. And he doesn't give a damn what happens to your show."

Each word was like a slap. Carisa could feel the impact of each one of them in the pit of her belly.

"No!" she cried. "No, that isn't true, Rolf. Papa will change . . . with time, he'll change, I know he'll do so. When the show is bigger, when we play before the President, before the Queen. . . ."

"He won't care if you play before the Almighty Himself." Rolf made an impatient gesture, a movement oddly like one her father might have made. "Anyway, what does it matter now? You're not going to be playing before anybody, because the show's closing."

"No. I won't close." Carisa, squaring her chin, heard the words emerge from her mouth with dim surprise.

"Oh, you will, you'll close, all right. As far as I see it, you've no other choice. Am I supposed to put on a circus with no help? And even if I could get the men I need, I'd still have to worry about the damned horses. There are already rumors that they're going to pass a law saying that circuses can't use baggage horses. Where do you think that will leave us, Carisa?"

Rolf's voice buzzed on with more arguments. Endlessly, Carisa thought in despair. As if he were secretly glad this was happening.

"And the Armies . . . if they happen to find us, Carisa, they'll take anything they need. Horses, wagons, supplies, food. They won't care. And they won't pay for what they take, either. Be realistic, Carisa. Sitting here at Hearts-ease in luxury as you've been doing, you surely wouldn't know. . . ."

"Be still!" she snapped. "Oh, just be quiet, will you, Rolf? I have to think."

"Think? What's there to think about? The only thing I see is for us to close up and have done with it, before we lose. . . ."

"Please, Rolf. I must think."

Rolf, offended, stood stiffly, staring at the scene of activity spread before them. Duddie staggered by with another bucket of water. The fat cook bellowed at five small boys from town, whom he had collared as temporary helpers. Marcella Duquesne struggled to carry her own costume trunk, her mouth pouting with outrage.

Carisa saw none of this. Her mind was working furiously. Rolf was right, of course—the show was doomed. Even if they could keep their performers, they could not put on even a matinee without the dozens of others, the men who sold tickets, hawked lemonade, ran the sideshows, put up canvas and rigging, lit the lanterns, cared for the animals, repaired the wagons and cooked the food.

But perhaps, she told herself, if she paid them enough—

No. Even if she could manage the extra expense, there was still the fact that their tour was curtailed. Where could they go now? Much of their circuit had centered about the southern states—cities with names like Charlottesville, Lynchburg, Greensboro, Rockingham, Red Banks, Cheraw, Camden, Columbia. It would be impossible to go to those places now. Northern soldiers had actually been stoned in Baltimore. The South was going to be a battlefield—

Carisa clenched her hands into fists, squeezing hard until her fingernails raked her own flesh. Panic rippled through her, a feeling that the world was tilting out of control, spinning away from her. First Adam, gone from her. Now this.

What was she to do? If she let the show disband, if she paid off all the employees and dismissed them, she would be left with nothing. A few wagons, some musical instruments, a calliope. Props and costumes and oil lanterns, boxes of circus banners, some paste buckets.

A circus was an alive thing. It did not take well to storage. Equipment deteriorated and canvas rotted; animals had to be fed and cared for, or else sold. A show had to be used, or, for all practical purposes, it died.

If only, she thought wildly, Richard Sands were here, so that she could talk to him, feed from his vitality, his endless store of ideas. She felt sure *he* would not have been defeated by something so frustrating as a war. He would have thought of something—

But what? Besides, Richard Sands had been defeated, too, she remembered with a dull feeling of loss. Yellow fever had bested him. He and several other members of his company had died in February when his show had been touring the West Indies.

Touring. Carisa's thoughts stopped short, and then skittered back to the word. Her heart gave a sudden jump. Of course. She should have thought of this before! Why hadn't she? She had been blind to think that her show had to be limited only to the United States—

"Rolf!" Her voice was rich with excitement. "Why do we have to stay here? We'll run away from the War . . . to Europe! We'll take the show on tour. To Paris, perhaps. And to England."

"To England?"

"And why shouldn't we?" she exulted. "What better time than now? The show is big, it'll draw big crowds, we've never been better. Oh, Rolf, we'll make a grand tour, we'll go to England and Scotland, and we'll show them all. We'll play London, we'll play Leeds and Manchester and Edinburgh and Chester . . . Rolf, it's the only way!"

"There's the little matter of a ship." Rolf's narrow face was stubborn. "Not to mention a few other things. Like roustabouts and tent men. Do you think that they'll come just because you make a pretty face at them and beg them to?"

"No. I won't beg them, I'll pay them. I'll pay them so well they'll *have* to come." She went on feverishly. "We'll go in one of my husband's whalers . . . why not? There are two available in the harbor, and we might as well take one of them before the Navy does."

She was caught up in the magnitude of her idea. "We'll take all of the performers, but only the men we'll need to handle the animals and equipment on board. The rest we'll hire when we get to England."

"*We?*"

The word stopped Carisa short as if it had been a wire fence.

She caught her breath, her enthusiasm seeping away. Of course. For a moment she had forgotten. She could not go. She was needed here, at Hearts-ease. There were the children, Katherine, the servants, all of whom would depend on her now that Adam was away. And there was Adam himself. She had to be here in case he came home, in case he needed her. In case he was injured or—She stopped the thought with weary effort.

"Go, Rolf. Call a meeting of the employees. I want to talk to them." She said it heavily. "No, I won't be coming with you."

Rolf's eyes glinted with triumph, and she knew what he was thinking. There would be a vast distance between them, an entire ocean, with no possible way to communicate save through letters, for the transatlantic telegraph had not yet been successful. Rolf would be free to do with the circus exactly as he pleased. His grifters, his gamblers, all of his other schemes, could be allowed a free hand. And there would be nothing she, Carisa, could do about it.

"Rolf . . ."

Then the words died on Carisa's lips. She buried her hands in the silky fabric of her gown, twisting and wrenching at the fabric until she was sure she must be tearing it.

If she wanted her show to survive—and she did—she would have to let it go from her, into the control of Rolf. There was no other way. There was certainly no one else in whose hands she dared leave the show—not even Duddie, much as she loved him, would be able to handle the complex job of moving a big circus across an ocean, plus the other problems which were sure to follow.

A smile was beginning on Rolf's lips, transforming his face into something greedy and clever and defiant.

"You needn't worry, Carisa. *I'll* take good care of the show." His tone stopped just short of insolence. "It'll be safe, and it will make good money, too. You can count on that."

"I'm sure I can." Her lips moved stiffly. "And I do want my show to be safe, Rolf. I'll pay you well if you bring it back to me intact when the War is over. There will be a bonus waiting for you. A very *big* one," she repeated. "And . . . I want you to start training Duddie as your assistant. There is much he can learn."

Rolf's grin wavered, then was back on his face. "Don't you fret, I'll see to it all."

Carisa nodded, dismissing him. She stood very still, watching as Rolf loped off to call the meeting, his stride light and taut, like the whippet he resembled. Difficult he was, but he would do as she asked, she knew. The promise of money would see to that.

The Phillips Circus was going to play before the Queen someday, she vowed to herself firmly. That was its destiny. Meanwhile, she must do anything she could to keep it alive until then.

"Heave it, weave it, shake it, take it, break it, make it, move along."

The voice was male, hoarse and full of rhythm. It was the chant of the boss-man who directed the tightening of the guy-ropes of the big top. And today the sound seemed even more poignant to Carisa, for she knew she would not hear it again for at least two years, possibly three or even more.

Today was their farewell performance. Rolf had wanted to use the big top, rather than the brick building which Carisa had built for winter rehearsals, and wordlessly Carisa had acquiesced. Today the show had to be under canvas, exactly as it had been on the road a thousand times before. This was something they all felt, from Rolf down to the smallest town boy who had rushed to the circus lot in the hope of being hired to do odd jobs.

Rolf, on Carisa's instructions, had billed the performance as "the last chance to see the Great Phillips Circus before its triumphant European Tour," and had even managed to spread the rumor that they were to play before Queen Victoria herself. This, of course, was an untruth. Yet the lie had brought in great crowds of people, all of them in a gala mood, for war excitement had swept over the city and everything was being treated as a holiday.

Carisa sat with Katherine and the children, trying not to think of Adam, by now on his way to . . . what? To death, to mutilation and injury? Shuddering, she brushed away the memory of the picture of Duddie's brother.

Even Julian had consented to attend the circus, and sat near his grandmother munching on a candied apple, exactly as if he were an ordinary carefree youth.

Two rows away sat Madeleine Kord with her brood of boisterous sons. These consisted of Calvin, her eldest, a plump, handsome boy of six with a pouting mouth, and three smaller boys. All four were pushing, shoving, jumping up and down on the board seats, and spilling lemonade on each other. Wearily Madeleine scolded them, then permitted them to do exactly as they pleased.

Even Eliza had attended the circus, her face hollowed and bleak, as if Samuel, in leaving, had borrowed his wife's vitality to take with him.

Just as the show was about to begin, Eliza brightened, and jabbed Katherine in the ribs. Carisa, too, turned to look. The four Henry sisters, flamboyant in silks and feathered bonnets, were parading into the tent. Their progress was marked by stares and furtive whisperings on the part of the ladies in the audience. The sisters seemed oblivious to this, but Poll gave a fierce stare in Carisa's direction, her eyes as black as two holes.

"Imagine," Eliza whispered, recovering from a hacking spasm of coughing. "Women the likes of *them*, here in the tent with decent people. They should be put out. I really don't know how they dare. . . ."

"They dare," Carisa said, "because they know perfectly well that it would cause a far larger scene if we were to throw them out."

"Still," Eliza muttered. "It's a shocking thing, truly it is, and to think that that woman was once an employee of yours."

"She was hired by my husband, if you'll recall, long

before I ever arrived at Hearts-ease," Carisa replied curtly.

With difficulty she turned herself to the circus, which was about to begin.

Band music rose, full of the heavy, swaying rhythm of horns, bells, and drums. The performers had started their "spectacle" around the ring, a grand march in costumes bright and exotic, flashing with spangles.

As always, on seeing the circus, Carisa felt a rush of bittersweet feeling.

How beautiful and unreal it all was. Clowns, somersaulting and flip-flapping, their grotesqueries endearing. A wooden house, rolled in on wheels, was "afire," and valiantly, with wild slapstick, the corps of clowns rescued a "baby," which was a trained pig dressed in infants' skirts.

Jugglers, adroitly balancing so many balls that the eye could not follow them. Liberty horses, white, curved-necked, intelligent, performing without riders, directed only by their trainer, who stood near them in the ring with his whistle. Marcella Duquesne, proud, regal, high overhead on her wire like a golden queen.

Then more clowns and at last Duddie, with his head thrust into a sack and his feet in wicker baskets, came staggering comically across the ring and did a quick fork leap onto a horse's back, to the screamed delight of the children in the audience.

Always, always, the shrieks of the children.

Carisa's eyes began to prickle with unshed tears. How long would it be before she would see her circus again? Would see *ever* see it again?

For she had no illusions. Ship travel always held risk, and a circus aboard a seagoing vessel was especially vulnerable. Animals were fragile, and could lose their lives in a severe storm. Crammed into close quarters, disease could mow them down. Cages could be washed overboard in high seas. Loading and unloading, always a problem, could turn out to be a nightmare. . . .

"Carisa, why the frown? It's a beautiful show, and should be a very great success in Europe."

It was Duddie, finished with his act now, but still

in his clown makeup and being goggled at by the Harts-horn and Kord children as he climbed the seats toward Carisa. Benicia shrieked in delight at seeing him. He reached into his baggy sleeve and produced a handful of paper-wrapped hard candies, which he tossed out. The children shouted and scrambled for them.

"*Am* I frowning?" Carisa got out of her seat, and maneuvering her hoop skirt with difficulty, managed to go and stand with the clown in the aisle, where they could talk with more privacy.

"You certainly are. You look grim indeed."

"I suppose I do. I've just been thinking . . . Oh, Duddie, what if our ship should go down! If the show was lost, I think I'd be lost, too. Something in me would die. . . ."

"Nonsense. Such talk from an old circus trouper. No, Carisa, you wouldn't die, you would go on as ever, and you would do it in the circus way, with a wave of your hand and a smile on your lips."

"I suppose so. Still . . ."

The French aerialists were performing now, twisting and whirling through the air like swooping birds. From below, their limbs seemed as fragile as flower stems, yet Carisa knew this was all illusion. These men were iron-strong, superb athletes with perfect timing.

"Carisa," Duddie said at last in a low voice. "There is something I must tell you."

"Yes?"

"I don't want to go to England. I want to stay here, at Hearts-ease."

"Why, Duddie!" She stared at the little clown, her mouth opening in shock. Duddie was as much a part of the Phillips Circus as Carisa's bones were to her arm. She couldn't imagine him separated from the show he loved.

And now he was indispensible to that show. Second only to Rolf, it was Duddie who oversaw the gate receipts and kept Rolf in check; Duddie whose laughter raised the morale of the workers after one of the accidents, wrecks or mudslides which plagued the life of a wagon circus.

"Duddie, you can't," she whispered. "You just can't! Whatever would we do without you?"

"Oh, I think the show would survive. I have to stay," he added simply. "Because of Benicia."

"Neecie!"

"She has promise, Carisa, perhaps more than you realize. If I go abroad for two or three years, who will train her? She must be given the chance to develop her potential."

The band had launched into rolicking drumbeats as trained dogs trotted about the ring, rolling balls with their noses.

"Benicia," Carisa repeated numbly. She clutched at the cotton fabric of Duddie's baggy, tri-colored costume, feeling the wiry flesh beneath. "Oh, Duddie, I beg of you. Please go to England with the show and see that it is all right. I have only you to do that for me, only you to keep Rolf in line and see that he does his job. He'll listen to you. He'll obey you. Please, Duddie. . . ."

"And Benicia?" The clown's eyes were stern, his mouth oddly sad. "You would sacrifice her, then, Carisa, in order to save your circus?"

"Of course not!"

"Then she needs her training now . . . not three or four years from now or whenever the War is finally over. An equestrienne has to be trained in childhood, Carisa, you know that. She can't wait."

"I . . . I know, Duddie. I'll train her myself."

"But Carisa, you. . . ."

"And why can't I do it?" she asked fiercely. "My legs may have been injured but my brain was not. I can work the mechanic belt as well as anyone. I'm still strong, Duddie, the years haven't changed that."

Duddie nodded, as if he had expected nothing less of her. "And your husband?"

"Adam is gone," she said grimly. "This is a decision I must make. I will teach her."

Her voice stopped, her words trailing off. Suddenly it was as if she could see all the long years stretching ahead. Years without Adam, without the circus to sustain her. Years and years, with only a small girl to train in the ways of the circus. . . .

Tears pricked at the backs of her eyelids, and fiercely she blinked them back. Then she lifted her chin and stared defiantly toward the circus ring, a smile fixed on her lips. People were staring at her. Speculating on her talk with Duddie, on her boldness in owning such a circus at all.

She must not let them see her terror.

At the end of the week the circus departed in the ship which Carisa—against the vehement protests of Mr. West, Adam's agent—had procured for them, the *Marie Galante.* The vessel had doubled as whaler and cargo ship, and Carisa forced its re-outfitting so that the circus and its animals could be accommodated.

On the morning of their departure, they spent a hectic morning loading animals and cages, observed by a curious crowd of townspeople.

Carisa paced about the wharf anxiously.

"Rolf?" She clutched at his sleeve. "Take care, will you, that the elephants don't injure themselves if the water should grow rough? They are fragile animals, really, and they. . . ."

"I know they are. I'll see to them." Rolf's face today looked narrow and eager, his eyes glittering like Papa's.

"And the horses? You'll take care of them, too? And inspect them often for disease?"

"Yes, I'll watch for them. You needn't fret, Carisa. It will be a good tour. *I'll* see to that."

Rolf turned away to see to the last-minute lashing of the cat cages, and Carisa bit her lip. Animals were so very fragile . . . a ship was fragile. . . .

"Carisa, you must try to smile," Duddie said. A brisk sea breeze was blowing across the wharves, riffling his hair. In civilian clothes Duddie looked small and deformed, and some of the dock workers were gawking at him. As if to defy them, Duddie gave them an impudent gesture and turned a series of rapid flip-flaps.

"I . . . I can't help it, Duddie," she choked when he had finished. "I know I'm being too anxious, but it's so hard not to be. Oh, at this moment I wish I'd never suggested this! The War will be over soon, Adam himself says so. . . ."

"Then Adam is wrong. The War will be a bitter and bloody one, Carisa, and I fear that it is going to last for years. There is too much bitterness in the country for it to be otherwise. I'm only glad I won't be here to see it."

They clung to each other for a moment, the slim woman and the short, dwarfish little man.

"Come back, Duddie," Carisa whispered. "I'll take care of Neecie, I'll train her well. Just come back and bring my circus with you . . . it's all I ask. . . ."

They were gone, on the tide. After the *Marie Galante* had disappeared from view, Carisa continued to stand on the wharf, staring blindly out at the water. She had brought the younger children to the wharf with her, and now they played at her feet, completely forgotten.

Adam was gone. And now the circus as well. What would she do? How would she ever survive? For always, these two, her husband and her circus, had filled her life to completion. Even her children, it seemed, had been but extensions of her life with Adam, parts of him. And now they were all she had left.

She felt something tugging at her hand, insistently.

"Carisa? Carisa, when are we going home? You said I'd ride today. You said. . . ."

It was Benicia, her dimples flashing, her face sturdy, determined, demanding.

"Ride?" Carisa repeated.

"Yes, in the ring. You said it, you promised! Duddie told me you promised!"

A headache had begun to radiate through Carisa's temples. It throbbed there, lancing pain through her head.

"I . . . I did say it, Neecie. You shall ride."

"But when? When, Carisa? I want to do it right now!"

"And so you shall."

Wearily Carisa took Vicki's hand and called out to

293

Matt, who had been playing at the end of the jetty with a stick of wood which he called his "musket." Adam, before he had left, had let Matt heft the considerable weight of his rifle, and it was an experience the boy had not forgotten.

Now Matt came wheeling toward her, a wiry little figure who resembled Adam in a dusty black woolen suit, making shooting motions with the stick.

"When's the circus coming back?" he demanded.

Again Carisa felt the unutterable weariness, the lancing pain in her temples.

"Not for a few years. We will have to wait until the War is over."

The three children gathered about her, next to her wide hoop skirt which swept the rough boards of the pier. Overhead, gulls swooped and cried, or plunged downward for fish. She could smell sea water and tar and rotting fish.

"I hope the War lasts a long time," Matt cried jubilantly. "So I can grow up and be in it, too!"

"Oh, I doubt . . ." began Carisa.

"But if I go to war, *I'm* going to sea," Matt announced. "Papa says the Hartshorns have always gone to sea, and I'm going to be like them. I'm going to be captain of a whaler!"

"And I'm going to ride," Neecie said, pulling at Carisa's hand and smiling beatifically. "Today, just as soon as I get back to the ring barn. Carisa said I could. Didn't you, Carisa?" Her face, turned up to Carisa's, was full of confidence and trust.

"Yes," Carisa whispered. "Yes, Neecie, you will ride."

The days inched by. Katherine and Eliza were both deeply involved in the collection of clothing and comfort boxes to be sent to the soldiers. They were forming groups to roll bandages, although where these were to be sent, no one yet knew.

Carisa spent her mornings with Benicia in the brick ring barn, training the child in riding and balance and timing, and working with the "mechanic," a waist belt to which was attached a rope suspended from a pole. This device required strength and alertness on the part of the operator, who had to jerk on the rope if the child fell, to prevent disaster.

Carisa could remember learning on it herself as a child, with Duddie to hold the rope. What a heady experience it had been, the horse swaying, herself tense with excitement and pride and concentration, balancing for a few glorious moments before tumbling off, to be safely dangled in mid-air.

Grimly, Carisa followed the program Duddie had outlined for her, adding other details she could remember from her own training, including the vari-colored "balancing ball," and other tumbling stunts.

One morning Katherine, coming out to the circus complex on some household errand, stopped in horror at the sight of the little girl clinging like a leaf to a pad atop the ring horse's back as it cantered around and around the ring.

"Why, you'll be making a freak of her, Carisa! What proper young man is going to want to marry a wild creature like that, a girl who won't even know what a side-saddle is, much less how to use it?"

"Neecie isn't a fine lady, she's a circus performer," Carisa said boldly, both hands on the safety rope. "And one of great talent, too. Even at her young age, she's exceptional."

"Exceptional! You're going to make a freak of her, Carisa! A creature fit neither for life in New London or for the circus ring either."

Carisa reddened. "I think the circus will be her life, Mother Hartshorn. When she is old enough to choose it, that is."

"And my son? My son, who adopted this child and who provides her support? What do you think he will say when he learns you're training his darling as a bare-back rider?"

With no circus business to occupy her, Carisa's days seemed to drag. She spent her afternoons with the children, playing games with them, reading to them, or

295

telling them stories from her own childhood in England, days which often seemed as vivid to her as if she had just lived them.

"Tell us again, Carisa," Neecie would beg. "Tell us about the time you were all hungry and Duddie stole four chickens!" "Tell us about the time Grandpapa chased the runaway horses through the village!"

So, smiling, Carisa would oblige. It was always Neecie who listened most eagerly, who plied her with question after question, until Carisa, pleading exhaustion, had to stop.

"There are other things besides the circus!" she would say laughingly to the little girl.

"No! No, Carisa, there aren't! *I'm* going to be in the circus someday! I'm going to ride like you and Aunt Anna and Aunt Stephana!"

It was at times like these that Carisa, staring at the little girl with her pretty, irrepressible face, was reminded, not of Anna, but of Stephana. Neecie possessed much of Stephana's boldness and spirit. And at times she could be as headstrong. . . .

Each day she also reserved time for Julian. She was teaching him to play chess, a game which Duddie had taught her long ago. She had learned that Julian had a sharply logical mind, although his moves were frequently so wildly aggressive that he overstepped himself and she was able to defeat him.

But on many days they could not play. Julian had taken to disappearing again, often for hours at a time. Twice Carisa had had to send the young stableboy, Tim Kelly, to Poll Henry's. Each time Julian had returned home white-faced and sullen, unwilling to talk to anyone.

Something would have to be done about him, and quickly, Carisa knew. But what? A new school, so that he could run away from it again? During the chess games, she had tried to draw him into talk, and one afternoon he had blurted out to her an ugly story of being stripped naked in the dormitory and forced to crawl around on the floor, while the other boys laughed and lashed at him with wet towels.

Carisa, sick with horror, had tried to find out more. Why hadn't he told a master, who could have stopped it? But Julian had tossed up the chess board, sending pawns and knights flying, and had rushed from the parlor.

Still, she decided, there would be no more schools, at least not for now. For now he had his tutor, and they would all have to pray he would grow out of this distressing phase of his life. And when Adam came home—

Adam. Letters from him had begun to arrive, addressed in his even, deliberate penmanship to Carisa, and also to Katherine. The letters were long and full of careful detail, names of men and regiments and cities, and Carisa stored them away carefully in a drawer, to reread a dozen times, and—she caught her breath painfully—to save for the children if he should never return.

But there were personal messages, too.

I think of that night it thundered and rained, he wrote once, and Carisa felt her heart thud with helpless joy.

Why didn't you disband the circus as I told you, you little fool? he wrote her once. *My agent wrote me of your audacity in commandeering the Marie Galante. Perhaps the Navy could use you, Carisa, in fighting its sea wars. You would make a formidable admiral.*

She crumpled that letter, her eyes stinging, then carefully refolded it and laid it at the bottom of the growing pile.

His regiment had traveled by train to Washington, he wrote, and was domiciled at a place called the Willard Hotel, although he anticipated being moved to a camp soon. *It seems one poor fellow fell asleep in our train and allowed his arm to dangle out of the window. When we came to a sudden stop his arm was broken and now he must go about sheepishly in a sling. Another man accidentally discharged his musket and shot himself in the thigh. So it seems we are already having casualties, but cannot call ourselves much proud of them. . . .*

Her nights were the worst of all, for without Adam the house seemed much larger, creaking with ghostly memories. Everywhere she looked there were traces of him: the gaming table where he had played back-gammon with Katherine, the glass *millefiori* paperweight which was his favorite, his gilded cigar box, the books he had loved.

After the children were in bed, Katherine and Carisa would sit in the parlor with their needlework. Frequently Carisa would ask Nelly to join them, for the maidservant's lively chatter did much to break the heavy silence. Some nights Katherine filled the parlor with her friends: Eliza, Madeleine Kord, young Betsy Martingdale, others. As they sewed or rolled bandages, someone would read aloud from one of the popular Beadle Dime Novels, an occupation which Katherine officially deplored, but seemed to enjoy as much as anyone.

Carisa sat listening to the turgid stories of engagements, jiltings, and girls of noble birth, her mind turning again and again to Adam and the circus. How soon would it be before Adam himself would become one of the casualties he had mentioned? She thought of him hurt as Duddie's brother had been—a double amputee—and recoiled. Oh, it must not happen! Dear God, it must not!

As for the circus, her mind plagued her with thoughts of all the New London ships which had gone down in storms. Over the decades, there had been dozens of them. Whaling widows were scattered all through the town of New London, owning tiny shops or living as best they could. . . .

When at last the women dispersed, their voices high in determined gaiety, Carisa would say good night to Katherine and then trudge upstairs to the bed which she and Adam had shared. How big that bed seemed now without him. How cold and empty.

She would lie staring into the darkness until her eyes closed and sleep possessed her. Often she dreamed, of thunder and gunpowder, of row upon row of ugly, snout-nosed cannons, of bodies lying open-mouthed in fields, scattered and abandoned like dirty laundry.

Another letter arrived from Adam, this one filled with brisk enthusiasm and asking her to send him a pillow, sheets for a bed two-and-a-half feet wide, and linen napkins for the officer's mess.

Troops are moving over the Potomac River every day, he wrote. *General Mansfield predicts that we, too, will cross the river soon. I hope so. There is little to do here except to parade around and inspect each other's finery, which, I might add, is truly splendid. My gray uniform is dull indeed compared to others I have seen. Some are attired like French Zouaves, with red breeches, blue coats, and gay yellow or scarlet sashes, even turbans and fezzes for their heads. There is a regiment from New York which calls itself the High-landers and wears kilts for dress parade. It seems we are all dressed in various shades of the rainbow, and now I am wondering how well such a rainbow will fight. . . .*

On July 23 they received word of a battle which had been fought near Washington at a place called Bull Run. That night Carisa clutched the New York newspaper in her perspiring fingers, feeling sick.

It had been a debacle. Thousands of young men in colorful assorted uniforms such as Adam had described, innocent of warfare, undisciplined, unhardened and in-experienced, had marched through the lush Virginia countryside. There, at a little stream called Bull Run, the two raw armies had fought each other in a valley boiling with dust and smoke and musket fire.

And somehow the Federal batteries had been over-run. Suddenly the whole Union army was in retreat, despite the efforts of Adam and men like him to stop the rout.

What a disaster! Adam wrote. *And worse yet, the folk in Washington seemed to think that the battle was staged expressly for their own pleasure. They took their carriages and buggies and plentiful hampers of food and drink, and drove to Cub Run, where they watched the spectacle as if it were a play or a minstrel show.*

Gradually, however, it began to dawn on these good people that this was indeed a war, and they themselves might get shot. Suddenly the picnic was over. What a melee it was, Carisa, women and children and holiday makers all wheeling onto the road in their carriages, trying to cross the bridge. Guns and battery wagons and carriages and military caissons, all in a fearsome tangle. Ladies were screaming and horses were rearing, and the road was completely jammed. . . .

Carisa put down this letter and closed her eyes. Thanks to Adam's precise script, she could see the scene as vividly as if she herself were there. What, she wondered, would she herself have done, if she had been one of the foolish women in those carriages? Would she, too, have screamed and fled?

I couldn't stop the men from running, Adam had written. *No one could. It was all such mass confusion. No one knew what to do, and no one seemed to be in command. Carisa, I think that our country does not yet know what war is. But I fear that we are soon going to learn. . . .*

19

For Vicki Hartshorn, the war was far away indeed. For her, that summer passed slowly, her life colored by fear.

It had begun on the day when Julian had locked her into the linen closet, with the hideous moment when her half-brother had jerked up the hem of her dress and tugged at the waistband of her petticoats, thrusting his fingers beneath them.

"Don't yell," he had hissed. "Or I'll put a pillow over your face and smother your breath. Do you hear?"

He would do it, too, Vicki knew.

"I . . . I won't tell," she wept.

"You'd better not. Now take them off, Vicki. Take off everything."

"But I . . . I can't . . . Mama said. . . ."

"I don't care what your Mama said. I tell you to take them off. Right now, all of them!"

He slapped at her, catching her on the tender flat of her chest, where Mama wouldn't see the bruises later.

Quivering, weeping, knowing this was terribly wrong, Vicki did as she was told. She sobbed with the removal of each garment, her tunic-dress, her stockings, her camisole, her little cotton drawers. At last she stood there shivering.

"Now get down on the floor," Julian commanded.

"On . . . on the . . ."

"Yes. That's right. Now you can crawl around. Crawl around, Vicki. Go on, do it!"

Trembling, weeping with fear, she did so. Her knees scraped the floor and a sliver thrust itself into her skin and made it bleed. But she was oblivious to the pain, her heart flinging against the cage of her chest as if it would burst out. And now Julian had grabbed a linen towel from the stack kept on the shelf. He was twisting it long and thin, lashing at her with it.

"You're ugly, Vicki, did you know that? Ugly, ugly, like a horrid little pig or toad. Say it, say it after me. I'm ugly. Say it, Vicki!"

"I'm . . . ugly . . ."

"I'm horrible. Go on, say it. I'm an ugly dong-sucker. Say it!"

"I'm an ugly . . ." But the unfamiliar word tripped her tongue, and she went into a fresh round of weeping.

"Oh, shut up, will you? Shut up or I'll hit you harder. Then they'll come running and they'll all laugh at you. They'll call you puny. They'll say things you wouldn't want. . . ."

Julian's voice seemed to pause. He sucked in air loudly. "Now I want you to go over there, Vicki. Over that chair. Just lie over it. There, that's right. Like that."

The intrusion of the closed jack-knife into her body was so hideously alien that Vicki could only jerk in helpless surprise. Pain arrowed through her, nausea crowding at the back of her throat. She wanted to shriek but her vocal cords were paralyzed. All she could manage was a groaning grunt.

"There," Julian said, jamming pain into her. "There,

301

and there, and there. See how *you* like that. And don't yell, not if you know what's good for you."

She didn't know how long it lasted. Only that she must not make any more noise or he would put a pillow over her mouth and then she would die without any air. Pain consumed her and she began to vomit, spewing out her insides onto the floor, retching and gagging and choking, until at last even Julian sickened.

"Ugh," he told her. "You're an animal, aren't you? An ugly little dong-sucking animal." She felt his fingers go around her neck, squeezing. "Don't tell, damn you. Don't tell or I'm going to get that pillow and fix it so you can't breathe. I'll do to you what they do to cats in the stables!"

"No!" she whimpered. "Tim never . . ."

"All the time," Julian hissed. "All the time they smother cats in the stable."

He was gone. Stiffly Vicki got to her feet. She wiped at her mouth, her hands shaking. Slowly she pulled on her clothes. A drop of bright red blood stained her drawers as she pulled them on, and carefully she wetted it with her saliva and rubbed the red liquid away.

No one must know. No one must ever know. . . .

Vicki's retreat was the attic. You reached it from a tiny little door in one of the back, unused bedrooms in the old wing. You climbed steep stairs upward and then two more steep steps down to the attic floor. Julian never came here; he didn't like enclosed places and said scornfully that the place stank of dead flies and mold.

Which was another reason for liking the attic. She avoided Julian now, could not even eat her dinner if he were seated next to her at the table.

But she loved to come here, with Matt and Neecie, or by herself, to sit curled up by the old wooden trunks which some long-ago Hartshorn had brought over by ship from England. On rainy days the rain pelted the roof, making tinny, cozy sounds. On sunny days it was hot and warm and safe, full of the sound of flies buzzing on the window panes, and the smell of warm wood and old clothes and herbs drying on sheets on the floor.

Sometimes she brought her dolls with her. At other times she amused herself by going through the trunks where strange old dresses had been stored. One was a wedding dress, its bodice high and its skirt skimpy. It smelled of ancient lavender and was so yellowed and crumpled from storage that Vicki couldn't imagine any real woman ever wearing it.

There were fragile old fans, faded lace collars and, seven or eight high, carved tortoise-shell combs, with widely-separated teeth, which Vicki loved to take out and arrange in a row on the floor, or to put in her own abundant brown hair.

Once, slipping downstairs after an afternoon spent in the attic, she encountered Brigid, the cook, near the back staircase on some kitchen errand.

"Hiding, Miss Vicki?" the servant had asked. She was an enormous fat woman whose breasts, mounded under her black dress, were as puffy as the bread dough she worked in the kitchen.

"I . . . no . . . I. . . ."

"Well, just don't let me catch you going near all them herbs I set out to dry, and them bunches of dried onions, or I ain't tellin' what might happen to you. I spent a long time, I did, picking them things and laying them out. I don't want no kids messing in them."

"Oh, I won't. . . ."

"You'd better not. Or I'll tell your Mama where you been all afternoon when you was supposed to be in your room, napping. Or maybe, just maybe, I might tell that half-brother of yours, Julian, where you like to go. . . ."

The little pig eyes sparkled with evil. How had she known? Vicki wondered in sick panic. She must have been watching the way Julian's eyes followed her about, she must have seen him follow her to the greenhouse last week when Grandmama sent her to fetch Mama. . . .

She turned and began to run toward her room. The cook's laughter trailed after her.

"Funny little mouse, ain't she? Skeered of her own petticoats, if you ask me!"

In late August, 1861, Papa came home from the war, looking handsome and jaunty in his new uniform. He brought Vicki a new doll, an odd creature with a face exactly like that of an ancient crone. Its wrinkles, in fact, were identical to those of Nelly's granny, whom Vicki had met once at the circus. The doll had been made of a dried-up apple, Papa explained. Her body, Vicki saw from peeking under her skirt, was made of rough twigs tied together with a scrap of cloth.

He had brought a doll for Benicia, too, but Neecie took hers down to the ring barn where she lost it in the tall grass there. Neecie wasn't fond of dolls anyway. Grandmama said she was "as wild and harum scarum as a boy. Neither fish nor fowl nor good red meat will that young person be, mark my words."

Vicki was secretly glad to hear Grandmama say such things. Everyone except Grandmama, she knew, loved Neecie more than they did her. She was glad that Neecie had lost her doll; she, Vicki, was going to treasure hers, as Grandmama did the big rolls of left-over fabric squares she kept from every gown she had ever owned. Then Papa would see how careful she was, how sedate and ladylike. He would love her and hug her and chuck her under the chin, as he did Neecie.

Papa brought Matt home a Confederate rifle, much to Matt's joy. He spent hours playing with the unloaded rifle, toting it about, thrusting the ramrod in and out of the barrel and pretending he was shooting down Rebels.

Vicki hated the musket; it was so heavy that she herself could barely lift it. Anyway, she disliked the idea of killing. They had driven by a carriage accident once and a little girl had been lying in the grass at the edge of the road, her head sunken and bloody where the horse had kicked her. No, Vicki hated pain and loud noises, and most especially did she hate blood.

She never saw what Papa brought back to Julian from the war. He gave it to him when she was not there, and later Vicki overheard Papa and Mama arguing about it in low, tense voices.

Julian, it seemed, had thrown the gift away, and Papa was very angry. He wanted to send Julian back to school immediately. Mama didn't think he should go.

She said he needed the attention of a father. And Papa shouted back that the boy had had the attention of a father, and what had it gotten them but sullenness and disobedience and constant running away?

And then Papa had said something else, something about a woman named Poll Henry, and Julian hiding in the bushes to watch what went on at her house. He had heard this, he said, from the barber when he went to town for a shave and a haircut. *"My son, the laughing-stock of New London,"* he had shouted in a terrible voice. The way he had said this made Vicki put her hands over her ears and crawl away, her body trembling.

Papa and Mama had quarreled again, too, about Neecie. Papa had discovered her in the ring barn one morning, balanced on the funny wooden ball Mama had had made for her.

"You're putting ideas into her head, Carisa," he had shouted at Mama. "Ideas that can't come true."

"And why can't they?" Mama had shouted back.

"Because, my dear Carisa, we live here in New London and not in a traveling circus. It's impossible for that child to go about the country in a wagon at her age, all alone . . . I won't stand for it."

"Adam, I'm not asking that. I'm just asking to let her be trained, that alone. The rest can follow later, if she chooses it, if she wishes it. Don't you see? It's her destiny. It's what she was born to do, meant to do."

Destiny. Vicki had no idea what that meant, but she did know that Papa had suddenly, abruptly softened, and then he had put his arms around Mama. Then Vicki had seen them embracing, their bodies pressed together so tightly that it seemed they would never come apart. Papa's hands had been on Mama's breasts, and there had been shiny tears rolling down Mama's cheeks even as she kissed Papa.

There were so many things, these days, that Vicki didn't understand. For example, she didn't know why Papa said he had to re-enlist in the War again. Vicki had thought the war was over—he had brought back gifts, hadn't he?

But Papa said in his deep, rumbling voice that the

305

War was not over at all, it had just begun. The country was going to learn a few things, he added slowly. And the lesson was not going to be pleasant.

Meanwhile Papa, it seemed, disapproved of her. He told Mama that Vicki was too quiet and wraith-like, and that she spent too much time in the stables and carriage house, following Tim Kelly about. Why, he wanted to know, wasn't she more like Benicia? At least Neecie had the spark and fire to ride her horses, and could speak up when she was spoken to, instead of hanging her head as if she were afraid someone would hit her.

These days Tim Kelly was Vicki's one real friend—besides Grandmama, that is. She didn't even remember when she had first seen him; it was as if he had always been at Hearts-ease. Tim, who was assistant to the coachman, had to be up early in the morning to feed the horses and clean out their stalls. Then there were the carriages to be washed, the harnesses and fittings to be cleaned and oiled and polished.

Tim also was in charge of the cats. He kept four large tiger cats in the carriage house to keep the mice down. Vicki's favorite times were when one of the cats had kittens and Tim would let her come and kneel down by the mother cat in the straw.

The tiny animal scraps were so achingly helpless. When she held a kitten close to her ear and heard the tiny buzz of its purring, Vicki felt strong and happy. And Tim did *not* smother cats, as Julian had told her. Tim was too soft-hearted to hurt anything. When once a kitten had died, stepped on by a horse, Tim had cried.

Tim was Julian's age, but smaller, with light blue eyes, reddish hair, and a wash of freckles across his nose. His family had come from Ireland. Tim could tell Vicki stories of fairies and trolls and strange lights seen in bogs. He himself had seen a leprechaun once, he told her solemnly. It had perched on his foot one night just as he was falling asleep and winked at him. Telling her such stories, Tim didn't seem to mind that Vicki was only six, and himself sixteen.

Vicki learned other things about Tim. He didn't like

blood or killing either. His Pa, his Ma and his little sister, Moira, had all died of influenza. Vicki, with her gray eyes and very white skin, looked very much like Moira, he said. And she was quiet like Moira, too.

They talked often about Julian. It was from Tim that Vicki learned who Poll Henry was, and why Julian wasn't supposed to go to her house. She ran a "bawdy house," Tim said, and bad things went on there. Men came there and paid Poll and her sisters to kiss them. They played the pianoforte all night long, which was very wicked. All of them wore bright colors and fancy silks and velvets, which was wicked, too, although Vicki did not know just how.

And now that the soldiers from the War were crowded all about the town, there were more men at Poll's house than ever before, Tim said. There were so many that sometimes they had to stand in line outside Poll's front door, and she had had to hire more boys like Tim to work in her carriage house. Poll paid poorly, and fed the boys skimpy food, Tim told her. But the boys liked to work for her because sometimes she let them go and kiss the girls, too.

"Would you ever go and kiss Poll and her sisters?" Vicki had asked one day when Tim was weeding the day lily bed—gardening was another of his chores— making a big stack of weeds on the grass.

She had been surprised to see Tim blush and shift his knees and look away.

"No," he told her at last. "No, I wouldn't want women like that. I'd want a nice girl, a girl I could talk to."

Their eyes had met and Vicki thought she heard him mutter "like you." But then he had turned away and began throwing more weeds on the pile, and Vicki decided that she hadn't heard him right after all.

"But why would Julian want to go and look at Poll Henry's house?" she persisted.

"Because he has the Devil in him," was all that Tim would say, and he stood up and gathered the weeds into a burlap sack. He was not very tall, but he was taller than Vicki by far. His hands were big-knuckled and strong from all the work that he did, yet so gentle they could cup a newborn kitten.

And Vicki, trotting along beside him to the refuse heap behind the carriage house, felt safe, safe with Tim. For as long as Tim was near her, Julian could not come and get her and put a pillow over her face.

Did you receive the last letter I sent you? The pilot promised he would send it along, Adam wrote Carisa in March, 1862. *We are traveling south on the steamer Fulton, toward a place they call Ship Island. We'll be used in the campaign against New Orleans, I suspect. We've had a good voyage so far, with only one moderate gale. I've been given a stateroom by the stairway. It's tiny, and too near the boiler, and three of us are crammed into it, but we are not complaining very loudly. . . .*

The months had passed for Carisa with leaden slowness. To her vast, shaking relief, letters from Rolf had begun to arrive; the show had survived its Atlantic crossing with only a few animal deaths. But, robbing her of her joy, arriving home from the Bull Run Campaign, Adam had almost immediately begun talk of re-enlisting. This time he planned to join his cousin in Hartford, who was recruiting a company for the Twelfth Connecticut Volunteers.

"Adam!" she had cried angrily. "Adam, how can you? To go and risk yourself again!"

"I must, Carisa."

"Nonsense, you don't have to go at all. No one would think less of you if you stayed here at home . . . Redlands Kord is going to do so, and countless other men who are over forty. They all. . . ."

"They are not me, Carisa. And this is something I feel I must do. Whether or not you can understand me."

The regiment had spent the winter in Hartford, drilling. They would serve under a Major General Benjamin Butler, Adam wrote her. Butler was a former lawyer with a bristly mustache, fat face, and pouchy, slanted eyes. *I pray, however, that he is capable enough. . . .*

Adam managed to get leave to come home and see

308

her just before his regiment left for New York. She spotted him from an upstairs window and went flying outdoors breathlessly to meet him.

"I don't have long," he told her hastily. "Only twelve hours."

"Oh, Adam." She clung to him and wept, pressing her face against the roughened woolen texture of his uniform. "Only twelve hours? It doesn't seem fair! I don't want to let you go, not again!"

Adam's arms had encircled her, pulling her to him. "It's too late for second thoughts, Carisa. I'm committed now."

They were still alone on the grounds, near the greenhouse. There had been a winter thaw, and the ground was frozen and derelict, the trees black skeletons, matching Carisa's own mood. Smoke rose from the flues of the greenhouse.

"Why?" she cried. "Oh, Adam, why? You didn't have to go again, no one asked you to re-enlist, I begged you not to."

He held her back from him, his eyes darkening. "I'm a Hartshorn, Carisa. Over the years, Hartshorns have given much for this country. I feel a responsibility. . . ."

"Responsibility! Bah!" She pushed away from him angrily. "Isn't it your responsibility to stay at home with your family? Oh, I hate war. I hate it! Taking my husband away, and my circus, which I might never see again. . . ."

"Your circus," Adam said quietly. "Yes, you would hate that, wouldn't you, Carisa, to have that taken away. My poor girl."

"No . . . No . . . it's not like that . . ." Carisa cursed herself for those carelessly spoken words.

"It is, Carisa. It's always been the circus for you, and you know it."

"No! No!" Some desperate impulse made Carisa press her body to Adam's and then—before anyone could spot them from the house—pull him fiercely toward the greenhouse.

"Carisa . . ."

"No, Adam, let's don't talk. Just come. I want to

309

show you something. How much, how very much I love you. . . ."

The greenhouse was damp and warm, filled with the heavy smells of potting soil and moist growing things. Plants were everywhere, lined on long benches in rows, or hanging in pots from the ceiling. Some rough sacks had been thrust under one of the benches, and boldly Carisa grabbed some and spread them on the floor.

"Adam?"

"Oh, God, Carisa . . ." Adam groaned. His arms encircled her fiercely. "My mother . . . the children . . . I should go and greet them. . . ."

"Do it later," she sighed. "For now, just kiss me. . . ."

His hands touched her, drawing fire from her. She was drowning in the hardness of his kiss, the urgent searching of his lips. Somehow they were sinking to the floor, and she was flinging off her gown, Adam helping her to tear feverishly at the buttons and hooks.

And then they were naked, lying full length on the burlap sacks, their bodies laid against each other in long, sweet embrace.

"It's because of me, isn't it?" she whispered at last, when they lay perspiring and spent. "It's because of me that you want to go to war, isn't it? You don't want to be around me any more. . . ."

"Carisa . . ." His voice was choked. "Oh, God, it isn't that simple. . . ."

"All those weeks and months, Adam, that you were gone that first enlistment. I worried about you so. I knew you wanted to get away from me. . . ."

He kissed her lightly, his lips barely touching her. "Let it be, Carisa. I'm here now, aren't I? We have twelve hours together. Let's enjoy them for what they are. Whatever has happened in the past, whatever wrong things I've done, or will do . . . it doesn't matter now. It's all over."

"Yes."

She gave herself up to his embrace again, refusing to allow herself to think of what Adam had said. *Whatever wrong things I've done, or will do.* What had he meant?

310

But she did not have time to ask him, for he was kissing her again, and then there was a banging on the greenhouse door, and Matt was crying out in a high, piercing voice that he wanted to see his Papa.

The last white clumps of snow on the ground melted away, and then were replaced by the white powder of a late snowfall. Fort Trumbull, it was announced, was now in a state of readiness, and a recruiting depot there met its quota of one hundred and twenty-seven men. Samuel Hartshorn had departed for the Navy, leaving Eliza behind, sallower and more dried-up and cough-ridden than ever. The streets of New London teemed with soldiers. There were incidents of drunkenness, shootings, fights and beatings.

Carisa saw with growing uneasiness that the shipping of the port had suffered. About one hundred and twenty-two vessels lay idle in the harbor, Adam had admitted to her on that twelve-hour leave. There were whalers, merchantmen, fishing boats and others.

"But of course all of that will change soon enough," he had assured her. He and Mr. West had wasted precious hours of the leave closeted in Adam's study making last-minute business arrangements. "Our ships will all be needed for the war. And there's talk now of opening a new supply route to the West Indies for fruit and vegetables, now that our Southern business has been cut off."

Carisa heard this gloomily. She had listened to enough of Duddie's grim tales of Balaclava to shudder. What if Adam and his agent were wrong? What if the War, instead of being a boon to shipping, proved to be a disaster? What if large numbers of vessels were to be sunk? And it was true that people had been using large amounts of the new kerosene these days instead of whale oil. . . .

The day after Adam departed, she drove to town and invested a large amount of the money he had left with her in the New London House Nail Company. It, like other industries in the town, was booming, men working night and day to make materials for the war.

311

This task accomplished, she returned home, rubbing one fist against her dry, burning eyes, puffy from crying. Nelly and Gaines had been married some weeks previously, when the men had returned home from the Bull Run Campaign. Now, in the barren hiatus caused by Adam's leaving, Carisa forced herself to take an interest in furnishing the couple's two-room suite in the servants' quarters. She gave them bedding, two rocking chairs, and a fine highboy, promising Nelly to find her a pair of good tinted lithographs.

Nelly was delighted. Gaines, she told Carisa bravely, would be surprised to see their rooms looking so fine when he returned home.

We are on Ship Island, near Biloxi, Adam wrote in mid-March of 1862. *Here the sand is a dazzling white during the day, and shines at night like fool's gold. We are camped in a rubble of sand hills, and haven't even any baggage wagons or horses.*

Horses, Carisa thought dully. How happily Adam's regiment would have grabbed the baggage and ring horses from the Phillips Circus and put them to work. Thank God she had had the foresight to send her circus to England. At least she had managed to save her show animals.

She read on. *We haven't a cook-tent, or lumber to build one. My men have to haul firewood on their backs, from miles away. We are all chafing for something to happen. . . .*

Near the end of May, Carisa was in her room dressing one morning, preparing to go to the ring barn with Benicia for their daily workout. She tugged irritably at the dark bombazine of her dress. Lately it seemed that all of her gowns had grown too tight. She had been feeling nauseated, too, in the mornings, and very tired at night.

She knew what this meant, and could not stifle a feeling of despair. Another baby now, of all times? With its father gone away to war, perhaps never to come back—

"Miss Carisa! Miss Carisa!" There was a loud hammering on her bedroom door, interrupting the gloom of these thoughts. Then Nelly burst in.

"What is it now, Nelly?" Carisa asked wearily.

"Oh, you'll never guess what I saw last night!"

"And what could that be?"

"Why, I was just sitting on the edge of my bed taking off my stockings when I happened to look out through the window. You know the windows in those rooms you gave us that look out toward the water?"

"Yes."

"Well, what do you think I saw? The ghost ship!"

"The what?"

"The ghost ship! Oh, it was just as plain as day, moving along so quiet-like it was scary! I nearly screamed. And you can be sure I crawled under my quilts as quick as I could!"

Carisa sighed. The legendary ghost ship, she remembered, had been seen shortly after she had arrived at Hearts-ease. She shook off an involuntary shiver. "Nelly, you don't really believe in that silly story, do you?"

The excitement left Nelly's face, and her mouth quivered. "Yes. I really do. If you'd seen it, Miss Carisa, you'd believe it, too. Anyone would."

"Oh, I'm sure it was just a fishing boat. Or a whaler. Remember, New London *is* a harbor, and we certainly don't lack for ships."

Adam, she was thinking in sudden panic. Adam, away at Ship Island, fretting to go into battle. What if—But with enormous effort, she pushed away the thought.

"No, this was real," Nelly insisted. "And it wasn't like any fishing boat *I've* ever seen. It was old looking, and even though there was a wind, the sails were slack. But still it moved." She shivered. "Anyway, now all we have to do is wait."

"Wait?"

"Until someone dies," the servant said somberly. "Isn't that what the ship comes for? To warn us?"

She went about her day's work, trying to push Nelly's fancy out of her mind. Because surely that was all it was—servants' excitement. Carefully she worked with

313

Neecie. In the afternoon she read to the three younger children and helped Julian with his lessons. Glumly she accompanied Katherine to a bandage rolling party, returning home in the late afternoon feeling tired and listless.

A stack of mail was waiting for her: a letter from Rolf informed her that the Phillips Circus was doing well on its tour and would shortly be heading north to Edinburgh. Marcella Duquesne had fallen from her wire and broken her ankle, and Rolf was trying to replace her.

You needn't worry, Rolf wrote in his sprawling script. *I can replace her here, there's lots to choose from. The show is in my good hands, as you know.*

Yes. She knew. Carisa crushed the letter into a ball and threw it angrily toward the waste-paper basket. Then, leaving the rest of the mail, she swept down the corridor to her bedroom. An odd, aching feeling pushed at the small of her back.

She would lie down, she decided dully. There was a new issue of *Scribner's,* and she would occupy herself with it.

However, by seven o'clock, she was turning and writhing on the bed, all thoughts of reading long gone from her mind. Nelly came, to hold her hand and to put cold compresses on her forehead. Katherine hastily sent for Dr. Arthur. She was having another miscarriage.

She twisted on the bed, clutching at the bedcovers as if that might help against the pangs. She wouldn't mind the pain so much, she told herself, panting, if at least she were to get a child from it. But a miscarriage . . . so empty, so sterile. . . .

Dr. Arthur strode into the room, bringing with him the smell of chemicals and carbolic.

"Well? And what did you do to bring it about this time, Mrs. Hartshorn?" He was referring to her previous miscarriage in 1859, she knew. She had suffered it on a steamer while taking a circus trip.

"Nothing!" she cried. "This time my husband can't possibly blame me . . . no one can!"

"Well, you must have been straining yourself some-

314

how. Too much activity on the part of a delicate woman can bring about abortion of the fetus, and that, my dear, is exactly what has happened to you."

"I'm not delicate!"

"Very well, then. But you're certainly losing your child, aren't you?"

She could not reply; suddenly she was possessed by a huge, grinding pain in her pelvis. It ripped and tore at her flesh. She arched her back and bit her lips to choke down a scream.

"Oh, dear God," Nelly wailed from somewhere near the window. "Oh, I knew this would happen, I knew it. Seeing that ship last night, and now this. . . ."

"N-nonsense," Carisa managed to say through clenched teeth.

"Oh, my." Nelly dropped the damp towel she had been holding to sink into a chair. "Oh, I wish I hadn't seen it. I wish I hadn't!"

"Do be quiet, you silly girl," Katherine ordered. She had just come into the room, and now she thrust a basin of water into Nelly's hands. "Busy yourself rinsing these rags and still your tongue. It won't help Miss Carisa to hear your babbling."

"I'm sorry, I'm sorry. . . ."

Carisa scarcely heard their wrangling voices, so intent was she on the tumult going on within her own body. All of this just to lose a child, she was thinking. How disappointed Adam will be. And it isn't my fault this time, it isn't. . . ."

Just before midnight she uttered a loud, piercing scream that brought Nelly and Katherine running toward the bed, and even made Dr. Arthur jump. Then she was delivered of two small, dead infants. A pair of sons this time, she heard Dr. Arthur say.

"Dead . . ."

"Yes, both of them," Dr. Arthur said briskly.

"No . . ."

They could not possibly have lived; she knew that, in her mind. But still her heart raged against it, against a fate which could casually create two little lives, then snuff them out.

"A pity, too," the doctor went on. "But they were only five-month babies and never could have survived. However," he added as Carisa did not reply. "I would not advise you to have any more children, Mrs. Hartshorn. With the condition of your female organs, it could be very dangerous for you. As it is, you lost entirely too much blood this time."

After he had left, Nelly came and sponged Carisa's body and changed the linen on the bed, her eyes streaming with tears.

"Oh, Miss Carisa, I wish I hadn't seen that ship. If only I hadn't looked . . . oh, this is all my fault. . . ."

"Of course it's not," Carisa whispered. She clung to the other woman's hands, squeezing at them weakly. "How could it possibly be your fault, Nelly?"

"You . . . you're so kind and good," Nelly wept. "They should have lived, they should have. . . ."

20

After a great deal of thought, Carisa named the two dead infants John and Dudley, for it grieved her to think that they should be buried without even names. There was a bleak little funeral, and when the two babies were at last laid to rest, Carisa felt as if she had aged a dozen hard years.

With aching guilt, she knew she had complained to herself at the thought of another pregnancy, a child to be borne alone with Adam away. But now that the boys were dead, she missed them with a wild, incessant grief. Small morsels of flesh, they had been a part of herself and Adam. A part of their loving. Oh, she would have cherished them if only she had been given a chance. It just wasn't fair!

Do not grieve yourself, Carisa, over something you could not control, Adam wrote her. *God wanted to take those children, and His ways must often be inscrutable to us.*

As if in keeping with her own somber mood, there came news of the war. There had been bloody fighting at Shiloh, and General McClellan had begun the siege of Yorktown. New Orleans had surrendered, and Adam wrote her of his part in this, which, he lamented, was very small.

The Twelfth Connecticut, now in the role of occupying troops, was camped near a levee. Adam's letters described gloomy cypress swamps, swamp fever, lush plantations of cane sugar, and people on the verge of starvation. It was these which bothered him more than anything else, he wrote her. He and some of the other officers had been saving their rations to give to the smallest and most emaciated of the children.

At the end of May, 1862, Julian ran away. At first no one considered this serious; the youth was often gone for hours at a stretch. Even his tutor, Mr. Waggoner, who found him gone at noon, his bed unslept in, felt that this was merely another of the boy's escapades.

Katherine agreed with him.

"Oh, what's all the concern?" she asked in her deep, husky voice. She was in the parlor counting out a new needlepoint canvas preparatory to an afternoon spent sewing and chatting with Eliza. "No doubt he'll turn up, as he always does. Especially if we send the buggy down to *that woman's* house." She emphasized the words with distaste.

"I don't know. I'm uneasy, Mother Hartshorn. Julian has seemed so very restless, so unhappy since Adam left."

"Because we forbade him to go to that place?" Katherine grimaced. "It's unnatural! Why would it fascinate him so, to see who goes in and out of that bawdy house? Ungodly, that's what it is. And if you ask me, Carisa, one of these days he's going to get a bit bolder and go inside."

Carisa licked her lips, for Katherine had never been told the full story of Julian and Poll Henry.

"I suppose boys do go into places like that," she ventured.

Katherine, reaching for a skein of Persian wool, paused. "I imagine so. But not boys of good family, boys who have been properly reared, and not like *that*, like a . . . a. . . ."

"Perhaps he . . . has his reasons."

"Nonsense! Wickedness is his reason, and none other."

Carisa paced about restlessly, unsatisfied. "I'm going to go and look for him," she announced at last.

Ten minutes later the small surrey had been harnessed and Carisa was on her way into New London, accompanied by Tim Kelly, who managed the chestnut mare with a practiced hand. It was a moist, cool May morning, the air full of sea tang. The mare was frisky, and required Tim's full attention.

Poll's house sat among its grove of trees, still and quiet. They made two circuits up the winding road which led to it, seeing no sign of Julian. A brindle dog came running out to bark at them, but other than this, there was no sign of life.

"Looks like they're all asleep, ma'am," Tim said.

Carisa drew a sharp breath. She was filled with a sudden dread of going up that bricked walk and knocking on Poll's front door. Indeed, she had never come here to see Poll as she had told herself last year she must do. Somehow there had always been a good excuse to put it off.

Now Tim, sitting beside her, seemed to sense her hesitation. "I'll go, ma'am," he volunteered quickly. "This is no job for a lady such as yourself."

"No," she said at last. "No, I don't think so, Tim. This is something I must do myself. Please wait here for me. I'll be back in a few minutes."

He helped her out of the surrey and she swept up the walk, keeping her chin high and thankful that she had chosen to wear a new gown of blue poplin, trimmed in black velvet ribbon.

It took a long time for her rap on the polished brass door knocker to be answered. Then there was a longer wait for the surprised little maid to admit her into the foyer, then trot upstairs to call her mistress.

While she waited, Carisa glanced about her with a piercing curiosity. The parquet floor of the large entrance hall gleamed with polish. One door stood ajar, revealing the sparkle of a crystal chandelier, the gleam of a white marble fireplace. An ornate brass statuette occupied the mantle of that fireplace . . . a naked nymph, Carisa noted with a catch of her breath.

"Well! So! It is Carisa Hartshorn again, is it?" Poll came gliding down the big, polished staircase, a black silk dressing gown pulled about her bony, cat-like body. When she had been a nursemaid at Hearts-ease, Poll had still possessed something of the soft, malleable look of the young. This, Carisa saw, was now gone. Now Poll was all hardness and glitter, from the jet buttons of her dressing gown to the similar jeweled blackness of her eyes.

"I came to talk to you," Carisa began.

"Talk to me? And what about?" Poll threw back her head and laughed. The long white column of her throat worked convulsively. "To beg me for a job? Oh, yes, a girl like you would do very well here! And I've so much business with all those men from the forts, I could keep you fully occupied!"

A girl like you. Hatred welled up in Carisa. How dare Poll Henry speak to her that way? Did she resent it that much that she, Poll, had been a servant and Carisa the mistress? That Carisa had married Adam when Poll could not?

"I've come about Julian," she heard herself say.

"Julian?" Abruptly Poll's laughter faded. "What about him?"

"He is missing. His bed hasn't been slept in. I want to know if he is here, or if he has been here."

Poll hesitated. "Come into the parlor," she said at last. We can talk there."

Poll pushed open a door, and sudden arcs of light and movement seemed to jump out at Carisa. Involuntarily she stepped backward.

319

"My mirror room," Poll said. "What's the matter, don't you like it?"

Carisa looked about her, at the walls hung with glass, each square edged in birds-eye maple. More glass adorned the ceiling, reflecting back the two women from a dozen fragmented angles. Around the edge of the room were settees upholstered in rich blue. These, too, were reflected again and again in optic illusion.

Carisa could almost see it, the rows of young women sitting on these settees in gaudy, daring evening dress, waiting to be inspected by the men who came here. And what else happened in this room? she wondered. There was an aura of sexuality here, heavy and palpable. Even a sexual smell. . . .

Poll's eyes were laughing at her.

"I didn't come here to admire your decor," Carisa said as coldly as she could. "I came to find out about my step-son. Has he been here?"

To her surprise, Poll again hesitated. "Yes. He was here last night. I tried to send him away, but he wouldn't go. He said that he was a man now, and he wanted what was his."

To Carisa's astonishment, Poll's cheeks had reddened faintly.

He wanted what was his. The words seemed to hang between them. Carisa could feel herself reeling with her shock.

"You . . . you didn't. . . ."

Poll's jet-black eyes glittered at her. "Make of it what you will. He was a beautiful boy once, and I did love him, in my way . . . but you wouldn't understand that, would you? And besides, what did you expect me to do? He was old enough. . . ."

"Where is he now?" Carisa whispered, feeling sick.

"Who knows? He left early this morning. Said he was going to join up and fight in the Union Army. He told me he was big enough and strong enough, no one would ask any questions of him. And he said he could shoot a pistol, too."

"No!" Carisa's cry tore out of her.

"Oh, yes, he's off like all the other men, to drink

320

his fill of killing. And nothing you can do will stop him."

"But where? Where did he go? Which road did he take?"

"How should I know that?" Poll's laughter was harsh. "But I do know one thing, Mrs. Circus Owner. You look down at the likes of me, don't you? You always did, even when you first came to Hearts-ease and weren't any better than me."

"That's not true!"

"Oh, I know it's true. You all whisper about me, don't you? I heard the tongues clack when I attended that circus of yours. But let me tell you something."

The other's voice had lowered to a whisper. "I know a lot more about you fine ladies than you could ever imagine. You see, I know your husbands."

I know your husbands. Sly words with an ugly, secret meaning.

Carisa's breath caught. "You don't . . . you don't know *my* husband!"

"Oh?" Poll's grin was triumphant. "I do know him. And I'll tell you this, Carisa Hartshorn, I know your circus folk, too. They come here often enough for their pleasure, from Rolf Taggart on down to that silly little midget man. And do you know, men like that tend to talk when they've liquor in them. And some of the things they say. . . ."

She advanced toward Carisa, the silk of her dressing gown rustling. A dozen images of her were duplicated in the glass behind her.

Carisa felt a sick squeeze in the pit of her belly. Poll knew something. Something horrid about Adam. She felt sure of it, something which would rip and tear like scissors across the fabric of their lives.

"Oh, yes, Mrs. Hartshorn. I could tell you things about that fine husband of yours. . . ."

"No!" Carisa screamed. "No, no, I won't listen!"

Reflections whirled as she clapped her hands over her ears and stumbled toward the parlor door. She plunged out into the entrance hall, her feet skidding on polished parquet. A maid gawked at her. Then she was outdoors, running toward the haven of her own carriage.

Behind her rose Poll Henry's laughter, mocking.

July came, and still they had had no word from Julian. It was as if he had disappeared into the seething vortex of the war, leaving behind him no clue.

Dutifully Carisa did all that she could to find him. She walked through New London, asking constables, merchants and firemen if they had seen the youth, or heard of him. She wrote to Adam in New Orleans, asking him to use his Army contacts to locate his son. She wrote to Samuel, temporarily stationed with the hospital transport, *Ocean Queen,* in the Chesapeake Bay. Dr. Arthur was now with that ship, she had learned, treating patients ill with typhoid, exposure, or hideous wounds.

None knew of Julian's whereabouts. Adam wrote her bleakly that many boys as young as fourteen had turned up among the soldiers, having lied about their ages.

Let us pray for him, he wrote. *I am afraid that it is all we can do now. My son was drawn to the glamour of battle. Now he is going to learn some of its reality, God help him.*

Adam himself had known little of the "glamour" of battle, but much of the drudgery. In New Orleans, because of some legal courses he had once taken at Harvard College, he had been appointed to conduct court-martials, an unhappy task to which he took with little enthusiasm. *I don't like being set up to judge other men, I don't have the stomach for it. Compassion, it seems, has little part in the affairs of the U.S. Army* . . . .

In August, Carisa received a letter from the headmaster at Julian's old school. A boy resembling Adam's son had been seen by one of the school's recent graduates, standing in line outside a hospital tent near Manassas Junction. The youth had been wearing bloody bandages around his knee and head. The other man had attempted to talk to him. But before he could be questioned, Julian had slipped away. . . .

During this period, life at Hearts-ease seemed to

slow, almost to stop. Now that Julian was gone, Vicki seemed to brighten. She spent long hours playing in the attic, or following Tim Kelly about. Benicia continued to ride and to train on the wooden ball, surprising Carisa with her skill.

And Matt had begun to beg Tim to take him to the waterfront, where he would play on the piers and watch the harbor traffic. He would captain a whaler one day, he announced. He, too, was a Hartshorn, was he not?

Eliza Hartshorn was now a frequent guest at Heartsease—perhaps because her own house, on Whale Oil Row, was desolate and empty with only one woman and a few servants to occupy it. She and Katherine worked long hours on the bandages they were rolling for Samuel's hospital ship.

Eliza's cough was worse than ever, and sometimes a paroxysm would seize her, leaving her perspiring and weak.

"If only Dr. Arthur were here," Katherine would lament. "He would at least mix you a poultice or a soothing draught."

Eliza nodded, her skin so sallow that her pale eyelashes stood out in dark relief.

"Never mind!" Carisa said sharply, touched with pity somehow for this women whom she had never really liked. "We can make one ourselves, can't we, from your *Mackenzies?*"

Katherine looked startled. "Why, yes, I suppose we . . ."

"Then let's get the book and see what we can concoct. Surely it will be as effective as anything Dr. Arthur might devise."

The thick household book, tattered from use, was the one to which Katherine had often referred during Carisa's earlier years as a bride. It contained a chapter on "useful domestic medicines," which included plasters, ointments, cordials, balsams and salves. Carisa found one formula for "Balsam of Honey," which looked easy. It contained opium, wine, honey and other things. Grimly she drove to town to purchase the necessary ingredients.

323

But the elixir, although it made Eliza sleepy and vague, did not stop her cough. One afternoon while she was sitting in the parlor she coughed up a bright red stream of blood all over the bandage which she was rolling.

Katherine, too, was ailing these days. Her migraine headaches, always incapacitating, had grown worse. Often she had them after there was a letter from Adam or Samuel. One morning she confessed to Carisa that there was also a large lump in her right breast which was bothering her.

"Perhaps we should find a surgeon," Carisa suggested, dismayed.

"What? And have him cut it out?" Katherine paled, for surgery was an excruciating process undergone only by the brave and the desperate. "I'll never do such a thing, I couldn't! And I won't fret myself unduly over this. Still," she added unwillingly, "I recall that my mother died of such a tumor. It grew very big and painful before her end."

Carisa felt her heart catch. Over the years, her relationship with her mother-in-law had subtly altered. Where once Katherine had openly disapproved of her, now there were moments of grudging respect. Occasional small acts of kindness too, although Katherine brushed off all thanks for these.

"Then we must find something in *Mackenzies* for you, too," Carisa tried to say cheerfully.

But there was nothing in the section on "diseases of females" which seemed to apply, and Carisa finally decided to give Katherine laudanum for her pain. Now she was sorry that Dr. Arthur had left for the war. Odious as he was, he would be better than no doctor at all, for most of the town's other physicians had left for the war, leaving the town's citizens to fend for themselves.

The days dragged. She received letters from both Duddie and Rolf. Duddie wrote that the show had been well-received in Scotland and Wales, and was now in France. Here Duddie had managed to attend a performance at the *Cirque Napoléon,* viewing the great Jules

Léotard in his "flying trapeze" act which had electrified the entire circus world.

Léotard, of course, was superb, Duddie wrote, *and I can see why he is the toast of Europe. Still, there are other things on my mind just now. I am afraid that Rolf Taggart, like a very proud and squawking peacock, is letting this tour in Europe go to his head. He is enjoying his power too much, Carisa. He is beginning to speak and act as if HE were the owner of the Phillips Circus instead of yourself. . . .*

Carisa crumpled this letter up, her cheeks flaming. She paced back and forth across the carpet in her office, her heart slamming with rage.

How dare Rolf act this way? It was not he who had schemed and struggled and dreamed and even married, in order to make the Phillips Circus what it was.

No, Rolf did not own her show. He never would. He was only a tool, a means through which she could work as owner. Surely he realized that. If not, she would soon make him see it.

She would write to Rolf immediately, she decided, reminding him of the sizeable bonus which awaited him. She would also remind him of his position as subordinate. Rolf *was* manageable, she told herself, if handled firmly, and she would get him under her control again, as she had always managed to do before.

If only she did not need him so desperately!

In September a sullen reply from Rolf came, ignoring all that she had said to him, and informing her that he had been in correspondence with John Phillips. Her father was now living in Brooklyn and working occasionally for an itinerant medicine show.

A medicine show! Carisa's heart twisted as she thought of the once proud and arrogant John Phillips reduced to hustling up sales for Hinkley's Bone Liniment or Dr. Jayne's Sanative Pills, or something else equally flamboyant and useless.

Her eyes focused again on the letter. *He has arthritis now so bad that he can hardly handle money,* Rolf wrote. *Why don't you send him something, since you're so rich and important these days?*

Carisa sat for a long time staring at the letter. She *had* been sending Papa a monthly stipend. She had been doing it for years, at least until he had moved without leaving a forwarding address. Never had she received one word of thanks from him, or even a letter.

He would suffer anything, even starvation, before he would humble himself before her, she thought angrily.

One rainy morning in September she boarded a steamer for New York. Gray rain lashed the deck and soaked her bonnet and mantle. She had to spend most of the voyage seated in the passengers' salon, which smelled of tobacco, damp wool and engine oil.

But at least she was traveling alone, she reminded herself—and that felt good. Katherine was unwell, and Nelly had had to remain to see to the children. As for the other servants, she would not consider having any of them along.

She found New York bristling with war fever. Soldiers swarmed the streets and were even camped on the Battery, waiting to be shipped to the front. There were placards everywhere, begging for volunteers, or for money. Buildings bore hastily-painted signs announcing Army offices, recruiting stations, or soldiers' relief organizations.

She stayed again at Mrs. Adair's. The small brownstone hotel was bursting with Union officers on leave from the front, giving the place a curiously raffish air. Dismayed, Carisa hurried at once to her room to change out of her damp traveling dress. A few minutes later, she emerged into the corridor, intending to go downstairs and ask the attendant to summon a hack for her.

"Well, haven't I seen you somewhere before?" A tall officer, reeking of whiskey, was lurching his way up the stairs.

"No, I'm sure you haven't," Carisa told him firmly, wishing she had selected another hotel. Mrs. Adair's had always been so respectable. Now it was filled with the loud noises and banging and guffaws of war-boisterous men.

But the officer leaned toward her. "Oh, yesh, I have. I'm sure of it." He was swaying perilously. "At a party,

326

thatsh it. A nice good party. An' you, pretty as a picture. . . ."

He laughed happily.

"Please excuse me." Carisa brushed past him, hoping he would not grab her. She hurried down the flight of stairs to the haven of the ladies' sitting room and the private ladies' entrance.

These, although deserted-looking and forlorn, were at least empty of soldiers. Carisa rang for the attendant, and asked him to hail her a cab.

The streets of New York clattered with carriage traffic, with the jostling drays, buggies, carts and vans which were the life-blood of this city. Smells rose about her: soot, dust, manure, the reek of industry. New York!

In spite of herself, Carisa felt her heart begin to pound a little faster. She had the wild thought that something was about to happen to her. Something to jerk her out of her cocoon and thrust her into the whirl of life again. Something . . . perhaps not altogether pleasant.

Oh, don't be silly, she told herself, as the hack swayed and rattled over the bricked streets.

She drove to the ferry dock and boarded the ferry for Brooklyn.

The little girl, grimy and untidy, came skipping down the front steps of the brick tenement. Her dress may once have been white, but now its shade was the color of diluted mud, its hem even darker from dragging in the streets. She paused to stare at Carisa with her thumb in her mouth.

"Surely this isn't the address?" Carisa asked the hackman she had hired after debarking from the ferry.

"It is. I told you it wa'nt no place for the likes of you. Who you got to see here, anyway?" The hackman, a freckled man of forty, had evidently taken a liking to Carisa, for he had chatted to her steadily ever since she had entered his hack.

"My . . . my father," she whispered.

His face seemed to change subtly. "Want me to wait, then? It'll cost you extra."

"Yes. If you would."

Silently he helped her out of the hack.

She stood for a moment on the bricked pavement, looking about her in growing dismay. The working-class street was lined with brick tenements, crammed in side by side. People were everywhere: screaming children, lounging men, housewives. A man peddled rags, and a boy hawked brick dust, to be used for sharpening knives. A woman wearily pumped water from an outside pump, a baby wailing at her skirts.

A fruit seller had set up his cart, and customers picked gingerly over his wares. Raising her eyes, Carisa saw that laundry flapped from someone's wrought iron balcony. In fact, laundry was everywhere, on ropes or draped over railings or hanging from windows. Even the balconies which projected from these grimy buildings were filled, either with drying clothes or with piled-up junk.

Her sense of adventure—if she had had one—had abruptly fled. Now she was only conscious of the feeling of nausea pushing at her throat. Papa—living here!

As Carisa approached the building, the little girl scampered away. The entrance hall was small and unlit, and smelled of boiling cabbage, fish and human excretions. A tattered sign was tacked to the bare wall announcing *Rooms, five cents a spot*. A hallway stretched before her, lined with doors.

Carisa hesitated, trying not to breathe too deeply. Just then one of the doors slammed open. A young girl came bursting out, her hair streaming down her back in a tangle.

"Could you tell me where John Phillips lives?" Carisa called out quickly.

"Who? Old Man Phillips? Up two flights and to your right."

The girl gave Carisa's gown a long, envying look, and then pushed past her and out the front door of the building.

Old Man Phillips. Carisa bit her lower lip. To her

328

right was a flight of steps and another sign saying *Rooms,* with the crude drawing of a hand pointing upward. Holding her hoopskirts against the narrowness of the passage, Carisa began to climb.

"What are you doing here?" Papa's voice said.

Carisa stood in the doorway of the room, frozen, unable to move.

Even if she had sat down and tried to imagine the worst possible habitation in the world, she could never have thought of this.

At least fifteen men were sleeping in this small room, no larger than twelve-by-fourteen. They were everywhere, on mattresses or quilts, huddled on crude board bunks built in an alcove, or in front of a huge, greasy black stove. Sounds of snoring and heavy breathing filled the air. There was the stench of unwashed feet and bodies.

Three of the sleepers had awakened at her entrance, and were now propped on their elbows, staring at her as if she were an apparition from another world. But these men (sleeping in the middle of the day! she thought wildly) were still not the worst of the nightmare. The worst of it was the appearance of her father himself.

It had been years since she had seen him. And the girl in the downstairs corridor had been right. John Phillips was now an old man.

Where once he had been tall and lithe, now he was thin, cadaverous. The once muscular arms and shoulders had dwindled, grown spindly. He seemed to have shrunk several inches.

But worst of all were his hands. These had turned into misshapen claws, the fingers thickened, swollen, twisted unnaturally.

"Papa . . ." She found her voice. "Papa, I am your daughter, I'm Carisa, don't you recognize me? And, please, couldn't we go out into the hall to talk?" She gestured toward the staring men. "I can't talk to you like this. Not with them. . . ."

Her father stared at her. His eyes were a chilly blue.

"Very well." His voice, unchanged, could have come intact from her childhood.

"Papa," she whispered as soon as the door had closed behind them and they were out in the foul-smelling hall. "Papa . . ." Her voice trembled. "Who are those men?"

"They are my lodgers."

"Lodgers!"

"Yes. They pay me to sleep here. I run two shifts of them, one at night and one in the daytime."

"But . . . oh, why didn't you let me know where you were? I would have sent you money, I would have sent you anything you needed. You had only to ask, and I would have. . . ."

"I didn't want your money."

The plaster in the corridor was oily and stained. Somewhere in the building a baby squalled, and two women argued. Carisa forced herself not to think about these sounds. She dug her fingernails into the flesh of her palms until the pain sliced at her. She must not weep. She must not lose control of herself!

His blue eyes seemed to burn at her. "I invested in a small medicine show which was to travel through upper New York State. I put everything I had into it. But it failed. My hands . . ."

"No. Oh, Papa. . . ."

Was she mistaken, or did his face seem to twist briefly? Did he seem about to move toward her, to say something else? But then the moment was gone, and she was not sure if it had even happened at all.

"You needn't have come here," he was saying. "I'll get along."

"Papa!" The word seemed to explode from some other woman, not from herself. "Papa, how many times did I write to you, begging you to come to Hearts-ease? Pleading with you to be in my show? I named my circus after you, Papa! *It bears your name.* You didn't have to start a medicine show, or to stay here in New York all these years. . . ."

"Enough." John Phillips' voice still held the old, thrilling timber which had been able to command circus audiences.

"No!" she stormed. "No, I'm not finished yet! Papa, why are you being so stubborn? I'm sorry about Stephana dying, I'm sorry about the *Flambeaux* . . . I wish *I* had been the one to die instead of Stephie! But I wasn't. It didn't happen that way. She died and I lived. And I wanted to make it up to you. . . ."

He turned, dismissing her. His back, clad in an ancient black suit, was oddly pathetic. It made Carisa think of a drifter who had come around once to panhandle at the kitchen door of Hearts-ease.

"Papa!" she screamed. "Papa, if you'd only once come to see the show, just to see what I've done. . . ."

"Go home, Carisa." John Phillips turned, his eyes glittering at her. "Go away from here, go back to the life you have chosen for yourself. Go back to that lecherous husband of yours."

"My . . . lecherous . . . what do you mean?"

She felt as if he had suddenly jammed a tent stake into her chest. Her mouth felt so stiff that her lips would barely form the words.

The blue eyes glinted. A gnarled hand lifted toward her. "I mean that it was *your husband* who debauched my daughter Anna and made her into what she was . . . a vile harlot!"

Anna, she thought wildly. *Anna and Adam. Oh, dear God.*

"Papa . . ." her voice said. "You can't mean that . . . you can't really mean what you're saying. . . ."

She found that, without being aware of it, she had backed away from him, that she was near the scarred bannister at the top of the stairs. She felt cold all over. Chilly perspiration ran down between her breasts and along her ribs.

"No," she whispered. "Papa, you're wrong, you must be. You can't mean that. . . ."

"Adam Hartshorn was the man who debauched my daughter," her father repeated implacably.

Carisa's mind was spinning, her thoughts jagged and painful. Suddenly it was is if she could see Poll Henry's face, alive with malice. *I could tell you things about*

331

that husband of yours. She could see Benicia, her eyes looking so trustingly up to Adam, her soft little voice calling him Papa—

Oh, dear God. Dear God, it could not be true, and it wasn't true. She refused to believe it.

"Papa, you're lying! Do you hear me? It's all a lie!" She was screaming it at him. "Anna herself told me that . . . that a man came to see her after the show one day, a rich man. She said that he took her out, to a beer garden. . . ."

"And so he did. He took her away to his fine rich hotel and he registered her there as his wife, and he kept her there and debauched her. It was he who did that, Adam Hartshorn, your husband."

A clawed forefinger was pointed at her, accusing. Carisa involuntarily shrank back.

"You, Carisa, you have tainted our family all of your life. First your mother. Then the *Flambeaux,* and finally. . . ."

But Carisa could not listen any longer. She staggered backward, catching herself on the greasy bannister. Then she had picked up her skirts and was fleeing wildly downstairs, away from the words she could not bear to hear.

Later she would never remember it clearly—her long, jouncing trip, in hack, ferry and cab, back to Mrs. Adair's and the dubious sanctuary of her hotel room. All she knew was the blinding fact that Adam had betrayed her—and with her own sister.

How could it have happened? How could Adam have done such a thing?

Well, you see, Carisa, he came the first night only to admire me, to tell me how much he enjoyed the performance. We talked for a while, for a very long while, really. He seemed very lonely. . . .

He seduced me, dear sister. Or perhaps I seduced him, I don't really know. . . .

He seemed very lonely. . . .

Very lonely. . . .

When she finally reached Mrs. Adair's, she paid the

cab driver, tossing coins into his hand without even looking to see what they were. She rushed into the hotel and made her way blindly upstairs to her room on the second floor. There she flung herself on her bed and, to the sound of bangs and shouts and laughter in the corridor, abandoned herself to weeping.

She wept, she cried, she raged. She slammed her fist impotently into the soft, goose-feather bolster.

It was as if, she thought desperately, a gauze screen had always covered the world she knew. Now that screen had been ripped off, revealing life as it really was. How often had she heard Katherine and Eliza gossiping about men who were unfaithful to their wives? How often had she pitied Eliza because Samuel was unfaithful?

A half-hour passed. There were guffaws from the corridor as a group of soldiers lurched past her door. At last Carisa sat up, conscious for the first time of the tear stains on the silk of her gown. They would make water marks. Well, she didn't care. What did it matter? What did anything matter?

She jumped off the bed and began to pace about the hotel room, hearing the angry swish of her petticoats and skirts. Anna had always had a weak, complaisant nature, she knew. Always her sister had sought the simple solution, the easy way. Had she loved Adam, or had he been merely a situation from which she could not extract herself gracefully?

Carisa found herself standing in front of the tall, wooden dressing stand. She leaned forward and stared at her reflection in the small mirror there.

How ugly she looked! How dull and puffy-eyed!

A basin of cool water had been provided on a lower shelf of the dressing stand. Towels and washcloths hung on pegs. Carisa scrubbed her face until her skin was red, then blotted it dry. Then, following an urge she could not explain, she fumbled at the front fastening of her gown.

In a moment it fell in a crumpled circle at her feet. Then, feverishly, she untied her bulky hoop skirt, tore

333

out of her corset cover, yanked at the laces and hooks which fastened her corset.

At last she stood naked.

She could see parts of herself in the mirror, her skin pale and glowing, like the flesh of some smooth fruit. Her body . . . how often had Adam caressed it, loved it, kissed every part of it? She herself had loved her own body because Adam loved it.

Angrily she picked up her tortoise-shell hairbrush and threw it at the small square of mirror, shattering its glass into a hundred accusing pieces.

Two hours later, dressed again, feeling drained and depressed and exhausted, Carisa entered the small main lobby of Mrs. Adair's. She would have dinner alone in her room, of course—she certainly could not enter the dining room by herself—but she needed something to read, anything at all to ease the frantic running of her thoughts. *Anna, Adam, Anna . . .* Their names beat at her, smashed at her heart just as she had splintered the upstairs mirror.

"Well, a male voice suddenly said. "I thought you would never get back from whatever gallivanting occupied you today. I waited here in the lobby all afternoon for you."

Carisa ignored the voice (surely it could not be speaking to her) and continued across the crowded lobby to where a stack of newspapers and periodicals were kept for the use of patrons.

"I said, I've been waiting here all day for you, Carisa."

Carisa, in the act of reaching for a copy of *Frank Leslie's Illustrated Newspaper,* nearly dropped it in her astonishment. She looked wildly about her, seeing nothing but Union officers and an old man snoozing in a corner chair. Then she realized that an officer was lounging in a settee, the *Evening Sun* held up in front of him.

Slowly he lowered the newspaper. Black eyes gleamed at her in amusement.

"Did I surprise you, Carisa?"

"Samuel! Samuel Hartshorn!" She shook her head dazedly. People were staring at them, and she lowered her voice hastily. "What are you doing here? In New York of all places! I thought you were on board a hospital ship in the Chesapeake Bay!"

"I was. I came here as a courier, on official war business." Samuel gave a vague, important wave of his hand, his eyes regarding her appreciatively. Then he rose, tossing aside the paper and extending his arm for her to take.

"Well, Carisa, now that I've spent all this time waiting for you, don't you think that the least you could do is to accompany me in to dinner?"

"D-dinner?" she stammered. "I just came downstairs to get a magazine. I was planning to take dinner in my room. It isn't proper for. . . ."

His teeth gleamed at her. "Since when did *you* become a slave to what is considered 'proper'? Besides, as your brother-in-law, I will make you a perfectly acceptable escort for dinner."

He is a womanizer, Adam had said once of his brother. Carisa felt as if events were bounding swiftly out of her control. "How did you know that I would be here at Mrs. Adair's?"

"I didn't, until Roger told me. Roger Utley lives at Mystic, and remembers you well from that party you gave when you first married my brother."

Roger Utley. Of course. The drunken officer whom she had encountered on the stairs. It was all coming back to Carisa, that hideous party when all of New London had snubbed her, and Samuel had kissed her. There had been so many faces that night, so many men staring at her. And Samuel's mouth, searching and brutal. . . .

Silencing her protests, Samuel forced her firmly in the direction of the tiny dining room, where guests were served at round, white-covered tables with bowls of fruit for centerpieces.

They were served terrapin soup, steaming and fragrant. Samuel ate with deliberation, his eyes pausing often to rest on Carisa with a disquieting glint.

"You look very beautiful tonight," he murmured.

"Then your eyesight must be very poor indeed, for I'm very tired and not in a good humor at all."

She lowered her eyes. Through the years Samuel had often stared at her with that bold urgency, but always she had been able to fob him off with a quick smile or a change of subject. Besides, there were rumors that Samuel had a demanding mistress in Groton Heights who absorbed all of his energies.

Now, it seemed, Samuel's energies were unhindered.

"Tell me of Navy life," she said hastily. "I have always wondered about it."

"I doubt that," Samuel commented dryly, his hot eyes brushing across her again. But nonetheless, he did as she asked, telling her of the severely injured cases his ship had treated, and hinting self-importantly of certain secret Navy missions, in which he, Samuel, was playing a key role.

"Have you heard from my fine and stalwart brother?" Samuel asked her at last, diffidently.

"He is still in charge of the court-martials," Carisa replied. "At a place called Camp Parapet, which is somewhere near New Orleans, I think. He hates that, Samuel. He wrote me that he didn't enlist just to be handing out sentences for petty thievery and desertion. And some of the sentences the Army forces him to hand down are far too harsh. In his last letter he wrote that he had to have one man executed. . . ."

Her voice shook. She could well imagine how repugnant such a sentence would be to a man like Adam.

"Kindness! My brother is a soft-hearted fool. What good is kindness when there are deserters involved? They should be shot, and as quickly as possible. Otherwise they infect the rest of the men with their fear."

"Shot! For being frightened of war, or for not believing in it? Oh, Samuel, how can you say such things? Adam writes me that some of the men have been addled in their minds by the terrible things they have seen. Their minds cannot adjust to it. . . ."

Speaking of Adam was almost like bringing him to their table, and suddenly Carisa was overwhelmed with

336

such a rush of pain and grief that she could barely sit erect. *Adam,* she thought wildly. *Adam, Adam, how could you have done it to me?*

"Nonsense," Samuel said. "Fear is fear, and it has an ugly stench." As Carisa lowered her eyes, Samuel added, "Have some wine, Carisa. I took the liberty of ordering some fine Bordeaux to relax us. You look as if you could use it."

They completed their meal. Carisa tasted the rare roast beef, swimming in its own natural juices, the stuffed potatoes and hot, spicy apple pie. She drank several glasses of the full, rich wine, letting it carry her along as it wished. The dining room was loud with boisterous laughter, with the trilling giggles of men. And with each swallow of wine, Carisa's pain seemed to recede from her, until at last it seemed only a dim ache at the end of some long, frozen corridor.

Samuel's hand lingered on her arm as he helped her up from her chair at last and escorted her to the lobby again. This time the room was deserted, save for the same old man, still snoozing in his chair.

Samuel took her hand and pulled her to him.

"Samuel . . . no . . ." She tried to push him away.

"Carisa . . . Carisa, you're so beautiful tonight, so desirable. . . ." His breathing had quickened, his face darkened with temper. "But never push me away, girl. I won't take that from a woman. I never have taken it."

She reeled and then had to cling to him for support, barely hearing what he had said.

"I think I'd better escort you to your room, my dear, you're swaying on your feet. Why, I believe you've drunk too much. You're shaking."

"No . . . no, I'm not. I'll be all right. And . . . and thank you for the . . . the meal, Samuel. And the delicious, delicious wine. . . ."

She *was* drunk. Her voice seemed to come from an enormous, echoing distance. When she turned toward the door of the lobby, the floor seemed to tilt up at her—the walls, with their heavy, dark paintings, to twist and swirl.

"The floor," she muttered. "It keeps moving. . . ."

"Here," Samuel said. "You'll never make it upstairs without me. My, you are a little wine-bibber, aren't you? Do you realize that I had to order two bottles in order to keep your glass filled?"

"I'm . . . not a wine-bibber! And . . . didn't drink all that much. . . ."

Why was her tongue so slurred? She clung to the solid support of Samuel's arm, ignoring the hot-eyed looks he was giving her.

"What if . . . Mrs. Adair sees me. . . ." Her laughter rose, sounding even to herself hollow and desperate.

"Didn't you know, Carisa? Mrs. Adair died last year. The hotel is being run by her son now."

"Oh . . ."

In a daze, she felt herself being escorted upstairs and down the corridor to her room, which was near the back of the building. Samuel took the room key from her fumbling hand.

"Here," he said. "Let me do that. You're much too tipsy to manage a key."

Somehow—she couldn't remember all of the details— they were lying together naked. She had a dim memory of Samuel's hands stripping the clothing from her body and kissing her, her neck, her breasts, her nipples, her thighs and belly, until a warm sweet bud of sensation grew and flowered in her groin.

"Samuel . . ." she groaned. "God . . . please stop . . . this is wrong. . . ."

"No, it isn't." His body covered hers, large and male and sensual, overpowering her feeble efforts to beat him back. "It's not wrong at all. God, Carisa, how I've wanted you. All these years. Remember that time I kissed you?"

"Yes . . ."

He kissed her again and she tasted wine. Involuntarily, her body arched to meet his.

"I wanted you then. I wanted to tear that tempting gown off you and rape you. Did you know that, Carisa? You are eminently rapable."

"You . . . mustn't say such things. . . ."

338

"I'll say them if I wish."

Carisa heard herself making some reply to this, but she didn't hear what it was. She felt suddenly wild and defiant and wicked. The events of today had already receded in her mind, like the tide going out. The pain was still there, but now it was numbed and distant. The only reality was now, this room, this bed, this man's naked flesh pressed against her own.

Her climax, when it came, was so violent and explosive that she shrieked out, and Samuel had to clap his palm over her mouth so that she would not arouse the hotel.

But even as she screamed, the pain seemed to flood back to her, filling every crevice of her body and mind. When their energy was spent, she lay quietly beside Samuel, tears rolling down her cheeks.

"You cried out a name," he said, his voice harsh.

"I did?"

"Yes, you little bitch. Damn you, you cried out for Adam."

After that, it seemed as if there was nothing left they could say to each other. Silently, Samuel rose and dressed, and then she heard the door click shut behind him.

She ate her breakfast in her room the next morning, barely able to touch the heavy plateful of fried eggs and steak and potatoes which the hotel considered suitable for its guests. Her head ached, and her mouth felt fuzzy and sore.

My God, she thought. *What sort of madness possessed me?*

And with Samuel Hartshorn, of all men! A man good-looking without a doubt, but stuffed with his own self-importance, ambition and greed. A man who could use and exploit women exactly as if they were fine Cuban cigars, or rum to be savored. Marrying Eliza for her money and family connections, then being ruthlessly unfaithful to her with a series of mistresses. . . .

Dear God, Carisa thought. Sickness choked up in

339

her. Now she, Carisa, was one of those women, however inadvertently.

If only she hadn't drunk all that wine!

She took another sip of black coffee, the only item on the breakfast tray which she could tolerate.

Adam had made love to her sister. Now she had made love to Adam's brother. In a hideous way, she had had her revenge.

Her head was aching. She pushed the tray away and got up and walked to the window, which looked out on a network of back alleys, where delivery carts jostled, and a stray cat prowled.

She would find an attorney today, she decided quickly, and arrange for more money to be sent to her father so that he would not have to take in derelict lodgers in that hideous room of his. Then she would leave for Hearts-ease immediately. She would put last night—and Samuel—out of her mind. She would never allow herself to think of him again.

21

If anyone had asked Carisa to describe the most unhappy period of her life, she would unhesitatingly have selected the war years.

The newspapers were full of accounts of battles with unfamiliar names: Chickamauga, Lookout Mountain, Spotsylvania, Cold Harbor, Petersburg. Casualty lists were long. Many times Carisa would find on one of them the name of a man who had sailed on a Hartshorn whaler, or who had worked for the Phillips Circus. Each time she would be seized with a wild, unreasoning grief. And each time, when she had come to the end of the toll of names, she would grow weak. Adam had not been on the list. Not this time. . . .

Adam's letters continued to come regularly. He wrote of forced marches as General Banks, who had assumed command after the hated General Butler had been relieved of his post, struggled to scatter the Confederates occupying the Teche country west of New Orleans.

In flat words Adam told of walking until he staggered, of blisters on his feet—dozens of them—as big as silver dollars. Of grown men dropping by the wayside to weep.

But at least they were going somewhere, he wrote cheerfully. They were doing something, they were a part of the war at last.

A dozen times after her return to Hearts-ease, Carisa had torn up letters to him. *I encountered your brother Samuel in Mrs. Adair's Hotel and I got drunk and made love to him . . . I had just learned about you and Anna, and that you are Neecie's father. . . .*

How could she write him such things? She could not. Especially when she might never see him again. If he died, and those were to be her last words to him, the ones he would carry in his mind to eternity—

So she wrote nothing except her usual letters full of household news. *We still have no word of Julian,* she wrote him. *Not since he was seen at Manassas, and even then it might not have been Julian at all, we were never sure about that. Only yesterday the wife of one of my Italian workmen learned that her sixteen-year-old son had been killed at Vicksburg. I went to see her, and she was so pitiable, I think she had gone half-mad with her grief. . . .*

There were nights when Carisa herself dreamed mad dreams. One night she awoke sweating after a vivid nightmare in which she saw Adam crouched beside a body which had been exploded into bloody, mangled fragments. Another time she dreamed of Julian, his torso and arm drenched with red, lying unconscious in some farmer's cornfield.

And once, hideously, she dreamed that she was again lying beside Samuel in that hotel room at Mrs. Adair's, that his naked arms were again reaching for her. . . .

By the summer of 1864, Carisa learned that Adam had been a part of General Sheridan's devastation of the

Shenandoah Valley, in the assaults on Winchester, Fisher's Hill and, a month later, Cedar Creek.

He wrote her poignant letters describing the soldiers, most of them achingly young, who participated in these battles. A youth killed in the act of telling a joke, felled by a bullet which pierced his blanket roll, his stuffed knapsack and the upper part of his chest. A sixteen-year-old who was afraid to discharge his rifle at the enemy. Wounded boys, crying out hoarsely for their mothers, or for water.

Never did Adam mention his own fear, although Carisa was sure that he felt it; at times his letters seemed filled with wordless longing. Sometimes they arrived smudged almost to illegibility. Once, to Carisa's horror, there was a drop of blood on the upper left corner of a page.

One December morning in 1864 Carisa was in her study writing a letter to Rolf when she heard Nelly utter a shriek and go clattering downstairs. Carisa felt her heart give a heavy, thick thump, as if it would push itself out of her chest.

She got up from her chair, fighting a sudden rush of dizziness. Then the vertigo left her, and she rushed out of the office and downstairs after Nelly, wincing as the tendons in her legs uttered their protest.

She ran outside. It was nearly Christmas, a few small, hard flakes of snow flying in the air, to evaporate as soon as they touched the ground. The sky was piled with more heavy, lowering clouds.

Stopped on the gravel drive was an old, wobbling farm wagon pulled by an ancient horse. Nelly was already there, embracing a tall, thin man who looked strangely like Gaines. Another man still sat in the bed of the cart, on a blanket of moldy straw.

Now Gaines put Nelly aside and turned to help his passenger.

Carisa stopped still, her hands clenched at her sides. The man's skin was as gray as tallow mixed with ashes, his eyes sunken. Tears were running down his cheeks. And—she saw this with an indrawn gasp for breath—his leg was wrapped in bloody bandages.

342

"Papa! Papa!" The children came running out of the house, shrieking. Brigid, the cook, fatter than ever, came waddling out behind them, followed by Editha, a new scullery maid. But Carisa stood paralyzed, oblivious of their startled exclamations.

She started forward, noting as if in a dream that the man leaned very heavily on Gaines. The manservant said something to him in a low voice and pointed toward Carisa. The man wiped his eyes and looked at her and now he was smiling.

"Adam!" The name tore out of her. "Adam, Adam, oh, my God, Adam!"

She was running, all of her muscles pushing her blindly toward him, and then she was in his arms.

"We'd been told to withdraw, ma'am, to a new area," Gaines told her later that day, after Adam had been put to bed and his injured leg washed and rebandaged. Gaines himself looked thin and drawn and tired, not at all the same taciturn man who had left for the war.

"Oh, it wasn't pretty, that it wasn't," he went on. "Bullets were comin' at us from all over. We was tripping over the wounded and the dead, and the poor devils just had to lay where they fell, there wasn't no choice in the matter."

Carisa thought of the ugly dreams she had had of bodies lying strewn about like tumbled laundry. She shuddered. "Tell me, Gaines. Tell me all of it. I have to know."

"Well, you know the smell of gunpowder? I suppose you don't, being a woman and all, but it's a terrible stench, like to make a man feel sick, just for what it reminds him of. And blood . . . it was everywhere. I never seen so much of it. Must of been the limestone soil or something that wouldn't take it, and no grass to cover it, either. It looked to be everywhere. Splashes of it, or zig-zag trails of it. . . ."

"Gaines!"

"Sorry, ma'am. Well, Captain Hartshorn, he kind of taken a liking to this boy that was with the Twelfth

343

Connecticut . . . couldn't have been no more than sixteen, he was, and scared to shoot his rifle for fear some Rebel might know he was shootin' and take a pot-shot back at him."

"Yes," Carisa breathed. "I remember Adam writing about him."

Gaines gave a hard, dry, bitter laugh. "This kid, well, he fell with a bullet in him and Captain Hartshorn went back for him. Right in the midst of heavy fire it was, men were dyin' all around. And he dragged this boy out of the worst of the fire. I saw it all and I couldn't get back.

"They had a makeshift hospital in a protected spot, and some doctors there, doing what they could. Captain Hartshorn carried the boy there, flung over his shoulder like a sack of wheat. But before he could make it to the tent, some sharp-shooter must of seen him, for he let out a shell and . . . wham! . . . your husband was shot directly in the thigh. The two of 'em fell to the ground together."

"No . . ."

"The boy was done for, he must of died while Captain Hartshorn was carryin' him. But I got two others to help, and we carried the Captain to the hospital tent. They staunched the blood, cleaned the wound and cauterized it."

Carisa swallowed, thinking of the pain Adam must have suffered. His flesh seared with a red-hot iron. . . .

"You are the one who nursed him, aren't you, Gaines?" she whispered at last. "You saved him for me."

The manservant shrugged. "Aw, I didn't save him, it was the good Lord done that. All I did was give Him some help. And keep soakin' the wound and keepin' the damn flies off."

Adam, however, was not fully cured yet and would not be for some time. Carisa was present when Gaines first stripped the slit uniform pants off Adam's bandaged leg. When he unwrapped the stained bandages, she had to suppress an exclamation of horror.

344

The gash, high on Adam's thigh, had been a deep one, taking with it a sizeable hunk of muscle and flesh. The Army doctor, after probing for the bullet, had cauterized the wound. The result was a livid, scarred hole which still had lingering pockets of infection.

"Adam!" she gasped, swaying. "I . . . I had no idea. . . ."

"Ugly, isn't it?" He tried to grin at her. She wanted to sob, for his skin was gray, his eyes almost quenched.

"Ugly?" She hesitated. Then she decided that lying would be useless. "Yes," she admitted. "It is. But I don't mind. And fortunately it will all be covered by your trousers unless you choose to wear a bathing costume."

Adam gave a bitter laugh. "I seem to remember that someone said something like that to you once, Carisa. Was it Dr. Arthur? Oh, I see that you and I are going to be quite a pair. You with your scarred leg, me with mine. Yours covered by skirts, mine by trousers."

"Adam . . ." She knelt by the bed and buried her face in his chest, heedless of Gaine's presence. She felt Adam's arms go around her and heard the click of the door as Gaines tactfully withdrew.

"Adam," she choked. "It . . . it was terrible here without you . . . Terrible things happened. I . . . I don't know how to say it . . . Samuel . . . at Mrs. Adair's Hotel in New York. . . ."

Adam put a finger to her lips, stopping her words. "I don't want to hear it, Carisa, whatever it was you were going to say. I sensed in your letters . . . well, perhaps there are mistakes which must be forever buried and forgotten and never spoken of again. I have made such mistakes. Perhaps . . . perhaps you have done so as well."

It was the closest either of them ever came to discussing it.

Knowing he must be told, as gently as she could, Carisa gave Adam the details of his mother's death. Katherine had died in her sleep only two months previously. Her last words had been of Adam, and of plans for the new species of day lily she had hoped to develop.

What Carisa did not add was that Katherine had lived her last months in great pain, shrunk to a suffering specter, taut skin stretched over her bones.

"I . . . I never thought you were right for him," she had whispered one night to Carisa after she had been given her nightly dose of laudanum so she could sleep.

Carisa could only stare at her mother-in-law, feeling frozen under the drugged brilliance of her eyes.

"But I've come to see that it doesn't matter," Katherine went on after a moment. "Not really. He loves you, Carisa. I only hope you love him."

"But I do . . . I do!"

"You married him for his money, Carisa. All of us knew that. The whole town knew it."

Carisa felt the painful blood beating in her face. "But it's all different now . . . it's all changed. . . ."

"Is it, Carisa? *He* doesn't think so."

Life went on. Adam's recovery was slow, but each day his complexion seemed a bit less grayish, his appetite stronger. The first week he slept nearly all day. By the second he was sitting up in bed and demanding to be brought old newspapers, books, ledgers. He did not mention anything about the letters he had asked her to save, nor did he speak much of the war, other than to add that he had also suffered from typhoid fever and had been quite weakened.

One day Carisa asked him about the letters. Did he wish her to help him compile them into some sort of order, so that he could edit them for publication?

"Oh, God, no," Adam said. He gave a rueful, bitter laugh. "Perhaps one day when I'm a very old man, I'll write my memoirs. Or my grandson can do it. As for today, I'm tired to the bone, tired of killing and carnage. Why? I keep asking myself. Why did it have to happen, young William, all of them, mowed down, gone, gone forever?"

He turned away and she saw that his eyes were moist, glistening with unshed tears. "Life, Carisa," he said.

346

"That's what's really important. That's what I learned at Cedar Creek."

January passed, and February. The Confederacy, sick and desperate, was in its last failing days. General Sherman's armies were marching north through South Carolina, burning, gutting, pillaging. On March 4 President Lincoln was inaugurated for the second time, and spoke movingly about forgetting vengeance, asking the people to "bind up the nation's wounds."

By April 9, it was all over. Generals Grant and Lee met at Appomattox Courthouse and came to terms. The South had surrendered.

Adam's leg, after days of poultices and damp cloths, had finally healed, although the muscle had been damaged and he would probably always walk with a slight limp. And gradually, over these weeks, Carisa attempted to fill him in on the events which had happened during his absence.

Within a month of Katherine's death, Eliza's had followed. The consumption, eating away at her lungs, had grown rapidly worse. Eliza lay upstairs in her columned old house on "Whale Oil Row," clad immaculately in a cambric nightgown as if she were merely taking a day off to rest.

All of Eliza's talk was of Samuel. Letters he had sent her, his speculations on the War, hints he had dropped to her that he was playing a key role in the secret wartime machinations. She reminisced over a trip they had taken together once to Paris, told Carisa of his favorite dishes, of the dog he had loved.

Carisa sat and listened to this, squirming with guilt. She, Carisa, had lain naked in the arms of the man about whom Eliza spoke with such longing. Had felt his fingers squeeze her arm in possessiveness. Didn't Eliza know of Samuel's many mistresses? Of his special one in Groton Heights? Oh, surely after all of these years, she must.

Yet in all of her rambling talk, Eliza said nothing of any other women. It was as if they did not exist for her.

Nervously Carisa paced back and forth about her

347

sister-in-law's room, trying to frame polite, noncommittal replies to go along with Eliza's fantasy of the loving, attentive husband.

One morning she penned Samuel a furious letter. *Your wife is ill and consumptive and probably dying. You managed to get to Mrs. Adair's Hotel once; why can't you come home to see your wife before it is too late?*

To her surprise, Samuel did come home. She never knew how he managed to wrangle it, or what strings he pulled, but he spent two days with Eliza in the house on Whale Oil Row. What happened between the two, Carisa was never to know, for to her vast relief, Samuel left again for the Navy without calling upon her.

But Carisa had the knowledge that whatever else she had done to injure Eliza, at least she had given her this. That much, she had atoned.

Cautiously, for she did not wish to further upset him, Carisa tried to fill Adam in on the state of the Hartshorn finances. As she had feared, the whaling industry, already sagging, had been further hurt by the war. Confederate raiders had sunk a number of New London vessels. Some idle whalers had been used to blockade Southern ports, by loading them with stone and then sinking them in strategic places. Now the fleet of the entire city numbered only 25. Worse, crews were hard to get and the new fuel, kerosene, had greatly lessened the demand for whale oil.

Adam heard this in silence, pain creasing his face.

"Do you know, Carisa," he said at last, "my father used to have an old newspaper clipping. A trivial thing, really, but it had been saved for generations, and when I was a boy sometimes he would take it out and show it to me. It was from the *New London Gazette* and it was written in 1785. 'Now my horse jockeys,' it said. 'Beat your horses and cattle into spears, lances, harpoons and whaling gear, and let us all strike out; many spouts ahead! Whale a-plenty, you have them for the catching.'"

He shifted on his pillow, looking weary. "I loved

that, it sounded like a war cry to me, a call to glory. And now, it seems, the glory is rapidly fading."

"But not yet gone," Carisa said quickly. "While you were away, I tried to invest the money you left with me. I put most of it into the New London Horse Nail Company. They were working night and day because of the war and my earnings were considerable."

Adam's face seemed to pale. "Do you mean that we, the Hartshorns, profited from the war? We made money off those poor devils lying there in the fields and woods shattered like meat?"

"Well, yes." She was miserably conscious of his displeasure. "And of course," she hurried on, "there is the Phillips Circus. As soon as the war is really over, I will write to Rolf and tell them to come home. People will be ready for amusement after so much heartbreak.

"And there is another thing. I've been asking questions in the town. . . . Redlands Kord has helped me with this. Do you remember that before you left, guano deposits were discovered on Phoenix Island? A firm has been organized, the Phoenix Guano Company, and it seems that they have started to do an extremely good business in the European market . . ."

"Guano!" Adam had stiffened. "You don't mean . . . *bird droppings?*"

"Well, yes. Except, of course, I've been told that these are the accumulated droppings of centuries, and they are very valuable, Adam, as fertilizer. . . ."

"I don't care how valuable they are, and I don't care if there is a million dollars to be made that way! We are Hartshorns! I will not have . . ." Adam began to cough.

"Adam . . . I'll get you something. . . ." Carisa hurried for a bottle of the cough elixyr she had made up.

"We have been a whaling family and a proud one," Adam told her after he had swallowed two spoonsful of it. "We will never ship guano, Carisa . . . not while there is any protest left in me."

"Very well."

She stared down at the elixyr bottle, flushing. She had thought it a rather good idea. It would have enabled Adam to make good use of the ships he still owned, and provided jobs for the captains and crews he still had.

"Then perhaps there is some other commodity we can ship," she said quickly. "For now, though, I feel we should cut back a bit. That house at Newport was one of your mother's extravagances, and I have been waiting for you to return so that we can complete the sale of it. I think I already have a buyer, a wealthy factory owner from New York. He makes shirt collars, I believe."

She waited for Adam to smile, but he did not.

"Fine," he said, looking away from her.

"And the circus, we'll always have that, of course," she heard herself babble on, knowing only that she had to fill the aching silence that suddenly existed between them. "I've been thinking and planning for months what to do. Once it returns I'm sure I can make a great deal of money. . . ."

"Money. Oh, yes, I'm sure you'll manage that," he told her. "Meanwhile, I'd prefer not to think of it just yet, if you don't mind. And now do you think that I might take a nap? I find myself growing sleepy; I still haven't got my strength back yet, much as I hate to admit it."

She had been dismissed, gently but firmly. She nodded, trying not to let her hurt show. Then she drew the coverlet up over him, kissed him lightly, and left the room.

Out in the corridor she leaned against the wall, where the portraits of past Hartshorns stared down at her.

"Well, I was only trying," she snapped at last to the accusing eyes of the first Adam. "Do you want your precious Hearts-ease, too, to be sold to a collar-maker from New York? Guano, it seems to me, is a lot better than poverty, if it should ever come to that."

But the oil-painted eyes were stony, giving her no answer.

*   *   *
350

In late April, 1865, Julian Hartshorn came home. He came walking heavily up the graveled drive clad in a tattered uniform made of "soddy," the poor grade of wool foisted off on the Army by unscrupulous woolen mills. Carisa and Benicia, on their way back from the ring barn after a morning's work-out, were the first to see him.

"Carisa? Who's that?" Neecie stopped suddenly, to stare at the solitary figure walking toward them. "That man. I think he's coming here."

Carisa stared, too. The man had that peculiar dazed, young-old look seen so often these days on the faces of returning soldiers. Although there seemed to be nothing wrong with his legs, he walked heavily. His left arm was in a sling, and seemed to end without a hand.

Carisa narrowed her eyes and then started forward. "Julian! My God, Julian, is it you?"

"I wondered if you would recognize me." His lips twisted bitterly, and she saw that his face was lean and weary, his eyes etched deep blue. He might have been almost handsome if his expression had not held such despair.

"But . . . but you've grown up!" she said stupidly.

"Yes. Haven't I?" The full lips quirked. "Aren't you going to ask me how I lost my hand? Everyone else has."

She licked her lips, conscious of Neecie's start of horror beside her.

"I lost it at Spotsylvania," he told her. "Five bloody days of trench killing. They tied me down on a table and chopped off my hand and cauterized it with tar. They were piling the left-over hands and feet in buckets."

As Benicia let out a sharp little cry, Julian glared at his half-sister coldly.

"They say we sustained twelve thousand losses. I can't even imagine it, can you? All those bodies . . ." He pressed his lips together and turned toward the house. "I don't know why I came home," he added. "But I did."

351

-≈⚜ 1872 ⚜≈-

22

The war years were over. And over, too, were some of the other bad times which had occurred in the years immediately following.

Yellow fever. In 1868 it had killed a number of New Londoners, including Dr. Arthur. The fever had touched Hearts-ease as well. To Carisa's vast relief, none of the children had caught it. But the fever had touched fat Brigid in the kitchen, some of the servants and circus employees, and Carisa herself. Few of these had died, but Carisa herself had lain weak and ill for weeks, nursed by a frantic Adam.

Sometimes in her dreams she could still hear Adam's shouts as he struggled with her in her delirium. "Live, Carisa, live! Struggle, will you? Fight for life as hard as you do for that circus of yours. . . ."

One morning she had awakened to find Adam sitting by her bed, looking pale and red-eyed. Beside him was Duddie, for the Phillips Circus had been home for a year now.

"Adam . . ." she whispered.

His hand found hers. "So you made it, my darling. I thought for a while that you weren't going to. We all did."

"Oh, she fought a good battle," Duddie put in proudly, as if he had managed it all by himself. "Real circus stuff she is. But I think your husband had something

352

to do with it, too, Carisa," the clown added. "He defied God with his voice alone. Never had I heard a man shout so loudly, or work so hard, or be so angry at the Fates. . . ."

"Adam did that?" She felt weak, soft, floating, with a curious sense of well-being.

"Yes, he did. So count your blessings, my girl. The show is well. We lost poor Major Ribinson and three of the tent men, and the circus people were all whispering about the famous Hartshorn phantom ship." Duddie gave a shiver. "But no one can prove that he actually saw it. Which, I might add, is just as well. By the way, your new color posters are beautiful. Rolf picked them up from the lithographer's yesterday, and the color fairly leaps up at you. They are not just posters, Carisa, they are works of art. Saloon owners will be fighting to hang them over the bar."

Carisa gave a weak smile, aware of Adam's answering scowl.

"Saloons!" he began. "Are you sure you want. . . ."

"Oh, but I do," Carisa whispered. "I want my circus paper in saloons. I want it on the sides of livery stables and barns, and in barber shops and millinery shops and rendering plants and gasworks. And on the sides of ice wagons. That's how Mr. Barnum advertises, and I want to do it, too. I want the Phillips name to be everywhere. It's the only way my show can grow."

"You want the Phillips name . . . and your own . . . bandied about the streets like . . . like cheap gossip?" Adam asked.

"Yes . . ." Sleepiness was falling over her like a veil, and she could not see Adam's face clearly. "It has to be that way, Adam, don't you see? Papa . . . sometime he'll come, and he'll see what I've been doing, and he'll be proud. I know he will."

"Carisa . . ."

"He'll love the show, Adam. And it will all be because of me, because of what I've done. Did you know that Rolf is arranging for us to play before President Johnson? A president, Adam! Can you imagine it? Maybe Papa will come to Washington to see that. . . ."

353

She let her eyes close, ignoring the look of pity which Adam and Duddie exchanged. She let herself drift off to sleep. *Someday,* she thought groggily. Someday they'd all see. . . .

Yellow fever had not been their only problem.

There had also been Julian. Sullen, erratic, his moods pervaded the house, disrupting the pattern of their days. He had taken one year at Harvard College, dropping out without explanation. After that he was at home, installed by Adam at his shipping office under the reluctant tutelage of Mr. West, Adam's whaling agent.

One day Julian would be quiet and civil, going obediently to work and surprising Mr. West with his grasp of business. The next morning he would disappear. Later they would learn that he had been seen galloping at break-neck speed along the bridle paths in the hemlocks near Hearts-ease, or in Bolles Wood. Or he had been spotted carousing through New London and Groton Heights with his friends, wild, unruly young men like himself.

In the kitchen Brigid and Nelly had whispered that Julian visited Poll Henry's frequently, that Poll herself was the one he called upon there, that she held a special regard for him. But when questioned by Carisa, Julian had denied all this. Why couldn't she and Adam just leave him alone and let him live his life? He had adjusted to the loss of his hand, and was working hard enough, wasn't he? What more did they wish of him? If they did not stop harping at him, he would leave home, permanently.

Vicki's nightmares had been another disturbing element. Oddly they had begun again just at the end of the war. Now, nearly every night, there were the piercing screams which signaled another of the dreams.

Carisa would leap out of bed, awakened by the shrieks which could be heard all over the house. Without even bothering to throw on a dressing gown, she would run into her daughter's room. There she would find Vicki, huddled shivering under her quilts.

"What is it, darling? What is it?"

354

Incoherent, wild, the sobs would pour out of Vicki. "I . . . I don't know, Mama. It was . . . *he!* He was after me again! Hurting . . . hurting . . . Oh, Mama, keep me safe. Don't let him touch me, don't let him. . . ."

She would lapse into muffled weeping. Then Carisa would light the lamp and sit with her until she fell asleep again. Whatever demon it was that came to Vicki, Carisa did not know. And perhaps, she thought, Vicki herself did not know either. For in the mornings, she would not even remember that she had dreamed.

Matt had also had his problems. Usually an obedient boy, he attended the Bartlett School in town. One October morning in 1869 when he was fourteen, he came home from school red-faced and trembling, to inform Carisa that he had hit his schoolmaster, Mr. Asa Billings, in the eye.

"You did what?"

Carisa could not believe she had heard him properly, for the school day was long and arduous, with the schoolmaster in full control. Few boys dared to defy authority.

"That's right, I hit him, and I'd do it again, too!" Matt raged at her, his amber eyes, so like Adam's, flashing. "He hits me every day, Mama . . . not just on the hands but on the shoulders and back, too."

"Oh, Matt, surely. . . ."

"No, Mama, it's true! Today he hit me on the cheek. On my face, Mama! I . . . I couldn't stand it any more. I grabbed the ruler away from him and I smashed him in the eye with it and then I ran away." Matt hesitated. "I suppose Papa will whip me for this, but I don't care. I'm glad I did it."

That night Adam made a visit to the school. He returned home with his eyes glowing yellow and the knuckles of his hands bruised and bleeding.

The next day the offending schoolmaster was gone, and people whispered that his face had been badly battered. Matt returned to school again, this time under the tutelage of a mild-voiced veteran of Gettysburg

355

who, if he did not laugh a good deal, at least smiled now and again.

One of Carisa's most difficult problems during these years, however, was Rolf Taggart. Rolf, it seemed, had grown accustomed to having the sole control of the Phillips Circus and did not wish to give this up.

For every plan which Carisa advanced, Rolf was ready with criticism. He did not think that colored circus "paper," or posters, would be very practical. He criticized her choice of performers and balked when she made a trip to Bridgeport to confer with P. T. Barnum, who was in retirement there.

To add more heat to the conflict simmering between them, Carisa had been eyeing with longing the burgeoning railroad lines. In the past, circuses had had to travel by wagon. This meant a slow, arduous pace and necessary stops at all towns, large and small. A few shows, she knew, had tried traveling by rail, but this had not been successful. Each short railroad line had its own track width. When a show reached the end of one local line, it would have to stop, unload and reload, sometimes three or four times in one night, in order to fit on the next section of track.

But now all of that had changed. A uniform rail gauge had been established, and now one set of cars could roll anywhere that rails went. P. T. Barnum and a showman named William Coup were about to start a railroad show which, they advertised, would be a "new Mammoth Enterprise . . . a great NATIONAL MUSEUM, MENAGERIE CARAVAN AND HIPPODROME . . ."

"Barnum!" Rolf scoffed one day late in 1871 in Carisa's office. "That man is a fool if he thinks his so-called 'mammoth enterprise' is going to do anything other than flop mightily."

"I think he's going to be very successful indeed. And, further, I think that the Phillips Circus. . . ."

But Rolf was not listening. Jerkily he had begun to pace about Carisa's office, his hands jammed into the pockets of his suit. "The Phillips Circus," he muttered, so low that Carisa could barely hear him. "Phillips! Always that name. What about Taggart? That show should be mine. It should be me who's doing the planning, not some rich little. . . ."

"Some rich little what?" Carisa challenged.

"Nothing," he mumbled. "All I can say is that you're a fool if you think that railroads are going to be the answer. Why, our wagons aren't even all the same size . . . how are you going to get them on the cars? Loading will be a nightmare."

"There must be a way." Already she had forgotten the words he had muttered, his sullen objections. Her mind was puzzling with the problems which lay ahead of them. "When I visited him, Mr. Barnum would not tell me much about the methods they plan to use, but I did manage to talk with one of his employees. He said that Mr. Coup is experimenting with four hooks on either corner of the flatcar, and. . . ."

"Experiments! That's all it'll ever be."

"No. It will be more than that, I'm sure of it. Don't you realize what this could mean to us? We could travel up to a hundred miles a night instead of being chained to every little one-horse village along the route. We could travel in good weather and in bad, and we'd never have to worry about mud, or spills, or accidents. . . ."

Carisa's eyes grew faraway as she recounted her dream. "We'd play big cities, Rolf, where the real money is. And *we* would be a city, too, a whole city on wheels! No more hotels and rooming houses! We'd have our own cook-car, and cars for the performers to bunk. We'd have a car for harness and repair, one for wardrobes and even for our blacksmith. . . ."

"Aw, you've gone completely feather-soft in the head."

She let her eyes challenge him. "No, I haven't." She chose her words deliberately. "If you do this, Rolf, and make a success of it, I'll raise your share of the proceeds by ten per cent. If you fail, you're through. I don't want you any more; you can go out and find yourself a job with some mud show."

Rolf stiffened. A "mud show" was a term of derision;

357

it meant the crudest of all shows, a few broken-down horses and performers, a rickety wagon or two.

"Are you saying I can't do it? That I can't manage a show on rails?"

"I don't know. Can you?"

His nostrils flared. Then he nodded curtly. "All right. Get me some railroad cars, then. And get them fast. This thing can't be done in a week."

23

Now it was 1872, at noon on a sunny July day. Carisa, in the midst of planning an essential circus trip to Philadelphia, had come to the beach at the begging of Neecie, who said she wished to talk with her.

Gulls wheeled and screeched overhead. A solitary terrier raced in and out of the waves, yelping joyously as the water touched his paws.

"Carisa!" Neecie said beside her. "Carisa, I don't think you've heard one word of what I've said!"

Carisa gave a guilty jerk. "Of course I have, darling."

"You have not. Your eyes have that faraway look again, that look you get when you're thinking about the circus."

Neecie tossed her head, and gave an angry swish to the hem of her dark blue walking dress. She scuffed with the toe of her shoe at the edge of a shell which lay embedded in the sand.

"Well, I guess I'll just have to tell it to you again. I'm ready, as ready as I'll ever be. If I have to do any more practicing, even another hour of it, I think I'll just die! Drill, drill, drill! Is that all you and Duddie can think of for me to do? I'll wager my Aunt Stephana didn't have to go through such babyish nonsense."

"Perhaps if she had had more of it, she would be alive today," Carisa reprimanded sharply.

"I . . . I suppose you're right." Neecie bent over and

picked up the large broken clamshell, which had been washed up on the shore by a recent storm. Frowning, she stared down at its ragged edges.

"Still," she burst out, "I'm sixteen now! If Papa had only let me go with the show last year when I begged him, I'd be a star by now. Instead I'm stuck here at Hearts-ease doing *drill*."

"You're too young to travel about the country by yourself," Carisa began, stifling a pang of pity for her niece. *Neither fish nor fowl nor good red meat.* Katherine's phrase popped into Carisa's head unbidden. In a way, Katherine had been right. Neecie really belonged nowhere fully—at Hearts-ease she was restless, yet there was no way that a girl as young as herself could be permitted to go alone from city to city. Even if Adam would permit it, which he would not.

"Neecie," she heard herself go on, "you must listen to me. Drill is a part of the circus. Ever since you were a child, I've tried to make you see that. The show lives by split seconds, and you must have constant, unremitting practice, so that you will never have to think about what you are doing, or your. . . ."

"I know, I know," the girl sighed. "You must never have to think about what your body is doing, it does all the work for you. Oh, I know all that! All I want to do is to perform! Is that so much to ask?"

Carisa hesitated, again feeling the stab of guilt. How pretty Benicia was, with her lithe, tall body, her shining blonde hair, her unexpected dimples which flashed and charmed. How much like Stephana she was, too. Yet Neecie's temperament was sunnier and more open. Her temper, although explosive while it lasted, was also quick to cool. And she attracted love to her as a magnet attracts filings. No one who knew Neecie escaped from her spell; even Carisa was unwillingly caught in it. Anna or no Anna, she loved the girl and always would.

"Darling," Carisa said. "I'm afraid you're going to have to wait a year or so, until. . . ."

"A year! Carisa, I'm *sixteen*." Benicia's blue eyes implored. "Didn't you hear me tell you that I'm ready?

359

I'm more than ready, I'm getting over-ripe. If I don't perform soon, I . . . I'll start to rot!"

Carisa stifled a smile. "You're not a fruit, dear, an apple or a pear."

Neecie made a face. "No, but it's still the same thing, Carisa, and you know it."

As they walked along, Carisa struggled with her guilt and anger. Everything that the girl said was true. She *was* ready to perform before a circus audience. In fact, if she had been a proper circus child, she would already have been doing so.

It was Adam who clung to Neecie, his favorite of the children, insisting that his daughter was different. She hadn't been reared in a show wagon but in a sheltered home. She knew little of the footloose and wild traveling life, and he did not wish her innocence and gaiety destroyed.

"The Phillips Circus certainly won't destroy them!" Carisa had raged at him. "Are we to throw away centuries of heritage, years of training? Adam . . ."

"*You* were the one who gave her that training, against my wishes," Adam said coldly. "You and Duddie took that responsibility upon yourselves. And now you can blame yourselves for the results."

"But . . ."

"Carisa, Benicia is not a circus child, for all that she was given the training of one. She is used to a pleasant and luxurious life. I have no objections to her riding for pleasure . . . you know that, Carisa, you know I wouldn't be so cruel. Still. . . ."

Adam would not be moved. And now, thinking of this, Carisa heard herself say lightly, "Surely, Neecie, you'll want to marry sometime?"

"Marry! Oh, Carisa, not me." Benicia, temporarily distracted, allowed her dimples to flash. "Vicki is the one who will be getting married soon. That fat old Madeleine Kord has given her son orders to court her."

"Orders!" Carisa laughed. "Calvin Kord is a very nice young man."

"For some other girl." Benicia sniffed. "But not for

our Vicki. Carisa, you know it's true. Calvin is much too pompous. . . ."

"Enough, Neecie." Carisa said this sharply, for Benicia's speculations had struck an answering unease in herself. "Adam feels that the boy is well suited for Vicki, and he certainly comes from one of the best families in New London."

"He is already running to fat, though, isn't he?" Benicia bounded a few steps forward to scoop up another shell. "He will be portly before he is thirty. And by the time he is fifty he will be as immense as his mother . . . I think that at least three of Vicki could fit side-by-side into one of her corsets!"

"Enough, enough," Carisa said, laughing. "Go along with you, Neecie! And don't you think that you'd better get back to the house? Madame Kouwen is coming at one, and you must be ready for her. You know how she hates being kept waiting."

"Ballet!" Neecie snorted. "Not that I don't like it, because I do. Still, it seems that I'm doing it all for nothing. For a career that never seems to get any closer, because Papa wants to keep me tied down here at home like a . . . a nanny-goat tethered to a tree!"

With this, she lifted the hem of her dress and began to run over the sparse sand in the direction of Hearts-ease, loping as easily as a boy.

Carisa shaded her eyes with her hand to watch her. How young, how lissom, how lithely perfect! Long ago, Katherine had predicted that Benicia would outshine Vicki, and so it had happened. When the two girls were in the same room, no young man spared more than a glance for shy, quiet, slender Vicki. Their eyes were all for this lovely minx, Benicia, who moved as freely as a gypsy, laughed uninhibitedly, and scorned all of them.

Anna and Adam's daughter. Carisa dropped her hand and turned to stare out at the blue expanse of water.

At last she turned and began to walk back toward Hearts-ease, for a deskful of office work awaited her. Benicia, running on ahead, was already out of view.

A hundred yards ahead, a stand of trees projected

forward like a wedge into the sparse beach sand, which the city fathers talked about augmenting with wagonloads of sand hauled in from elsewhere. Here, she saw, the terrier had raced ahead of her, still clamping the dead fish in its mouth. A man was standing beneath one of the trees. The dog skittered toward him, stopped, barked, and obediently dropped the dead fish.

When the man turned his face in Carisa's direction, she saw that he was Samuel Hartshorn.

Instantly she veered toward the tumbling waves, placing her back to him so that he would not recognize her. Why had this man the power to make her feel so furtive and guilty?

She had made a mistake that night at Mrs. Adair's, during the war, a mistake which she had never stopped regretting. For Samuel had arrived home from the war newly widowed and eager to take up with Carisa where they had left off.

Desperately she had returned his letters, avoided his overtures at family gatherings. "Samuel, it's over, can't you understand that? Or, rather, it never existed, I don't want any part of it, or of you."

She could still remember it, the way his face had twisted with a glowering anger. "No woman tells me that!"

"This one does," she had heard herself reply defiantly.

For a moment she had been afraid, for Samuel had lunged toward her almost as if he intended to hit her. Then he had stopped, turned and walked away, fury evident in every jerky motion of his body. Carisa had been vastly relieved when rumor said that her brother-in-law had taken up again with Jennie Wynn, his temperamental mistress in Groton Heights. Jennie, Carisa had told herself, would surely keep him busy with her tantrums and her demands. . . .

Now, as she heard Samuel calling her name, she turned and whirled toward the curling foam of the waves, heedless of the moisture that soaked the hem of her gown.

"Is that all you can think of to do when I appear,

Carisa? Turn tail and run like this puppy of mine? I'm sick of being treated like a leper."

She hurried her steps as fast as her legs would allow.

"Of course you're not a leper," she heard herself snap. "But I'm a woman thirty-five years old, Samuel Hartshorn, and I'm married to your brother. Or had you forgotten that?"

"Had *you?*" He was grinning. He strode beside her, tall and lean and arrogant, filled with his own self-importance as Adam never could be.

"Please, Samuel. Why did you have to come here? All I wanted to do was to walk on the beach alone. What do you want?"

"I just want to talk. Why is it that you make such a huge effort to avoid me, Carisa? You've done it for years, and I'm getting tired of it."

"What else do you expect me to do? Why don't you go and see Jennie Wynn, Samuel? I'm sure *she* would be happy to talk with you."

Samuel's face darkened. "Leave Jennie out of this. Besides, she and I have quarreled."

"I thought so." Samuel had grasped her arm, and in vain Carisa tried to pull away. "Samuel . . . please . . . please just let me alone. I made a mistake years ago, that's all it was. I'd had too much to drink, and I. . . ."

"Not a mistake. You wanted me then, Carisa. You responded to me, just as you're responding now."

"I am *not* responding! How dare you imply such a thing! I . . ."

To her horror, she found that he was pulling her toward the thicket, dappled with sun and shade.

"I didn't come upon you here on the beach by accident," he was telling her. "I overheard your quarrel with Adam this morning. I had come to call on him about some shipping matters, and there you were, the two of you, shouting at each other. Over the circus, some trip or other that you insist on taking. . . ."

Carisa flushed, feeling as if her and Adam's most intimate privacy had been violated. "It's true. We did quarrel. I must travel to Philadelphia to solve a problem

363

with the circus. I don't trust it to Rolf, and . . . and Adam objects."

In spite of herself, she could not help sighing. Adam still resisted her circus travel and was jealous of the time she spent with it. Couldn't he understand how much she loved them both? Her husband and her circus. For her it was never a question of loving one *or* the other. She loved both, she always had.

"You and Adam should never have married," Samuel was saying. "It was an impossible union from the start. A woman like you, bold, passionate, as ambitious as a man. And Adam, the same, a man sprung from privateers and sea captains, yet for all of that a dreamer, too, a man of words and ideas."

Was Samuel sneering? Carisa felt an angry chill. "My husband would make six of you," she replied coldly. She lifted her skirts and moved backward, intending to be on her way again.

Samuel lunged at her, grabbing her. "Damn you! Damn you little circus bitch! All of these years you marched around with that chin of yours high in the air, as if you were too good for me! Well, we all know what circus women are like. I've always known, and that night in New York only proved it."

Samuel's mouth pressed down on hers, brutal, demanding. She fought off his lips, his hands, the urgency of his embrace.

There was a noise behind them, a crackling of dead leaves.

"Well," Julian's voice said. "I didn't expect to find my step-mother here with her lover."

"It's nothing like you thought! Nothing at all!"

Carisa raced after Julian, who was striding toward his tethered gelding.

"Isn't it? Why would Uncle Samuel look as if he wanted to hit me, then?"

"Perhaps he did want to hit you," Carisa said furiously. "Julian, I swear I'm not his mistress, I swear I never knew he was going to come here to the beach today or I wouldn't have come. You've got to believe me."

It was ten minutes later. Samuel had gone stalking off down the beach with his dog, leaving her to deal with Julian as best she could.

"Julian, you must listen to me. Your father and I . . . had a disagreement this morning. I had to get out of the house. Neecie and I went for a walk and then she went back for her ballet, and . . . and Samuel must have followed me. He . . . He has always been. . . ."

She stopped. This was impossible to explain to a young man like Julian.

He grinned at her, fumbling one-handed for the bridle of the gelding, which was tethered to a sapling. With an easy motion he swung himself onto the horse.

"Should I tell, Carisa? Or shouldn't I? I guess it boils down to how much do I really owe you for all those games of chess we used to play?"

"Julian . . ."

"My father has always put you on a pedestal, Carisa, did you know that? He is besotted with you, and always has been. And you . . . you betray him with your circus. And now with his brother?"

"Julian, that's not so, and you know it's not! I . . ."

But Julian had wheeled down the beach, the gelding's hooves kicking up spurts of sand as it galloped in the direction from which Carisa had come. Distantly, rising in the hot summer air, she could hear his laughter.

Philadelphia was hot and humid, its cobbled and bricked streets still moist from a recent rain.

Carisa spent her trip in agonized thinking and wondering. Why would Samuel suddenly explode with desire for her after all of these years? Had he had some quarrel with Adam which he wished to avenge? Or had he simply been brooding until his thoughts had at last festered to a head?

As for Julian, she couldn't understand him at all. It was as if, in some terrible, toying way, he had actually been teasing her. As if he had no intention of telling

Adam what she had done, but only wished to see her fear that he might.

But once in the city itself, and then on the big ten-acre circus lot on its outskirts, Carisa forced away these trepidations, and made herself concentrate on the business she had come for.

Illness had caused a disastrous thinning of the clown ranks, and now Carisa bored into this problem with the determination she reserved for circus matters.

"We'll have to get some new clowns, that's all," she told Rolf. "I've heard of an English clown named Little Wheal, who is supposed to make his entrance with a hundred consecutive somersaults. Perhaps I can get him. Meanwhile, I think we can manage a wire-walking clown, and some more *augustes*. . . ."

Once more she was able to submerge her personal worries in the problems of her circus. That night, after viewing the evening performance and making careful notes, she returned to her room in a small but elegant hotel situated on Gaskill Street, on the southern boundary of Society Hill.

Samuel Hartshorn was lounging in a chair in her room.

"Samuel!" Her voice went high and squeaky with her shock. "Samuel, how did you ever get into my room!"

"Hello, Carisa. Why are you so surprised to see me? Your little Nelly told me what hotel you were staying at. And you know that I always finish what I start. Haven't I told you that once already?"

Samuel's black broadcloth suit, fitted tightly, emphasized the maleness of his body as he rose casually from the chair. The male body which many women had yearned for, Carisa told herself disjointedly. The body which had cheated on Eliza so many times—

"What . . . what are you doing here?" she demanded. "If the hotel manager knew you were here, in my room. . . ."

"He does know. I told him I was your husband, and had decided to rejoin you here at the last moment. He never even questioned me."

She had brought a large canvas reticule to the circus lot with her, crammed with papers, and now she clutched it to her breast, her fingers perspiring against its fabric. Samuel was smiling at her, full of male confidence and swagger.

He expected to make love to her. No, Carisa told herself feverishly, that wasn't it exactly. He expected to use her. To put her body to his service exactly as he had utilized all the many other women he had known. As if they were fine Scotch whiskey, or expensive Cuban cigars. . . .

Involuntarily she shuddered. At least when Adam took her into his arms, he loved *her,* she was not an object, something to be used and savored and then thrown away. . . .

"Samuel," she whispered. "You must leave here at once."

He laughed dryly. "And what will I tell the manager, my dear? That we've suddenly had a little marital spat? This time I don't feel like passing you up. You're too beautiful to let go . . . I want to hold you, to experience your charms. . . ."

"No!" she cried. "Please, Samuel, just leave. I beg of you. Whatever we had, whatever we did together, it happened years ago. I had too much wine to drink, I wasn't myself. And it's *over,* Samuel, can't you understand that?"

"For me it isn't over. And it isn't for you, either, my dear. Do you think I can't tell when a woman desires me?"

"No . . . please . . . I love Adam. . . ."

"No, you don't love my brother, Carisa. You don't love anyone but yourself and that circus of yours. *That's* your real lover . . . sawdust and spangles and cotton candy!"

"It's not true . . . You don't know me, Samuel, and you don't know our marriage. Please, all I want is for you to leave me alone. . . ."

You don't love anyone but yourself and that circus of yours. Samuel's accusing words seemed to whirl in the air in front of her. Why? she wondered desperately.

367

Why would he say that? And Julian? Did she give the impression that she put the circus before her husband?

Adam, she thought desperately as Samuel lunged forward and clamped his hand over her mouth. *Adam, I do love you, I do. . . .*

"No, Carisa," Samuel said. "I won't leave you alone. I want what's coming to me. I've waited enough years for it, haven't I?"

Vicki Hartshorn, seventeen this year, reached into her apron pocket for a pair of scissors. Carefully she clipped off a pink rosebud and added it to the others she carried in her basket. The atmosphere of the greenhouse, warm, moist, full of yeasty plant and earth odors, was like being in another world. Safe, close, comforting.

More and more these days she seemed to find the greenhouse her refuge. Since Grandmama had died, there had been no one to take an interest in the flowers, the night-blooming cereus, the fragile roses, the tropical orchids. Mama was too busy with the circus to pay attention to flowers. Neecie didn't care about them at all—her life was in the ring barn with her horse, Helen of Troy. Only Tim Kelly enjoyed the greenhouse, and it was he who helped her to clean it, to stoke its fires, and to haul the large amounts of water it needed.

So, by default, the greenhouse belonged to her. Carefully Vicki shopped the seed catalogs. She subscribed to *Parks Floral Magazine,* with its tantalizing array of bulbs, seeds and perennials, its gossipy letters to the editor mingled with advertisements for tea sets and consumption cures.

She was involved now in breeding tuberous begonia and hybrid gloxinia. One day, if she were careful, she would have a display worthy of *Parks Magazine.* Occasionally she saw advertisements there, put in by people who had extra bulbs and wished to sell them.

Sometimes, in her rambling daydreams, Vicki dreamed of growing bulbs for sale. But she knew she never would. She was too painfully quiet, too retiring, ever to do anything like that. In fact, she still couldn't understand why a man like Calvin Kord persisted in paying calls on a girl as shy as she. Was his mother forcing him to do it? The Kord Axe Company, she knew, had fallen on hard times. While the Hartshorn money, because of Mama's circus, was growing. . . .

Uneasily Vicki laid the last rosebud in the basket. Then she walked further down the row of green plants to inspect the Chinese Sacred Lily she had recently ordered from *Parks*.

One of its leaves was pock-marked, and Vicki touched it sadly. Some mite, she thought, some invisible insect pest. Grandmama would have known how to kill it. Grandmama had had a big book full of receipts, page after page, which told how to mix paint and varnish, cosmetics and perfume, soaps and rose waters, cordials and wines.

The only thing that Grandmama had not been able to mix was the elixir that would have cured her tumor.

Vicki sighed and pulled off the offending leaf. How she missed Grandmama! More than anyone else in the family, she was sure. Mama was absorbed in her own life. Neecie, too, had her circus, Matt his plans to go to sea. Even Julian had his raucous friends and secret pastimes, and for them all Grandmama had slipped back into the distant past.

But Vicki remembered. She still kept in her room the big fabric roll that Katherine had used to save, squares of material from every dress she had ever owned, stitched into one big roll. Calicos, silks, *gros de Suisse*, *mousseline de laine*. And across the corner of each square was stitched the trimmings for the dress it represented: lace and satin ribbons, fading delicately.

Just then there was a noise outside the greenhouse, and Vicki turned with a start, thinking that it was Tim, who had promised to bring her a barrel of mulch.

"Vicki, are you in here? Your mother told me that you would be."

It was not Tim. It was Calvin Kord, dressed imposingly in what *Godey's* Magazine called a walking suit. His coat was a fashionable dark blue, his trousers buff. He wore a white waistcoat and carried a gray beaver hat in his hand. Calvin, at nineteen, was already slated to go into his father's business. He was tall and stoutly built, with a soft chin and a little paunch already visible beneath his waistcoat.

"I am . . . just looking at my bulbs," she muttered. She wished Mama had not sent him out here. She was not dressed to receive callers. She wore the old dove-colored gown she saved for gardening, which was too small for her and hugged her breasts tightly.

"That old dress makes you look very fragile and breakable," Neecie had teased her last week. "Men like that. It makes them feel very powerful and they start thinking of all the things they would like to do to you."

Vicki had not been amused. She had thought it a horrid thing for Neecie to say, and was quite angry with her. Neecie's words had made her belly feel all sick and churned up—

Now she saw that Calvin was moving restlessly up and down the rows of low tables, batting with his hands at spiky green leaves and curling tendrils, dismissing all of her work as if it had been weeds.

"I've been wanting to talk with you, Vicki. And I haven't had a chance because you never seem to come to any of my mother's music nights or parties. Have you been sick?"

"Sick? No . . ." She slipped off the gardening gloves and laid them on a table. She stood awkwardly, wondering what to do with her hands now.

"You haven't been avoiding me, have you?" Calvin gave a hearty, confident laugh, and Vicki knew that this was supposed to be a joke.

"No . . ."

"It sure is hot in here. How can you stand it? So wet and muggy, ugh, it's like a jungle."

"I like it."

"You like it? Oh, I suppose you do." Calvin's shrug dismissed her preferences. "Listen, Vicki, I came here to ask you something."

"What?"

"I came here to ask you to marry me."

"You came . . . for what?" She stared at him dumbly. Her hands twisted themselves together.

370

"Why, to ask you to marry me, of course." Calvin gave another hearty laugh. He sounded exactly like a man of thirty, she thought dazedly. A man who cannot imagine being turned down.

"B-but why?" she burst out.

"Why? Well, because I want to." He took a step closer to her and she could smell hair pomade, shirt starch, laundry soap and male perspiration, all very clean. She shrank back, terrified that he was going to touch her.

"Just because I want to," he repeated, licking his lips. "Because I think you'd make a decent wife for me, you're very quiet and ladylike and proper, and that's the kind of wife I need."

"Oh."

She must have backed away from him, for the edge of the plant table was pressing cruelly into the flesh of her thighs, and her back ached from holding herself so rigidly. She could feel her lower lip tremble.

He was talking to her now, telling her of his plans to build a house in New London. It would be in the Gothic style, big, rambling, adorned with carved wooden pediments, and there would be a low stone fence surrounding it on all four sides, for privacy. A recent inheritance from an uncle would finance the house. And since Calvin himself had come to work for the Kord Axe Company, the profits would soon take a turn for the better, so naturally. . . .

Vicki heard not one word of this. Marriage! Her head felt as if it were swimming in flowers. Realistically she knew that this proposal was probably the only one she would ever get. Neecie was the one who had already received eight proposals—and turned down every one. Neecie was the one who was vibrant and beautiful, not herself.

"Well?" Calvin leaned closer to her, and she saw that his cheeks were flushed dull with color.

"I . . . I don't know."

Her mind was moving rapidly. If she married Calvin, she would be mistress of her own home. She could have her own greenhouse, her own carriage to drive to town

371

as she pleased. She could even ask Mama to let her bring Tim Kelly to her new home as gardener and coachman. . . .

"Well, will you, Vicki? If you say yes, I could go and talk to your father today. I'm sure he would approve, our families have been neighbors for many years now, even if your mother does own a circus."

"I . . ." Vicki swallowed convulsively, suddenly terrified by the enormity of what she was doing, by an odd, spinning sense of fright. "Yes," she gasped at last. "I will."

"Carisa," Adam said one night, after they had made love by gaslight. "What's that bruise on your thigh? And on your right breast?"

She could feel color flooding over her entire body.

"It . . . it's nothing. I think I fell one morning last week when I was hurrying too fast down the circus path. I tripped on a stone."

She could barely look at him. The bruises—yellowed and fading now—were the mark of Samuel's greed and brutality. He had used her repeatedly, muttering gutter words in her ears as he had ravished her. Used her, as if she had been a waterfront whore, a receptacle for semen, nothing more. As if he had much anger in him, to spend on her. . . .

Afterward, when he had finally left, she had wept and sobbed and scrubbed herself until her skin was raw.

Now Adam touched her gently, running a thumb down the longest bruise, his eyes distant and thoughtful.

"I wonder," he said quietly. "Nelly came to me with a very strange story, Carisa. She said that Mr. Samuel was extremely insistent on knowing just which hotel you planned to stay in when you were in Philadelphia."

"I . . . Did she?"

Carisa could barely move her lips from fright. She knew Adam's fearsome temper, so quickly aroused, so dangerous while it lasted. She remembered the master who had had to leave town suddenly with the battered face. And, too, the story Adam had told her of the man who had died in the saloon in Reykjavik. If Adam were ever to learn that Samuel had raped her—Well, he must not know. That was all. He must never know.

"Do you know, Carisa, if I didn't know your aversion for my brother, I could almost begin to think. . . ."

"No, no, no," she burst out. "Adam, whatever it might look like, it's just not true. Samuel has . . . has perhaps been attracted to me, and he is undoubtedly lonely since his mistress and he . . ." She stopped, then hastily went on. "He has never remarried, but . . . but I certainly have never encouraged him. I would never dream of doing such a thing. . . ."

"Good. See that you don't then," Adam's voice was cold. "My brother is not a savory man. As for his mistress, rumor has it that she died recently after trying to abort herself of Samuel's child. Whatever her morals, that shouldn't have happened. And I am severing all business dealings with him, Carisa, an act which I should have completed years ago. I am divesting myself of all my property held jointly with him, and he will never be invited to our home again."

"That's fine," she said weakly. She reached for the bedsheet and pulled it up over her body and the incriminating marks.

"Carisa," he whispered, his voice changing. "Don't pull up the sheet. Not yet. I want to see you. I want to make love to you again. . . ."

Three months later, in late September, 1872, plans had been made for a glittering two days which would begin with Benicia's equestrienne debut and climax with Vicki's marriage to Calvin Kord. The drama of these two juxtaposed events appealed to Carisa, but they were also being staged together for a practical reason, too. The circus would be in New London for the debut and then Duddie and a few of the other performers could remain to attend the wedding as guests.

Besides, as Vicki nervously insisted, "I can't imagine having a wedding without Duddie around to pull candy out of his sleeve and throw it at the children. And me. Do you think, Mama, that he'll pull rice out of his sleeve and throw that, too?"

373

Benicia had wanted to make her debut in New York, where she would receive the most attention from the press. But Adam had bluntly refused. The show must take place in New London, he insisted, among friends and relatives, rather than in the impersonal surroundings of a big city.

Then, he said, Benicia was to forget the circus and turn her thoughts back to the ordinary life enjoyed by a young woman of her age and social status in New London.

Carisa was horrified.

"But Adam! Surely she is going to travel with the show after this! You can't expect her to . . . to just make her debut and then stay here at Hearts-ease and forget it all?"

Adam shook his head. "Now you are beginning to sound like Neecie herself, Carisa. Begging, blandishing me like a child for a bauble."

"Adam . . ."

"You both informed me that she deserved a debut, and I gave in. If I didn't, Neecie insisted, she would rot away like a grape on a vine. Well, heaven forbid that anyone in my household should be asked to endure that fate."

"But . . . but merely making a debut isn't enough! *One* performance, and then to tell her that she must take up an ordinary life? It's cruel, Adam! Neecie is a circus performer! She has more than just a talent for it, she has a genius. . . ."

"Nonsense. Genius in a girl of sixteen? I'm willing to let her have her debut, get this circus business out of her system. Then she'll be ready to settle down and pay some attention to those young men who have been lounging about our parlor recently."

"You just don't want to let her go," Carisa muttered. "She's always been your favorite, and you. . . ."

They had been eating breakfast together in the master bedroom, as was their custom, and now Adam smiled at her sadly. "You identify with that girl, don't you, Carisa? You imagine yourself in her place. But can't you see that she is not like you? She wasn't reared a

374

circus child, as you were, trained like some little animal from infancy to perform in the ring. No, Neecie was given the upbringing of a proper New London girl. She can read, and she can write in beautiful calligraphy. She can speak French and play the piano, albeit reluctantly, and she can do perfect embroidery when she chooses. She can converse at a dinner table exactly as other young girls of her breeding are trained to do. That is what you blind yourself to, Carisa. This girl has delicacies, fancies. She wouldn't be able to endure the privations of circus life."

"That's not true!"

"Isn't it? I've seen your new circus train myself, Carisa. The rooms you provide for your female performers are like boxes, the entire berth no bigger than a couch, tiny, cramped and miserable. Neecie will have to be alone on holidays, she'll have to perform every day whether she wishes it or not. . . ."

Carisa sprang out of her chair and stood trembling. "Other women in the circus endure such things! This is one time when you're wrong, Adam Hartshorn. Neecie is a strong girl, and she's capable. She can endure anything, even circus quarters. Just you wait until she makes her debut . . . then you'll see!"

The band struck up a lilting, sensual Eastern march. A caged lion roared, a child cried out in excitement, and it had begun.

First there were four male equestrians, dressed in exotic Eastern costumes, their robes and turbans glittering with sequins. Then Benicia came riding into the ring, reclined on her snow-white mare, Helen of Troy.

The show audience, which crammed the brick building to capacity, with people standing at the back, let out a combined gasp.

Benicia was beautiful. She wore a costume patterned after the Harem girls of the Arabian countries, composed of filmy leggings and ornate jeweled bands of fabric, carefully sewn over flesh-colored tights so that it looked as if she were nearly nude.

Lithe, curved, bold, she was the most fascinating

creature New London had ever seen. And artfully applied cosmetics heightened the exotic illusion. Benicia's eyelids had been darkened, her lips and cheeks reddened like fruit. Corn-yellow hair streamed loose down her back, and the unexpected little dimple creased devilishly—

Carisa sat stunned beside Adam. Matt was on her left, and in the row behind her, Vicki and Calvin sat with the rest of the Kords. She could hear Madeleine's startled gasp, and felt like uttering one herself.

She, Carisa, had supervised the costume and had pronounced it daring but still within the bounds of modesty. It was Neecie herself who gave the costume such an aura of sexuality, riveting all eyes upon her.

The stolid ring horse cantered around the ring as it had been taught, its gait eight miles an hour, as regular as a metronome. And on its back, Benicia danced.

Twisting, swaying, bending and curving with lissom grace.

It was more than ballet, Carisa realized, dazed. Benicia had taken the ballet steps as her start, and then she had improvised, bending and moving her body in ways that no ballet master had ever envisioned. Each pose she struck was perfect. Each jump, each somersault, was an execution of fluid, rippling lines.

Flawless. And completely new.

For Benicia had abandoned the careful routine which Carisa had designed for her, and which she had supposedly been practicing all these months. Instead, this was her own creation, and boldly she performed it, knowing that Carisa could not stop her now, that in the ring she was free to do as she pleased.

Like Stephana, Carisa thought in mounting horror.

The performance went on, radiating magic, and a wild sexuality. Somewhere high in the rafters of the gloomy brick building, Carisa imagined that she could hear the ghostly laughter of Stephana, the whisper of Anna, the protest of John Phillips. . . .

She shook away the fancy.

"Adam!" She nudged her husband in the side.

"Adam, she's not doing the routine we'd planned. She's improvising!"

"Is she?" Adam's eyes were fixed upon his daughter.

"Adam, we've got to stop her! Some of those somersaults and turns . . . they're really very dangerous! She's not ready for them yet. One slip and. . . ."

"Hush, Carisa, and let her alone. This is your doing, you brought her to this. I think she is doing very well. At least we can let her have her show."

Carisa settled back in her seat, flushing. The horse wheeled about in the ring and Benicia artfully managed to complete her act in a spot which faced her parents. She gave a graceful leap down from the mare's back and bowed low in their direction, like a collapsing flower. The crowd roared and screamed for more.

Benicia rose from her bow and stood proudly straight, her eyes gleaming with triumph.

The next day was Vicki's wedding, the whole affair badly eclipsed by the sensation which Benicia had provided for them. The wedding guests could barely stop chattering long enough for the wedding vows to be spoken.

Benicia's performance—Benicia's daring costume and exotic looks—all were hashed over and over in tones of shock and amazement.

Was it true that Benicia had been nude beneath the gauzy costume she wore? Was it true that her parents had quarreled bitterly about the girl making her debut, and after the wedding Adam planned to place his adopted daughter in a convent?

Was it true that the girl was engaged to marry a clown in the circus? A millionaire in New York? A Turkish prince?

Carisa pretended that she did not hear the speculations. She moved through the day mechanically, supervising the many wedding details, and comforting Vicki, who had vomited twice from nervousness. She inspected Matt in his new suit, and scolded Julian, who had chosen today, of all days, to appear downstairs drunk.

377

All the while she tried to comfort herself with the knowledge that Neecie *had* made the debut for which she had longed. And now it seemed that she had even agreed to comply with Adam's wishes and begin to concentrate on an active social life. With her beauty, Adam was sure, her suitors would be more than willing to overlook her defiance of convention.

Why, then, did Carisa feel so depressed and uneasy? If Neecie herself agreed that there was to be no more circus. . . .

Vicki and Calvin were about to leave for their wedding trip, which was to be a voyage to Paris, a gift to them from Adam and Carisa. Vicki had changed to her traveling garb, a walking dress of claret-colored silk, with an overdress in camel-hair of a lighter shade. In it she looked fragile and frightened, and Carisa forgot her worries over Benicia long enough to feel a pang.

"Mama! Mama!" Vicki threw herself into her mother's arms, clinging to her.

"Darling, don't carry on so," Carisa said gently. "You're married, you have a husband to care for you now, and I'm sure you're going to be very happy," she added, hoping that this was indeed to be the case. "You're staying at the Kords' tonight, and then tomorrow you will leave for New York. Then a boat to Europe. And you'll love Paris. It's a wonderful city."

"Paris. Yes."

"Our ship sails in four days' time," Calvin put in officiously. "So we will have plenty of time to sight-see in New York as well."

"That will be pleasant." Carisa patted her daughter's back, wishing that her son-in-law were just a bit more nervous himself. Dressed impeccably in the latest fashion, Calvin seemed so very sure of himself.

"G-goodbye, Mama!" Vicki stammered. She gave Carisa a moist, convulsive kiss. Then she threw herself into Adam's arms.

"Papa . . . Papa . . ."

Adam looked stricken. "Now, Vicki. Paris isn't the end of the world. You'll be home by spring, and by

378

then your new house should be nearly done, and you'll be busy furnishing and decorating it. . . ."

"Papa . . . Oh, Papa! Mama . . ."

And now, looking discomfited at last, Calvin led Vicki away to the brougham which awaited them. Tim Kelly stood beside it, his gray eyes somber. He helped Vicki into the carriage, and then stood stiffly at attention as Calvin climbed in after her.

24

Night had fallen, and the gasolier had been lit, sending warm flickers of light throughout the bedroom at Kordlands, and softening the gold-leafed carving of the bedroom mirror. Vicki's nightgown, stiffly new and heavily trimmed with *Valenciennes* lace, had been laid out on the bed by the maid.

"Now . . . I think I'd better go into my dressing room." Calvin said this rapidly, drawing in a deep breath of air and then letting it out with an explosive noise. He had, Vicki saw, spilled lobster salad on his fine new waistcoat.

"Oh . . ." she murmured.

"You can call the maid if you need help. There's a bell-pull over on that wall. I'll be back in a few minutes, or however long it takes you to get ready."

Vicki pressed her lips together nervously. *Surely you will want to rest here for a night first, in familiar surroundings,* Madeleine Kord had said firmly.

What familiar surroundings? Vicki had wanted to retort. This is your house, not mine. But she had not dared. Madeleine Kord was to be her mother-in-law. And an imposing one she would make, with her huge body swathed in whalebone and black bombazine, her little dark eyes almost lost in the flesh of her face.

"Well . . ." Calvin cleared his throat. "I'll be back in

a little while, I guess. I'll knock when I'm ready to come in."

"Yes. Very well."

Calvin stumbled as he moved toward the door, but he managed to close it behind him quietly. After it had shut, Vicki stood stiffly in the center of the room, trying to stifle the smothered pounding of her heart.

Was this how it all happened? she wondered desperately. With this awkwardness, this feeling of reading lines aloud from a very bad play? She and Calvin seemed to be actors in a drama about which they knew nothing.

Panic began to skitter through her belly. She took a jerky step toward the drapery-swagged window, seeing to her left her reflection moving in the gilt mirror. She saw that her face was as white as the linen pillowcover.

Men like that fragile look, Neecie had teased. *It makes them feel very powerful and they start thinking of all the things they would like to do to you. . . .*

Why, Vicki wondered, had Neecie to say such a terrible thing? It made her think of ugliness. Of hands touching her body, fingers ramming, violating—

Vicki gave a violent whirl and began to pace in the other direction, toward the looming bed. Julian. Bad, screaming, ugly dreams—No, she mustn't think of those now. The nightmares were over. She was no longer a frightened child of six, or ten. She was grown now, a married woman.

Next door, she knew, Calvin was undressing. She could hear a floorboard creak as he moved about. He was putting on his night things. What would he look like in them? Hastily Vicki pushed that thought away, too. Her hand moved toward the bell pull, then stopped.

Slowly she lowered her hand. No, she didn't want to call the maid. She didn't want the girl up here, with her sly, knowing eyes, her giggles, her knowledge of what was to happen. More knowledge than Vicki herself possessed. . . .

No, there would be no servant to stare boldly and then to go down to the kitchen and report that the new

Mrs. Kord looked pale, that her hands shook and her eyes were filled with tears.

Vicki began to tear at the fastenings of her dress. She was in a frantic hurry now, for Calvin might come into the room at any second, and she did not want him to find her half-naked. She ripped ruthlessly at the jet buttons, not even noticing when one of them snapped off and rolled onto the carpet by the bed.

She pulled off the gown and flung it at a chair.

She stood now in her undergarments, layers of whale-bone and muslin and lace, which, save for her arms, covered her almost as well as the dress had.

Petticoats. She fumbled at her waist, jerked at the strings which held them there. These, too, fell to the floor. She dumped them on the chair. Then she stumbled over to the bed and picked up the ornate, lacy nightdress.

She settled it over her shoulders, thankful for its shelter. Then, from beneath it, she began to struggle with the rest of her undergarments—the embroidered corset cover, the corset. Fortunately, her corset was one of the new, modern kind with metal front snaps and a latch which prevented it from opening accidentally. Her fingers flew at it. At last she squirmed out of it and let it drop.

Her underdrawers, which came nearly to her knees, she left on. Surely, she thought to herself, surely it was proper to do so. She could not possibly be expected. . . .

Calvin's knock at the door made her jump. Her heart convulsed into her throat, and then seemed to fall down again with a swoop. She stood paralyzed, one hand clutched to her chest, her fingers feeling the physical pounding there.

He knocked again. This time she managed to propel herself toward the bed. She lifted the embroidered coverlet and slid under it just as Calvin pushed open the door.

"Yes?" Her voice was a low gasp. She looked up and their eyes met.

"Vicki? May I come in?"

Later it all became blurred in her mind, the hideous nightmare which began the very moment when Calvin stepped toward her, looking unfamiliar and faintly ridiculous in his blue silk dressing gown worn over his nightshirt.

"Well." He cleared his throat.

After he had turned out the gasolier and climbed into bed beside her, they lay for long minutes side-by-side. Neither of them spoke or moved. Somewhere in the house they could hear the sound of a clock striking the hour. Was it midnight, twelve strokes? Vicki lost count of the booming strikes.

At last he turned to her. In the darkness his hands fumbled for her. They brushed over her hip, closed down on the flesh of her thigh with a moist, meaty, warm feeling that made Vicki cringe.

"Well. I suppose . . ." Then Calvin stopped and gulped. Even Vicki knew it had been a ludicrous thing to say. She stiffened her body, closed her eyes, and held her breath.

It was a nightmare, all of it. From the first cloyingly warm touch of Calvin's hand to the shocking moment when he lifted the hem of her nightdress, ran his fingers up her legs, encountered the cloth of her drawers, and did not know how to get them off.

She felt him tugging at the waistband ribbon. "Please," he muttered. "Please, Vicki, you've got to. . . ."

She barely heard him. She lay enduring it, fighting a sudden nausea, a squeezing in her belly. She would not scream. She *would not*.

"Please, you've got to let me. It's what I'm supposed to do. You're supposed to. . . ." Calvin paused and swallowed. He jerked again at her drawers, and this time the ribbon pulled away, cutting the flesh of Vicki's waist as it did so.

"Vicki. You've got to. You're my wife now, you've got to."

"No."

"I said you're my wife. It's what women do. Didn't anyone tell you? My God. . . ."

382

As he spoke, Calvin was doing unspeakable things. Pushing at her, forcing her legs apart. Lowering himself on top of her, his breath panting and rough.

God—God—Mama—Grandmama—

She stiffened under him and sobbed and endured the frightful pushing pain. Calvin panted hideously above her like an animal, crying out muffled words, words she didn't even hear.

Then it was over. Calvin uttered a strange, muffled cry. His body jerked and convulsed. Then he collapsed on top of her. He lay limp and breathless, the weight of his body pushing down on her chest so that she could scarcely catch her breath.

From somewhere she found the strength to push him away. He rolled to one side and lay beside her, breathing heavily.

As soon as she was free of him, Vicki sprang off the bed. She fumbled around on the floor for her underdrawers, did not find them, and finally grabbed for the clothes she had flung onto the chair.

"What . . . what are you doing?" Calvin muttered groggily.

She did not answer but went on dressing, her haste so desperate that she did not care now if he saw her, she didn't care about anything except getting away.

Calvin rose on one elbow. "Hey! You can't get dressed now! What would Mother think? It's after midnight! Where do you think you're going?"

"I don't know. Home, I guess."

She pulled the dress around her, fastened some of the jet buttons, gave up on the rest, and fled from the room.

"Vicki!"

Calvin's voice, thick and plaintive, floated after her.

Once she had reached home, breathless, weeping, her ankle twisted from where she had stumbled over a rock, she did not know what to do. It was a cold night; the golden September day had faded and now a chilly salt wind blew from the Sound, ruffling the tops of the trees. Hearts-ease lay like a long rectangle in the darkness. No lights were burning. Even the circus compound was dark, for the show had left tonight to resume its interrupted tour.

She hesitated on the gravel drive, staring at the silent house. She knew the door would be locked. She could pound on the door, of course, but that would arouse the whole household. Servants would come running. And Mama. Papa, Matt, Julian, Neecie. They would all gather about her and demand to know what had happened. What was she doing here, at past midnight? Why had she run away? She was a wife now, she belonged with her husband.

Vicki swallowed hard. Then she began to look about her desperately. The night was cold and would grow more so; she would have to find some shelter.

Her eyes fixed on a dark, low shape almost invisible against a backdrop of trees, shards of moonlight sparkling dully on its surface. The greenhouse. Of course. It would be warm there, and she could find burlap sacks to sleep on. . . .

Stumbling over roughened tufts of grass, she made her way toward the greenhouse. Its door yielded to her hand—she never kept it locked—and she half-fell inside. Immediately the earthy yeasty smell surrounded her like a breath of familiar air.

Here, she thought. Here I'll be safe. Among my flowers.

The plants were arranged in rows on long tables, or hanging on hooks from the ceiling, and she sensed their presence, all of them waiting and listening. In the dark she could not see where the burlap bags were—had she left them on a shelf at the end, or had she tossed them under one of the tables? She had never expected to have to use them in this way. . . .

She fumbled around and found the stub of a candle, and a little metal box of matches. She struck a match, and the candlelight sent a flickering glow of warmth through the greenhouse, revealing the shadowy plants.

The sacks, she saw, were under the farthest table. She stooped and pulled them out, wrinkling her nose at the scent of grain and earth which came from them. She tried to arrange them into a pallet on the floor.

Suddenly she was tired, exhausted deep to the bone. Without even bothering to snuff out her candle, she collapsed on the burlap and fell asleep.

Five minutes later she felt someone shaking her.

She struggled upward through thick, gluey sleep.

"What . . . What . . ." She could hardly wrench her eyes open, they felt nailed shut by exhaustion. She did not recognize her own voice.

"Hey, hey, what is this? Vicki, my God, is it you? What are you doing here? On the floor!"

It was Tim Kelly, holding an oil lamp which blazed through the greenhouse, causing black shadows to move and jump. He looked rumpled and sleepy, having pulled on a pair of trousers over his nightshirt. His reddish hair seemed to glow in the lamplight like flames.

She struggled to sit up. Then she felt his hand beneath her arms, helping her. He lifted her to her feet and she stood swaying, feeling sleep-drunk and disoriented. Involuntarily she clung to him for support. She could smell the scent of his body, very male and clean.

"What in the name of the dear lord are you doing here?" he asked. "You were married this afternoon! I myself drove you to Kordlands."

"I know, I know, I know," she wept. His arm went around her. She couldn't help it; she pressed her face into the broad expanse of Tim's chest and began to sob.

"Vicki." His voice had roughened. "Vicki, he didn't . . . he didn't harm you, did he? Is that why you ran away?"

"No!"

"Shall I call your father?"

"No! Oh, no!" She clutched at him. "No, I couldn't face them tonight. I'm never going back to Kordlands again, Tim. Never, ever. Not if Papa whips me for it, I don't care. I never should have married him!"

"Vicki . . ."

"No, I tell you, I won't go back, I won't!"

They stood together for a moment and she noticed that Tim had not let go of her. If he had, she would have fallen. He was her friend, she assured herself. He

385

always had been, since her early childhood. She could not remember a time at Hearts-ease when Tim had not been there.

"I saw a light in here," he said in a low voice. "I pulled on my pants and I came out, thinking it was a thief. Or perhaps a tramp, come in here to sleep. They do that sometimes. I never knew it would be you."

She did not reply. Her heart had begun to pound again, this time in a new, slow, throbbing way.

"Well," Tim said. "What are we going to do with you, Vicki? You certainly can't sleep here in the greenhouse like a wanderer."

His voice was roughened. Different somehow, and tender.

Carisa awoke at dawn with one of her dreams. In it, a baby was crying, and when Carisa went into its room to quiet it she saw that Vicki was bent over the cradle, her mouth curved into a smile. *Thea*, Vicki was saying. Her name will be *Thea*.

She rose on one elbow to glance at the ormolu clock which sat on the small dressing table. Dawn. She sank back onto the feather mattress, hearing Adam's soft breathing beside her, and looked at the ceiling.

Surely it was natural for her to dream of Vicki having a baby, wasn't it? After all, the girl was newly-married, and what else could be expected but for her to have a child? But a name like Thea! Why should that particular name, rather unusual, have popped into her dream?

Puzzled, uneasy, Carisa turned over in bed, and that was when she heard the noise in the corridor. Furtive, light footsteps, and then the creak of floorboards.

She pushed back the coverlet and got out of bed. She reached for her dressing gown and pulled it about her, belting it as she went. One of the servants? But they never came upstairs this early.

When she reached the corridor, it was empty. But there was still the faint scent of rosewater, Vicki's fragrance, in the air, and the door at the far end of the hallway, Vicki's door, gave a light click.

Without stopping to think, Carisa moved swiftly

down the hall and pushed open the door to her daughter's room.

Vicki, looking disheveled, her hair streaming out of its pins, was sitting on the edge of the bed. Her gown, too, was rumpled, the jet buttons fastened crookedly, the silken fabric smudged with bits of garden earth and dried leaves. She was staring straight ahead, her expression strange. Her skin was linen-pale, yet her cheeks glowed with hectic color. Her eyes dark and lambent, her lips slightly swollen.

Bruised with love, was Carisa's first, involuntary thought. But if that was the case, then why—

"Vicki. Daughter, what are you doing here?"

Vicki jumped like a startled small animal. Her eyes widened. Her mouth dropped open, then closed again firmly.

"I came home, Mama. As you see."

"But why?"

"Because I just had to, that's all. I *couldn't* stay there, I hated it, I hated it, I tell you, Mama!"

Yet there was still that strange, glowing look in her daughter's eyes, as if something uplifting had happened to her.

"But Calvin is your husband," Carisa heard herself repeat stupidly.

"No! He isn't! I hate being married to him. He . . . He . . ." Vicki averted her face and Carisa saw the grim line of her chin, so much like Adam's when he was angry.

"Vicki, darling. Was it the sleeping together? You do know that is a part of marriage, don't you? Didn't we talk about that? It is something which a woman must. . . ."

"I don't care! I hated it . . . with Calvin, he's a . . . Oh, Mama, it was awful. A nightmare, a terrible nightmare. I'll never go back to Kordlands again."

Why was it that even as Vicki said these words—and her fright was genuine, Carisa was sure of it—her face again got that closed, exalted look?

"I won't go back to the Kords," the girl repeated hysterically. "I won't, Mama. You can do anything you wish to me, you can punish me, but I'll never go back to Calvin again. Never, for the rest of my life, do you hear me?"

"But Vicki . . ."

"Just leave, will you, Mama? Leave me alone! I want to take a nap. I'm very tired and I . . . I have to think."

Carisa felt helpless, as if matters had slid entirely out of her control. Her daughter had left the house a nervous bride. She had returned like this, hysterical, exalted, stubborn.

"Very well, darling. Would you like me to mix you a sleeping draught?"

"No."

"Then do try to sleep for as long as you can. I'm sure that when you wake up you'll feel better, and then we can send a note to the Kords and straighten all of this out."

"Mama, when will you see?" Vicki asked impatiently. "I don't want this straightened out. *I don't want anyone to do anything.* I'm going to stay here. I'm never going back to the Kords' again."

But the news of Vicki was not to be the only shock of the day. Carisa and Adam breakfasted, as was their habit, in their bedroom, lingering over coffee to discuss what should be done.

"I'll talk to her," Adam said grimly. "Or perhaps you should, Carisa. Maybe this sort of delicate thing is best handled by a mother."

Carisa hesitated. "I don't know. She seems so very determined. She says she's never going back to him. She virtually dared us to punish her for it, and I think she meant every word."

Adam scowled. "That young puppy. If he did anything to harm her. . . ."

"Oh, surely he didn't. Insensitive he may be, but I'm sure he's decent enough. I think it's just that she didn't . . . the physical side of marriage. . . ."

"*You* didn't object to that."

"No. But I was . . . circus children are given much more freedom in their upbringing, Adam. Oh, I did talk with her, Adam, before the wedding. I tried to explain. . . ."

Adam got up from the small, oval table where their breakfast was laid out. He began to pace about the room, limping slightly on his war-injured leg.

"I'm beginning to think we've sheltered her too much, Carisa. She always had her grandmother to run to, or the attic, or that greenhouse where she could hide herself from the world. What good to anyone is a wife who flees the marriage bed? She might as well be a. . . ."

He stopped. The word *cripple* seemed to float uneasily in the room.

"No!" Carisa cried. "I'm sure it will be all right, Adam, once Vicki has had a chance to think. She was always a delicate child. And now perhaps she needs time to adjust. . . ."

Hollow words. Carisa was almost thankful when there was a knock at their door which proved to be Annie, the young upstairs maid, come to fetch their breakfast things. Nelly, who often performed these services, was now in her eighth month of a difficult pregnancy, and Carisa had been giving her light duties.

Annie peeped at them furtively. "Are you finished, ma'am?"

"Yes, we're finished," Adam told her. "Take the dishes away. And wipe that silly smile off your face, too, if you please. Our daughter Victoria has come home again, and we are pleased to receive her. Kindly convey that information to everyone in the kitchen and ask them not to gossip about it further."

"Yes, sir." The little maid, who was Brigid's niece and already growing as plump as her aunt, flushed and bit her lip. Reaching for a plate, she nearly knocked over a cup.

"Annie?" Carisa asked. "What is it?"

"Oh . . ." The girl hesitated. A look of fright passed over her features and the saucer she held rattled loudly.

"Annie! You'd better tell us."

"I . . . I. . . Oh, Ma'am, when I saw it I run straight down to the kitchen to tell Aunt Brigid, I don't know what to do, I swear I didn't, and she said to keep quiet about it, you'd find out soon enough for yourself. . . ."

"Find out what?" Adam's voice was dangerous.

"Why, find out . . . See, the circus left last night. For its next show or wherever it's to go. And all of us went down to the train siding to see it off . . . *you* know, you were there. . . ."

The maid's lips were chattering now, and she had dropped all pretense of clearing away the tray.

"Get on with it, Annie. Please tell us."

"Well, it's Miss Benicia. She . . ."

Neecie.

Carisa drew in a sharp breath, knowing what was to come, and already regretting the pain that Adam must feel, for Benicia had been his favorite. Yet for herself, she could feel only an absurd rush of gladness.

"See," the girl went on, "Miss Benicia wanted to go with them. She told me about it, she told all of us in the kitchen, she always talked to us as if we were just as good as quality. She told us how her Papa wouldn't let her, he wanted to keep her here. He wanted her to make her debut and then just drop it, like. He thought that would satisfy her. But it wouldn't, we all knew that. She's a performer, see. Born to it, she said."

Adam had turned a sick white. His eyes blazed with their old tawny fire. "What you are trying to tell us, then, is that our daughter has run away with the circus. Is that it?"

The maidservant shrank toward the door.

"Y . . . yes . . ."

Adam plunged out of his chair and strode out of the room, in spite of his limp moving with all the power of an angry stallion. Carisa and Annie looked at each other. Silently they both waited for his return.

"Her bed's not been slept in." Adam said it heavily, his face looking weary. "She's gone, all right. After promising me she would not! She was to get the circus out of her system, out of her blood . . . After all, her heritage is Hartshorn, too. . . ."

He paused, pressing his lips together. "Where have they gone? South? You have the schedule, don't you,

Carisa? I'll send a telegram to that rogue Rolf Taggart. He must have known about this. I'll have his hide for allowing this, he . . ." Adam stopped, his eyes suddenly chilly. *"You* had no part in this, did you?"

Carisa made a gesture to dismiss the maidservant, who ran off with relief.

"No!" she cried. "Of course I didn't! Adam, I would never go behind your back."

But she *had* gone behind his back, a cold little voice of reality spoke in her. She had trained Benicia without his knowledge, knowing he wished her to have another sort of life.

"Oh, I know how you must feel," she hurried on quickly. "I know what Neecie meant to you and the hopes you had for her. But perhaps this is all for the best. I mean . . ."

"The best!" Adam's tone was of chilly fury. "How can it possibly be for the best? A beautiful girl like Neecie, traveling about the country like a mountebank. Men after her, swarming back after the show to accost her. Publicity, stares, snickers. Sleeping in cramped quarters that I wouldn't offer to a chimney sweep . . . no roots, no home, no one to depend on but herself. . . ."

Carisa let her voice match his in coldness. "Neecie will not be a mountebank, as you call it. She'll be a featured performer. As for her quarters, they will be good ones. And she'll be as safe with the circus as she would be at home. Duddie will be there to watch out for her, and we have a separate railroad car with the very strictest of rules and chaperones."

Adam's fist pounded down on the tea table, rattling china and pewter, and causing a fork to skitter off onto the floor.

"Dammit, Carisa, I don't care about chaperones! Neecie is my daughter. And I don't want her haring about the country like a gypsy. I want her home, where she belongs."

"Even if she no longer belongs at home? Even if she *belongs* in the circus?" Carisa felt a wild, flowing anger, and she knew that she was about to say things that she

391

would regret later. But she could not stop herself and did not want to.

"Yes, Neecie *is* your daughter . . . she is your child and Anna's, isn't she?"

Adam's face had turned very pale. His golden eyes were somber. "Yes. I'm sorry, Carisa. I tried to keep it from you."

"I've known it for years," Carisa said dully. "Neecie is the result of your lust for my sister. I've tried to accept that, although it's been very hard. And I've tried to love Neecie, too, and I think I've succeeded in that. But once I loved my sister, too. And I made a promise to her that her child would remain with the circus. I promised her, Adam. And I owe Anna that much . . . *we* owe her."

Adam's face had turned into a granite mask.

"Anna is dead. And we did rear her child, better than any circus youngster ever had a right to expect. We gave her an education, Carisa, we gave her a veneer of polish and confidence, an upbringing far better than anything the circus might ever provide. . . ."

"I lived that life for years, Adam," Carisa whispered. "The life of the circus. And I loved every minute of it."

"Yes, and now you're trying to relive those years through Neecie, aren't you? That's the real reason you've pushed her all of these years. Your career is over, and you regretted it. So you took possession of a little girl. You trained her in that ring barn of yours like a dog or a horse. . . ."

Adam made a savage gesture. "You taught her to jump through hoops, didn't you? And I mean that literally. And now she has really pleased you, for she's run away to *live your life.*"

"No! No, Adam, it's not like that at all! Neecie loves the circus, I know she does, she always has. She. . . ."

"And what of all the stories you told her, the wonderful stories of your circus childhood? And Duddie, whom you allowed to be with her day after day, teaching her tricks even as a small girl of four?"

"Adam." She could feel the blood leaving her face, and knew that she must look pale and coldly furious.

392

"You're acting as if I did that girl a wrong. I didn't! I only gave her her heritage! The life she was born to lead! That's all! And how can you possibly object to it? After all, *I* am a circus performer, am I not? You saw nothing wrong with marrying me . . . you *wanted* to marry me . . . you loved the circus once, Adam!"

Savagely Adam stepped toward the bedroom door and twisted its brass handle.

"Yes. I loved the circus once. And I loved you."

He was gone, slamming the bedroom door behind him.

25

When she was upset, her office became her refuge, and this was where Carisa fled to now, to pace back and forth on the Turkish rug, trying to assemble her thoughts. She felt as if she could no longer understand Adam—if indeed she had ever understood him at all. What a mass of contradictions he was! He loved the circus—she was sure he did, for she had seen his eyes at the performances of the Phillips Circus, alight with bemused excitement. And yet he could fight to keep Neecie at home, could delude himself that she would be contented to appear in the ring only once. He blamed Carisa for encouraging the girl to be a performer—yet hadn't Adam himself given in and permitted her training?

It was as if, she thought slowly, he was always torn —between love for the circus and dislike for it, between love for her, Carisa, and anger with her.

Where would it all end? For she knew she could not give up her circus. And neither could she give up Adam, who, despite his faults, was the only man she had ever loved, or would love.

She continued to pace, seeing in her mind her husband's face as he had slammed out of their bedroom.

Never had she seen Adam look so grim and strained, so . . . yes, so old.

When had it happened? she wondered dully. The network of wrinkles scoring Adam's forehead, lining the corners of his eyes and mouth with stubborn strength. Had she been so deeply immersed in her circus that she had not seen these changes in him?

She heard shouts in the corridor and knew that Adam was summoning Gaines. No doubt he would send a telegram to Rolf, demanding that Benicia be sent home at once. Probably she would be clapped onto a train and bundled home like an errant prisoner, she thought angrily. Punished and humiliated because she had wished to fulfill the destiny that was hers.

Fury rose in her.

Well, she, Carisa, could send telegrams, too. And Rolf would listen to *her* because he had to.

They shared their bed that night in stony silence. Nor did Adam speak to her the following day, save to inform her that Vicki was to be given her old room back and treated exactly as before. If Calvin Kord came to the house, he, Adam, would receive him.

The days wore on. A week later Carisa received a letter from Rolf. They were in Philadelphia now, he wrote, and Benicia had been an instant success. She had been the talk of the entire city, with every performance sold out. The following day, Adam made an unexplained trip, and came home three days later in a sullen and silent mood. Carisa knew he must have gone to talk with Benicia—where else could he have gone? But what had passed between the two, or what strength Neecie had shown in defying her father, Carisa did not know.

During this time, Julian came and went erratically, and was seldom home for meals. When he was, he and Adam got into angry disagreements, and on one occasion nearly came to blows because Julian had neglected his work at the shipping office.

Vicki moved through the house like a thin little ghost. She avoided all social activity, and could scarcely be persuaded even to go to town to shop. She spoke little, and spent nearly all her time in the greenhouse, caring for her plants, with Tim Kelly to assist her.

Even Matt's usual seventeen-year-old boisterousness was dimmed. He and Julian argued and sniped at each other, until Carisa despaired of them. The younger boy seemed restless, and once at the dinner table, when he began to speak of taking training in navigation and going to sea, Adam cut him off sharply.

"Isn't one vagabond in the family enough?" he snapped. "As for your going to sea. I'm sure your mother will be happy to inform you that the whaling industry is dying. Haven't you seen the loafers lounging on the corner of State and Main street? The sidewalks are filthy with tobacco juice. Forty years ago those men would have been at sea."

"But Papa . . ." Matt began in a choked voice.

"Enough. You would do the Hartshorns a far better service if you were to go to Harvard College and distinguish yourself there."

At this remark, Matt scowled, and Adam's face held such a tormented look that Carisa felt a pang.

More days slipped by. Carisa began to grow almost accustomed to this new, silent life they led. Duddie wrote her that the Phillips Circus was playing to sellout crowds wherever it went, and that Benicia had been written up and illustrated in *Frank Leslie's* as "the equestrienne angel."

In November a suffragette named Susan B. Anthony and a group of her women supporters tried to vote in the presidential election and were arrested. Carisa, in a mood of defiance, telegraphed Miss Anthony a money order for fifty dollars.

She received weekly letters from Benicia, each glowing with enthusiasm. *You've no idea how wonderful it is, how thrilling, to take my bows at the end of my act and see people's faces and know that they like me. It makes everything worthwhile.*

Do tell Papa that I love him. I miss him so much and I will always adore him for letting me do this, because he is letting me, isn't he? And against his better judg-

*ment, too. And I love him for it. When we get back
to New London for the winter, I will give him the biggest kiss and hug in the world. . . .*

Carisa pushed this letter under the door of Adam's
study. She never knew if he had read it. But later in the
day Adam called for the surrey and drove in to New
London. He returned very late, smelling of whiskey.

In late November the circus returned to winter
quarters. It arrived at the train siding in a display of
show and color, and then paraded in full pageantry back
to the circus complex at Hearts-ease.

Carisa and Adam had come out to the road with the
children and servants to watch the parade as it came
near. They heard the bubbly, brassy, incredible notes of
the calliope from a long distance away, even before they
could spot the first wagon.

After what seemed like many minutes, the first
wagon, pulled by eight magnificent matched black geld-
ings, pulled into view at a bend in the road. Gold leaf,
fanciful with carving, flashed in the sun.

Adam narrowed his eyes at the approaching procession, and Carisa knew that he was searching for
Neecie.

"Soon I plan to build a railroad spur so the parade
won't have so far to go," Carisa said. "Oh . . . look . . .
there she is, in the Arabian wagon, waving at us!"

Adam sighed. "She's home, then. For the winter, at
least."

"Yes." Carisa glanced at her husband. "It was most
generous of you not to interfere with her," she added
with difficulty. "It meant so much to her to be a part
of it."

"I am not a villain, Carisa. To take her from something she loves that much . . . perhaps I didn't have it in
me to do that after all."

In February of 1873 she received a telegram from the
firm of attorneys whom she had engaged to see that her
father received his monthly money. John Phillips was
dying of heart failure. They had taken the liberty of
having him moved to a small nursing home where he

could receive better care. She should come at once if she wished to see him alive.

Carisa let the telegram drop from suddenly lifeless hands.

She was alone in her office, and had been going through the papers stacked helter-skelter on her desk. Designs for future circus posters, fan letters, communications from France, Germany and England. And—symbol of a dream come true—a letter marked with the Royal Crest, from a secretary on the staff of Queen Victoria, stating that the old Queen herself wished to see the glories of the Phillips Circus.

But Carisa saw none of these. Papa, dying!

She felt stunned. Surely this could not be true. She could remember so vividly the Papa of her youth, tall, regally arrogant, utterly in command of himself.

No, she prayed wildly. Let it be a mistake. Doctors don't know everything, no one does. Let this be a mistake.

She let her eyes rove jerkily around the clutter on the desk, fastening them at last on the letter from the Queen. A command performance! The Phillips Circus was at last renowned across the country. They received hundreds of fan letters weekly, as well as requests for performances and tickets. They played to sellout crowds, were written up glowingly in newspapers and magazines. And now they were to play before the Queen.

Carisa sat staring numbly at the letter, unable to summon the energy to get to her feet. Packing, travel arrangements, all of it must be done quickly. Still her limbs felt leaden, and she could not move.

In the corridor she heard the rapid sound of masculine steps, and then Julian's voice, shouting a command to Annie.

"Y-yes, sir," the girl replied, and Carisa, even in her shocked state, could sense the unease in the girl's voice. All of the servants were afraid of Julian.

Carisa let her hand reach toward the stacked-up letters on the desk. She picked up the royal letter and balanced it for a long moment in her palm. She handled it gingerly, as if it were spun of gold leaf and might blow away.

She would take it to Papa, she decided. Even if he had never attended a performance, at least she could present him with this. At least he would know that his dream had been realized; she had really done it. . . .

She blinked back sudden hot, aching tears, and rang for Nelly.

Leaden clouds were piled up in the sky, holding snow in their depths. A gray light pervaded the borough of Brooklyn, lending an ugliness to its chunky skyline, the partly-completed foundations for the Brooklyn Bridge.

The nursing home was located on Albany Avenue, near a red-brick building called St. John's Hospital. A white-clad nurse peered out of a window as Carisa's cab clattered up.

"Wait here, please," she told the driver.

"How long will you be, ma'am?"

"I . . . I don't know. Not long, perhaps. Anyway, please just wait, no matter how long. I'll pay you well."

The man shrugged. "Sure."

He helped her out, and then she stood on the sidewalk, pulling her cloak about her against the chill fingers of wind. With the wind came the odor of the sea, and of horse-droppings from the street. Carisa clutched at her reticule, which contained the letters from Queen Victoria, and hurried up the walk toward the nursing home.

Her ring was answered by a maidservant. Carisa stated her business and the woman grunted, telling her to come inside.

The home itself, Carisa saw, was clean enough. Floors and walls were immaculately scrubbed. But it smelled of carbolic, lye soap, and illness. Carisa tried to breathe as shallowly as possible, fighting off the urge to turn around and run.

"You want old Mr. Phillips? He's a cantankerous one, that one is."

The servant, chattering dourly, led Carisa up a wide

398

flight of stairs and then down a long corridor. They passed several opened doors, through which she could see old men lying in bed, their cheeks caved in tooth-lessly.

Papa, she thought in despair.

He had evidently been placed in a four-bed ward, and Carisa had to suppress a start of horror as she entered the room, which was crowded with beds, chairs, tables and "commode chairs," all of it lit by two gloomy tall windows.

One occupant of the room lay yellow-faced and seemingly semi-conscious beneath his coverlet, tossing and muttering. Another sat up in bed trying to eat from a tray, his hands shaking so violently that food flew about his bed. A third—

Carisa averted her eyes. None of these was her father. She must have been brought to the wrong room. She was just about to say so when the maidservant said, "Well, there he is. That last bed, that's him. And ornery enough he is, too, when he don't get his own way."

The servant gestured, and Carisa's eyes moved un-willingly to the far corner of the room, where a thin old man sat propped up by four pillows. His lips and skin were bluish. Gnarled, twisted hands, also bluish in color, rested on top of the coverlet. Only the eyes were the same, blue and piercing. They seemed to blaze at her.

"Papa!" Her heart thudded.

"You. What are you doing here?"

She faltered. "I came because the law firm said you were ill. They said . . . they said you might like some company."

The gnarled old hand made a contemptuous gesture. "Company! Bah! I have that right here, don't I? The dying and the senile. They're my company."

She felt herself recoiling from the bitterness in his tone. "Papa . . . Papa, I wanted to see you. . . ."

"Then look at me, if that's what you want. For it's your last chance. I've not very long now. Heart failure, the doctor tells me. Says it's a miracle I've hung on this long, and God knows why I am hanging on. This world hasn't anything to offer me now and it hasn't in a long time."

Silence settled in the room. Her father coughed agonizingly, wheezing and choking. As he did so, Carisa found a chair at the foot of his bed. She settled herself in it with a rustle of skirts and petticoats.

He had stopped coughing now, and was looking weak and drained.

"Papa. Have they been sending you money regularly, as I asked them to do?"

"Oh, yes, on the dot of the month, as steady as a metronome." The slack old mouth twisted. "Not that I wanted it. I didn't spend any more of it than I needed to. There's plenty of it left, you'll find it in my things."

"You could have lived comfortably, Papa!" She found that she was twisting her hands in her lap until her rings cut into her flesh. "Why didn't you come to Hearts-ease to live with us? I would have treated you well. You could have been a part of the circus. You could have. . . ."

"Didn't want that."

Carisa felt as if she couldn't bear this. She jumped convulsively from her chair and fled to the window. The view looked out on a barren little yard, half-covered in melting snow, where trash barrels awaited pickup.

"Papa, you never answered my letters, not one. You had grandchildren whom you never knew. You never came to anything . . . not to the circus, not even to Benicia's debut. When we played before President Grant you wouldn't come. You wouldn't even come when the show was in New York."

In spite of herself, her voice was rising, thready with tears.

"Daughter, I . . ."

John Phillips gave a breathy gasp, and when Carisa turned she saw that he was straining forward. There was a bell-cord beside his bed, tacked to the wall, and he fumbled in its direction.

"Call," he gasped. "Call the nurse. Need . . . need my pillows higher. That . . . always helps. . . ."

She rushed to the bed, jerked hard on the cord, and then plumped the pillows herself, pulling the fragile old body forward.

A young nurse hurried in, followed by an older one, and then they converged on the bed, manipulating the old body, putting medicine into its mouth, piling up more pillows.

Carisa drew back and waited for them to finish. Involuntarily her hand went to her reticule, where the letter from the Queen waited. She had forgotten to show it to him.

But, the aching thought came, would he really have cared? She had created the Phillips Circus from almost nothing. From a little mud show playing in small towns it had grown to be one of the best known circuses in the country. The Phillips name was now as famous as that of P. T. Barnum. And what had it been for? For this ravaged dying old man who would not even speak decently to her on his deathbed?

Why had she never admitted it to herself? she wondered slowly. John Phillips had resented her very birth. No matter what she had done with her circus, she never could have satisfied him.

"Miss," the young nurse said rapidly. "You'd better come now. I think he's dying. There isn't anything we can do for him, you know."

As if in a dream, Carisa came forward. Her father lay very still on the piled-up pillows. His lips were dark blue now, his breath so shallow that it seemed as if he were not breathing at all. The blue eyes were focused somewhere in the distance. They did not notice Carisa.

"Papa," she whispered, choking. "I'm sorry for the accident. You've got to believe me. I spent all my life trying to make it up to you. The circus . . . the Phillips show . . . and you never cared, did you?"

Her damp hands squeezed the folds of her skirt, pleating it. "Papa, did you know we're to play before Queen Victoria? Her secretary wrote us a letter. She loves circuses, you know . . . she always has, even before Prince Albert died. Probably next fall we'll go over,

401

after the regular season. We'll winter in England and we'll play before a Queen. Papa! Your dream . . . I made it come true. . . ."

She was sobbing openly now, unaware of the nurse's pitying look.

"Miss. He's gone. Didn't you know it? He must have died right away, as soon as we spoke to you."

"No! He can't have! He didn't!" Carisa wrenched the letter out of her reticule and stood crumpling it. "He hasn't seen this yet. I was going to show it to him. We . . . My show is to play in England, you know, before the Queen! I . . . I wanted to tell him. I wanted him to know. . . ."

"I'm sure he does, dearie." The nurse—she was younger than Carisa, a plain girl in her early twenties—took Carisa's arm and led her away, out of that close, crowded room reeking of death.

"I'm seen some things about dying that might surprise you, Miss. So come on now, honey. Come to our office. It's small, but it's tidy, and I can heat you some tea. And we've some muffins which aren't too stale. Come, it would do you good. . . ."

Numbly, Carisa allowed herself to be led downstairs and to the small nursing home office. There she sat and sobbed into her tea, until at last the young nurse took it away. Then the girl shut the door and left Carisa to weep in privacy.

An hour later, Carisa left the nursing home, after arranging for the body to be brought back to Heartsease for burial. With her she carried two cardboard boxes filled with her father's possessions—boxes crammed with money, with papers, circus programs and posters, newspaper articles about the Phillips Circus dating back to its first performance. There was even the article about Benicia, "Equestrienne Angel," which had been in *Frank Leslie's* magazine. The clippings were dog-eared, and some of the names—her own, Rolf's, Duddie's and Benicia's—were underlined in pencil.

Papa, she thought as she climbed wearily into the waiting cab. *Papa, oh, Papa.*

Pity overwhelmed her, a pity as heavy and hopeless as her grief.

John Phillips' body was brought back to Hearts-ease. Defiantly Carisa had it buried in the circus compound, inside the octagonal brick building which they used for winter performances, his headstone level with the flooring.

The stone said simply, *John Phillips, Phillips Circus, 1800-1873*. In England, such burials had once been common in older times, inside churches or cathedrals, and Carisa thought this one somehow very fitting.

Adam did not.

"Carisa," he said, shocked. "Don't you think that the man should be buried in consecrated ground?"

"Then let a minister come and consecrate it," she said sharply. "I want him here. He refused to come and see my show during his lifetime . . . now he will *have* to see it!"

Adam stared at her for a moment. Then suddenly he threw back his head and uttered a peal of laughter. It was the first time that she had heard him laugh in weeks.

"You'll have your revenge, won't you, Carisa?"

"Revenge?"

"The man treated you as dirt. He took your money and ignored you. Ignored the circus which bore his name. Why shouldn't you resent it? And what better way to wreak your revenge than to stick him under the ground in a ring-side seat, so to speak?"

She hesitated. "I wasn't thinking of revenge. Not exactly. I just wanted him to . . . to be here, that's all. Oh, I know he can't really see the show, that's silly. Still . . ."

"Still, it's a fine turn-about. And it'll be the talk of New London, I'll guarantee you that. You always did know how to generate gossip, didn't you, Carisa?" Adam's voice half-teasing, half-serious.

Suddenly it was May. Winter had come and gone again, and with it went the Phillips Circus, heading out once more on its seasonal circuit. Benicia had left with it, her wardrobe trunk stuffed with a half-dozen diaphanous costumes stitched for her over the long winter months by Mrs. Wiggins and her staff, which had now grown to twelve.

There had been some stormy scenes. Benicia was hot-tempered, and she could shout and slam doors with abandon when she wished. If she didn't go again with the circus, something in her would wither, she pleaded eloquently to Adam. She was meant for that life, discomforts and all—it was what God had created her for. If she disobeyed her calling, she would be disobeying God.

Besides, she had added slyly, she could always run away again, couldn't she? Only this time she would go with Mr. Barnum's circus where her family would have no control over her. What would Adam think of that?

"All right." Adam had said it reluctantly. "Go, then, Neecie, if it will bring you happiness. You know I wouldn't stand in the way of that. But please don't tell me it is God who wishes you to be an equestrienne. That is all your own and your mother's desire, my beautiful little wild thistle."

To satisfy Adam, however, a tall, rawboned niece of Nelly's had been found to travel with Neecie as her maidservant and dresser. The girl would be both protection and chaperone, and could also report back to the family if Neecie were in any need of assistance.

"You mean she is to be a spy, Papa," Neecie teased, only half-jokingly.

"Yes, I suppose she is," Adam admitted. "But she's also being sent because we love you and we want you looked after. I don't trust those circus chaperones. As for Duddie and Rolf, they are men, and you've always been able to twist men around your little finger, my sweet!"

"Men!" Benicia tossed her head. "I don't care about them. Getting married is the last thing I want right now . . . unless it's to a man in the circus, of course," she added thoughtfully.

"A man in the circus!" Adam's face grew thunderous.

Benicia seemed unaware that she had provoked his wrath. "Why, of course, Papa. A circus performer must

404

marry within the show . . . otherwise how could she travel? Perhaps . . ." Here the girl's eyes began to sparkle. "Perhaps I'll marry a geek . . . that's a snake eater in circus talk. Or a juggler. . . ."

"You will do nothing of the kind!" Adam roared. "If I hear even one more breath of such talk, I'll. . . ."

"You'll do what, Papa?" Neecie giggled. She threw her arms around her father and kissed him. "Oh, Papa, can't you take a joke? Do you think I would ever marry a man who swallowed snakes? Or ate live chickens, the way they do in the carnivals sometimes? Don't be silly! No, I don't intend to marry anyone at all."

Carisa, who had been listening to this exchange, smiled to herself wryly. She imagined that fiery, lovely Benicia would not long lack for a husband. Despite her flamboyant occupation, she was entirely too delectable and tempting. And one day some young man, stronger and bolder than the rest, would succeed where others had failed. . . .

After the circus left, it was Vicki to whom Carisa's thoughts turned. Throughout the winter, Vicki remained stubbornly at home, refusing to go to social functions or to any event where she might expect to encounter one of the Kords.

Four times Calvin Kord had called at Hearts-ease, the last time accompanied by his father. Vicki had locked herself in her bedroom, refusing to come downstairs. The marriage was over, she insisted. Over forever. It had been a terrible mistake. Let the Kords make of it what they would, she never wanted to see Calvin again.

By late November they learned that the annulment Adam had been hoping to obtain for his daughter was not going to be possible. Vicki was two months pregnant and would give birth to her child sometime in June.

Carisa felt heart-sick over this news, but Vicki had remained surprisingly calm, her oval face placid as she worked in the greenhouse with new cuttings.

"I don't mind it, Mama, really I don't." Vicki lifted a plant with deft fingers. "I want a child. This child, anyway."

"You want it?"

Vicki stared at her daughter. The pregnancy had added extra flesh to her body, rounding her cheeks and softening the texture of her skin to a rich cream. Her eyes seemed luminous, contentedly self-absorbed.

No girl who had run away from her marriage bed should look like this, Carisa told herself.

"Yes, I want it," Vicki repeated. "Not Calvin's child. But . . . a child." Her lips tightened, and she would say no more.

May. It was a perfect month, lambent with promise. The air was rich with the tang of growing things. Vicki, heavy now with her child, moved slowly about the greenhouse, or the outdoors, where she now presided over glorious tulip gardens, blazing with reds and yellows.

Old Mrs. Wiggins—at 70 she could still wield a needle with precision—had been set to sewing a wardrobe for the baby. A whole chest of drawers had been filled with fluffy embroidered and lace-encrusted robes, caps, saques and dresses. Additional items had been ordered from town. Vicki's child, whether its parents remained married or not, would surely have the most magnificent layette in New London.

Then, on the night of May 12, the event happened which was to shatter the soft spring tranquility forever.

It began with Julian. Julian, in the years since his return from the battle of Spotsylvania, had been extremely difficult to live with. He loathed his mutilation, refused to be fitted with the metal and leather hook which Duddie devised for him, and continued to behave in every way possible as if he still owned two normal hands. He rode, fiercely and desperately. He jumped his mounts over stone and wooden fences, beating at them with his quirt if they hesitated or balked.

He socialized with all his friends in the same reckless mood, visiting with them all of the gaming houses, saloons and pleasure palaces which the city of New London and surrounding area could offer. Whispers came to Carisa that Julian and his friends went often to Poll Henry's, that Poll kept a special room upstairs for Julian alone, that she gave him large sums of money.

Then, too, there was Julian's work in the shipping office. Mr. West, Adam's agent, admitted that the young man had a sharp mind, and was even good at the tedious work of doing accounts. Yet on some days, Julian did not come to work until noon. On other days, he arrived punctually, but smelled of brandy. On rarer occasions, he arrived without the liquor smell, but still acting oddly, his pupils dilated, his talk curiously garbled. On these days he botched up the accounts and had to be sent home.

"I think he's taking some of that cocaine stuff," Mr. West whispered darkly to Adam one day. "I've read about all them writers and actresses and singers that take it. They think it's going to cure all of their aches and pains. A good strong cup of coffee would be a lot better for 'em, *I* say."

It was true that Julian did complain about pain in the hand that was no longer there. "Phantom pain," their new doctor, a man named Morton, called it.

Adam scoffed at this theory. "The boy is just a spoiled young ruffian. If it were not for his handicap, and the fact that he is still my son. . . ."

"You've always hated him, haven't you, Adam?" some dark impulse made Carisa ask.

Adam was silent for a very long time. "I didn't want to," he said at last. "God help me. I didn't want to."

The day of May 12 began normally enough, with Julian leaving for the shipping office, and Matt for a session with his tutor, for he planned to enter Harvard in the fall. Vicki had gone to her greenhouse and Carisa was in her office, Adam his study. In the kitchen Nelly pressed with hot flatirons Carisa's fine lace petticoats and underwear.

A normal day.

At four o'clock Carisa laid down her pen and pushed aside the letters she had been trying to answer. She fled outdoors with a novel, and spent the rest of the afternoon reading in guilty abandon. The sun was warm on her shoulders, and she felt lazily content, almost happy. As happy, she thought with sudden perception, as she might ever be. . . .

Dinner was a quiet affair, for both Matt and Julian were absent tonight. It seemed that the two had gone off together for the evening.

"The wolf and the lamb, going out to supper together?" Adam asked dryly. "I wonder what brings this new-found friendship? As far as I can see, the only thing that Matt and Julian have ever done together is to argue."

"Perhaps it's a good sign," Carisa said.

"A sign of trouble, most likely."

Carisa felt this, too, but she tried to push away her unease and listen as Vicki and Adam talked of Adam's new shipping ventures. He was building a pair of steamers, the *Vicki* and the *Benicia,* to add to his fleet.

When dinner was over, Adam left for a meeting in town, and Vicki retired early to her bedroom, saying that she was sleepy. Carisa climbed the stairs to her office, shutting the drapes against the soft May night and trying to forget Adam's parting comment to her:

"I suppose that while I'm gone you'll go up to that office of yours and work. I think you're as addicted to that circus, Carisa, as a man is to whiskey. Your father's death taught me that. It was never him you were struggling and scheming for, was it? No, my dear, I think you did it all for yourself. Yourself and no other."

The words had stung. Hurt her badly. Addicted—selfish—scheming—How could Adam have said such things to her? Pressing her lips together, Carisa bent over her correspondence, trying to shut Adam's accusations out of her mind.

The clock in the downstairs hall struck ten, its gongs echoing. With an abrupt gesture, Carisa pushed away the letter from Germany she had been trying to decipher. How dull, she thought with sudden anger, to be stuck here with a pile of letters, while Benicia, out in the real world, toured with the real circus and did the things of which Carisa could only write.

It must be the May night, she decided quickly. It was making her restless.

She got up and began to pace about the office, an odd sort of tension beginning to tighten in her. Something, she thought uneasily. Something was about to happen. . . .

Then she heard it, almost as if it were a cue. Footsteps sounded on the stairs. Then voices came from the upstairs corridor, muffled, sharp, full of fury and hatred. Carisa froze, recognizing Matt's choked bellow. And, yes, Julian's voice as well.

The two had evidently returned from their evening together. Now they were disagreeing violently about something.

Carisa hesitated. Then, pushing open her office door, she went out into the corridor.

They were at the end of the hall by the windowseat on which Poll Henry and Julian had once sat, gazing out of the window and plotting blackmail. Now the two young men faced each other like belligerent alley curs and, it was plain, both of them had been drinking.

She hurried toward them. "Matt, Julian, what's the trouble? You're certainly being very noisy, and Vicki is trying to sleep."

"Go away, Carisa," Julian said harshly. "This is between Matt and me."

"Yes, Mama. Please go away." Perspiration shone on Matt's upper lip. He looked very young, Carisa thought. And rather shaken, as if something had happened to jar him from the protective cocoon of his youth.

"No, I won't go away," she told him sharply. "Not until you tell me what this is all about."

Julian shot a hard look at Matt, then lifted his handless arm mockingly. "There's nothing to tell, dear Carisa."

"Perhaps not. But I think that the two of you are acting like a pair of livery-stable boys who have had a falling-out."

"He's the one acting like a stable-boy!" Matt suddenly accused. His face was flushed an ugly dark red. "*He,* Mama, not me! He likes practical jokes, it seems! And so does. . . ."

"Matt . . ." Julian said it warningly.

"Oh, yes," Matt blurted. "Julian put her up to it, I'll warrant! Why else would she do it? Julian and his

409

nasty idea of a joke, all he could think of to do was . . .
was . . ."

"What?" Carisa stared at her son, apprehension pushing through her. Matt was usually a level-headed youngster, simple and uncomplicated. He loved horses, he loved his family, he loved the sea. That was Matt. She had never seen him so furious. And, yes, drunk. Evidently Julian had seen to it that his half-brother had consumed great quantities of alcohol. And what else had he introduced him to? she began to wonder with a sensation of dread.

"Mama . . . oh, I can't tell you, Mama, it's too terrible. Just too terrible." Matt reeled backward against the wall, his shoulder knocking askew one of the family portraits.

"You won't tell . . . you damned little bastard . . ." Julian suddenly leaped forward at Matt, catching the youth off balance. He attacked him with his one good hand, clawing, hitting, smacking, jabbing his knee upward into Matt's groin.

It was an action so sudden and vicious that Carisa stood stunned, unable to react.

Matt let out a cry and clutched at his belly. "Mama . . ." he groaned. "Julian took me to Poll Henry's! And he . . ."

"No! Shut up, you!"

Julian sprang again, shoving Matt, who was loose-muscled with drink, to the floor. Blood ran from the youth's nose, spurting out in dark red streaks along the carpet.

Carisa, starting forward in an attempt to pull Julian away, was roughly knocked backward. Matt let out a roar of rage. He staggered to his feet. The dull red of his face had turned to white, and his nostrils were flaring, as they had done that day long ago when he had hit the schoolmaster.

Carisa found her voice and began to shout for help. "Gaines! Jed! Nelly! Anyone, please come, please. . . ."

They were vicious in their power. Fists smacked and breath panted heavily.

"You did it," Matt kept muttering. "That girl . . ."

filthy . . . you set her to it . . . you and Poll . . . God, God, so filthy and dirty . . ."

Fists slammed into flesh, blows pounded. And now Carisa heard footsteps hurrying up the staircase. Gaines, followed by Jed, the yard boy, and Tim Kelly.

Carisa sank backward against the wall, perspiration damp on her forehead, as the servants broke up the fight and subdued the two young men. *You set her to it, you and Poll—so filthy, so dirty—*

What had happened tonight?

26

It was after midnight. Carisa and Nelly had finally bound up the numerous cuts and bruises on Matt's face, applying a piece of ice to the worst of the swellings. Julian, now in his own room, was similarly marred, but Carisa, burning with a slow, hard fury she had not known she possessed, had as yet done nothing for him.

Let him suffer, she told herself grimly. He had started this: there was no question about it. Let him now reap the consequences, whatever they might be.

She had elicited enough information from Matt to fill her belly with dread. Julian, pretending jollity and friendship, had lured Matt into going out with him and some other friends to a well-known saloon in town where Julian had procured whiskey for all of them. Afterward, Julian had suggested going to Poll Henry's.

"Mama, he said . . . he said . . ." Matt began shamefacedly. His skin was flushed as red as the quilt which covered the bed on which he lay.

"Go on, son," Carisa encouraged, although she was sure she could guess what was coming next. Why was it that men always had to indulge in these manhood rites? she wondered angrily. So sordid, ugly and dangerous.

411

"Are you sure, Mama? I . . . wouldn't want to offend. . . ."

"I'm not easily offended," Carisa told him dryly.

Matt hesitated. "Well, there was a girl there, Mama. Her name was . . . Violet, I guess, some flower name like that. She was very small and pretty, and she wore a short evening dress, pulled way down off her shoulders. . . ." Again Matt flushed. "I suppose you can guess what happened. I went upstairs with her, and . . . and later we all drank some more whiskey and then we came home."

Carisa stared at him. "But, Matt, when did you and Julian. . . ."

Matt put one finger up and gingerly felt of his right eye, which was swollen shut. "Julian had drunk more than any of us, but you would never have known it. He seemed so jolly all evening. Laughing a lot . . . making jokes . . . you almost forgot he was . . . you know, your brother. And then, when we got home, he told me."

"Told you what, Matt?"

"Why, that the girl was diseased!" Matt closed both swollen and blackened eyes and lay back on his pillow. "Mama, it seems that he and Poll decided to play a trick on me. This girl, this Violet or whatever her name was, Poll was about to fire her, because the doctor said she had a disease. So Julian paid her extra to . . . to be with me . . . to . . . give me the pox. . . ."

Syphilis. A disease known and feared by the circus folk, it could cause insanity, blindness, ugly, open sores, paralysis.

Shock caromed through her. "Oh! Oh, Matt, surely you are mistaken. Surely Julian would never. . . ."

"*Wouldn't* he, Mama? He told me he did. You and Papa have always blinded yourselves to him, haven't you? Julian is wicked. Mama! Wicked! He used to do terrible things to all of us when we were children. To Vicki, especially, because she'd never fight back. You never knew. You didn't want to know."

"Matt . . . that isn't true. . . ."

"It is true." Matt suddenly struggled forward and reached for a basin which had been sitting on the table by the bed. He began to retch into it. When at last he had finished, his face looked pasty and drained.

"A dirty disease," he muttered. "The French pox . . . the disease of kings . . . whatever they call it, I'll wager I've got it. Mama, I don't want to stay here any more. I want to go far away from here . . . never come back again. . . ."

Twenty minutes later, Adam came home. Carisa met him at the front door, and, in his study, quickly told him all that had happened.

"That devil . . . that young devil. . . ." Adam slammed his fist onto the top of the oak desk. Never had Carisa seen him so angry. Huge veins stood out on his neck and temples.

"Adam," she begged. "Please calm down. Perhaps it's not all as it seems. Perhaps . . ."

He pushed her aside. "I won't calm down, I can't. Not until I get to the bottom of this."

From somewhere she found the strength to throw herself between Adam and the door of the study.

"Adam! Don't you see? We mustn't be hasty. We must stop and get Julian's side of this first. Suppose . . . well, just suppose that Julian was only joking when he told Matt the girl was diseased? Suppose that *was* the joke? To scare Matt, to upset him. That might be something which Julian would do, his sense of humor is very strange. But surely not. . . ."

With one powerful twist of his shoulders, Adam had shoved her out of the way. "You've always stood up for that boy, haven't you? Well, you're wrong, Carisa. And this time when I find him I'm going to break his goddamn neck, a job which should have been done years ago!"

"Adam . . . Oh, Adam . . ." She raced after him.

"He's gone, Carisa. The young devil is gone."

They stood in the threshold of Julian's room, staring in at the crumpled, empty bedclothes, lit by a flickering gas lamp. The tall window near the bed was wide open, an oak tree leaning near it, and this was evidently how

Julian had made his exit. A boy's trick, Carisa thought dully. Yet Julian was not a boy any longer.

"He's r-riding, I suppose," Carisa heard herself stammer. "That's what he always does when he is upset. When he returns he'll be calmer, and in the morning you can talk with him."

"No. I want to see him now. And I'll do it before he founders another horse, which is what he's very likely to do," Adam added grimly.

"No, Adam, please. Wait until your temper has cooled. And Julian's as well. It's dark outside, it's past midnight. . . ."

Her words might as well have been mosquitoes. Adam paid them no attention, striding downstairs and toward the side door which gave access to the carriage-house and stables. Her heart beating in her throat, Carisa followed him.

Tim Kelly waited by the stable door, looking anxious, and Adam limped into the stable, ordering him to saddle Samson, a big fast gelding.

"He's gone toward the woods," Tim said. "But are you sure you want to. . . ."

"Dammit, of course I'm sure! Saddle him up and be quick about it!" Fury glowed in Adam's eyes, reminding Carisa of the look she had sometimes seen in the eyes of the Bengal tiger, Herod. Herod had long since died of old age, but sometimes Carisa dreamed of him. And tonight Adam was like that, all coil and spring and hot fury.

"Tim, get me a horse, too," she ordered. "Give me Cleo, she'll do. She's docile and won't be too skittish in the dark. And don't bother with a side-saddle, I'll ride bareback."

"No," Adam growled. "This is no night for a woman. You stay here, Carisa."

"I'm coming. And don't you dare to stop me, Adam Hartshorn."

In a few minutes they were heading down the path which led to the circus complex. It was a soft, moist, humid May night, full of the sound of croaking frogs and insects. Somewhere a dog barked insistently.

414

Adam rode fast, and Carisa had to urge her own mare on, praying that the animal would not stumble over any obstacle in the dark. Her skirts were uncomfortably bunched, and she knew that in her long, silken skirts she looked faintly ridiculous. But that didn't matter. There was no one save Adam to see. And she couldn't let Adam ride out alone. His mood was too dangerous tonight, and Julian's as well.

The moon, which had been full, went behind a barrier of silvery clouds. It grew harder to pick their way along the path, which branched out as they neared the circus quarters into a maze of bridle paths, some of which would take them into the virgin hemlock forest.

At last Adam pulled his gelding to a halt. The path had divided, and it was impossible to tell in which direction Julian had gone. The moon came momentarily from behind its cloud shield, and then disappeared again, as if mocking them.

"Adam," Carisa whispered. "Don't you think we should turn back? We'll never find him out here. This is madness."

"*You* go back if you wish. But I'm going to find him if it takes a week. Listen . . . I heard that dog bark again. Perhaps he's been following Julian. Or has seen him." Adam pointed toward the path which led into the forest. "We'll go there, Carisa. Come on!"

Inside the forest it was so dark that they had to slow to a creeping walk. Carisa's little mare tossed her head, moving restlessly. Dark bulks of trees seemed to lean in on them from every side, and Carisa had to suppress a shriek as the mare stumbled on a stone in the path, then caught herself and went on.

"Adam! Oh, surely this is insane! Julian can't be here. And even if he is, what good will it do to talk with him? Tonight, when you are both so angry?"

Adam was not even listening. Grimly they pushed on. The moon reemerged, floating clear and mottled-pale above them, illuminating the trail.

Carisa caught her breath. "There," she whispered. "Adam! Ahead there, just at the bend in the trail! Isn't . . . isn't that another horse?"

Adam sucked in a quick breath. He had seen the dark outline of horse and rider at the same time she did. Now he dug his heels into the gelding's sides.

"Julian! Stop, Julian, you damned young devil. . . ."

The shadow which had been the other horse suddenly melted into the darkness of the surrounding trees. Adam lunged ahead.

"Papa! Go home, Papa! Go home and leave me alone!"

"No, I won't! I'm coming, damn you, and when I do. . . ."

"Papa, I never meant. . . ."

There was the sound of crashing as Julian attempted to turn his mount off the trail and into the shelter of the underbrush. And then a sudden, louder crash and the agonized squealing of a horse.

Later Carisa's mind would mercifully blur the memory of the gasping, ugly labor of getting Julian back to the house. He had been crushed beneath the weight of his horse, the slim body smashed and broken. Blood seeped from the well-tailored evening suit Julian wore, turning the black fabric muddy. The horse, a valuable jumper, had had to be shot.

But Julian was still alive. Adam dispatched Tim Kelly for the doctor, and then he and Carisa began the work of trying to staunch the flow of blood, knowing all the while that their efforts were useless. Julian lay semi-conscious, tossing his head from side to side. His head was the only part of his body that did move, Carisa noted with a lurch of fear.

She had a sudden, wild memory of the boy Julian had used to be. Round-faced, angelic, with a mass of honey-colored curls. But grimly she forced the image back. She must not think of that long-ago boy now. In his place was this dying man with a tallow-yellow, perspiring face, muttering incoherently.

Adam, too, looked ashen.

"I killed him," he kept mumbling. "I killed him, Carisa."

"No, Adam. It wasn't your fault . . . ."

"It *was* my fault. I wanted to kill him, Carisa. I lusted for his blood."

"Poll!" Julian cried out in a sudden, choked voice. "Poll!"

Later, after Dr. Morton had arrived, Julian's delirium grew worse. He began to mutter to himself, to cry out snatches of words and phrases.

"Poll! Poll!" A pause. "No . . . Weston, Barriden . . . no . . . stop it stop it stop it you're hurting, you're . . . Oh, God, oh, God, don't . . . I'll give in . . . I'm an ugly dong-sucker . . . *God.* . . ." A sudden change of tone. Julian's voice abruptly became soft, childish. "Papa, Papa, give me some candy. I want some candy, I tell you . . . And I want you to go riding with me. Not with Matt, with *me,* Papa! Me! Why won't you look at me, Papa?"

Adam listened to all of this, his face an expressionless mask.

"He is in very bad shape," Dr. Morton said at last, calling Carisa and Adam into the hallway. "He has a spinal cord injury and has lost much blood. He also has a punctured lung and broken ribs . . . I don't hold out much hope for him."

"But of course he will live!" Adam burst out. "He survived the War, I tell you. He's as strong as a horse. And he's young, he. . . ."

Dr. Morton looked at him with pity. "I beg to differ, but he's not strong at all. And he doesn't seem to have much will to live. By the looks of him, he's been battered by brawling, and debilitated by alcohol and perhaps worse. Have you any idea of how thin he really is? But I'll do the best I can for him."

"Doctor . . ." Adam's eyes were glittering. "Doctor . . ."

"Yes?"

"Could I speak with him? Just for a moment?"

"He is incoherent and he's not going to make any sense. I think he should save whatever strength he has for surviving. *If* he survives. And again, I must repeat, the chances are not good."

For long hours, during which Julian sank in and out

417

of consciousness, Carisa and Adam sat by his bed. Adam's face was savage, and he seemed so engrossed in his own thoughts that Carisa dared not speak to him.

At dawn Nelly came upstairs and insisted on taking a turn with Julian while Adam and Carisa ate some breakfast.

"I'm not hungry," Carisa said dully.

"Oh, but you must eat something or you'll faint dead away," Nelly urged. "And Mr. Hartshorn, he looks worse than you do."

"Very well."

"Five minutes," Adam muttered. "That's all I'll take."

But it was less than five minutes later that Nelly came stumbling and weeping down to the dining room, where Adam and Carisa had not even been served yet.

"He's gone!" she sobbed. "Oh, Miss Carisa, he's gone. He looked right at me, he did, and he said the strangest thing. *'Matt,'* he said. *'Papa went riding with Matt and not with me.'*" The servant shook her head. "Oh, Miss Carisa, those were his last words. And I wonder what they meant?"

Adam opened his mouth to speak, and then closed it. His face had gone ashen.

He stumbled forward, out of the dining room and toward the stairs. When Carisa followed him she saw that he had gone to Julian's room. He was kneeling beside the bed, looking down at the face of his son.

The barrier of trees had grown thicker about Poll Henry's house, the forsythia hedge larger and more imposing. In the bright light of early afternoon, the painted bricks looked pale and secretive. Carisa wished that she hadn't come.

As if celebrating some cosmic prank, Julian had died without revealing the full extent of his "joke" on Matt. And Adam, after coping with the horrors of making funeral arrangements for Julian, had finally collapsed gray-faced into a chair.

"I'll mix you a soothing draught," Carisa told him.

"Laudanum, do you mean? God, no, I don't want anything. Tell Tim to harness the surrey. I'm going out."

"Oh, no, you won't," she said, for she knew what he meant. "You'll do no such thing."

"Stand aside, Carisa. I've got to talk to that woman. I must find out about Matt."

"I'll do it," she insisted firmly. "Do you think that she would tell you? She would just laugh in your face. But perhaps she will tell me, another woman."

But now, as the surrey swayed up toward Poll's front door, where a worn carriage block awaited, Carisa's optimism began to seep away. She thought of the last time she had been in this house and shivered violently.

Five minutes later Carisa had an odd, jolting sense of *déjà vu* as Poll Henry swept down the stairs wearing a black dressing gown trimmed with feathers and jet beads sewn on its flounces in an elaborate pattern. As Poll moved, the beads caught the light.

Carisa could not take her eyes from this woman who had, long ago, been her servant. No longer, it was clear, was Poll anyone's servant, nor would she ever be again. Little dry wrinkles creased the corners of her eyes and framed her mouth. Her eyes were hard.

"Well, my maid tells me that the great Mrs. Carisa Hartshorn is here to see the likes of me."

"I . . . I had to talk to you."

"Oh?"

But before Carisa could go on, there were the sounds of running footsteps in the upper corridor of the house, and then the high, laughing voice of a child. A woman shushed him lazily.

"Is there somewhere we could speak privately?" Carisa asked. "There is something I have to ask you . . . and something I must tell you."

Poll eyed her suspiciously. "What? What have you got to tell me?"

But she led Carisa to a door at the rear of the square foyer, and then down a short corridor. At the back of the house was a small pantry which Poll evidently used as her office, for most of its space was filled with a huge, pigeon-hole desk stuffed haphazardly with papers.

419

The reek of Poll's musky perfume was strong in the air, along with the fainter odor of cigarette smoke. A child's lead toy soldier lay on the floor, and Poll gave it a kick.

"The girl hasn't cleaned in here yet," she explained. "This is where I do my accounts and such. I'll bet that you didn't know a house like mine has to keep accounts, eh?" She gave a short, dry laugh. "Oh, yes, we've got household accounts and liquor bills just like the quality . . . and a lot of other records to keep, too."

"Records about the sickness or health of your employees?" Carisa heard herself ask.

Poll narrowed her eyes and sat down at the desk. "All right, Mrs. Hartshorn. Speak your piece, whatever it is, and get out of here. I've got a lot of work to do this afternoon before the night crowd gets here. We've got a special coming this afternoon. And my kid, he wants some time from me, too."

"You . . . have a child?"

"Why not?" The black jet beads winked as Poll shrugged. "Usually we ship out the girls that are carrying brats, but this kid is special. I wanted him, God knows why."

Carisa's eyes, which had been roving restlessly over the desk, had suddenly stopped at a small charcoal portrait of a child. A handsome boy he was, or at least the artist had sketched him so, with his round cheeks, full, little mouth and head of curly hair.

Exactly like Julian's hair, Carisa found herself thinking in dismay. And the set of his mouth, the merry yet willful look of it. . . .

She wrenched her thoughts away from the picture.

"It's about my son, Matt, that I've come. It seems that my step-son Julian has played a prank on Matt. He brought Matt here and . . . and initiated him with one of your employees. Later he told Matt that the girl was diseased."

Poll leaned back in her velvet upholstered desk chair and regarded Carisa from slitted eyes. Her mouth twitched.

420

"Well?" Carisa asked nervously. "Is it true or not? That the girl was diseased, I mean?"

Poll began to laugh. "Why don't you ask Julian? How would I know which girl it was? Do you think I spend all of my time seeing which girl goes with which customer? I don't, I haven't time, I've a business to run." Her laughter rang out in heavy, malicious peals. "Julian could tell you what you want to know."

"I don't think so."

"And why shouldn't he?" The voice was honeyed, malefic. "Julian is perfectly at home here, he knows the girls as well as I do." Poll held up a heavily be-ringed hand and began to count off on her fingers. "Let's see. Did the boy go with Annie? No, not Annie, not that night, for Annie had a steady that night, a man who asked for her alone. Then perhaps Gayla? Gayla especially enjoys the young ones, she likes breaking them in. But Gayla . . ."

"I think you know which girl it was, Mrs. Henry."

"Oh, ho. So the woman has a back-bone. Are you threatening me, Miss Circus Tramp? You? A little sawdust cunt who has jumped herself up to better things?"

As Carisa stiffened, Poll Henry rose from her chair, the black silk quivering.

"And let me tell you one more thing, Mrs. Circus Owner. My name isn't *Mrs.* Henry . . . it's Miss. Do you hear? I've never been married, and I don't hide be-hind a married name. I am what I am, and those who don't like it don't have to come here."

Carisa did not know what to reply. "I just wanted to know whether the girl was . . . is clean," she blurted out. "If she had a sickness my son wants to know so he can seek medical treatment. Surely . . . oh, surely you would be kind enough to tell me which girl he went with. He said she had a flower name. Violet, he said. Do you have a girl here by that name?"

Poll took two quick steps across the thick Bokhara rug, scattered with cigarette ashes, which carpeted the room. She picked up the small, framed portrait of the child and stood balancing it in her hands.

"Violet?"

"You must have a girl by that name! Matt specifically mentioned her. He said . . ."

Poll set the portrait down with a heavy click. She opened the front center drawer of the desk and pawed among its contents. At last she drew out a wooden card file. With long, oval fingernails, she flipped through the cards.

"Rose . . . Daisy . . . hmmm . . . yes, Violet. Violet left my employ just this morning, as it turns out."

"This morning!" Then Poll had known about Violet all along, Carisa thought angrily. She had only been playing with her, as a barnyard cat toys with a sparrow.

"That's right, she left on the train early this morning. I fired her."

"For what?"

Poll was silent. She closed the card box with a snap and shoved it back into the drawer.

"For two things," she said at last. "One, for insubordination. She was threatening to go to the Police Captain on me, and of course I can't afford that kind of thing. And the other reason. . . ."

"Yes? Yes?"

"The other reason was that she was sick. Ill, you know? These girls, they lead a dirty life sometimes. . . ." Poll's eyes sparkled with malice.

Carisa felt her hands clutching the carved back of a mahogany chair which stood against the wall. Its wood seemed to cut into her flesh.

"You're . . . you're joking, aren't you?" she whispered. "This is not a jest, Miss Henry. This is a young man's life we are talking about. A decent young man, who will someday want to marry and start a family . . ."

"He should have thought of that, then, before he came here."

Poll rose from her chair, standing straight and thin and imperious. Her flat, dark eyes challenged. "Well, Mrs. Adam Hartshorn? Had enough? Want to go home now? You found out what you came here to learn, and now you can go home and tell that fine big son of yours that he's got the pox. . . ."

Carisa's hand whipped out and slapped Poll Henry across the face.

Poll staggered backward under the force of the blow, her skin reddened where Carisa's palm had struck her. Carisa regarded her in horror. She had not known she was going to slap Poll; it was as if her hand had darted out of its own volition.

"Damn you! Damn you circus harlot!"

"And damn you," Carisa heard herself cry. "Poll Henry, why couldn't you have left my family alone?"

"I had a right. . . ."

"What right? What right did you ever have? But this time you went too far with your maliciousness. This time God, or fate, or whatever, has seen fit to punish you."

There was a dulled, obstinate look in Poll's eyes like an animal which has been clubbed. "Punish me? What do you mean?"

"I mean that Julian is dead," Carisa said cruelly. "He was thrown from his horse and crushed. He died this morning. His father and I were with him."

"No! It's a lie!" Poll's face had gone the sickly color of separated milk.

"On the contrary, it isn't a lie at all. His funeral will be in two days. And you contributed to his death, you and that vicious prank of yours. You helped to kill him."

As if by some irony, Julian's funeral took place on one of the loveliest and most lissom days of May. The sky was a pure, deep bowl of blue, the air full of the freshness of green growing things and the tang of the sea.

The funeral was to be a large one, for the Hartshorns had many connections in New London, and Julian himself had had a number of acquaintances among the wild and rakish young men of the town.

But those representing their own immediate family were few in number. Benicia had wired her apologies: the Phillips Circus had just reached Georgetown and they were playing to sellout crowds, she did not feel that she could come home. As for Matt, he had left late in the day after Carisa had returned home from Poll Henry's. He planned to ship out as a third mate on the *Winthrop,* a cargo vessel bound for the Indian Ocean. Nothing Adam or Carisa could say would dissuade him, not even Carisa's suggestion that he wait and see Dr. Morton.

"No, Mama, I can't wait, I won't. The *Winthrop* sails on the tide and I want to be aboard her. Besides, what can a doctor do? Even I know it's too soon to tell if I have the pox."

"But, Matt, couldn't you wait at least until after the funeral?"

"Why should I?" Matt made a contemptuous gesture. "What did Julian ever do for me but try to give me the pox?"

"Matt! I told you about the spitefulness of that woman. I think she would have said anything just to hurt us. Her enmity goes back many years, Matt. Your father has hired a detective agency to try to trace that girl, that Violet. . . ."

"He won't find anything. Girls like that, Mama, they probably change their names in every new city."

Carisa stared at him. Her cheerful, innocent boy, she thought despairingly. How quickly he had grown up. And if he really did have syphilis—oh, but she wouldn't think of that. She refused to do so. It simply was not true. Poll and Julian had lied, of course. Had wished to hurt and wound. And had succeeded, well beyond their imaginings.

"I should never have gone to that house," she heard Matt mutter. "And now all I want to do is to get away from here, forget I ever did it. Say good-bye to Vicki for me, Mama. I'll write, when I get to a port where I can, and maybe you can let me know about Vicki's baby, whether she had a boy or a girl."

Suddenly Matt was her own son again, and Carisa hugged him to her, trying to conceal her own tears. "Matt," she whispered. "Oh, Matt, I'm so sorry. . . ."

"Don't be, Mama." He pushed her away. "This isn't your fault. And I'll be back here to see you, in a year or two, whenever I can. Take care of the circus for me,

424

will you? And tell Duddie good-bye. Tell him I'll bring him some ivory from China . . . a carved elephant. He can pull that out of his pocket whenever he wishes to show the children a trick."

So, with a forced smile and a promise, Matt was gone.

Now Carisa stood beside Adam at the grave site, dry-eyed, the words of the burial service only a distant buzz in her ears. Beside her Adam stood frozen, his eyes focused on a distant small cloud which floated, like a fluff of Persian wool, in the sky. Vicki, large with her pregnancy and draped in a concealing cloak, stood beside her father, gazing stonily down at the black-draped casket.

Why, she hates him, Carisa thought suddenly. She glanced to her left, where Nelly stood with Gaines, her face expressionless.

Benicia had not come to the funeral at all. Matt had run away.

Was there no one who would weep for Julian?

And then, slowly, she realized that there was. The sound of muffled sobbing came from somewhere at the back of the large, silent crowd which had gathered to attend the funeral.

Carisa could not help turning to see who it was. And just then the crowd shifted and she glimpsed a woman, swathed in black, wearing a black bonnet and veil. Beside her, clutching at her hand and looking about him with wide, frightened eyes, was a little boy.

Carisa caught her breath, a wild, irrational anger swirling through her. Poll Henry! How dare she come here so boldly?

The service was coming to a close, and people were beginning to shift their feet and make the little movements which were preparatory to leaving. In a moment, Carisa knew, they would lower the casket into its gaping hole and begin to throw the first shovels of dirt upon it. She swallowed hard, choking back nausea.

Then, before she had realized she was going to do so, she found that she had turned and was pushing her way back through the crowd.

"Carisa!" Adam's whisper was angry. "Carisa, where are you going? You can't leave yet, you little fool. . . ."

Blindly, she stumbled on. She darted between two startled women, both of whom she knew, although she could not remember their names today. Faces turned to stare at her and she heard the whisper of voices.

Anger and grief hummed inside her head like a violin string drawn too tight.

But when she got to the place where she had seen the woman in black, she was gone and so was the boy. There was only a toy lead soldier, dropped in the trampled grass as if to mock her.

27

At the end of June and nearly two weeks late, Vicki gave birth to a baby girl. Her labor was long, nearly forty-eight hours, but at last the child was born, a six-pound infant with a full head of pale blonde hair.

The baby screamed furiously at the indignity of being born. Vicki lay in her bed, pale and exhausted. Her hair hung in damp strings on her pillow, and dark smudges discolored the skin beneath her eyes. Yet her eyes held an exultant look.

Carisa and Nelly washed the infant and brought it to Vicki, swaddled in clean linen.

"She's beautiful!" Vicki breathed. She caught her breath. "And crying so loudly, Mama, you would think she hated to be born!"

"And maybe she did," Nelly put in. "Imagine, all that messiness, and being crushed in a dark place and pushed around and squeezed, and all."

Vicki reached out her arms to take the infant. "Well, it's over for her now, thank heavens. And, Mama, I want to see her. All of her. I want to strip off those cloths so I can be sure she is all right."

Carisa hid a smile, and did as her daughter asked.

For long moments Vicki marveled over her child, counting the minute toes and small fingers, inspecting the little ears and nose and genitals. At last she covered the baby and sighed.

"I want him to see her, too, Mama. I think he deserves to."

"Who, dear? Do you mean Calvin?"

Vicki made a weak gesture and sank back into her pillows as if all of her strength was gone. "No, Mama. Not Calvin. I mean Tim."

"Tim?"

"Tim Kelly, Mama. Whom did you think I meant? He is the father of my baby. Surely you, of all people, must have guessed that. I want him to see his daughter, how beautiful she is."

"But Vicki . . ."

Carisa stopped. She caught her own breath, remembering Tim's strong, freckled face, those steady eyes and firm chin. Tim Kelly. She remembered the proud way Vicki had carried herself these past months, her dreamy contentment.

Tim Kelly! A stable-man.

But when, she wondered, could it have happened?

Then she remembered. The night of the wedding, when Vicki had arrived home at dawn, looking at once frightened and exalted. The skirt of her gown had been covered with leaves and dirt. Dirt which might have come from the greenhouse.

Yes, Carisa thought. Of course. Somehow Tim had found her, somehow it had happened.

"Mama . . . Mama, don't look at me like that. Mama, if you knew Tim as I do, you would understand. He's not like Calvin. He's gentle, he's warm and kind. He loves me, he would never hurt me. . . ."

Carisa held herself very still. She could not speak. A stabbing, unfamiliar ache seemed to pierce her chest. Adam, holding her with fierce tender joy, the two of them soaring together, beyond daily concerns or anything worldly. . . .

"Mama," she heard Vicki whisper in that exhausted, drained voice. "I know it was wrong, at least you and

Papa might think it was. But Tim and I don't. We love each other, Mama. We want to be married. We will be married as soon as we can." She paused. "It doesn't matter that Tim is only a . . . that he works in the stables. I don't care about that. I'll go to work, too. I'll go with him anywhere. We'll start a plant nursery together. We'll raise bulbs and flowers. . . ."

Carisa could not stop the tears that sprang to her eyes. "Darling . . . Darling, I understand. And I'm so happy for you, happier than you'll ever know. But . . . the problems, all the problems! You know, don't you, just how angry your father is going to be?"

"As he was at Neecie?" Vicki sighed. "I don't care about that, Mama."

"And the Kords . . . they'll be furious."

"I suppose they will be. But they don't seem to matter to me any more. It's Tim, Mama. Tim who is real to me."

Thoughtfully, Carisa went downstairs. She found Adam in his study, bent over a stack of papers on his desk, scowling at them. He looked up as she entered.

"Vicki is fine," she told him. "The baby was a girl, and she is fine, too." She hesitated. "Adam. . . ."

"Yes, Carisa? What is it that you wish to tell me?"

She ran her tongue over suddenly dry lips. "It's Vicki," she said at last.

"And Tim Kelly?" Adam's expression was unreadable.

"Why . . ." She stared at him. "Why, yes. It is Tim. He is the father of her baby, Adam. She told me so herself, just now. She says she loves him and wants to marry him."

Adam, with slow, deliberate care, put his pen back into its holder. "Does she, Carisa?"

"Adam! Adam Hartshorn! You knew all about this, didn't you? You don't seem surprised!"

"I'm not. I've known of this for weeks. I'm amazed that you haven't guessed, Carisa."

"You've known this all along . . . then why didn't you tell me?"

428

"Tim asked me to keep it secret until they had finished making their plans. He does not want any more gossip than necessary. I'm afraid that with the divorce, there will be more than enough talk anyway."

"But . . ."

"But what, Carisa? You thought I would be furious. Well, for a time I was. I was ready to horse-whip that young man. It was only the fear of doing murder that held me back, I'll confess it. But then, after Julian. . . ."

A grim look came into Adam's eyes. "After Julian died, I began to think. A girl who would flee home from the marriage-bed . . . she would be like a cripple, Carisa. A girl who could never become a woman, a cripple in a different way than Julian was." Adam's voice stopped, painfully. "But something happened to change that in our Vicki. Tim. He changed her. And perhaps we must accept it. And be thankful for it."

Carisa moistened her lips. She stared at this husband with whom she had lived all these years and had thought she knew. "But, Adam, Tim is a stable-man, a servant in our employ."

"And you were in the circus, as I recall," Adam said dryly. "Tim has been a good worker, don't you think? He is a good man. Better than my own son, Julian. Better, too, than that sniveling Calvin Kord who came here with his father and wept, and would not even fight like a man to get his wife back."

She would never understand Adam, she thought later, as she helped Nelly to bathe the baby before it was brought to Vicki for its feeding. What a complicated man he was, with his quick enthusiasms, his equally quick angers, his prejudices and generosities, his tenderness and obstinacy, his. . . .

She stopped, blinking her eyes to rid them of sudden moisture. His secret mind, she thought miserably. The privacy of him, the thoughts which he shared with no one, and especially not with his wife. Were all men like that? All *people*? How much did any married couple ever really share with each other?

Adam, she thought dully. *I love you. I always have. And you will never quite believe it, will you?*

429

She bent her head, applying her attention to the small, wriggling infant with her bright eyes which gazed at her grandmother as alertly as a young bird.

Later that day, Vicki announced that the name of the baby would be Timothea, Thea for short.

Thea, Carisa remembered with a faint rising of the hairs on her neck, had been the name of the baby in her dream.

England. The country of her birth, of rolling, sheep-cropped hills, of dusty lanes bordered by wild hedgerows. Childhood memories: of a pet rabbit, of bathing in a swift-running little creek, of two gypsy women dancing in a village street.

Six months later, Carisa stood with Duddie on the Isle of Wight, off the southern coast of England, and thought of these things, and of Papa's dreams.

"Well, we're here," Duddie said. "How many years have you wished for this, Carisa? And now it's all coming true. When I first knew him, your father used to say that it would be a fine day if he ever played before the Queen . . . the young Queen she was, then, soft and pretty and shy. Now she's an old woman, but she's always loved the circus, Carisa, and she's seen the best. Van Amburgh, Seth Howes and Joseph Cushing, 'Lord' George Sanger. Now it's our turn."

"Yes." Carisa tried to look pleased. She drew her wool mantle more tightly about her shoulders against the chilly, mid-December breeze. How many times, she wondered dully, had John Phillips dreamed aloud of playing before the Queen? And yet they had never even come near her. It had always been the tiny stone villages in the Cotswolds, or the Mendip Hills, the little seaside villages of Cornwall.

"I wonder what it is she plans to give you?" Duddie's voice went on. "She's always awarded circus men with a jeweled tie-pin, but, of course, a woman would require something else, something more feminine. . . ."

As Duddie speculated, Carisa bit down on her lower lip until pain coursed through it. *A dream come true,*

430

she thought bitterly. Then why was it that the dream tasted so gritty, ashes in her mouth?

The Isle of Wight was a curiously wild and lovely place, and ordinarily Carisa would have reveled in its beauty remembering a time long years ago when the small caravan had been stranded here by a storm. There were great stretches of moorland and downs, brooded over by Carisbrooke Castle, an old Roman fortress where Charles I had once been held prisoner. There were spectacular shores and chalk cliffs: the Undercliff, Blackgang Chine, Freshwater Bay.

And, of course, Osborne House, the Queen's winter retreat, reigning over the island in Florentine splendor. Built to resemble an Italian palazzo, Osborne House had been considered by many to be a wicked extravagance. It was made of pale stone, massive, sprawling, ornate. It had what seemed to be miles of stone railings, and florid statues set in alcoves. There were two square towers with additional wings, it seemed, almost at random.

And all of this, Carisa thought dully, for one aging and widowed Queen, who had never fully recovered from the death of her consort, Prince Albert, and who still dressed in mourning after twelve years.

Devoutly, she hoped that the Phillips Circus might do something to lighten the burden of the Queen's grief.

If there were only something she could do to make her own heart light. . . .

Duddie's words seemed to come from very far away. "Yes," he was saying. "In a way, at least, your father's dream has come true . . . or will soon. The Phillips Circus, his own daughter. . . ."

"Oh, don't let's pretend," she said sharply. "Papa never wanted *my* dream . . . he wanted his own. And even if he were alive today, he would never have come here to be with us . . . not if Queen Victoria herself were to write him a letter and invite him to Osborne House for tea. No, he would have stayed at home and read about it in the papers, then clipped it all for his scrap box."

The little clown gave her a penetrating look. "I've never seen you like this, Carisa. So very bitter."

"No, Duddie. I don't think I'm bitter, not exactly. Just tired. And, oh, I don't know. I can't explain. Perhaps it's just that I'm growing old."

"Old? You? I've never seen you more beautiful, and I think that in the last few months your energy has trebled. It isn't healthy, my girl, to be as intense as you've been recently. To bury yourself in the circus as if it were your salvation. Which it isn't, you know. And can't ever be."

Carisa nodded. She gazed unseeingly at the scene which surrounded them——the rows of side-show tents with their big canvas banners, the "big top" flying with flags and gala bunting, in honor of the occasion. The hubbub of wagons, horses and performers lining up for the parade which was to begin in a few moments. Hundreds of men and animals, all of them paid and fed by her. . . .

A bugle sounded, a last-minute call to those performers and workers who were dallying elsewhere.

"I'd better go," Duddie said quickly. "Rolf may lose his temper if he doesn't see me in my place. He's grown erratic lately, Carisa . . . his temper has not always been pleasant."

Dully, Carisa watched him go. How many years? she asked herself. How many years had she longed for this moment? Longed for today, and even planned it, down to the last detail. The elephants, the gorgeous parade wagons, many of them made by Fielding Brothers in New York, all of them glittering in their splendor of carving, ornamental mirrors, and gold leaf. The noise, the crowds, the cheers, the sweetness of recognition.

And now that the dream was finally here, it meant little.

An elephant trumpeted, followed by another, and a tiger roared as if in response. She could hear Rolf, shouting orders through a megaphone, his voice harsh as he marshaled all of them, hundreds of horses and men, dozens of wagons, thousands of dollars worth of costumes and equipment, into parade order.

Carisa began to pace about. The December wind picked up the folds of her severely tailored walking skirt and pushed it against her legs. It was chilly, but it was not a strong wind, and should pose no problem for the circus, she assured herself automatically.

The parade—more than one solid mile of it— would be perfect. The performance, to follow in two hours, would be equally perfect. And the Queen would surely be pleased.

Most of the circus employees had viewed this European trip as an unexpected bonanza—for otherwise they would have spent the winter loafing, until it was time to sign up for another season. And this, the winter of 1873, was an especially good winter to have work. In September the respected banking firm of Jay Cooke and Company had gone bankrupt, ushering in what some already called the "Panic of '73." Thousands of businesses had folded. Tens of thousands of people were jobless and homeless. Many pitiable folk even had to sleep in the streets.

"Perhaps by the time we return home the panic will be over," Carisa had remarked hopefully to Adam shortly before their departure.

"Don't be foolish, Carisa. High finances are a precarious thing. And monetary crises are not as easily mended as your circus wagons."

She had flushed; was he belittling her? There was such a distance between them these days. It had seemed to begin with Julian's death, and the gulf grew wider every day.

"Well, at least the depression shouldn't affect us very much," she had remarked quickly. "People will always need entertainment, to forget their worries for a few hours. They'll dig and scrape for their last pennies, just to come and laugh and enjoy themselves."

"And when their last penny is gone?"

"Their last pennies won't be gone. The panic isn't going to last forever . . . and I refuse to think that it will. The Phillips Circus is the best it's ever been, the biggest and strongest. Nothing can touch us now . . . not even a panic!"

433

So, she had put the financial crisis out of her mind, and concentrated on her plans for bringing the circus abroad.

"You won't care if I don't go with you," Adam had said without expression one morning, just as she was beginning to plan that he *would* go. "I'm working on plans for my two new steamers . . . ugly, squat things they are, but I believe the future lies with them. You won't notice if I'm not there, will you, Carisa? You and that circus . . . it's your lifeblood, isn't it? If it were to disappear, I think you'd evaporate, too, like a cloud of sea-mist."

"Don't be silly, Adam. Please, I want you to come. I'm planning that you will. Once we're in England, we can enjoy London, take some side-trips, have a vacation. . . ."

"Vacation? I am never going to take another vacation surrounded by clowns and calliopes," Adam had said firmly. "No, my dear. This time I will stay and you will go. You can gloat over your fabulous show in privacy."

"Gloat! I don't gloat! I've never done such a thing! I . . ."

"You do, Carisa, your face goes all soft and dreamy. Most women, when their face gets that tantalizing expression, are dreaming of a man. You? You dream of gate receipts and lithographed posters, and aerialists and clowns and jugglers. . . ."

Now, with a sudden, violent gesture, Carisa pushed away the sound of Adam's voice, so full of bitterness. The wagons, she saw, were ready. Rolf waved his megaphone at the driver of the first one, a tableaux wagon with its sides elaborately carved in scenes depicting ancient Egypt. Four lady aerialists, dressed as Cleopatra and her attendants, graced this wagon. Cleopatra, young and dark-haired, smiled as Rolf, clad as their harem servant, swung himself aboard. He waved at the operator of the calliope.

The operator slammed his fingers down on the keys for the first ear-shattering notes. A dream, Carisa thought wildly. A dream was about to begin to come true.

434

Why couldn't she let her heart lighten with the absurd rollicking music of the calliope?

The truth of it was that she was lonely. Lonely as she had never been in all the years of her marriage. In all her fantasies of playing before Queen Victoria, somehow there had always been her family. Adam, at her side, to marvel and admire. The children—Matt, Vicki, Neecie, Julian—to gaze goggle-eyed at clowns and elephants, somehow always ten years old.

And Nelly, too, bubbling over with enthusiasm, wanting to see everything, oohing and ahing and jumping up and down.

All of them to see her triumph. Happy because she was happy, glorying in her success.

It hadn't happened that way. She had come here to England—save for the show itself, and Neecie, of course—alone.

Adam had resisted her persuasions to the end. He had grown increasingly absorbed in his shipping, spending long hours on the waterfront in his office there, or in his study with his agent.

"Steam, Carisa; in a generation or two, it will supersede sail. The *Vicki* and the *Benicia* will be the nucleus of my new fleet. New London's whaling business may be dying, but the seaport itself does not have to."

"But Adam," she had faltered. "You work so hard, so many hours. . . ."

He had scowled at her. "I work no harder than you do. Often these days I think of my ancestor, the first Adam Hartshorn. The sea, Carisa. We Hartshorns have always been entangled in her, for better or for evil. It can't change now."

She had stared at him, her heart sinking. "You don't *want* to come to England with me, do you, Adam? That's really what you're saying to me, isn't it?"

He had hesitated, his amber eyes gleaming at her as if fires had been banked in their depths. "Perhaps I don't, Carisa. Perhaps I don't."

Vicki had not come either. She said she did not wish to subject the baby, Thea, who was delicate, to the rigors of a winter Atlantic crossing. Besides, there were problems with the divorce she was seeking from Calvin.

"How can I leave, Mama, in the midst of all this?" she had pleaded to her mother. "Calvin is being so stubborn . . . there are lawyers and arguing and ill feelings. Mama, I love Tim, I want to marry him, and if Calvin won't step aside, I—I'll do something anyway. I'll run away with Tim and live with him, I swear I will, Mama!"

And she would, Carisa knew, gazing at her daughter with astonishment. Where had the shy little girl gone? The fearful little girl who fled to the attic or the greenhouse, who whimpered with fear whenever Julian teased her?

"Mama?" Vicki was asking. "You don't hate me, do you? For . . . for being so very troublesome? *You* learned to defy gossip when you were young . . . Nelly has told me all about it. You knew what you wanted and you went after it."

"Yes," Carisa said. "But I . . ." She stopped, unable to explain. *Because I took what I wanted, I was denied what it turned out I really wanted. And so I got nothing.* How could she ever tell Vicki that?

"I want to be like you are, Mama. As strong as you are. And as determined."

For this, Carisa could find no reply.

Matt, of course, could not accompany them to England either, for he was far off on his travels now. He had sent them a hastily penciled letter from faraway Batavia, in the Dutch Indies. *I am learning much,* he wrote. *Although I grow very tired of the monotony of the ship's diet, I do enjoy putting in at strange ports, seeing all of the bright colors and strange people and odd foods. Captain Walker says I have real talent for navigating and has taken pains to teach me all he can.*

No mention of his health. Carisa read the letter with a sinking heart. Why couldn't he have said something? she wondered angrily. Something, at least, to ease their minds?

But he was young, she reminded herself at last. And

syphilis was a disease upon which the young did not like to spend thoughts.

Even Nelly had been unable to accompany her. At the last minute Nelly had found herself pregnant again, and reluctantly Carisa had insisted that she remain behind.

"You've had difficult pregnancies and two miscarriages. I have no intention, Nelly, of having you lose your baby on my account," she told the maidservant.

"Oh, but Miss Carisa . . ." Nelly looked at once relieved and guilty. "You know I would go if. . . ."

"Of course you would. Instead, why don't I bring Rosie with me? She's a niece of yours, and surely she'll do a good job. And as long as you have a continuing crop of nieces . . ." Here Carisa tried to force a smile, for the loss of Nelly had been a real blow. "Why, I'm sure I'll get along very well."

The voyage to England had been smooth enough, marred by only one storm which had tossed the ship about, causing nearly all of the passengers to become seasick, and injuring four horses, which had been thrown against stanchions in the quarters provided for them. But no other animals had been hurt, and once the sea calmed, Carisa's nausea, along with everyone else's, abated.

The ship was large, clean, and run with efficiency by Captain Driesbach. Carisa traveled first class, along with Rolf, Duddie, Benicia, and the other star-billed performers. They made a colorful group in the dining salon, and attracted considerable attention.

Carisa felt oddly removed from the chatter and laughter of the other passengers. She spent much of her time pacing the deck in the chilly sea wind, defiantly aware that she made a solitary and unapproachable figure. She felt as if there were an empty, hollow void at the center of her, deeper than loneliness and worse than grief. Near midnight of the fourth day of the voyage, she actually peered over the railing at the oily, rushing water and thought about jumping.

Who would miss her? she wondered dully. They all had their lives without her, even Adam. As for the Phillips Circus, even that functioned without her. And

Rolf was standing ready to snatch the reins of that away from her . . . he would be glad to assume the show as his own.

I won't do it today, the thought came in her at last. *Not now, not yet. But sometime, perhaps sometime. . . .*

It was the closest she had ever come to suicide.

On the seventh day, after the storm had blown over, Carisa was walking on deck when she was approached by a tall, sandy-haired man with impossibly good-looking features, marred by a broken nose. That nose, bumpy and pugnacious, gave him a rakish attractiveness and saved him from looking like an effete actor.

"Mrs. Hartshorn, you have been as elusive as a wraith," he said to her. He bowed slightly and gave her a long, steady look. "I have said hello to you on the deck at least four times, and each time you have snubbed me roundly."

"Snubbed you?"

"Yes, snubbed." He was grinning. "It's a fine way to treat a fellow passenger, especially when we have been formally introduced. But I suppose you've forgotten that, too."

She flushed painfully. "I'm sorry . . . I really don't remember . . . I guess I've been preoccupied. . . ."

Smiling, ignoring her embarrassment, he told her that he was Justin Whitfield, an artist for *Harper's Weekly,* traveling to London to send back some political drawings and sketches. And while he was there, he added, he also planned to depict the Phillips Circus and its command performance before the Queen.

"What a coincidence," she said slowly. "That you are taking the same ship we are."

"Not a coincidence, Mrs. Hartshorn, but a wicked plan. Your intentions have been printed in every New York paper, and I would have had to have been illiterate not to have known them. Besides, I've been fascinated with . . . with the brilliance of the Phillips Circus for some time. I illustrated the article on your daughter, you know. The one which first referred to her as the 'Equestrienne Angel.' "

"Oh . . . that was you. . . ." Carisa could remember

438

the article, accompanied by the painstakingly lavish lithograph, its lines vital and flowing.

"Yes, and one of my better drawings, if I do say so myself. And your daughter is a charming girl, I might add. Unaffected by all of her fame, and quite capable of freezing off any man audacious enough to approach her."

"Yes," Carisa said thoughtfully. "She is. She tells me, Mr. Whitfield, that she won't marry, that she has no intention of doing so. And if she ever does, I imagine that it will be to someone in the circus."

"Is that so?"

He gazed back at her, rakish, handsome, his blue eyes sparkling with mischief and confidence. Yet there was a rugged strength in the muscles hidden beneath the well-tailored suit.

It was Benicia he wanted, she realized. Benicia whom he was pursuing. Did he hope to charm Neecie's mother and enlist her in his behalf? Was that why he had followed her here on deck? If so, he was making a mistake, for she—

"Would you like to take a turn around the deck with me, Mrs. Hartshorn?" he asked her. "Surely you must be lonely walking about all by yourself, especially in this cold wind."

"No," she told him. "I'm perfectly content. And if you wish company I am sure Neecie will be glad to stroll with you. I last saw her in the passengers' lounge and she looked very bored."

He nodded. "Very well. I have enjoyed meeting you, Mrs. Hartshorn. And now I see from where your daughter gets her beauty."

He left her, and Carisa walked to the rail and stared out at the horizon, pewter sky meeting gray sea, bleak and limitless.

He didn't even know that Benicia is not my daughter, she told herself slowly.

As she stood there, her feeling of aloneness increased, and for the first time in many years she thought about Poll Henry's curse, shrilled at her so many years ago.

I hope God takes away your husband and your circus

439

*and every other goddamn thing that you love, and I
hope that someday you'll die lonely, lonely and old and
ugly and forsaken.*

Involuntarily, Carisa shuddered. She stared out toward the gray sea, and the words seeped into her heart like acid.

"Carisa," Rolf said. He leaned back in his wood and canvas chair. "I want to talk to you."

"All right, Rolf. What is it?"

The parade was over. Carisa, following it in a pony-cart, had seen the old Queen herself, standing on a balcony at Osborne House with her attendants and grandchildren, looking old and tired. Yet Victoria had watched while the entire parade passed before her, showing no signs of weariness. Now, in less than half an hour, the Royal party was scheduled to arrive here, at the tent, for the performance itself. Special bunting-draped seating had been set aside for Victoria and her entourage, and seats were also reserved for the Osborne House staff and certain other families on the island whom the Queen wished to include. No other audience would be permitted.

"The old girl really stood up well, didn't she?" Rolf was saying. "That chin of hers was lifted the whole time. Guess she's used to standing at attention, eh?"

"Yes." Carisa said it dully.

They were inside Rolf's office tent—a makeshift affair, for usually he had a portion of a railroad car to himself. But, of course, they had left the railroad cars at home, reverting back to wagons for this overseas journey. But for all its makeshiftness, the tent, like Rolf himself, was fanatically neat. It contained a battered wooden desk, two canvas chairs, a metal safe imprinted in black, stenciled lettering, and a kerosene lamp.

Rolf had lit a cigar. Now he leaned back in his chair, blowing thick blue fumes in Carisa's direction.

"I plan to get married," he announced.

"Married!" Carisa stared at him, startled out of her gloom.

"That's right, why so surprised, Carisa? Surely you're

440

not all that taken aback! I'm by no means an old man yet . . . I'm only ten years older than yourself, or had you forgotten?"

"I . . . I didn't mean your age," she stammered. And it was true. Rolf Taggart was one of those lean, muscular men who remain ageless until they are elderly. Thus Rolf looked exactly as he always had, tall, whippet-lean, with a narrow, handsome wedge-shaped face, and piercing eyes much like John Phillips'. He was her half-brother, Carisa reminded herself with a shiver. So often she forgot that. . . .

Now Rolf leaned toward her, toying with the cigar. "Well, Carisa? Aren't you going to ask me who the lucky girl is? Or what my plans are?" His eyes glinted at her.

Carisa caught her breath, fixed by an odd sensation of unease. Outside the small tent she knew they must be wheeling the cat cages by, for she could hear the rattle of wheels, and a throaty, rattling, feral growl. There was, too, the sudden hot stench of jungle.

"All right, Rolf. Who is she? And what *are* your plans?"

"Why, I'm planning to marry Eleanora diRicci." As Carisa looked baffled, Rolf explained. "She's the new little aerialist, and she plays Cleopatra in the parade. Don't you remember? The Egyptian tableaux wagon?"

"Yes, but she. . . ."

She's only a girl, Carisa wanted to protest. A child of fifteen or sixteen, younger than Neecie, with black, glossy hair and the smooth, rounded, soft, innocent flesh of youth.

"She's young, I'll admit that." Rolf lifted his angular chin. "But she wants me, and I want her, so what does it matter? She's good, Carisa, the best. I can make her a queen, a real star. We'll start a dynasty of our own, what do you think of that?" Rolf's eyes flashed. "I'm going to have children, a dozen of them, and they'll all be in the show . . . my show. . . ."

"Go on," Carisa said coldly. A sudden leap of her heart told her what was coming.

"My show," Rolf repeated. "Eleanora and I have

441

agreed on it . . . we want the Phillips Circus, Carisa. I've saved all of what you paid me, and all of what I earned otherwise . . . you didn't know that, did you? Saved and invested it with Mr. Samuel Hartshorn . . . oh, yes, he took great delight in advising me. Said I was a born financier and he was going to help me all that he could."

Samuel. Damn him. So, after all these years, he had had his revenge on her after all. Carisa could barely hear her own reply over the rush of blood that had flooded to her face and temples. She sat with her hands clenched in her lap, trying to force her face into an expressionless mask. She couldn't let Rolf see her fear and her dismay.

"Did he help you?" she heard her voice say.

"Yes," Rolf mocked. "And what's more, little Ellie's family has some money saved up, too, and they plan to come in with me on this."

"On what?"

"Why, you know what. I want the Phillips show. I want it, I tell you, and I mean to have it. That name . . . it should have been mine . . . all these years it should have been mine. . . ."

Rolf's eyes glittered with an intense light, and Carisa knew with a sudden, sick feeling that he was telling her things about which he had brooded for years.

"*I'm* the one who made the Phillips Circus what it is today," his voice went on. "Not you, my dear. Oh, you owned it, you paid the bills and hired a few of the performers, but that's all you did. *I* did the work. The sheer, gut work. I saved your show for you when we got mired in mud and everyone said we'd never get out. I bailed you out of storms and put you ahead of Sands and Nathan, Ezra Stevens and all of them. I put you on railroad cars and made it work . . . better than Barnum's show, better than anyone's."

"That's not fair. . . ." She started to rise furiously out of her chair.

"Fair?" Rolf's eyes glittered at her with that fanatic light. "Nothing is ever fair in this life, didn't you know that, Carisa? If life was fair, *I* would have the same as you. But because my mother was Marta Taggart, poor

442

half-mad Marta, my father wouldn't marry her. Instead he married that milk-sop woman who gave birth to you, a weakling who couldn't even survive childbirth. . . ."

"Mama . . ." she whispered. "Mama was no weakling. . . ."

"Oh, nothing is fair, nothing, and well I know it! Take me. I did all the work for this show, but never got fair pay for it, never what I was worth, what I was entitled to. So now I *am* going to take what's mine. I have the money, I have the backing, and I'm going to take all of it!"

"But . . . you can't . . . it's my show. . . ."

Now Carisa did jump out of her chair, all of her pretense at calm gone. Suddenly she felt trapped in the smothering canvas walls of the little tent. With a furious gesture she jerked at the rope which moored the side canvas to the ground. Canvas flapped upward. Instantly sunlight poured in, and the chilly December wind.

"What are you doing that for? Look, Carisa, you can have all the tantrums you wish. The fact is, you *will* sell . . . willing or unwilling. You didn't think I would work for the rest of my life like this, did you? As your servant, your lackey? What kind of a man did you think I was? To follow your orders, you, a damned woman, when all the while I knew I could do the job better than you?"

His words seemed to beat at her like the wings of some huge bird. "I'm a Phillips, too!" his voice grated on. The words poured out in a torrent. "Oh, you'd never talk about it, would you? You'd never admit it, not even once, but it's true. Maybe I'm not legitimate, maybe it was on the other side of the blanket, but I'm just as much John Phillips' son as you are his daughter. Dammit, *I* have a circus heritage, too. This show is my heritage. And I want it. I'll force you to give it to me."

As she paced about the cramped tent, fear raced through Carisa. She knew Rolf meant everything he had said. And what if he really could make her sell? The circus business had often been dirty, she knew, rife with cheating and battles and cut-throat dealing. Rat-bills and paper-tearing and betrayal. In her childhood they had even heard rumors that a man had been murdered for his show by a son.

And Rolf was a master at such techniques—if not murder, then everything else. He had had many years to grow very good at them, for she, Carisa, had allowed him those years. In order to keep her circus, she had closed her eyes and let him undercut the competition. Weakly she had protested—against gambling, against short-changing. But still she had let Rolf work. She had used him as a weapon against her rivals. Well, hadn't she? A keen-edged human weapon which could slash and rip. . . .

What a fool she had been! Keeping Rolf all these years, knowing full well how dangerous he could be. Deluding herself that she had him under her control. When in fact he had never been under her control at all. Instead, he had been nursing his resentment of her, his jealousy and hatred. . . .

Sudden resolve poured through her, strengthening her. Rolf had not won yet. This was still her circus. And she would fight for it.

Instinctively she stopped her rapid pacing and turned to face Rolf. She held her hands quietly at her sides to stop their trembling.

"I'm happy that you are marrying, of course," she said in a low, clear voice. "And I hope that you will be very happy. But I can't sell my show to you. And I won't."

"You will."

Rage screamed through her and for a wild moment she felt the urge to claw out at him, to scratch at his face, to let all of her strength pour out in one furious attack on him.

Instead, with enormous effort she controlled herself. Only her nostrils flared slightly as she said, "Rolf, it's impossible. Now that you are marrying, I'll give you a wedding gift of five thousand dollars. But you will continue to be my manager and to take the same percentage as before."

Rolf's upper lip twisted and lifted, revealing white teeth. "Not good enough, Carisa. As I told you, I want more. I want the Phillips Circus. And I mean to get it. If you won't sell, then I'm going to take it from you."

"How, Rolf? How will you do that?"

"Oh, don't you worry. I've had time to think about this . . . years! Performers can be bought out . . . it happens all the time." His eyes glinted. "As I recall, you've done it yourself, Carisa, when you stole Marcella Duquesne from Richard Sands. Accidents can happen, too. Bad ones. Animals poisoned, ropes breaking, fires. . . ."

Fire. The gut-cramping, very real fear of all circus folk.

She must be calm, she ordered herself shakily. She must not show her fear. She must not antagonize Rolf any further. She must think. . . .

But her mind seemed separated from that small, sensible voice in her head issuing such orders. Instead she heard herself speak in a low voice she did not recognize as her own.

"Rolf, you're fired. As of now, today. Pack your things and get out of here. And take your little Eleanora with you. I don't want her around any more either."

Rolf did not move. His eyes fixed hers, as black and depthless as a snake's.

"You don't mean that."

"Oh, yes, I do mean it. I made a mistake, a terrible mistake, in keeping you all of these years. I should have fired you, Rolf, when I first learned that you were mixed up with grifters and gamblers and short-changers. I should have listened to Duddie, I should have fought for my show on my own. But I didn't. I didn't listen to anyone. Instead, foolishly, I kept you. I thought I needed you. . . ."

Her voice had gone low and she whispered this last sentence more to herself than to Rolf.

Rolf slammed his fist down on the desk top and kicked his canvas chair backward from beneath him.

445

Then he advanced toward her, his face flushed a wild, purplish color.

"You can't . . ." he began in a choked way. "You can't do this . . ."

"I can and I will. Go, before I call for help. Duddie carries a pistol in his trunk and he'd be willing to use it on my account. And if he isn't, I'll use it myself."

They faced each other.

"I have a pistol, too," Rolf muttered. His eyes darted from side to side and his tongue went out to moisten his lips.

"Go," Carisa repeated, although her heart was leaping now with her fear. Rolf was mad, she knew. Crazed from years of brooding, years of resentment. And how much of his madness was her own fault? The thought chilled her.

But if Rolf had a pistol concealed in his desk, he did not move toward it.

"You can't get along without me," he muttered. "What will you do, line up the parade yourself? Fix your own wagons?" He laughed, derisively.

"I'll manage. As soon as today's performance is over, we'll go back to New London. I'll find another circus man to take your place, Rolf. It's something I should have done years ago."

She narrowed her eyes at him, forcing into them all of her will and her anger. "Go, Rolf. Leave at once."

A long silence. A silence so profound that she could hear the clicking of her own pulse in her throat.

"All right then. All right! If that's the way you want to play it."

Rolf flung out of the tent, leaving behind him his cigar butt still asmolder in an ashtray. Blindly Carisa reached for it and stubbed it out. Then she sank weakly into one of the canvas chairs. Outside the tent she heard a shout and knew, without having to be told, that the Queen's entourage had arrived.

She rushed to the flap of the tent. There they were— five splendid carriages manned by uniformed footmen and coachmen, and filled with the Royal party, the Queen and her grandchildren. At one of the carriage windows she glimpsed the Queen herself, a dumpy, dour-faced old woman.

For a moment, a few brief seconds, Carisa's eyes and those of the old Queen met. It was as if Carisa could sense the grief in Victoria, the slow, heavy sorrow which was always with her now. And it was as if, too, the Queen could sense Carisa's own isolation.

It had been a brief moment of eye-communication between two women from widely different worlds.

Then it was gone, the Royal carriages had moved on toward the tent. Soon the Queen and her party would take their seats in the big top.

Carisa sighed and closed the flap of the tent. The show—the dream, Papa's dream and her own—was about to begin.

28

They arrived back in New London in February, after having been delayed by an epidemic of influenza which had spread through most of the circus employees, sparing only a few. Carisa herself had been very ill, nursed by a worried Benicia.

She had tossed and turned in her delirium, plagued by frightening dreams. Dreams that Rolf had taken over the Phillips Circus, wrenching it from her like a bauble snatched from a child's hand. Dreams that she had been left alone by Adam, to grow old and ugly and lonely. . . .

"Carisa!" Neecie had cried, trying to sponge her forehead. "Carisa, you're babbling so, it frightens me! You've been saying such wild things about Papa. And the circus . . . you're not going to lose it, why ever would you talk that way? How could anyone take it from you? What could they do?"

"Do . . ." Carisa jerked about on her sweaty bed-covers, barely seeing the young, anxious face bent over

447

hers. "Oh, there's so much he could do. He learned how . . . managing my show. . . ."

"Don't be silly. Carisa, it's all a dream, nothing more. This is 1874, not the Dark Ages. People don't do things like that."

"Neecie!" Carisa struggled unsuccessfully to sit up on her bed in the small hotel room. "You don't know. . . ."

"I do know that you had better drink this broth which the landlady made for you. Drink all of it that you can. And Justin has managed to round up a good doctor for you. He's coming in an hour or so, on the ferry from Portsmouth."

"Justin?" Carisa shook her head in bewilderment. Her brain felt so cloudy. And her skin was burning.

"Why, Justin Whitfield! Surely you remember meeting him on the ship? He stayed here to write about our performance before the Queen, and to draw the illustrations. Oh, Carisa, they are splendid! He has already sent them back to New York, and he let me read it before he sent it. He said some wonderful things about all of us. He called you a 'grand circus lady, a real queen in her own right.' What do you think of that, Carisa? Aren't you pleased?"

"Pleased. . . ." Carisa sank back into the rough muslin sheets provided by their frugal landlady. The room was spinning around and around like one of the metal hoops Matt and Vicki had used to play with.

So, she thought confusedly. That man, that Justin Whitfield, had stayed here on account of Benicia. She, of course, was the real reason for his interest in the Phillips Circus. . . .

But why would he say such astonishing things about herself?

Overdramatization, Carisa told herself, sinking down again to dizziness. Newspaper men exaggerated. It was part of their trade, and they must be excused for it. She was no grand circus lady. God, no. She was nothing but a fool. A frightened fool. . . .

New London lay under a new coat of heavy, moist snow which mingled with the mud in the streets to form icy clumps. Red-faced men were in the streets, shoveling great loads of snow onto the bare spots, so that the blades of the cutters could slide.

Carisa sank back in the Hearts-ease cutter, trying to suppress a feeling of unease which grew stronger with each foot the vehicle's metal runners slid toward home.

With difficulty, she turned her thoughts to the unloading of animals and equipment which was still going on at the wharves. Duddie was supervising this. Carisa had asked him to be her circus manager and the little clown, after swallowing back his surprise, had accepted.

At first dumbfounded and amused by the fact of the small misshapen clown taking over, the circus people had accepted Duddie's authority. They had known and liked Duddie for years, and he knew how to get along with them.

Benicia, of all people, had been the one to suggest to Carisa that she do this.

"Carisa, why are you going to go back to the 'States and hire some strange man to take over our show? Don't you realize that we already have a manager right here?"

"We do?" Carisa had stared at her.

"Of course. Duddie, who else! He knows how to do everything, he's watched Rolf for years, and we've always depended on him. Everyone likes Duddie; he hasn't the temper Rolf had. And, Carisa, remember that he is the son of an Earl. He may not look it, but he is smart, and he can make people do as he wishes."

Duddie, Carisa had thought dully. All of those years there had been Duddie, so familiar a part of her environment that she had not even seen his possibilities. So she had hired him, giving the clown the same percentage which Rolf had enjoyed. He would be an honest manager, she knew, without ambitions for control himself. He would be content to take her orders, to work selflessly for her, and for the good of the circus itself. Why had she not seen this years ago?

They had not seen Rolf again. He had left, together with Eleanora diRicci and the entire diRicci troupe. No one knew where they had gone, and Carisa tried not to think about it. Many things could happen, she tried to assure herself. Perhaps Rolf would buy another show, or go elsewhere.

But she knew he would not.

Hearts-ease occupied its snow-covered grounds like a proud villa, its white clapboards and dark shutters giving it an austere dignity. Over the years Carisa had come to love the old house as Adam did, and now she gazed at it fondly, her eyes moistening. *Home,* she thought.

They were all in the front foyer to greet them: Adam, Vicki and her wispy, blonde-haired daughter; Nelly, plump with her latest pregnancy. Behind Nelly clustered the other servants, Gaines, fat Brigid, Annie, various of Nelly's nieces who had been hired over the years as parlor maids and scullery girls. Tim Kelly hovered in the background, standing away from the servants yet not with the family either.

Benicia tore away from Carisa and ran to throw herself into Adam's arms.

"Papa! Oh, Papa, Papa! How good it is to see you! Oh, I only wish you could have seen us playing before the Queen. It was marvelous, we've never been better, even Duddie said that. And the Queen loved us, I know she did, I saw her smiling twice. . . ."

Adam held his daughter tightly, although his eyes, Carisa noted with a pang, seemed to have lost some of their golden fire.

"So it was a success. I'm glad, Neecie. Glad that you are happy. And now you are going to be at Hearts-ease for the rest of the winter."

"Oh, yes, for months and months at least. Of course, I have a lot of practicing to do. A new back-twist flip, Papa! And in the spring I'm going to jump through hoops of fire! It's going to be spectacular, people will never have seen anything like it. . . ."

Adam's mouth twisted into a smile, and for the first time his eyes met Carisa's. She sensed some emotion in them, although she could not tell what it was.

But whatever emotion it was, it fleeted away almost

at once, and then she heard Adam ask her in an ordinary voice if she had brought all of her luggage with her.

"Some of it," she replied. "They are bringing a few trunks now, and the rest will come later, when the ship is fully unloaded. I have brought home some porcelain, Adam, and some very nice damask. And some carved furniture which I bought in London before we left there. It is all very ornate."

Adam frowned. "Furniture? But we have plenty of furniture, Carisa."

She felt her chin lift. She had shopped compulsively, as an alcoholic imbibes whiskey, in order to deaden her fears about Rolf, her terror of losing Adam.

"Oh," she told him. "But this is carved in the most exquisite detail and is very expensive, Adam. And I thought. . . ." For an instant her voice wavered. "And I thought we needed a change or two, something more up-to-date and modern. Wait until they bring the things up and you can see them for yourself!"

Carisa had the feeling that she was talking too much, and too fast. Babbling, she told herself angrily. She was babbling like a silly girl. But why didn't he say something to her? Why did he just stare at her, his eyes so golden, so leonine and piercing?

"I assume that you wish to rest before dinner," he said at last. "I've ordered a good New England meal for tonight. I thought you would enjoy it after eating English food for so long."

"We had German food on the ship, Papa . . . both ways!" Neecie put in, unaware of any deeper undercurrents. "Our captain on the way home was fat and from Dusseldorf, and I swear I'm so sick of sausages and sauerkraut that I could shriek. . . ." She linked her arm with her father's and dragged him off toward the parlor, leaving Carisa to gaze after them.

With a start, she noticed that Vicki and the servants were staring at her.

"My . . . my luggage," she murmured to Nelly.

"Yes, Miss Carisa. I'll have Gaines see to it."

451

Carisa's eyes met Nelly's brown ones. In them, she saw pity.

When Carisa walked into the master bedroom which she and Adam had shared, she found it looking exactly the same as before. A fire crackled in the fireplace, making cozy noises as it heated the room. The Turkish rugs, freshly beaten, reflected their jewel colors, the intricate oriental patterns. The Chelsea porcelain tea service still sat on its low table, awaiting their breakfasts together.

However, when she walked into their small adjoining bathroom, made from a closet many years before, she saw that it was bare of all Adam's personal effects. The room was clean, smelling of lye soap and rose-petal sachet, but it also smelled stale. As if no one had been in it for months, Carisa noticed uneasily.

She turned to Nelly who, white starched apron drawn over her rounded belly, was busily unpacking Carisa's small steamer trunk.

"Nelly?"

Nelly gave a great deal of attention to a stack of petticoats which she was removing from the trunk.

"He has been sleeping down the hall and in one of the extra bedrooms," Nelly remarked at last. "He moved out of here soon after you left. He said he didn't like rattling around in such a large room all by himself."

"Well, now he won't have to rattle around any more. He can move back."

Nelly did not say anything. She went to the polished low bureau and pulled open its bottom drawer, rearranging some of Carisa's clean nightgowns and petticoats in it. On the floor, she was making a heap of soiled clothing.

"Nelly . . . ?"

"It's none of my business, Miss Carisa."

"But . . . which room did he move to?"

"The last one in the old section, next to the one Julian used. He has had it repainted in yellow, and he had new Wilton carpeting put in."

"Oh?" Carisa felt her throat give a dry convulsive

452

swallow. "Well, Nelly, I think that will be enough unpacking for now. I think I'll take a nap before dinner.
I had the influenza while I was in England and I've still
not quite recovered from it."

"You did? Oh, Miss Carisa, and I didn't even know!"

Nelly was instantly contrite, making a fuss over
Carisa. Numbly, Carisa allowed herself to be undressed,
cosseted and covered up with a soft quilt. When at last
Nelly had gone, closing the door quietly behind her,
Carisa closed her eyes. A tear pushed from under her
eyelids, hot and burning.

Somehow, she endured dinner. Endured, too, Neecie's
lighthearted account of all they had done and seen.
The way the old Queen had looked, the way she had
turned to her youngest grandchild to point and whisper.
The play they had seen in London, the odd way in which
Rolf Taggart had suddenly deserted the show just as
they were about to perform before the Queen.

Neecie talked on, her spirits irrepressible, her voice
filling the silences that seemed to lurk at the corners
of the room.

"Did you know, Mama, that Papa's new steamers are
going to be a wild success?" Vicki said at last over
dessert, a blackberry pie. "He is shipping goods to
England and the Continent now, and his last voyage
made a very hearty profit indeed." She giggled. "Redlands Kord is angry at Papa because the profit *is* so
very good. Why, he's called Papa a modern-day pirate
who deals in contracts and bills of lading instead of in
ransom."

"Oh, Adam!" Carisa forgot her hurt and bewilderment, and allowed herself to be transported by pleasure.
"Then your new steamers are going to be successful.
Why, that's wonderful, I'm so glad. You just can't
imagine how really glad I am for you. . . ."

"Enough, Carisa. Please don't gush. It doesn't become you."

Carisa stared at her husband, the color flooding to
her face. She felt as if he had slapped her—as, indeed,
in a way he had. Thankfully, Benicia burst into the

awkward silence with a story of what Justin Whitfield had said about the Queen, and the moment was past.

By the end of the meal, Carisa's temples were throbbing with a headache. She excused herself and went upstairs to the bedroom they had once shared. In a drawer of her dressing table she found a leather-bound copy of an old book, giving some of the early history of New London.

In fascination, she began to read. In clear, lucid prose the author had caught it all—the blustering passions and forces which had driven the early New Londoners in their assault upon the sea and upon the leviathans which lived there. And prominent among these men was the first Adam Hartshorn, forceful in his dark energy. His descendant, her own Adam, possessed much of this same vitality. . . .

With a start, she heard a bedroom door close in the corridor and realized that several hours had passed. Benicia and Vicki, talking among themselves, had gone to bed. Then, half an hour later, Adam came, too. She recognized his footsteps, forceful yet irregular due to the old war wound.

Did the footsteps seem to pause at her door?

No. Evidently they did not, for they moved on again, to the far end of the corridor. Again a door clicked open, then shut.

Carisa could stand it no longer. She flung down the book and jumped out of her chair. She hurried down the hallway, heedless of whether anyone heard her.

Boldly she burst into Adam's room without knocking. She found him standing at a window, the room still dark, for he had not bothered to light the gas. Instead, he had pulled aside a corner of the pale damask drape to stare out at the blackness of the night, specked with white dots of falling snow.

"Adam." She whispered it. "Why don't you light the lamp? It's dark in here."

He did not turn. "Go away, Carisa."

"No, I won't." She marched over to the gasolier on the wall and lit it herself with hands that shook. Light flared into the room, sending wavering shadows up the newly painted walls, and making Adam's face look grim.

"Adam! What's wrong?" she demanded. "I arrived home to find you'd moved out of our bedroom."

"Yes. I did move out. I thought it would be more comfortable here."

"But . . ."

"It's over, Carisa," he said. *"That."*

"Over?" She could only stare at him, not believing she had heard him correctly. A little tic had begun to beat at the corner of her right eye. She could feel it tugging at her flesh like a gentle butterfly.

"I mean us. You and I, Carisa. We made a mistake all those long years ago. Or rather, I made a mistake. I let my desire for a lovely, lissom girl get in the way of my common sense. I let you blackmail me with your beauty."

"Blackmail! What on earth are you talking about?" She cried it impatiently. "Adam, we're married. We're husband and wife. We have children, and responsibilities."

"Oh, I know that. And I don't intend to ask for a divorce, unless you wish me to do so. We'll continue as we are. We'll live together under the same roof and I'll try not to embarrass you in any way. But we are finished. You and I."

"Finished . . ." One part of her knew what he was saying. But the rest of her recoiled from it. She thrust her hands in front of her, making an instinctive, denying gesture. "Oh, Adam. Surely you're just upset about something. Depressed . . ."

"No. I've had a long time to think about this, all of the time you were away. You're not much of a correspondent, are you, Carisa? I guess you were too busy with the circus to write me many letters."

"I did write you!" she replied hotly. "But you're right, I was busy, and I was also ill, don't you remember my telling you that at dinner? I was sick with influenza and Neecie had to nurse me. . . ."

She stumbled toward him. Desperately she threw her arms around him. If their bodies could only press to-

455

gether and touch, then that stiff expression would leave his face. His eyes would soften and he would hold her the way he had used to do, and it would be all right again.

"No, Carisa." He moved away from her. "Don't try your wiles on me. I'll give in to them, and I don't want to. Don't you understand? You can't use me any more. I'm through with that."

"Use you?" She heard her voice come out as a frightened squeak. She wanted to scream at him in her anger and grief and fright. Instead, all she could do was to croak at him. Like a silly, scared mouse.

"I mean that you utilized me, Carisa, as you have used every other man in your life . . . Rolf Taggart, Duddie . . . absolutely without conscience or compunction."

"What . . . what are you talking about?"

"Don't you remember, Carisa?" And then Adam's voice changed, and he repeated, " *'I will marry you if you will buy me the William deBord circus and let me run it and do with it whatever I please. It is absolutely the only condition under which I will marry you.'* I can remember that statement word-for-word. Do you know how many times I've thought of it over the years?"

Carisa's whisper—her protest—sank away. As if it came from an impossibly far distance, she could hear Katherine's voice, feeble with the effort of dying. *You married him for his money. All of us knew that. The whole town knew it.*

Her mind seemed to whirl back, to that day long ago when she had been carried for the first time to Hearts-ease, when she had first seen the rare, rich oak bedroom paneling, the lush Turkish rugs, the furniture gleaming with the polish and patina of age. Well? she asked herself harshly. Wasn't Adam right? Hadn't she coveted these? Hadn't she recognized them for what they were—an opportunity?

"But . . . I was only a young girl then," she heard herself plead. "A girl of seventeen. Young . . . foolish

456

... I didn't really know what I was doing, or what I wanted. . . ."

Adam threw back his head and gave a bitter laugh. "Oh, come, Carisa. Surely there was never a time in your life when you didn't know exactly what you wanted. You wanted a circus and you married me to get it. It's that simple."

"No . . . No . . ." She was weeping. "Adam . . . I fell in *love* with you. Don't you realize? I've loved you, all of these years. I have, I have. I still love you."

"Do you?"

Why wouldn't Adam touch her? She knew that he wanted to. She could sense it, the desire radiating from him as he stood stiffly by the bedroom window staring out at the snowy night. He wanted to pick her up and fling her down on the bed and make love to her. And she wanted it, too. She wanted him to do that, no matter how rough he was. She would revel in it, glory in it . . . God, dear God, how she loved him. . . .

Adam had begun to talk, in a husky voice that she barely recognized. Like the snaps of firecrackers, certain phrases seemed to explode out at her. *"My brother Samuel . . . you were his lover, weren't you? His mistress. . . ."*

She shook her head wildly. Was Adam accusing her of—with Samuel—

"Adam, whatever are you saying? I was never . . . Samuel's mistress," she whispered.

"You were. He told me so himself, two weeks after you left for London. He taunted me with it, telling me how he had been with you in a hotel in Philadelphia. . . . I nearly smashed his face to blood and pulp. I almost killed him, Carisa. I don't know what stopped me, I wanted to see him dead."

"Adam . . .." Her lips were dry. "You don't understand. It isn't like it sounds. Samuel . . . that day in Philadelphia . . . he forced himself on me, I had no choice. . . ."

Carisa could feel the blood seeping away from her face. Little black dots of dizziness had begun to dance in front of her eyes. Ugly pictures tilted and whirled in her mind. Samuel, lunging at her that day long ago at Mrs. Adair's. Samuel lowering his body onto hers that night in Philadelphia, his face disfigured with anger and hatred . . . hatred for Adam as well as for herself?

"Adam," she began. "Don't you see that Samuel hates you? Perhaps he always has. You were the one who inherited Hearts-ease from your father . . . you've always been your mother's favorite. . . ."

Adam turned. "We won't speak of it again, Carisa. What's done is done. It's finished now. You have your own bedroom now, my dear wife, and it is large and comfortable, far more luxurious than any circus wagon could ever be. Go to it, will you? Go to it and do not ever speak to me of Samuel Hartshorn again."

There were a thousand things she could have done or said. She could have screamed at Adam, raged at him out of the tornado of her own grief and fear. She could have thrown Anna into his face, reminded him that Anna had once been *his* mistress, as had Poll Henry.

She could have shouted out that his brother hated him and had used Carisa to further that hatred. She could have blamed Adam for not seeing this. For being blind and pig-headed and obstinate, just as he had been with his son, Julian.

She could have run to him. She could have stripped off her gown and flung herself into his arms, forcing him to pay attention to her, to release his sexual tensions with her. Once their bodies blended in the act of love, he might have forgotten his anger. He might have softened toward her. . . .

But she did none of these things. She couldn't. She wasn't the sort of woman to scream out in rage, to grovel, or to cheapen herself before a man who didn't want her.

So she went back to the master bedroom, as he had instructed her, and she closed the door behind her. Mechanically she took off her dinner gown and put it into the mahogany wardrobe. She pulled off her ruffled petticoats, her corset cover, her underthings. She found a nightgown and managed to get it on. Then she turned

458

off the gaslight and crawled under the covers, into the big, barren bed which was so empty without anyone to share it.

Just as she fell asleep, she was almost certain that she heard a woman's laughter. Poll Henry's laughter, low, malicious and mocking. Then she was asleep, falling down to a darkness so profound that it might have been death.

The next morning she awoke to the dim, watery light of winter. It was still snowing, and the specks of white had frozen to the panes of the bedroom windows in a lacy pattern like a bridal veil. . . . Hastily Carisa pushed away the thought. She sat up in bed and rang for Nelly.

"Well, you certainly slept in, didn't you?" Nelly bustled in, looking plump and happy and ordinary. She was carrying Carisa's breakfast on a tray, oatmeal and toast and sausage and stewed dried peaches.

"Did I?" Carisa asked dully.

"Oh, my, yes, it's nearly ten o'clock. I would have waked you sooner but you looked so pale and tired that I decided to let you rest. Mr. Hartshorn's already gone out," Nelly added in that same determinedly cheerful voice. "He had a meeting in town with some of the men on the steamship company board. He said to tell you not to expect him until after dinner."

"Oh."

There seemed nothing else to say. Carisa eyed Nelly, and knew that the other woman knew. She realized also that Nelly would never say anything, that here a wide gulf separated them. It was going to be very lonely, she realized with a sudden, bitter pang. Adam . . . living with him under the same roof, yet so far apart from him that they might as well be strangers.

She could barely touch her breakfast. She let Nelly dress her in a soft, yellow-green silk that covered the curves of her body sensuously, flowing outward at the rear in the bustle style so fashionable these days. Examining herself in the wavy mirror, she knew that she looked her best. But what good was her beauty, she wondered dully, if Adam was not here to notice it?

459

"Well, Miss Carisa?" Nelly took away the untouched tray without comment. "And what are you going to do today, your first day home? Are you going to work in your office? You should see the stack of mail waiting for you there! There are boxes and boxes of it. The postman said he'd never seen anyone get as much mail as you do, not even the banks in town! Or maybe you'd want to come downstairs and look at all the new boxes and things waiting in the hall. They delivered them all this morning."

"Delivered?" For a moment Carisa was puzzled. Then she remembered the furniture and fabrics she had bought in London. It seemed a thousand years ago since that frenzied, driven shopping spree, and now she could not even recall clearly what she had bought.

Oh, she thought in despair. What did it matter?

She moved toward the bedroom door, hearing the silken rustle of her skirts. "First I suppose I had better go downstairs and see to the unpacking of the boxes," she heard herself say. "I'll have to decide what to do with everything."

She swept downstairs, trying hard to think about furniture instead of about Adam.

The days passed in a slow, numbed parade, and grimly Carisa set herself to get through them. She dove into spring plans for the circus, closeting herself in her office for hours every day to pore over drawings for new costumes, letters negotiating for new acts, all of the activity which once had been able to absorb her so fully.

A letter came from Matt, written in faded, closely-spaced ink, the copperplate lettering almost illegible. He was well, he wrote, although he was now recovering from a broken wrist suffered in a storm when he had been flung by the wind against a stay.

But no pox, he wrote joyously. *Mama, I'm sure.*

In spite of her relief at the news from Matt, she couldn't seem to concentrate. Costumes, musical scores, even the challenge of planning Benicia's new "firehoop" act, all of it seemed far away and dull, a chore which

460

she had to drag herself through each day. A job without meaning.

Restlessly, escaping from her office, she drove to town and consulted with a new interior decorator who had recently come to the city from New York. She and *Madame* Eglantine spent hours together, planning the arrangement of the new furniture Carisa had bought, and the redecorating of much of the downstairs of Hearts-ease.

It was, Carisa thought sometimes, as if she could not help herself. Relentlessly she pushed the plump little decorator to work long hours, until the woman complained and eyed her with secret hatred. Never before, insisted *Madame,* had she ever met any woman who insisted that all of her decorating be accomplished in only a few short weeks. These things took time, surely any real lady knew that.

Carisa did not care. Work was her anesthetic. She was busy eighteen hours a day, driving herself mercilessly, until at last she would stumble into bed, to drop immediately into dreamless sleep.

Two weeks later, most of the labor was done. One morning Adam stalked through the drawing-room, white-faced and angry. He gave a contemptuous kick at the carved pediment of the small Italianate wall table she had purchased. Porcelain and glass, crowded together on its surface, rattled perilously.

"Carisa," he exclaimed. "All of this stuff is just Victorian garbage! Tasteless and ugly. Why, it would take a maid hours just to dust all of these little carved leaves and flowers and cupids. . . ."

"We have a maid, don't we? In fact, we have several of them." Carisa's voice was as cold as his. "And I don't think it looks all that bad. It's fashionable, Adam. It's what all the wealthy people are putting into their drawing rooms and parlors these days."

"Let them, then! Carisa, don't you realize that Hearts-ease was built in 1715? It's a noble house, it has beautiful lines and it has character. And it was furnished very carefully by my family; each piece belongs. Don't you see what you've done to it?"

461

Carisa reddened. "I made it fashionable, that's what I've done. I made it look like the homes of the wealthy businessmen here in New London, people in society, Adam."

"On the contrary," he snapped. "You've made this house look like a brothel."

"A brothel! Adam . . ."

But he had slammed out of the room, banging the door behind him.

Carisa stood with her fists clenched in the middle of the room she had labored so hard to decorate. She looked about her, trying to quell her rage. Yes, she assured herself, the room *was* fashionable, no matter what Adam might think. It was the match of anything to be found in London or New York.

She let her eyes range about the room, seeing the heavy gilt-covered octagonal mirror, so encrusted with carving that it looked more like a confection than a looking glass. A naked porcelain nymph crouched on the table beneath it, her hands coyly covering her bareness. Beside her were ranged other smaller pieces Carisa had bought, and a group of small daguerreotypes. The room's heavy furniture was in much the same style. There were rich damask drapes, dozens of pictures, and everywhere—hanging from the swagged drapes, from the table covers and plump cushions—were tassles and fringes.

For some reason a thought popped into her head. Of Poll Henry's crowded little office, crammed with glassware and bibelots in imitation of this very style. Dear God, she thought suddenly. He is right. This room does look like a brothel.

In the clutter on the table beneath the mirror was a little porcelain shepherdess, her left hand lifting a fold of her delicately tinted skirt. "Prettily sentimental," *Madame* Eglantine had said of this piece. Slowly Carisa let her hand reach out for it.

I did this to punish Adam, a cold little voice spoke up inside her. *I couldn't hurt him, so I hurt Hearts-ease instead. I made a mockery of this lovely old house.*

With a swift, savage motion, she hurled the shepherdess at the gilt mirror. It sailed through the air, smashed into the frame, and shattered. Bits of gilt and china flew.

"Damn!" Carisa cried out in anguish. "Oh, damn, damn!"

But in her new, strangely despairing mood, Carisa did not take away the furniture, as was her first impulse. Instead she decided to keep it where it was temporarily.

She would give a party, she decided abruptly. A party so splendid and so smashing that Adam would have to pay attention. And—she decided quickly—it would be an event which would also include a private, exclusive showing of the Phillips Circus.

And somehow, when it was all over (she lay in bed until nearly dawn that night, planning it all in her mind) she and Adam would be drawn closer. Adam would come to see just what the circus meant—not only to herself but to others. He would perceive the magic of it, he would see why she loved it so.

Then, she mused dreamily, after the party, in the warm, mellow after-glow, they would finally be able to talk. First, she planned, they would survey the party debris and talk in low voices as all married people do. Pleasant, open, free. Then they would go upstairs arm in arm.

But instead of walking alone down the corridor to his own room, Adam would come into the master bedroom with her. They would not even bother to turn on the gasolier. Instead, they would undress in the darkness. Slowly, sweetly, savoring it. Then he would turn to her, gather her up in his arms, carry her to bed. . . .

At first light she fell asleep, the picture of Adam's face still in her mind, soft with tenderness and newfound love.

In the late morning, when she finally awoke, the dream seemed blurred, unclear, not real. A party? How could a party possibly bring Adam to her? But as she got up and dressed, somehow the notion persisted.

She *would* give a party, a splendid one, and somehow something would happen. She would make it happen!

463

Anyway, she told herself feverishly, she had to do something. She had finished the house, and she had to have some project to occupy herself wholly, something into which she could throw all of her energy and ability. Something which would keep her so busy that she would not have time to think. . . .

Rapidly she made her plans. The circus was about to begin its new season, and would leave in mid-April for its tour. Plans for its new format were now well underway, and Neecie's new act—the dangerous leap through a row of fiery hoops—would be a sensation. Also, they had recently acquired a new group of Italian aerialists, the Ciprianis, a troupe justifiably famous in Europe.

Why not? she thought. Why not unveil it all here at Hearts-ease, creating the event of the year?

She would invite all of the society people of New London, of course—names like Coit, Brandegee, and Waller. She would also ask newspaper people from New London and neighboring towns, from New York and Boston and Philadelphia and Washington. And—yes, why not?—Justin Whitfield from *Harper's Weekly*. She would ask them all, anyone who was anyone in the newspaper world.

First, she planned, would come the party. Elegant, sumptuous, expensive. Then the circus. To it, she decided, she would also invite the children of the party guests, for a circus, she felt strongly, must never be without children. She would also invite the residents of a small orphanage which had recently been started in the town, and some old sailors cared for by the Seaman's Friend Society.

They would stage the show in the octagonal brick building—no; immediately she discarded that thought. The octagonal building was now too small. It had only one ring, and the Phillips Circus was now a three-ring show.

So, they would use the canvas big top, and they would decorate it splendidly, with flags, banners and bunting, as they had done for the Queen. They would create special, ornate costumes. They would buy a new

464

albino lion, extremely rare. They would have new clown acts—her mind flew.

"A circus party?" Adam stared at her. It was the following day, and she had managed to stop him on his way out of the house. He spent much time these days in his shipping office, closeted there with his agent, Mr. West, and with the three men who were his partners in the new steamship company he had formed. It was as if, Carisa thought dully, Adam, too, sought to bury himself in the solace of work.

"Oh, Adam," she heard her voice go on. "It's going to be spectacular! Everyone will be fighting to come. Neecie's new fire-hoop act is going to be a sensation! She'll make all of the papers, we'll be the talk of the entire country. Well, I should be more modest. Of the Eastern seaboard at least."

Adam shrugged. "Oh, I've no doubt of that. Well, do it if you must, Carisa. I really can't stop you, can I? But don't plan on my help with it, or my attendance. I don't feel very festive these days."

"But . . ." She stared at him, shocked. "But you must come!"

"Must I?" Adam's eyes, glowing yellow, seemed distant, far away. It was as if he were a stranger to her.

The days passed quickly, and Carisa flung herself into her plans with renewed energy. Adam *would* come, she assured herself daily. No matter what their private quarrels, he had never humiliated her in public and surely he would not begin now.

And, she had to admit, this party was going to be a challenge. Not only must the Phillips Circus be more sparkling and spectacular than ever before, but the party itself must be unforgettable. It must shimmer with glamour and wealth!

She enlisted Duddie's and Nelly's help, longing in spite of herself for Rolf's genius at organizing details. If only Rolf were here—or at least Rolf's managerial ability. . . .

But he wasn't, she reminded herself, and for that she had to be grateful. No one had seen him in weeks, nor

Eleanora diRicci, the girl whom he was to have married. Even Duddie, who had many contacts in the underground circus gossip network, could pick up no signs of him. It was as if Rolf had vanished from the world Carisa knew.

The party plans progressed. Carisa took Mrs. Wiggins an issue of *Godey's,* in which was pictured just the gown she wanted to wear. Of violet colored silk, the skirt was embellished with lavish puffs of fabric and panels that ran lengthwise. It was trimmed with shirred ribbons and matching lace.

When she saw it, Mrs. Wiggins clapped one wrinkled old hand to her equally wrinkled face. Over the years, the seamstress seemed to have shrunk inside her skin, growing tinier and more bent over. Only her eyes, bright black, remained the same.

"Dear sweet heavens," she said now. "Such a complicated dress, with all them panels and ruffles and puffs . . . t'would take three weeks to do it right. And I haven't the time, what with all that extra circus sewing you give me. What do you think I am, one of them new dress factories in New York? Work, work, work, and on things so queer and fancy that no other seamstress would ever touch 'em."

"You have plenty of assistants and you have twelve sewing machines," Carisa said sharply. "Surely you can get this done, and finish the rest of it, too. Why else do I pay you?"

Mrs. Wiggins' black eyes snapped. "You pay me to make that there Phillips Circus look good, that's what. And by God, I do it. If it weren't for me, you'd all look like a bunch of shabby gypsy beggars."

Silence hung between them. Then Carisa drew a quick breath. "Oh . . . Oh, I'm sorry, Mrs. Wiggins. You're right, you have done so much for us. You and your helpers have toiled for thousands of hours, sewing tiny sequins and spangles on hundreds of costumes. I don't know what I ever would have done without you."

Impulsively she hugged the older woman.

"Oh, all right," Mrs. Wiggins said grumpily. "I can do it, I guess. I make costumes for clowns and jugglers

466

and fat ladies and them skinny men that fly through the air . . . If I can't put together one fancy dress, I guess I don't deserve to be in the business."

"T-thank you, Mrs. Wiggins."

Carisa's eyes pricked with sudden tears, and she had to turn away to hide them. Weeping, in front of Mrs. Wiggins! What on earth was wrong with her? These days it seemed that her eyes watered at anything. She was far too busy to cry!

29

Vicki held up the issue of *Godey's* to the light and stared for a moment at the drawing of five female figures, posed stiffly against a backdrop of artfully disarranged drapes and gold candelabra.

At last she let the magazine fall to her lap.

"Oh, Mama. It's a lovely dress, and it's so kind of you to think of ordering it for me. But I can't wear it."

"Of course you can! What sort of talk is that?"

They were in the parlor. Baby Thea, ten months old, played at their feet as they sat, Vicki with some embroidery, and Carisa with a penciled list of newspaper people whom she wanted to invite to her party.

"Mama," Vicki began. "I just can't come to the party. Can't you see, I'm neither one thing nor the other. I'm not married to Tim yet, but neither am I divorced from Calvin. I'm . . . just in limbo. And notorious! I can't face all those people."

"Are you having regrets then?"

Vicki's lips pressed tightly together. "No, Mama, I'm not. Not about Tim, anyway. It's just that . . . Oh, I hate the thought of all those people looking at me and laughing behind their hands at me. Sniggering, asking themselves why I ran away from Calvin. As if it were something dirty!"

"Then would you like me to ask Tim to the party as your escort? I will, if you wish."

"No!" Vicki made a violent gesture. *"You're* very brave, Mama, I suppose I've always known that. But I'm not. I can't defy gossip as you do. No, I don't want to come and I'm sure Tim doesn't want to, either. We're finished with this kind of life. As soon as the divorce is finished, we'll leave."

"But, Vicki, with Calvin so stubborn there's little hope. . . ."

"There is, now. Tim went to Kordlands and talked to Calvin. He told him that he is Thea's father. I think that was enough. Now that Calvin knows, he will give me a divorce."

There was a short silence, broken only by the baby's babbling. Then, suddenly ashamed of herself, Carisa said, "But the baby, it will be her first circus. Surely you will allow Thea to come."

"Thea?"

"She is getting to be a big girl now," Carisa said, hating herself for the calculation, the sudden upsurging hope that surged through her. "And if you don't want to attend, then perhaps her grandfather will bring her. To the circus, not to the party."

"Well," Vicki said. "I don't see why she couldn't go. If Papa wants to bring her. . . ."

The days plunged quickly past. Carisa went to New York and came home triumphantly with a find: *Monsieur* Oulette, who had once, he claimed, been a chef for Ward McAllister, the great arbiter of New York and Newport society. *Monsieur* Oulette, Carisa noted dubiously, had the reddened skin and puffy eyes of the alcoholic, but he had promised to come, and surely she could contrive to keep him sober on the night of the party.

The menu would be fashionably French. There would be *trout à la meunière* and *noisettes d'agneau cussy,* which was lamb chops, boned and rolled, served with artichoke hearts and mushroom puree. There would be potatoes stuffed with a mixture of poached oysters, mushrooms and white wine sauce, and an array of sweets: *Baba au Fruits, sorbet pamplemousse,* and *gâteau meringue.*

It was not a style of eating to which the Hartshorns were daily accustomed: Adam clung stubbornly to his New England fare. But Adam did not inquire about the menu, and Carisa did not discuss it with him. He would only call her pretentious, she told herself defiantly. And she could not serve plain food for such an important occasion, could she? If she did, everyone would laugh at her.

There would be flowers. Carisa planned to fill the house with all the blooms—forced hyacinths, daffodils, and tulips—which Vicki could produce in her green-house. She was also having thousands of hothouse roses shipped in from New York. Each woman guest would also receive as a favor a perfect, sculpted rose, made of English bone china.

To Carisa's vast regret, however, Hearts-ease did not have a large ballroom as did some of the newer mansions being built in the city. But there was a small one in a newer section of the house, with a graceful cove ceiling, drapes in a buttery gold damask, and an Aubusson carpet. It had seldom been used in recent years, and the furniture was all in dustcovers.

Carisa had the covers taken off, and the elegant Chippendale chairs reupholstered in a matching yellow. She engaged an eight-piece orchestra to play for those who wished to dance.

Later, in the circus compound, there would be more roses, huge banks of them to spell out the name of the Phillips Circus. There would be a red velvet runner on which the guests might walk to their seats, which were also being upholstered in sumptuous velvet. There would be champagne and petits-fours to sustain them, and lemonade and popcorn balls for the children.

Perhaps the rich nabobs of New York and Chicago might entertain more lavishly, Carisa told herself. After all, they had homes far larger than Hearts-ease, and millions of dollars with which to work. Still, she assured herself, none of them could offer the Phillips Circus as an entertainment. That, at least, would be a first.

The house fell into a mood of frantic hurry. Uphol-
sterers and carpenters came and went. Nelly was inter-
viewing extra servants, to clean and serve on the night
of the party. To Carisa's relief, Vicki took over the
chore of seeing that the house was prepared. She drove
the servants in her soft, firm little voice until Hearts-
ease was redolent with the smells of bees-wax, lemon
oil and silver polish.

Unfortunately, several unpleasant notes happened to
spoil the planning. In New London one afternoon, shopping for ribbons to trim Thea's new little party frock,
Carisa encountered Poll Henry. They were in the dry
goods store, with its creaky flooring covered in green
carpeting, its wires strung overhead for the transport of
money in little baskets to the cash office.

Poll, dressed in sober brown, was examining a roll of
ribbon. At first Carisa did not even recognize her, so
ordinary did she look. Then Poll looked up.

"Oh, the grand lady of the circus, is it? Come here
to the shops to buy ribbons just like the rest of us?"

Carisa felt the color flood to her cheeks, and began
to edge toward the door.

"Oh, yes," Poll went on. "I got time to read the latest
magazines, and that Mr. Justin Whitfield, he said some
mighty fancy things about you, didn't he? A 'grand lady'
indeed! Why, you're no better than I am. Wedging yourself in at Hearts-ease and turning Adam's head like
he. . . ."

"Please . . . I haven't time for this . . ." Carisa began
faintly.

But Poll blocked her way. "Time! Oh, you're so busy
giving your fancy balls, with your little china roses for
favors and your hothouse flowers, you've hardly any
time at all, do you? I even heard you're putting up some
of the newspaper men at the Crocker House. I'll wager
I'll be seeing some of them before that night is
through . . . in fact, I might be seeing some people you
don't even know about."

But Carisa was not even listening. Stores, she was
thinking wildly. Why do I always see Poll in a store?
I've got to get away from here—get away from *her*—

She dropped the cardboard round of white eyelet ribbon she had been holding and fled around Poll's skirts and toward the door. Her flight was followed by Poll's harsh, bitter laugh.

The encounter with Poll had made her uneasy: were all of her entertainment plans common knowledge in New London, enough so that a woman like Poll Henry would know about them? Yet evidently they were.

The following day she was in her office, going over the new season's band score, when Nelly told her that Rolf Taggart was waiting in the parlor to see her.

"Rolf!" The pen dropped from her fingers.

"That's right. Pacing about he is like a wild tiger, won't even sit down. Shall I tell him you can't see him today? That you're busy? It'd be the truth, sure enough, what with this party coming up in only a few days."

"No. No, that's not necessary. I'll go down."

She paused to touch her hands to her hair, assuring herself that it was in place, before descending the staircase. She found Rolf in the parlor, striding back and forth restlessly. When Carisa entered the room he was in the act of sweeping all of the backgammon pieces on the gaming table into a disordered heap. *Violence,* she thought. Always there had been that violence in Rolf, that urge to push and shove at things. Why had she never seen it?

"Hello, Carisa," Rolf said. "You're looking pale today. Are you worried about your circus?"

"No," she replied coldly. "I'm not. But I really don't have time to talk today. Please tell me why you've come."

"As if you couldn't guess. The Phillips Circus, of course. I'll make you a good offer, Carisa, better than anyone else would ever give you."

He named a price.

Carisa lifted her chin. "Rolf, I told you in England that I wouldn't sell, and I won't. I'm just not interested."

"Why not? Dammit, Carisa, what good does that show do *you,* sitting in your fancy mansion with your fancy, rich husband?" He gave another shove at the backgammon pieces, knocking half of them onto the rug.

"Rolf. If you continue this way, I'm afraid I'll have to ask you to leave. This is our home, not a saloon where you can do just as you please."

"Not yet. I won't go yet. Not until I get what I came here for." Beads of perspiration dotted Rolf's forehead. She could actually smell his anger, thick, frightening. *"You* don't need that show, girl . . . but I do. I'm a circus man, the show is my life, it's all I've ever known. I built that circus, Carisa, I gave it my sweat and my guts."

For an instant she felt a spurt of pity. This, too, Rolf's anguish, was her fault, for if she had dismissed him years ago he could have found his destiny somewhere else.

"I'm sorry, Rolf," she began.

"Sorry! You're sorry! Damn!" Savagely Rolf's palm caught the underside of the George I mahogany gaming table and sent it flying on its side. Dice cups, dice, backgammon pieces, and two candelabra which had been placed on its corners went tumbling. "That show is mine, you little bitch, mine by right and by birth!"

"I've said I'm sorry, Rolf, and I am." She tried not to look at the havoc he had made. "But the Phillips Circus is just not for sale. Good-bye, Rolf. I'm sorry that it had to end this way. I hope you find another job soon, and that you're very happy in your marriage."

He made a contemptuous face, his eyes, as blue as John Phillips', glittering with the same mad tenacity. "Marriage! A job! Bah! The Phillips Circus was my job."

Gaines, drawn by the sound of raised voices, was hovering outside in the corridor, and Carisa nodded to him.

"Good-bye, Rolf. My butler will escort you out."

"Your butler, is it? Oh, fancy, fancy! Well, damn you and all of your servants and your rich name. . . ."

Rolf pushed past Gaines, elbowing him viciously, and was gone, slamming his way out of the house.

Carisa and Gaines exchanged glances. "I saw men

like that in the war," Gaines muttered. "Half-crazed with killing and death they were, you could see it in their eyes. They didn't even think like the rest of us any more."

Carisa shivered. "Oh, don't worry, Gaines. Rolf is just angry and thwarted, that's all. He'll cool down when he realizes there is really no hope of buying my show."

"I hope you're right, Miss Carisa."

The days, which at first had dragged, began to pick up speed as the date set for the party approached. Carisa alternated between nervousness, hope, apprehension and frantic worry. Would the thousand threads of circus and party she had labored over these weeks blend into one smooth weave? Would it all go well? Would Rolf manage to cause her any trouble? What trouble *could* he cause?

On the night before the party, she could not get to sleep, but tossed and turned in her bed for long hours, listening to the wind in the night, banging a loose shutter against the house. Slap! Slap! Its erratic pounding seemed to beat away at her nerves.

At last she jumped out of bed and padded barefoot to the window, intending to throw it open to see which shutter was making the noise. She did so. Instantly the chilly wet April wind whipped into the room, grabbing up the folds of the drapes and snapping them at Carisa's face.

She leaned out of the window, drawing deep breaths, forgetting about the loose shutter. The moon, she saw, was full. Its pale light spilled down onto the grass, silvering the treetops and turning the outbuildings of Hearts-ease into a fairy-tale world. Down the hill and to her left was the water of the Sound. Here, too, the moonlight was at work, glittering the waves like gilt.

It was then, leaning out of the window and still reluctant to go back to bed, that she saw it. A dim, white shape, barely visible on the patch of water where moon-grayed sky met silver sea.

A ship.

Carisa drew in her breath and stared, suddenly appalled, although she could not have explained just why. New London was, after all, a harbor, and it was hardly unusual to see ships of all descriptions.

Still, this ship—she squinted at the shrouded shape. Misty it was, dim and unclear, the square patches of sail nearly fading into the moonlight. It was two-masted, she observed, and constructed in an odd style not much in fashion now.

Some impulse made her run to get the opera glasses which she kept in a top drawer of her bureau. She lifted them to her eyes, adjusted them, and peered intently.

Now she could see it more clearly. An ordinary ship, she saw with sudden relief. A fishing boat, perhaps, or a small brig—

She caught her breath. For, although the wind was high, the sails were not bellied out with wind. Instead, they hung limp and lifeless, absolutely still. As if the ship were caught in the doldrums, as if there were no wind.

But there *was* wind, she told herself in confusion; it had been banging at the shutters. *And the ship was moving.* Even without wind to propel it, strangely, eerily, its sails hanging slack, it moved.

Perspiration, beneath her nightgown, began to trickle between her breasts. The ghost ship! The phantom ship that had been seen when she had first come to Hearts-ease and Cook had died. The ship, she remembered feverishly, that Nelly claimed to have seen on the night before Carisa's two sons had been still-born.

No. The protest rose in her. *Oh, dear God, no.*

Who? she wondered, feeling sick. Who was to die tomorrow?

Morning brought birds twittering in the elm outside Carisa's window like children waiting for a circus to begin. Early house sounds came to her: the sound of pans being clattered in the kitchen, a bang as someone dropped a heavy box on wooden flooring. Carisa stretched, yawned, turned over in bed.

Then, groggily, she reached out for the other half of the bed—the half that should have contained Adam, her husband, sleeping beside her. Her fingers moved, searched, sought. But the linen of the sheets was cold to her touch.

We are finished, you and I. . . .

Carisa made a choked little sound in her throat, and sat up abruptly, throwing off her quilt. The ship, she remembered with a swift surge of terror. The ship—

She jumped out of bed and stumbled over to the window, where she jerked open the drapes. Sunlight flooded in, revealing the ordinary world, the lawn tinged with the first vibrant green of April. She could see a patch of garden, a segment of graveled walk, immaculately raked in preparation for the party tonight. To her left was the patch of Long Island Sound, its waters placid.

A ghost ship indeed, she told herself. She was almost laughing with the relief of it. She must have been half-dreaming last night, she told herself quickly. She had been jittery, anxious, and she had seen only a real ship, caught in some fluke of nature, or vagary of wind. Her imagination had done the work of transforming it into a phantom.

Today was going to be a fine day, a perfect day. She herself would see to that. . . .

She breakfasted in her room, eating sparingly. The newspaper men, she knew, had already arrived at their hotel. Justin Whitfield would be among them. She supposed he would soon come to the house, hoping to see Neecie. He was in love with the girl, in England he had made that very obvious. And Neecie liked him, too. It was only, Benicia explained laughingly, that she did not wish to marry yet. She wished to savor her freedom, she wanted to be able to travel with the Phillips Circus for many more years yet. . . .

Carisa sat sipping the hot, thick coffee, well-flavored with sugar. *I might have said that once,* she thought to herself unwillingly. *If I had not had the accident, if I had not met Adam. . . .*

"Miss Carisa? Miss Carisa?" It was Nelly, rapping at her door.

"Come in," she called quickly. There were some thoughts it was not good to dwell upon, she reminded herself as the servant entered. She had made a choice at age seventeen which had changed the entire structure of her life. One choice had led to another, down a whole row of choices and decisions, all of which, it seemed, had driven Adam further from her. If she had ever had him at all. . . .

"Well, it's the day, isn't it?" Nelly was bubbly with excitement. "Everything's ready. Lordy, they're already going crazy down there in the kitchen trying to do things for that Frenchman. He wants everything done his way and no other. Brigid says she doesn't know how she's ever going to put up with him. And she's got Annie watchin' him so he don't tipple too much before the dinner starts, just like you said."

Carisa forced a smile. "Good. I'm sure Annie will manage that very well. Brigid will manage, too. We all will. Everything will go well, you'll see."

"I hope so. Anyway, I guess you're not going to get much rest today. Tim Kelly, he wants to see you about the roses, where you want them put. They just came an hour ago and need wàtering down. And Duddie wants to know where you want those special circus seats and what you want to do with that extra bolt of velvet."

Nelly's eyes were sparkling as she continued the litany. "The champagne, they're putting it on ice, ten big tubs of it, and Miss Vicki, she wants to know when she should start arranging all the flowers in the ballroom. And Miss Neecie, she's all excited and dancing about in her room and laughing because that artist man, that Mr. Whitfield, he just sent her a diamond lavaliere. . . ."

"A diamond lavaliere!"

"Yes, and he sent her a little note with it, with a drawing of herself on horseback, oh, pretty it was! She showed it to me. He wants her to wear the lavaliere tonight and to think of him. And he says that the next diamond he gives her will be a ring. Oh, that young man, he's been pursuing her with a vengeance, and all Neecie does is to smile and flash those dimples of hers.

The little minx, she'll lead him a merry chase before she makes up her mind!"

"Still," Carisa said dubiously. "To accept a diamond of any kind. . . ."

"You don't think that's the first jewel she's been given?" Nelly threw up her hands. "Oh, my, no. You should see the collection she has, all crammed into a pretty little shell box. Cameos, topaz, lockets, bracelets. Everywhere that girl goes, she has to fight off the men, Miss Carisa, and she does it as easy as a mare twitchin' off flies. She'll twitch this Mr. Whitfield off, too, mark my words."

Carisa could not help smiling. "I doubt if Mr. Whitfield would enjoy being referred to as a fly on Neecie's back. And I doubt, also, that he is easily twitched away. Newspaper men can be very persistent, Nelly, that's how they make their living."

Carisa's mood was improving. She put down her coffee cup and allowed Nelly to dress her in a serviceable day-gown. Energy began to flood through her. First, she told herself, she would see Duddie and Vickie and the others, and answer all of their last-minute questions. Then she would check the kitchen. . . .

"You look . . . oh, beautiful! Like a great lady!" Nelly caught her breath in admiration.

It was now five o'clock. Carisa stood very still in front of the wavy mirror of her dressing table, gazing at the image of the woman who looked back at her. A creature clad in lush, rich velvet silk which caught the light each time she moved.

How self-assured that woman looked, Carisa thought dazedly, with her delicate, high cheekbones, her red-gold hair artfully piled on her head and secured with velvet ribbons and small sprigs of flowers.

But beautiful? No, she thought regretfully. It was her sister Stephana who had been that. Anna had been the pretty one, Carisa the most striking. . . .

She whirled about, pushing away the thought of those three long-ago girls.

"Now, Miss Carisa, you stand still or you're going to

ruin that hair-do," Nelly rebuked. "You're acting like Miss Benicia, you are, all restless like a young filly. Not that you don't look young," Nelly added, stepping back to examine Carisa judiciously. "A person would never know you're thirty-six."

Carisa did not reply, turning to stare again at the woman in the mirror.

"Now, let's see," Nelly went on happily. "I think the pins in your hair are pretty secure, but you'd better be careful just the same. And if you get messed up, I'll be in the powder room and I can fix things again."

"Yes, Nelly."

She could hear voices coming from downstairs. Doors slamming, people arriving, the clatter of voices. Laughter flooded up the staircase like quicksilver.

In the corridor, Vicki slipped up to Carisa and gave her a hug. "Good luck, Mama. Not that you'll need it. Your luck has always been of the best."

"Has it, Vicki?"

Carisa drew a long breath and moved lightly toward the stairs.

Feeling as if she were moving in a dream, she made her entrance down the long, gracious staircase, moving with her head held high, the way Katherine had taught her years ago. *Glide, Carisa, glide like a flower floating on a pond, and smile ravishingly. Your legs have healed surprisingly well, and in spite of your circus background, there's no reason why you can't look and act like a lady. . . .*

A lady. That was what Nelly had said. Justin Whitfield, too, in his article. Carisa wondered if it were true. And she wondered what Katherine would think if she could see her tonight.

At the foot of the stairs she stopped, her heart suddenly slamming up into her throat. Adam. He was standing in the entrance foyer talking with a group of men in formal frock coats. He had come to the party after all.

In a moment she had recovered herself, and forced herself to continue the long, smooth flow of her walk as

478

if nothing had happened. She could feel the color pounding to her cheeks, hear the decorous rustle of the short train of her skirts. Men were staring at her, but she did not see them. There was only Adam. His eyes, sherry-colored (or the color of lion's fur, she thought wildly) seemed to burn at her dangerously. To hold her and draw her, weak and trembling, toward their depths.

"Adam . . ." she began.

"Darling," she thought she heard him reply. But then he paused and cleared his throat and she knew that she had been mistaken. She had only created the word out of her own wish.

"Carisa, I would like you to meet Mr. Josiah Smith, who is one of my new associates in the steamship company . . ."

Men gathered about her, murmuring compliments. Smith, Brandegee, Williams, their names swirled about her. There were wives, too, splendid in long satin gowns with imposing bustles. Mrs. Brown, Mrs. Boss, Mrs. Congdon . . . everyone came. Fleetingly Carisa thought of another party, long ago. How different it had been then! Then she had been snubbed and ignored; today she was being fawned upon. Samuel Hartshorn, she thought dryly, had been right. People did respect success. . . .

The party surged on. Adam left her side to greet another arriving group of guests. Carisa, too, was kept busy meeting people. Newsmen arrived in twos and threes, already flushed with drink. Laughter rose and hummed. Carisa walked with one group to the drawing room, accepting their compliments for the cut flowers banked there, daffodils shining out in yellow glory.

Then Samuel Hartshorn arrived, jaunty, arrogant. A bluish-yellow discoloration on his cheekbone and a scar at his lower lip marked the damage that Adam had done to him.

"Samuel . . ."

"Your night of glory." Did his lips twist? "I wouldn't have missed it for anything."

Carisa's hands moistened in her dismay. Mentally she went over the guest list. Surely they had not invited

479

Samuel! Not after he and Adam had quarreled, after Adam had beaten him so savagely, had said he would never have him in the house again. Yet he was here.

"No," Samuel went on, as if reading her thoughts. "I wasn't invited, was I? But I came anyway, to see the show." He gave her a mocking look and leaned closer. "After all, my brother can hardly kick me out tonight, can he? Nor can he attack me physically, which, I gathered, he would very much like to do. No, tonight he'll just have to suffer me. Unless he wishes the press writing about our little disagreements."

"Samuel! How dare you . . ." But before Carisa could finish her furious reply, she was drawn away to the door again, for Madeleine and Redlands Kord had arrived.

"Carisa! What a party! I'm afraid you're going to be very famous, if the number of newspaper men lodged in the Crocker House is any indication of that."

Although Madeleine's voice trilled, her eyes hid resentment. Tonight she wore bottle-green *faille,* her flesh billowing out above and below her corseted waist. The Kords were still angry over Vicki's rejection of Calvin, Carisa knew, but there was little they could do about it openly. Roger Kord had been hard hit by the Panic of '73, and Adam had loaned him a large sum of money.

"Yes," Carisa murmured automatically. "I hope you'll enjoy it. We're unveiling a new aerial act which is absolutely new in this country, and our Benicia will be performing a leap through fire. . . ."

"And your other daughter? The charming Vicki? Where is she?"

"Oh, she's indisposed tonight. I am afraid the doctor has put her on bed rest for a week."

Carisa saw Madeleine's eyes glance away resentfully, and she could not suppress a shameful moment of satisfaction. How things had changed! Twenty years ago, it had been Madeleine who had snubbed her. Now it was Carisa who had that power. . . .

The house soon became crowded, with women opulent in silk and velvet, with men equally well-dressed, smelling of hair pomade and whiskey and cigars.

480

People flowed from room to room. They laughed and chatted of the weather, of Adam's new steamship company, of the circus to come, of a wedding soon to be held in the White House, between President Grant's daughter Nellie, and a man named Algernon Frederick Sartoris.

Newsmen thronged around the punch bowl and surrounded Benicia three deep. Neecie, splendid in *chambray* gauze and wearing the diamond lavaliere which glittered from her neck, laughed and flirted. Justin Whitfield glowered at his rivals. . . .

Supper was served in the ballroom. Long tables had been brought in and set with English damask, heirloom silver and crystal. The eight-piece orchestra, set on a dais, played softly in the background. The food was served deftly, course after course, and Carisa began to relax, knowing that *Monsieur* Oulette, whatever his drinking habits, was not going to fail her.

"Enjoying yourself?" Adam murmured next to her at the table.

"Yes." She said it defiantly. "Aren't you? All of your friends are here, Adam, all of the people you enjoy."

"And one I don't enjoy . . . my brother." Adam's eyes flashed dangerously. "Did you invite him, Carisa?"

"No! Of course I didn't! He came without invitation. He is arrogant, Adam, and he knows we don't dare to send him home without causing a disturbance. And he is doing little harm. He is amusing himself flirting with the ladies, as is his usual custom . . ." Deftly Carisa led the talk away from this dangerous topic. "And," she added, "just see how much fun Neecie is having, too, keeping all of her admirers at bay."

"Yes, I see." Adam was somber. "I also see a party which is far too lavish, too extravagant, to be in good taste. All of this French food. . . ." Adam jabbed with his fork at the rich lamb chops in distaste. "This is the sort of menu, Carisa, which is served by the *nouveau riche,* by people who feel they must impress everyone with just how rich and successful they are."

Carisa felt the color rushing to her cheeks, pounding through her temples. "Then I'm *nouveau riche,*" she

481

said quietly. "And proud of it. I worked hard to get where I am, and now I think I have a right to show people what I've done. I see nothing wrong with that. . . ."

"Carisa." Adam put down his fork. All around them the party buzzed—the lilting violins of the orchestra, the chattering diners, the clink of cutlery against china. But neither Carisa nor Adam heard. Their eyes blazed at each other in anger.

"Carisa, you don't understand. You never have, have you? It's not that I resent your success . . . if I had, I never would have let you continue with your show all of these years, defying convention to do so. No, it's that I resent being used. Used, Carisa! Put to the service of your circus like . . . like a prize elephant or a piece of equipment. All I really am to you is one of the rungs of that everlasting ladder to success which you keep climbing."

Hot tears sprang to her eyes. "Adam! That's not true! It isn't!"

But just then the man on Carisa's right, Ervyn King, a short, balding ship-builder, turned to Carisa to offer her a compliment on the dinner. Carisa, her cheeks flaming, was forced to turn to him and respond.

The meal wore on. As if their previous conversation had not occurred, Adam devoted his attention to the lady on his left, the wife of a prominent banker. Carisa sat fuming, barely tasting the *Baba aux Fruits,* with its rich cake, its currants and candied fruits, its thick *Baba* sauce laced with rum.

Adam did not say anything more to her. Yet occasionally she was aware of his eyes on her, mocking, yet curiously sorrowful. . . .

As the serving waiters, hired for the occasion, were clearing away the dessert plates, a late-arriving couple entered the ballroom. Gaines, who would otherwise have intercepted them, was busy attending to a gentleman from the *Evening Telegram* who had had too much to drink.

At first Carisa, sunk in her sudden, bitter depression, barely gave them a glance. She was vaguely aware that the woman, thin and dark, had black hair piled high on her head, gleaming with ribbons and pearls. Her dress, of elegant black silk, had a full-trained skirt. And her escort, who had turned to speak attentively to her, was equally well-dressed.

But beyond that, Carisa did not see, or care. The couple, whoever they were, had arrived late; she supposed she should rise up from the table and go to greet them. Yet she did not want to. She did not want to do anything except sit here at the table, frozen behind her mask of gaiety.

The couple, smiling, moved forward, skirting around a large display of hothouse roses. Carisa darted another startled glance at them.

And then she knew. With mounting horror, she knew. The man was Rolf Taggart. And the woman, dressed so elegantly in black, was none other than Poll Henry.

Ice seemed to course through Carisa. She felt as if it were cracking at her, splintering at the facade of her mask.

"Adam . . . " she murmured.

Beside her, Adam had stiffened. "I see them." His voice was harsh. "Come, Carisa. We've got to get rid of them."

He was already out of his chair, his movements seemingly casual, yet carrying him toward the door with muscular grace. Her heart thumping, Carisa followed him. She prayed that few of their guests would realize just who the woman in black actually was.

But why were they here? Why would Rolf bring Poll, the most notorious woman in New London, to her home? Who had put him up to it?

For she was sure that someone had. And now, as she passed the end of the first long table and sensed Samuel Hartshorn's eyes fixed on her, she realized who that someone was. Samuel! Proud and arrogant, Adam's brother was not the sort of man to accept rejection easily. Nor was he the sort of man who would allow himself to be beaten and humiliated without seeking some sort of revenge. . . .

Thinking of this, she crossed the ballroom where, overhead, an Italian chandelier cast glittering light on Poll's hair ornaments. She was barely conscious of the people who nodded to her as she passed, or who stared at her curiously.

Adam, however, was the first to reach the two. He strode up to Poll Henry, smiled, bowed, and linked his arm with hers. Then he turned and escorted her toward the main foyer with such grace that only Carisa knew he was actually twisting her arm.

"Don't . . . damn you . . ." she heard Poll mutter, although her lips were smiling.

Adam's answering smile was equally grim. "I think we'll be more comfortable in my study, don't you? We can talk there in peace. And I've a side entrance onto the garden where you can leave quietly."

"No . . . we won't leave yet. Not until I get what I came for." Rolf sprang forward, whippet-lean. The fruity smell of brandy emanated from him.

"Mr. Taggart, this is my home," Adam said coldly. "And you have not been invited here. I must ask you both to leave at once."

"Not until I talk some business with your wife. Dammit, I have a right. . . ."

But Poll had wrenched herself away from Adam and now she backed away from him, her full skirts sweeping the floor. "No!" The sinewy cords in her neck worked. "No, Adam, I won't be pushed out! Not like that, not as if I were a . . . I came here as a lady, I look as respectable as any of *them*." She jerked her head contemptuously in the direction of the ballroom, where strains of music and female laughter could be heard.

"Mrs. Henry . . ." Adam's voice held the chill of December sleet. "I really must ask you to leave now."

"No! I won't!" Poll edged away from the half-opened door of the study. Thank God, Carisa thought frantically, that here in the corridor they were out of

484

view of the ballroom. All of those people, the newsmen she had so foolishly invited—

Words poured out of Poll's mouth, low, choked. *"Mrs.* Henry! Once you called me Polly, Adam. Don't you remember that? Polly! And you and I, we slept in the same bed. Oh, I was good enough for you, then, wasn't I? I satisfied you. Oh, yes, you liked it, didn't you, you liked everything I did for you *then.* . . ."

Adam's face had darkened. "That was years ago. I was a different man and you were a different woman. Now it's time for you to leave here, before I. . . ."

"Before you what?" Poll's eyes were dark frantic holes, smudged in her face. "Before you strangle me?" She gave a bitter laugh. "Oh, yes," she told a horrified Carisa. "That fine, upstanding husband of yours tried to kill me once. I'll wager you didn't know that, did you? But it's true. He came to my house one afternoon and he walked in and he put those big hands of his around my throat!"

"No . . . it's a lie . . . Adam would never. . . ."

But even as she said these words, Carisa looked at Adam's face and knew that what Poll had said was true.

"Adam would, my dear." Poll's words were a sneer. "I awoke with nightmares for weeks after that, feeling his hands on my neck. And there were witnesses. The glazier was here, and saw him leave. As for my sister, she's in New York now, but she'd come back if I asked her. . . ."

"Carisa, please go." Drops of perspiration had sprung out on Adam's forehead. "Go back to our guests. I'll explain all of this later."

"Adam . . . there's no need to explain, I want to be with you. . . ."

"I said please go. I'll take care of this."

"No, Adam, I won't go. No matter what you think, I belong here, with you."

"Whatever happened between us, Poll Henry, it's over now, it was finished years ago," Adam said. "It does not give you any rights now. As for your other accusation, I don't believe you can really produce any witnesses.

485

And even if you could, it wouldn't matter. Because I didn't kill you, did I?"

Poll lifted her chin sullenly. "No, but you tried. And what would people say if they found out? You, the great Adam Hartshorn, pillar of New London society . . ." Her voice mocked. "You, trying to strangle the town's madam, owner of New London's most exclusive brothel! Oh, what a good story that would make! What gossip! And with all those newsmen here tonight. . . ."

"Enough. I think you'd better leave."

"And what if I don't want to?"

As Adam stepped toward her in rage, Poll laughed. "Well, don't worry. We won't soil your precious house for very long, Rolf and I. We just came to see the circus, that's all. Rolf and I . . . we're old friends, and he came along to escort Jimmie and me. My little Jimmie is waiting outside in the carriage. He's never seen a circus, and I told him he could come."

Jimmie. Poll had said the name with odd emphasis, her eyes glinting.

Adam, too, had evidently seen this, for his face had gone abruptly white, except for two stains of color painted on his cheeks. Carisa caught her breath, for there was a look about Adam at this moment, a deadly, coiled-spring look—

"Adam!" She threw herself in front of her husband. "Adam, please. Please don't cause any trouble tonight. . . ."

He shook her away as if she had been a wisp of embroidery silk. "I told you to go back to your party, Carisa."

"No . . ."

"And *I* won't leave either," Poll announced with relish. "I don't have to, I got a right to be here. You see, Adam, Jimmie is your grandson."

"No."

"Oh, yes. He's Julian's son, and I should know, Julian was the only man I'd slept with all that year, and my sister and the girls can tell you it's God's truth. What's more, your son acknowledged the boy and sent him money every month until he died. If you don't believe me, go to his banker."

"His banker," Adam repeated dully. He stood frozen as if paralyzed, unable to speak. Then, shaking his head like a wounded lion, he lunged forward.

Again Carisa, moving faster than she had thought possible, sprang between her husband and Poll Henry.

"Adam . . . no, I beg of you . . . the child. . . ."

"What about the child?"

"Why . . ." Carisa thought of the drawing she had seen on Poll's desk, the curly-haired boy with the full, humorous, willful mouth. Julian's mouth. . . .

"Why . . . he is just a child, Adam. An innocent child who does not understand any of the terrible conflicts between adults. He has been told that he is going to attend the circus. And he expects to go."

"Very well." Adam stood very still, his mouth twisted. "Very well, then. If you insist, Carisa, the boy may see the show. But I'm afraid you'll have to make all the arrangements. I must go back to the ballroom and see to our other guests."

30

Later, Carisa would never remember how she managed it all, the herding of nearly two hundred people outdoors and into carriages, to be whisked down the small back road which would take them to the circus lot. Poll and Rolf had, thankfully, gone to their carriage, and she had managed to fend off Madeleine Kord's curious questions.

Although her hands were trembling, she held her chin high. She forced herself to laugh, to nod, to smile. She oversaw Gaines, who, with the aid of Tim Kelly, was seeing to the details of bringing the carriages up.

Lanterns flickered in the darkness as the line of carriages moved slowly. Shrugging on a wool evening cape,

Carisa herself boarded one of the first ones, leaving Adam to follow her with baby Thea, whom he had promised to bring.

Lit by kerosene lanterns, the circus tent loomed up from its grassy lot like the dwelling of some desert king. Never, Carisa thought with a pang as her carriage rattled up, had she seen anything more beautiful. The towering canvas was peaked and sculpted by the four tall main poles which supported it, and by the double rows of quarter poles. Flags rippled from the main poles, snapping in the crisp evening wind. Red and blue bunting adorned the sides of the tent in extravagant loops, all of it outlined by the oil lamps, glowing in the night like cat's eyes.

Papa—The thought rose heavily in her mind. Papa, Papa, wherever you are, are you watching? Do you see me? Do you see the Phillips Circus and what it's become?

People were arriving. Ladies in long skirts stepped decorously out of buggies and surreys, assisted by husbands or coachmen. Children squealed and ran about, their dresses white flashes in the dark. One little boy raced perilously close to the row of lamps which illuminated the tent area. His mother gasped and pulled him away.

The little boy howled, knuckled at his eyes, and followed her into the tent.

The line of carriages became clogged. Stable-boys, set to directing traffic with lanterns, began to shout at each other, and at the perspiring coachmen. The calliope had begun to play, sounding its irresistable call to excitement and glamour.

At the head of the line now, Carisa saw, was an open buggy bearing the emblem of a local livery stable. Out of it piled three newsmen, pads of paper in hand. One of them was Justin Whitfield, who grinned jauntily at Carisa.

Samuel Hartshorn had arrived in a small surrey, driving it himself. Then a black cabriolet, with ornate brass trappings, disgorged its occupants. A man jumped out, and then reached up to help a little boy down. The child, with a thatch of crisp, light curls, laughed. He was followed by a woman clad in black silk. Carisa looked up and met Poll Henry's hot stare.

The night had begun.

"Carisa, darling Carisa!" Duddie, waiting at the "back door" with the other performers scheduled to go on, was the first to spot her. He rushed up to her, a small machine of energy, turning cart-wheels as he came. At last he bounced up, smiling, and produced a small box from his costume sleeve.

"For you." He handed it to her with a flourish. People had started to gather about her—clowns, aerialists, animal trainers, jugglers, Egyptians, equestriennes.

"Me?" Absurdly her lips had begun to tremble. "Duddie . . . all of you . . . you shouldn't have bought me a gift."

"And why not? Who deserves it more than you, Carisa? After all that you've done for the show? You made us, Carisa, we all know that. But this isn't much," the clown added, mugging a face. "Just a little thing I had a jeweler in New York make up for us. It's from all of us."

The little pin, made of sterling silver, sparkled up from Carisa's palm, its detailing exquisite. A silver circus tent, complete with flags and bunting, the Phillips name etched on its sides.

"Oh . . . Oh, Duddie . . . everyone . . . it's perfect, I don't deserve it. . . . She stood foolishly holding the box, fighting back tears.

Voices clamored. "Put it on, Carisa. Wear it, that's what it's for."

Numbly, she fumbled with the little pin, her hands shaking so violently that she stabbed herself with it. A little red dot of blood appeared on the end of her left forefinger. Carisa stared down at it, her heart beginning to race.

Bad luck, a voice whispered in her. *Bad luck to bleed on opening night—*

Quickly she wiped away the blood before any of the

performers could see it, and managed to attach the pin to her collar.

"There," Duddie said. "That's nice. You look like a real circus lady, Carisa."

Somehow Carisa managed to wish Duddie luck, to give personal messages to all the other performers, to smile and laugh normally. She showed her new pin to Benicia and accepted her compliments, her exuberant hug.

"Oh, Carisa, it's going to be a wonderful night, a wonderful show, I can just tell! The reporters have already been swarming back here, asking me the most absurd questions. . . ."

Benicia was beautiful tonight, as shining as the diamond lavaliere which encircled her throat. Carisa tried to smile at her, pushing away the worry that consumed her. Poll—Rolf—she had given instructions that they be seated in one of the darker, emptier sections, where they would not be as easily seen by her other guests. Would they cause any trouble? What trouble *could* they cause, other than the rippling of unpleasant gossip?

"And Justin Whitfield?" she asked Benicia. "Has he been here, too?"

Neecie's hands flew to the diamond at her throat. "Oh, yes, he has given me his very best wishes. And . . . I suppose Nelly has told you that he gave me this lavaliere as well."

"Yes," Carisa said dryly.

"Well, I took it." Neecie lifted her chin. "Perhaps I shouldn't have, perhaps it's not considered 'proper,' but I don't care. I like Justin, I like him very much, and he wanted to give this to me. I couldn't hurt him by refusing."

If this had been any other night, Carisa would have scolded, or teased, or probably both. Instead, she forced a smile. "Never mind, Neecie. I hope it brings you luck. Are you nervous?"

"No . . . yes . . . I don't know." Neecie's dimples flashed as she arched her back and spread her arms wide. "Oh, I feel just so wonderful tonight, so splendid . . . it's as if nothing could ever go wrong!"

Benicia's joy was so innocent, so transparent, that Carisa felt her heart sink. "And your father?" she asked in a low voice. "Has he been here to wish you luck?"

"Yes, he just came, and he did not approve of Justin's lavaliere. He brought Thea to see me . . . I gave her a big kiss." Neecie's forehead had wrinkled. "Carisa, why did Papa look so glowering? And yet so sad and upset, too. It was more than just the lavaliere, I know it was."

Carisa licked her lips. "I suppose . . . perhaps he has something on his mind."

"Oh, do you mean me? My act? Now, you know I've told Papa over and over that this act is perfectly safe, nothing is going to happen to me, it only looks dangerous." Here Neecie's eyes began to flash with her pent-up excitement. "Besides, I don't mind a little danger. It only excites me, Carisa, it makes me feel real, alive!"

"Perhaps."

Try as she would, Carisa could not capture the mood of exhilaration that gripped her step-daughter.

Neecie's voice bubbled on. "Did you see that Rolf Taggart is here? Rolf, of all people! Carisa, I saw him just a few minutes ago, walking by here as if he were still the manager. Angry, scowling as if we'd all done something terrible to him. . . ."

But the bugle was sounding, a signal that the show was about to start, and there was no more time for talk. Carisa gave Neecie a quick hug. To her dismay she found that her eyes had filled with sudden, hot moisture.

"Best of luck, Neecie. And . . . may God be with you."

"You, too, Carisa." Neecie's hands squeezed hers tightly. "And . . . and thank you, Carisa. For all you've done. I'll never forget it."

For Carisa, her memory of that circus night would always be irretrievably mingled with the brassy, metallic sound of the band. It was the circus band which provided the pulse-beat of the show—loud, gaudy, irresistible. Drums, horns, cannons, anvils, sleigh bells, marking off the cakewalk rhythm of magic.

Seldom was the audience aware of this, but it was the circus band which played in time to the acts, rather than the reverse. For this reason Carisa's band director, William Mack, stood in his white suit with his back to the band, so that he could see the performers.

Now, to a vigorous march, the performers began their grand entry around the hippodrome track—bright costumes, gilt wagons, ponderous elephants, rattling cat cages, clowns and more clowns—all of the splendor and panoply derived from years of planning. Above them, dwarfing them, the canvas made a pale dome, criss-crossed by a network of ropes, quarter poles, wires, pulleys, other apparatus, all of it lit by lanterns hung high from ropes.

Carisa watched this spectacle from an aisle. A child gave an excited squeal, spilling its lemonade. Across the center ring, Carisa could see her distinguished guests, already enjoying their champagne. To her left, in a row of seating heavily in shadow, Carisa knew that Rolf Taggart and Poll Henry, together with Poll's son, were seated. Carisa had glimpsed Poll's face as she was being directed to her seat by a uniformed usher—it had boiled with hatred and resentment.

But that, Carisa told herself dully, could not be helped. The proper women of New London would have been scandalized to learn they had been seated with a brothel madam.

Well, she wouldn't think of that now, she decided, as the band began a rattling roll of drums to mark the passing of the cat cages before the block of seats occupied by the party guests. Big Sheba, the golden Bengal tiger, gave a coughing, irritable roar.

Carisa walked down the aisle to the hippodrome track and, slipping past the still marching performers, crossed to her left toward the block of seats which held not only Poll and Rolf, but also the orphans from the asylum and a contingent of retired sailors, the latter beginning to grow thoroughly tipsy on the beer which she had provided for them.

She paused, staring across the tent to the reserved

492

section. Was that Adam, standing by an aisle seat, lifting up little Thea so that she could see the parade?

Then she saw him look in her direction. For one wild moment, his eyes met hers across the bright movement of spangled costumes. Or *did* his eyes meet hers? Almost instantly Adam had turned away, and Carisa knew, once more, that it had been only her wish to have it so. Adam had not been looking at her, or for her, at all.

Music: cakewalks and marches and rollicking polkas, beating out the pulse of the circus. Carisa, sitting with her guests in the reserved section, in a seat upholstered in red velvet, felt numb, possessed with such a sense of impending doom that she felt she must burst with her anxiety. Rolf Taggart and Poll Henry. Both of them here, seated across the expanse of rings, their presence a dark smear to cloud this gaiety. . . .

Marcella Duquesne, long ago recovered from her broken ankle and now wearing a costume glittering with sequins, balanced on her high wire like a silver flame. The Italian aerialists, wingless birds, looped through the air with heart-stopping precision. And now Neecie, balanced upon her white horse like a swaying yellow flower, was cantering into the center ring.

"She really is lovely, isn't she?" Adam's voice was hoarse. He sat tensely, his eyes fixed upon the ring, and upon his daughter who whirled and pirouetted there.

"Yes . . ."

Too lovely, Carisa thought suddenly. Too innocent, too secure in her energy and talent, too vulnerable. . . .

Abruptly she rose from her seat. Poll Henry was here, she reminded herself. And Rolf, who wished only to take her circus from her. Rolf, who had hinted at mysterious accidents, ugly mishaps—my God—

"Carisa! Where are you going?"

"I don't know, Adam. I suppose it's nothing, but I only know I have to get up. I'll walk around the track a few times, make sure that everything is all right. I won't be long."

Not waiting to hear his protest, she simply fled, lifting her skirts and maneuvering down the narrow aisles, past the lemonade and peanut "butchers," the girl handing out clown dolls and cheap concessions.

"Jumpy tonight, are you, Carisa?" It was Rolf, of course, come out to the hippodrome track to join her. He was grinning at her, his teeth gleaming wolfishly in the glow from the lantern which dangled above their heads, safely out of the reach of curious children. Again Carisa smelled brandy fumes and she knew that, like the newsmen, Rolf had been drinking heavily before he came here.

"Jumpy?" She tried to still the tremor in her voice. "Why, no, of course not. I'm just . . . checking things out, that's all."

"Really? I've never seen you quite this restless, dear sister. Pacing up and down as if you were afraid something might happen. But what could happen, eh, Carisa? What could possibly happen?"

Carisa stared at her former manager. She had seen Rolf in a mood like this before—just before he pounced on a town alderman who had tried to thwart him, or a foodseller who had cheated him. But tonight she sensed that his mood was even more erratic than that. Beneath the fuzz of alcohol there was a wildness, a sense of nerves frayed ragged. . . .

"You're missing the show, Rolf," she heard herself say. "Neecie's new act. Isn't that what you came here to see?"

Rolf shrugged. "Poll is fetching her boy some popcorn and lemonade, and as for myself, I had some business to discuss with you. Right here and now is as good a place as any."

"Here?" She looked about her in bewilderment. They were standing at the far end of the three rings, near an entrance, viewing the rings through a network of poles and ropes. This was a poor vantage spot, and thus the seats here had been left empty tonight, although the block of seats to the far right was filled with the charity guests Carisa had invited.

"Yes," he mocked. "Right here in the middle of the show . . . *my* show, Carisa. It's private enough."

494

And so it was, Carisa knew. For, although they were in the full view of hundreds of people, no one was looking at them. Instead, all eyes were fixed on the moving figure of Benicia, a golden flame etched against a background of canvas and crowd faces. Benicia, blooming on her horse's back in full ballet grace. . . .

With a start, Carisa realized that Rolf was speaking to her, and had been for some minutes. He was telling her what he had done for the Phillips Circus, repeating in painful detail the events of storm, mud, disease and catastrophe with which he had coped. As he spoke, his hand played convulsively with an end of paper bunting which had come loose from its tack and hung down. Duddie had painstakingly decorated the tent in streamers of red, white and blue bunting, and now Carisa had the irrational urge to dart forward and snatch the bits of colored paper from Rolf's hand.

". . . we had a tent collapse on us the next year, Carisa, during a wind storm, but you wouldn't remember that, would you? No, you weren't even there. You were sitting home at Hearts-ease in your fancy office." Rolf made a contemptuous gesture. "In your office, writing letters. You were out of it, Carisa, out of it. *I* did the real work! I always did!"

"Rolf . . ." Rage pelted through her. She was only dimly aware that the lemonade vendor was hurrying past them with a refill tray of bottles, his tray wobbling. A small crowd of people had grouped about him to buy.

"Rolf, you're not being fair! You did the managing . . . no one ever said you didn't! But I worked, too. I did the planning. I was the one who got us the calliope, who found us the colored banners, who arranged for wagons, who hired the best performers, who put us on railroad tracks. . . ."

"Did you?"

Rolf's eyes had gone small and glittering as he leaned against the quarter-pole which supported the canvas immediately above them. Suddenly he gripped the guy-rope and swung himself upward. He moved monkey-like, hand-over-hand, like the circus performer he was.

495

Almost instantly he had grasped the oil lantern from its dangling rope, and had pulled it downward with him.

He landed on the cinder track again with a light, graceful bounce.

"Rolf! What are you doing with that lantern?"

"Why, I'd like to smoke a cigar. But I forgot to bring my matches." Rolf dug into the pocket of his suit, and produced a fat Havana cigar, which he tossed casually into the air and then caught.

"A cigar! But, Rolf, you know we don't allow anyone to smoke inside the tent. We never have. You know how dangerous it can be. . . ."

"Fire. Yes."

Carisa felt as if he had slammed a fist into the center of her chest.

"Rolf." She said it through stiff lips. "Rolf, you can't really mean this. You wouldn't . . ."

"Oh, yes, he would. He does mean it. He's talked of nothing else for two months. And I should know, he's been living at my house all of that time." The voice was Poll Henry's. Carisa whirled about to see the brothel madam advancing toward them, holding two bottles of lemonade. In the dim, shadowy light of the tent, Poll's black skirt seemed to draw all light toward it, extinguishing it. Only her face was distinct, a glimmering white.

But there was no time for her to cope with Poll Henry now. Not with Rolf staring at her, his eyes so fanatic and determined.

"Put the lantern down, Rolf," Carisa managed to say, in the firm, level voice which she had been taught to use with animals, especially dangerous ones.

"No. I won't."

The crowd clapped as Neecie executed a perfect somersault, flinging her body into the air in a tight, perfect arc.

"Rolf, you will, you must. There are people in this tent, hundreds of them. Children . . ."

This was not real, the thought rippled through her. This was surely a dream, a joke, a jest. She could not

496

really be standing here in full view of hundreds of people arguing with a madman.

"Put the lamp down," she repeated. "The lanterns were never meant to handle like this, Rolf. You yourself taught me that. You were always so careful . . ."

"Sell to me, Carisa. Sell me this show."

"No, Rolf, you know I can't."

"I want this show, I deserve it." Rolf tossed away the cigar, a spinning arc into darkness, and then his hand began to play with the piece of bunting, twisting it, crumpling it. "We started out as a shabby little mud show, with five rotten wagons and a couple of moth-eaten tigers. Now look at us . . ." Rolf gestured toward the center ring, toward the banked tiers of seats filled with people. "We have reporters here, the whole country looking at us. I want that, Carisa. I need it, all of it."

"No. Rolf, please . . ."

Carisa had forgotten about Poll, she had forgotten everything except that Rolf still gripped the lantern in his hands. He cradled it, his fingers caressing the stained metal surface, inching the piece of bunting closer and closer to the heat.

"It's my show, Carisa. *I* worked for it."

"Rolf . . . Oh, Rolf, I'm so sorry, but you know that it isn't, you know that it was my husband's money which financed us right from the beginning. If it had not been for Adam, we would have been nowhere, we would have had nothing."

The lemonade vendor had moved on, but one of his customers still remained, leaning in a patch of shadow near some empty seats, watching Benicia's performance intently. Carisa wanted to scream out to him, but she was afraid to. She was afraid of what Rolf might do, those nervous fingers toying with the bunting. Playing, teasing . . .

"Sell, Carisa, sell."

Deliberately Rolf lifted the lantern.

It edged perilously close to the twisted bit of bunting. Beside her, Carisa was dimly aware that Poll Henry had

497

dropped one of the bottles of lemonade, had drawn in her breath in a sharp gasp.

The lantern moved still closer to the bit of paper. Now only a fraction of an inch kept it from ignition.

In her dream she had first became aware of the smell. It smelled . . . burned. Yes, that was it. The black, oily stench of something which has been consumed by flame. And it was a smell so strong that she realized this was no stove or trash fire gone awry. Many things had burned. Canvas, rope, wood, cloth, straw.

And flesh. Yes, flesh had burned, too. Carisa could smell it, pungent and sickly . . .

"No!" she screamed, darting forward. "No, no, for God's sake, Rolf, don't do it! Please don't!"

"Be still, you bitch. And stay back, you." Rolf's voice was a dagger. He lifted the lantern, gesturing savagely toward the man behind them, who had abandoned all pretense of watching the circus and had started in their direction.

"I'm John Phillips' son, as much his son as you are his daughter. The Phillips name is my name, too. At least it would have been if he had ever legitimized me."

"Rolf . . . I'm sure Papa didn't mean to hurt you. . . ."

She heard her own voice babble on, trying to reason with Rolf, to get him to see sense. But she knew he wasn't listening. He had gone beyond reason to a terrifying outer world where even the grotesque seems natural.

This was real, she told herself feverishly. This was really happening. If she didn't give Rolf her show, he would burn it up. Put to the flames all of the gorgeous gold-leaf wagons and ponderous elephants and curved-neck horses and valiant performers.

Neecie, a golden flame on her horse's back. Duddie, loving and loyal.

And the audience, all of the people in the bleachers, the wealthy party guests, the children, the old sailors she had invited, the orphans. All of them trusting her.

And Adam. *My God,* she thought. Adam is here with little Thea. And Poll's son, Jimmie, is here. Adam's grandson. . . .

All of them were to be consigned to horror, to the flames eating up the guy-ropes until the support poles collapsed, bringing the canvas down with them in a sheet of flame. People would struggle to get out. They would scream and climb over each other. Some would make it, while others would be smothered beneath the burning canvas . . .

A deep, squeezing ache seemed to push outward from the center of her chest.

"Please. Put down the lantern, Rolf. Your threats aren't needed any more. As soon as the performance is over, I'll make out the necessary papers."

Rolf lowered the lantern a fraction of an inch. "What?"

"I said I'll sell to you. The Phillips Circus is yours."

Even Rolf seemed bewildered at what she had done.

"I love the Phillips Circus," she heard her voice go on, a voice stifled and strange. "But I love my husband much more. And I love my family. Do you think I'd ever take a chance that my circus might kill them, might kill the innocent, might kill my own employees who trust me? No. It's all over, Rolf. Do the best you can for the show. It's all I ask of you."

She didn't want to look at the triumph dawning in Rolf's eyes, the incredulous victory. She only wanted to get away, now that she had said the unthinkable.

"Please, Rolf . . . Poll . . . let me pass. I want to go home. I . . . I have to go home now."

As she pushed past Rolf, past Poll whose mouth seemed to hang open, the tent seemed to whirl unsteadily about her. It was over, she thought dully. All of it, the years of work and hope and pushing and planning. The sacrifices she had made, the barriers that had sprung up between Adam and herself, so that the show might play before two presidents, before Queen Victoria. . . .

She could not seem to grasp it. She had given up her circus. She had given it up.

In the ring, Neecie was cantering in a tight circle, while two assistants prepared the hoops through which she would soon jump. The band was rolling drums and banging cannons, building up the crowd's excitement.

Blindly, hearing none of this, Carisa pushed her way toward the exit.

"No!" Poll Henry blocked her way. "No, Rolf, she can't go, not yet! You can't let her off so easy, she's got to pay! Pay for all she's done. Pay for her hoity-toity ways, the little whore . . . pay for taking Adam from me and for slapping me in the face, pay for putting Jimmie and me in the seats with the orphans . . . I'll have her skin for that. . . ."

Carisa was aware that the man standing near them had turned, that his face somehow was Adam's. Perhaps she must have known it all along. But before she could move, or open her mouth to call to him, Poll lunged toward her in a swirl of black skirts.

"Stop her . . . stop her, the little circus bitch . . ."

Poll skidded, grabbed at Rolf for her balance. And somehow, the lantern went flying through the air.

Liquid spilled, and flames flashed up. Poll Henry's black skirts blossomed orange.

Poll's scream rose to the top of the canvas and hung there, a distillation of terror. Over and over her voice screamed, gasped, bubbled, sobbed.

Someone else shrieked. Neecie, in the center ring, turned her head. The band director raised his hands.

It seemed as if minutes had passed, yet Carisa knew it could only have been a few seconds. She started toward the flaming woman, throwing her evening mantle off her shoulders as she went.

"Give me that," Adam ordered.

She felt the mantle snatched out of her grasp, and then Adam threw it on Poll, tumbling her to the ground and rolling her over and over. Flames leaped and danced like wild creatures through Adam's spread-out fingers.

"Adam, Adam, oh, be careful . . ." Carisa did not know what words she screamed, or even that she was screaming.

500

"Don't just stand there, Carisa. Start getting people out. And . . . the baby! My God, hurry!"

Flames had started to spread along the loose sawdust. Turning, Carisa saw with horror that the baby, Thea, crowing and laughing, toddled straight toward the place where a little patch of orange-red licked at a trailing rope-end.

Band music struck up in sudden nightmare gaiety—a rollicking march, the circus disaster tune.

Carisa ran. She ran, her feet skidding on sawdust, to snatch up the baby. Then she was dodging backward to get out of the way of the lemonade vendor who raced toward them, leading a stampede of terrified people.

Someone screamed.

She caught a wild glimpse of Adam crouched on the ground beside the form of Poll Henry. Then bodies blocked her view, filling all the air, all the space.

"Adam, Adam," she sobbed. "My God, Adam!"

Clutching the baby, she fought to get to her husband, to the safety of his arms. But the circus crowd knew there was a fire now. They had panicked. Crying, screaming, cursing, they swarmed over seats—men, women, weeping children. They came rushing up the hippodrome track toward the entrance behind Carisa, not realizing that they could have slipped beneath the edge of the canvas at any point.

Nightmare. Of struggling bodies, moving faces, opened mouths, arms that pushed and shoved. Carisa glimpsed Neecie, off her horse now, trying to direct the crowd. Clowns and roustabouts wrestled the people, trying to drag children out. Justin Whitfield fought to get to Benicia.

A woman—Mrs. Pugh, the banker's wife, her face distorted by terror—came staggering toward Carisa and shoved her in the breast. The baby shrieked and Carisa stumbled, swimming downward through a mass of rushing feet and skirts and legs.

"Carisa!" She heard Adam shouting for her. "Carisa . . . my God, darling. . . ."

"Adam! Adam!"

501

A foot kicked her, something slammed her in the rib. The baby was sobbing. She knew she had to struggle, had to get to her feet again or she would be crushed beneath the press of all these people.

"Adam . . . Adam!"

Then something fell on her head. It sent a wave of pain through her so sickening and brutal that she was conscious only of surprise that anything could hurt quite that much.

That was all she knew.

She was dreaming it again. That eerily familiar nightmare which had haunted her sleep for so many years. Again she was running across that darkened expanse of grass, again she saw the shrouded shapes, smelled the sickening stench of roasted animal flesh.

"Adam!" she screamed. "Adam!"

Burned things, she thought hysterically as she ran. Things burned and charred and blackened. . . .

She struggled to find her way in the choking gray mist, dodging between eerie black humped things which lay deathly still. These objects—God! They were bodies! —seemed to waver and shift in front of her eyes, and then she saw that they had become stones. A ragged jawbone of stones, hugh monoliths protruding through the mist like teeth. Old stones, redolent of antiquity, of evil, strange rites. . . .

She sobbed and uttered a hoarse cry and pushed past the stones. Then she thought she could hear a woman's voice, warm, rich, full of urgency.

"John . . . you must tell her . . . tell her . . ." The voice stopped, as if it were very weak, but from somewhere it found the strength to go on again. *"Tell her that she . . . she must love . . . give up what she must, but . . . love. . . ."*

The voice, weak, but so warm and caring, was gone. Carisa was left again on the field with the burned, charred shapes, and now she knew how alone she was. How very alone. Never again would anyone love her, or hold her, or speak gently to her, or even quarrel with her. Never again would she know the love of a man.

"Adam," she choked. "Adam . . . please . . . I love you . . . don't go, please, don't. . . ."

She lifted her skirts and began to run, hurtling herself across the scattered field, racing faster and faster in her desperation. There was still a chance. Yes. A chance. If she ran fast enough, if she ran until pain pounded her chest and her heart stitched her ribs and her legs trembled with exhaustion. . . .

"Adam!" she screamed. "Oh, Adam! You've got to believe me! You've got to. . . ."

Someone was tugging at her shoulders. Shaking at her, shaking her awake.

Carisa wrenched open her eyelids. Light flashed at her, paining her. She seemed to be lying in light, swimming in it. Her head ached. Her entire body ached. She felt as if she had been picked up and smashed against a wall.

"What . . . what . . . oh. . . ."

"You're back home in bed," a familiar voice said. "In our bed."

"Our . . . our bed?"

Something rough touched her forehead, something scratchy. With difficulty it smoothed back her damp, matted hair.

"Yes, Carisa, you're in our bed and it's morning again. You got a vicious concussion when that quarter-pole hit you. I'm afraid you spent the night dreaming the grimmest of dreams. But Dr. Morton says you'll be fine, thank God. All you need is a lot of rest."

"Adam," she whispered. She was unable to say more. Her eyes had filled with tears and helplessly she let them run down her cheeks, for she did not have the strength to wipe them away.

"Yes, it's me. At your service, darling." He was smiling. She saw that his hands were encased in bandages, that there was a bandage across his jaw line as well.

"Your hands . . . oh, Adam, your hands, your face. . . ."

"Just a bit of a burn. It'll heal and I'll be as good as new. Which is more than I can say for poor Poll

Henry. Her burns weren't so bad, I don't think, but she was trampled in the rush to get out of the tent. I'm afraid I couldn't save her, Carisa, although I tried."

"Oh . . ."

Carisa closed her eyes. *The fire.* My God, she thought. The fire. With enormous effort she opened her eyes again and struggled to sit up.

"Adam . . . you've got to tell me . . . what happened? What's happened to them all, to Neecie and Thea and Duddie and . . . and all of them. . . ." She thought of her dream, and felt as if a heavy iron stake were twisting in her chest. "Adam . . . they aren't. . . ."

"Lie still, darling. You've been badly battered, and if you struggle you'll only feel worse." Adam's voice was husky. "I suppose you must know that the big top is gone, and most of the rigging and equipment. We lost two elephants, Carisa. They . . . they had to be shot. And six horses."

"Oh." She swallowed hard, racked with the loss of it, knowing full well how much Adam was *not* telling her. She found that her fists were clenched tightly, that perspiration was moist on her face.

"Go on, Adam. Tell me. How many. . . ." She licked her dry lips. "How many people?"

"No deaths, Carisa, other than Poll's. We were incredibly lucky. We did have some injuries, though . . . some broken arms and legs, and one poor old woman who fell and broke her hip. But they'll all live, thank God, and I'm sending money so that they'll have the best of medical care."

Adam's voice broke. "Poll's son, Jimmie, has a sprained arm. I'm bringing him here to Hearts-ease to live with us. I hope you don't mind. I've already brought him, I did it last night. He's a fine-looking boy. . . ."

Here to Hearts-ease to live with us. The words seemed to echo in Carisa's head. And, like another echo, came the image of Julian, a school runaway, sitting defiantly on the carriage block near the octagonal barn, his eyes blue and proud and desolate.

"I'm glad, Adam," she whispered. "I'm so glad. I think perhaps Julian would like that, if he could know."

504

Adam's eyes misted.

"Neecie is all right," he went on after a moment.
"And Duddie, and all of the other members of our
family. Duddie made himself quite a hero . . . he personally saved at least fifteen children, Carisa, dragging
them out from beneath the edge of the tent. Rolf,
too . . . I never thought he had it in him. It was he
who pulled you out, Carisa."

"Rolf! Rolf pulled me out?"

"Yes, he did. And he saved Thea as well. Both of
you owe your lives to him. He worked hard, until everyone was safe."

Rolf Taggart. Hungry, ambitious, angry, thwarted
Rolf. But a real circus man after all. People, Carisa
thought dazedly. How strange they could be, how terrible and wonderful.

For a long moment she was silent. "My dream," she
said at last. "Adam, that nightmare . . . how many
times I had it over the years, and always it was the
same. Me, rushing across a field littered with burned
bodies, so alone, so lonely, knowing only that I had
to get to you. To . . ." Her voice wavered. "To reach
you before it was too late."

"Darling . . ." Adam put his bandaged hand on hers.
"Darling, you have reached me."

"What?"

Adam's mouth was quirked tenderly. "Yes, Carisa,
you reached me . . . by loving me. By loving me enough
to give up your circus to save me, and to save all of us.
You see, darling, I was worried about you and what
that Taggart man might try to do. When you left, I
followed you, I heard it all."

"Oh . . ."

Somehow their hands found each other and clasped.

"I wronged you, darling." Adam's voice was thick,
husky. "Will you ever forgive me? I just didn't see. . . ."

"And I didn't see either," she said. "I did use you.
You were right. Oh, Adam, I know our marriage hasn't
been the best. I worked too hard and was too grasping
and made mistakes, so many mistakes. . . ."

"Hush." He put his bandaged hand over her lips.

505

"Hush, darling. That's all in the past now. We'll build a new circus . . . if we did it once, we can do it again. The two of us this time, working together, as we should have done all along. And we'll build a new marriage, too. A better one, a stronger one. There's time. Many years left yet."

"Yes . . ." Her eyes stung with tears, and now they were flowing down her cheeks, happy ones, sad ones, all mingled together.

"I love you, Carisa. I always have, and I always will."

"Adam . . . oh, Adam . . ." She clung to him, and gently, gently, his lips touched hers. Then they were holding each other and half-laughing, half-crying, Carisa burrowed herself into the center of Adam's arms, where she belonged.